THE STUFF OF
HEROES

miguel delibes

THE STUFF OF
HEROES

translated from the spanish by
Frances M. López-Morillas

PANTHEON BOOKS · NEW YORK

This translation was made possible in part through a grant from The Wheatland Foundation.

Library of Congress Cataloging-in-Publication Data
Delibes, Miguel.
[377A, madera de héroe. English]
The stuff of heroes / Miguel Delibes; translated from the Spanish
by Frances M. López-Morillas.
p.   cm.
Translation of: 377A, madera de héroe.
ISBN 0-394-57746-9
I. Title.
PQ6607.E45A61313   1990   89-43253
863'.64—dc20

Book Design by Anne Scatto
Manufactured in the United States of America
First American Edition

To the memory of my friend of childhood and adolescence, Luis María Fernández, whose tomb is in the sea.

Honor to the dead; a warning
to the living . . .

*(From the monument at the Dachau
concentration camp)*

PART
ONE

CHAPTER

■

The first time that the boy, Gervasio García de la Lastra, experienced those strange symptoms, which the more pious members of his family attributed to supernatural causes and the others, more skeptical, to purely physical phenomena operating on a delicate sensibility, was—as recorded in the diaries of the late cavalry colonel Don Felipe Neri Luna (1881–1953)—at the family gathering of Saturday, February 11, 1927, although, as can be deduced from those same notebooks, certain signs had appeared three days earlier when the little boy had burst like a hurricane into the study of his

maternal grandfather, Don León de la Lastra, while the old gentleman was having his usual afternoon snack of chocolate and fried
bread, and asked him point-blank, "Papa León, can I be a hero
without dying?"

(The grandchildren called him Papa León, just as Crucita, the
firstborn, had always called his wife Mama Obdulia; she was a
woman of oaklike strength and majestic appearance who, by some
inexplicable paradox, lost her equanimity if she heard the sonorous
terms that evoked death and last things in any way. In the diction-
ary there were forthright words, such as catafalque, sepulcher, and
miserere, which could not be pronounced in her presence. According to reliable testimony, however, she made no objection to the
word "grandmother" until her daughter Zita, who greatly to her
mother's displeasure had married Telmo García, M.D., gave birth
to a fine nine-pound girl and elevated Mama Obdulia to that noble
status. After this event Doña Obdulia noticed something which,
though it was perfectly obvious, she had not taken into account
before: namely, that the grandmother, as head of the family clan
and in the logical course of generations, was, along with the grandfather, the most likely candidate for decease and in consequence
closest to precisely that catafalque, sepulcher, and miserere, con-
cepts that had been abolished from her domain. In view of this
troublesome evidence, the term "grandmother" joined the repertory of forbidden words; and considering that this word was really
only a redundancy (mother of one's mother or one's father), the
question was resolved in a sort of judgment of Solomon by embel-
lishing the Christian name with the rank of maternity. The expression "Mama Obdulia" thus became not a frivolous substitute but
a valid formula (Mama's Mama) to indicate her preeminence in the
family. And since her legally recognized spouse, Don León de la
Lastra, shared assets, titles, and honors with her, he also ceased to
be "grandfather" and became Papa León, a euphemism that his son
Vidal, the only male among his children, described as "Mama's
typical nonsense," but which his daughters Zita and Cruz, abject
admirers of their mother's resourcefulness, accepted blindly.)

Papa León stroked his thin yellowish beard, peered at his grandson through the oval glass of his lenses, raised his scanty eyebrows
(which repeated themselves in deep wrinkles on either side of his

forehead), and answered with innocent solicitude:

"Hee, hee. Of course you can be a hero without dying, though it's easier to be one with four bullets in your belly."

The little boy's anxious smile showed his preference for the heroism of survival, but still he tried to obtain a guarantee of wholeness.

"And without winding up lame or anything?"

"Winding up lame, I should say not." Papa León gave his spontaneous schoolboy laugh again, at the same time trying to get inside his grandson's thought processes. "Do you mind telling me what bug has bitten you today?"

The boy thought for a moment and then, without answering, awkwardly rolled up the sleeve of his jersey and gestured with his bare arm at the big green horn of the phonograph that rested on the desk in the corner.

"If you play some music from your war," he said in a confidential tone, "I'll tell you a secret."

(At the time it occurred, Papa León had received the birth of his grandson with the disproportionate joy of those who believe that only males are worthy propagators of the line. He hardly noticed the girls, Crucita and Flora, but saw in the chubby-cheeked baby who arrived in third place, and whose howls denoted gifts of command and virile demands, not only a proud heir but a soldier worthy of the succession. Spurred by the baby's innocent gaze, Papa León often reconstructed the glorious days of the siege of Bilbao, the calculated strategy of General de la Concha, and the rash courage of Don Cástor Arrázola, whom he had served as aide-de-camp for more than a year. The child incarnated everything worthy and courageous that his past contained—his opposition to King Amadeo and the First Republic, his proven fidelity to the legitimate claims of the pretender, Don Carlos. Papa León saw himself in the child, watched over his sleep, supervised his meals, took great interest in his development, and as soon as the boy could get around by himself would take him to his study, seat him in the low armchair, and make him listen to military marches on the old phonograph for hours on end. Later, when Gervasio grew older, he enjoyed telling him warlike episodes in so lifelike a way that, from the age of four, the boy began to think of the fairy tales that Aunt

Cruz told him, during his long convalescences from flu, as mere mellifluous pastimes.

"Don't you like the story?"

"No, Auntie."

"Why don't you like the story?"

"It's for girls."

"Who says it's for girls?"

"I do, Auntie."

Aunt Cruz's floury white face, so like a circus clown's, became slightly flushed. She picked up her knitting and went to the sewing room to let off steam to her sister.

"Zita, I wouldn't be a bit surprised if Papa León were putting ideas into the boy's head. He seems strange to me."

Later, when Gervasio told Papa León about the incident, his grandfather laughed till he choked, administered a little tap with his fingertip on the upper part of the boy's chest, over the breastbone, and said with a conspiratorial wink, "You're a soldier, aren't you, you little rascal?")

This time the child's poise had impressed Papa León to the point that his skinny hands, furrowed with protruding blue veins, fumbled as they tried to attach the speaker to the phonograph and wind it up. When at last the grandfather succeeded and the first fuzzy notes sounded, Gervasio stood motionless with his elbows on the round table, his fine head on one side, his straw-colored eyes blank, his ears alert (like Don, the old pointer that Papa León, along with his old comrades Trifón de la Huerta and Mikel Lecuona, used to take with him to hunt woodcock in the oak groves of the Basque country at the turn of the century), and as the thump-thump of the march grew more emphatic, acquiring rhythm and vigor, the boy moved his bare arm forward until he had placed it right under his grandfather's straggly beard.

"Look," he said in a tearful voice.

Don León de la Lastra brought his old man's spectacles close to the little boy's forearm and observed with stupefaction that the tiny blond hairs that covered it were standing up one after another, like a troop coming to attention when the bugle sounds, and that the skin was puckering like a plucked chicken wing.

"But . . . you've got gooseflesh!"

His shrill voice became almost grave as he observed the phenomenon, but the child stood there imperturbably with his little bare arm resting on the table, until Papa León got up and disconnected the phonograph in consternation. Then Gervasio seemed to emerge from his reverie, looked at his grandfather in surprise, rolled down the sleeve of his jersey and, like a docile patient after a doctor's meticulous exploration, sat with crossed arms awaiting the diagnosis. But Papa León, completely taken aback by this unexpected revelation, could only manage to say, "How . . . how long has this been happening to you?" His spectacles with their thin silver rims slid down to the end of his nose.

The boy shrugged his shoulders shamefacedly, as though he had been accused of some misdeed.

"Ever since Christmas," he said.

"And tell me, my boy," continued his grandfather, "apart from the gooseflesh, what do you feel?" He crossed one leg over the other (with the thigh showing through the flannel of his trousers, thin, unyielding, and hard as rope) and brought his face close to his grandson's.

"Like a cold shiver down my back; as if my back had turned to soda water."

"Soda water?" He smiled. "That's odd. And this only happens to you when you hear music?"

"Yes, grandfather," he said, breaking the household rule. "But it has to be music on your phonograph."

This was the manner in which the singularity of little Gervasio García de la Lastra began to reveal itself. On the following Saturday, February 11, during the tumultuous family gathering, among the heavy furniture and dark oil paintings of the drawing room (presided over by a copy of Giotto's *Resurrection*, which crowned the mantelpiece and whose sleeping sentinel, according to Uncle Vidal, was the living image of Mama Zita), Papa León, after a number of roundabout remarks and circumlocutions, imparted his discovery to his children and children-in-law: his grandson Gervasio seemed called to a very high destiny; perhaps to be a hero. Military music affected him to the point that he underwent a real metamorphosis.

As was usually the case at the weekly family gathering, reactions were contradictory and violent. Aunt Cruz was deeply moved, though her chalk-white skin barely allowed her feelings to show through. Her husband, Don Felipe Neri Luna, cavalry major (who for some minutes had been struggling with the nausea that was stirring on the right side of his stomach and showed in the rubbery grimaces of his colorless lips), commented in a shaky voice that something indefinable in the boy's eyes had occasionally led him to believe that he was not a child like other children, a comment that annoyed Uncle Vidal (seated on the quilted divan beside Aunt Macrina, his wife, opposite the copy of Giotto's *Resurrection*, and always jealous of his own progeny) and led him to shout that Papa León, with his damned war stories and his nonsense, was responsible for the child's abnormalities, which besides being a serious crime was an abuse of authority. Aunt Macrina, his wife (who had beautiful blue eyes set very close together and an unfashionably turned-up nose), supported her husband and added, with lucid good sense, "Just tell me of one boy, just one," she repeated, "who at seven didn't aspire to be a hero or a fireman." Her remark wounded Mama Zita to the quick; she was the one most directly affected, and Papa León's words had sounded to her like high praise (as if he had predicted that his grandson Gervasio would wear a cardinal's hat). This led her to emphasize the pride of being mother to that extraordinary child, and to ask for understanding from those who hadn't been so lucky, an allusion that Uncle Vidal picked up instantly and that caused him to stand up and move toward her in a rage, murmuring between clenched teeth his favorite word for describing his sisters: "Foolish, foolish, foolish." And immediately afterward, with that refined contempt that an only son customarily feels for his sisters, he shouted that she needn't think that heroism was a profession, but a gift that came down from heaven some fine day to adorn a person who might be the most insignificant being in the world, to which Papa León, proud of the rumpus he had stirred up, argued that that didn't prevent God from showing his preferences by a visible sign, and that when he said that his grandson Gervasio seemed called to a very high destiny he didn't say it without foundation, but based it on a number of indications that he had observed in him. Uncle Vidal's rosy, shining bald head began to spin like a satellite among the dark shadows of the furniture, impatiently denying, and Uncle Felipe

Neri, who had momentarily succeeded in fighting down his nausea, addressed Papa León and asked him whether, apart from the child's obvious wishes, any signs had appeared to corroborate them. Papa León, with his sly gaze and his scanty yellowish whiskers, nodded twice and ended by saying in his shrill little voice, "Why, naturally they have appeared!" Uncle Vidal received this exclamation with a sarcastic wave of his hand and a hollow, helpless, exaggerated laugh, trying to destroy the wonder-working climate that was being created in the gathering, and that was accentuated when Papa León dragged the mahogany table (on which he had previously placed the phonograph) over the carpet to the center of the room and said to his daughter in an aside, as if it had all been rehearsed, "Cruz, do you mind bringing the boy in?"

And as soon as Aunt Cruz appeared in the doorway holding the child's hand and Papa León said, "Don't be frightened, my boy, we're going to try something," rolling the sleeves of Gervasio's jersey up to his elbows and placing him in front of the table with his bare arms raised, an expectant silence reigned in the room. Before the astonished eyes of the persons there assembled, Papa León started the machine, the cylinder began to rotate, and the martial and romantic strains of "Red Berets" (a little scratchy, a little harsh, a little distant, owing to the cylinder's great age) were wafted into the room. And as the tone of the piece became more stirring, the little blond hairs that lay on Gervasio's forearms began to stand straight up, and his soft, silky skin bristled like the surface of a liquid starting to boil. The awestricken stare of those present, fixed on the child's arms, failed to observe the hairs on the back of his neck, which were also starting to rise, or those in his bangs, which curled up as if he were walking in the teeth of a wind, or the progressive rising of the hair at his temples and the crown of his head, which, as it lifted away from his scalp, turned the little boy into a sideshow freak. Papa León, who had sought the surprise of others, could not overcome his own; stupefied, he raised his right eyebrow (tripled by the wrinkles on his forehead), and observing the unexpected growth of the phenomenon, shouted with senile excitement, "Look, his head, d'you see? His head, too!"

In a hysterical seizure that was half sentiment and half fear, Aunt Cruz took one of the little boy's hands between her own, as if to protect him against some evil, and screamed, "It's icy cold!" while Mama Zita, very frightened, covered her eyes with her hands and murmured in a tone so low it could scarcely be heard, "My son, my son." But the boy, pleased at being the center of attention, stood quietly with his eyes half closed, his bristling arms raised, his lips compressed, his unruly hair pointing toward the ceiling. At that instant the light went out and Aunt Macrina screamed, "That's done it, this is the devil's work!" Uncle Vidal grunted, Papa León placed himself between his children and the phonograph, and Uncle Felipe Neri made odd little sucking noises, all of which caused the gathering, barely illuminated by the red coals in the fireplace, to assume a phantasmagoric appearance. Uncle Vidal's well-polished bald spot spun in the half-light, and his strident voice startled everyone present.

"Are you trying to get us all excommunicated? This is worse than a black mass!"

Mama Zita cried out in anguish, "The boy, the boy!" and at that moment the light came on. Gervasio was still standing motionless, his arms held high, his eyes half open, his hair standing on end, but as the phonograph ran down and the march grew slower, his forearms gradually recovered their habitual smoothness, the blond down lay flat, and the enormous leonine head grew visibly smaller, like a deflating balloon. Still conscious of his accomplishment, he noticed a stir of expectancy around him, but as soon as Papa León disconnected the machine he lowered his arms, turned his head, and flashed Mama Zita a smile for which she rewarded him by pressing him fearfully to her bosom, as if the little boy had lost some of his earthliness in the experiment.

Gervasio felt proud to be the center of general attention, the cause of the angry, gesticulatory controversy that was taking place before his eyes. But as if he knew intuitively that the process would not develop fully while he was present, he feigned irresistible drowsiness, a problem that Mama Zita solved by putting him down in an armchair in the library, hardly reached by the light from the drawing room. As she returned, Mama Zita collided with Aunt Cruz at the door and the two hugged each other in silence, deeply moved, and Cruz mused amid her tears, "You'd think it was a sign from heaven." But Uncle Vidal, trying to get his own back, started to yell again, "Nonsense, nonsense, pure physical phenomena!" and Aunt Cruz, in her sister's arms, made signs to him that the child was nearby, to make him lower his voice and not wake the boy. But Gervasio, kneeling in the armchair, was watching the scene over the chairback and saw the funny faces Papa León was making as he bent over trying to protect the phonograph from the hubbub, saw Uncle Felipe Neri approach Aunt Cruz, kiss her, and murmur, "Portentous, portentous," squeezing his eyelids together as if he were trying to produce a reluctant tear, while Aunt Macrina, always ready like a good Madrilenian to discern provinciality in the manners and statements of her sisters-in-law, who were almost twice as old as she, called them credulous and simpleminded, thus giving her husband the opportunity to repeat, "Nonsense, nonsense, pure electrical phenomena. The human body is like a voltaic cell." And as they argued, the group, sounding for all the world like a nest of crickets, was moving toward the sliding doors. But before anyone could open them Mama Zita interrupted, and wiping a furtive tear with a lace handkerchief, lifted her meek, cowlike eyes and implored them, "Not a word to Telmo, I beg you. It would be horrible if he heard about this."

Uncle Vidal, who hated to see women give themselves airs, smiled scornfully and objected that nothing was as grotesque as attributing supernatural influences to members of one's own family for insignificant and easily explained occurrences, and that they only needed to remember the embarrassment that had been caused by a local lawyer, Emigdio de Lucas, when he had had a pamphlet printed practically canonizing a son of his who had died some months before; but Aunt Cruz, who had been frightened of her brother's outbursts since childhood, gave him little conciliatory taps on the arm, calling him an old heretic, trying to make it clear that the Emigdio de Lucas affair was different, that nobody in this house was trying to beatify Gervasio. Still, Uncle Vidal's irritation, far from abating, increased; and loftily refusing to quarrel with a woman—a typical ploy on his part—he rounded on Papa León and accused him of having turned the house into an insane asylum with his phonograph and his war, an imputation to which the grandfather listened in cowed silence, gazing at his son through the lenses of his spectacles, his pupils staring like two lentils, his eyebrows multiplied into wrinkles on his forehead. He was speechless, like a schoolboy afraid to answer, until, after Mama Zita had opened the sliding doors, he escaped down the hall and didn't stop until he bumped into Amalia, the maid, who with her cap on her head was standing stiffly, holding the street door, as she did every time she heard Mama Zita's warning double ring of the bell. And behind Uncle Vidal and Aunt Macrina, who were excitedly discussing the night's events, Aunt Cruz and Uncle Felipe Neri descended the stairs in awed and reverent silence, as if accompanying the viaticum, while Papa León observed all of them over Amalia's shoulder with ill-disguised peevishness, like a child who, tired of playing all afternoon with a possessive friend, gratefully watches him go in order to keep on playing with his toys by himself.

Two days later, when Flora and Gervasio came home from school, Papa León hissed at them from the door of his study and, after making sure that no one was in the dark hall, shut himself in with the children, telling them to be quiet. Having discovered his grandson's peculiarity, he was planning to test its limits, but because he was aware of the family's extreme sensitivity, he had decided to act with discretion and avoid subjecting the child to deceptive emotional states. Hence, at first he concerned himself with stimuli; that is, whether Gervasio, so sensitive to military music, would react as strongly to incentives of a different kind. The child played his part as protagonist by adopting an attitude of weary availability (like the one he showed in the presence of Don Justino, the family doctor, when that personage was drumming on his belly with short, brisk fingers to gauge the extent of an indigestion), reserving his boastful face for his sister Flora, who had always had the better of him in their relationship because of her greater age, liveliness, and imagination. But now, every time that Papa León in the course of his investigations told them stories about saints, the boy looked over his shoulder at his sister as if to say, "If I wanted to, I could be like them," while the grandfather cautiously observed the child's temples and the crown of his head to see if any change was taking place. But the literary test was a failure; neither tales of saints nor epic poems nor legends awoke the slightest emotion in the child. Only if Papa León accompanied them with a faint musical background did Gervasio show emotion, and even the stirrings of a display. This caused Papa León to lead the investigation in another direction. He called on the great masters (Beethoven, Mozart, Haydn, Bach, Chopin, Schubert), but Gervasio heard roll after roll of music without a flicker of emotion, except for one afternoon when listening to the "Slaves' Chorus" of Verdi's *Nabucco,* the hairs on his nape began to stir and fanned the back of his neck twice, on the point of standing up. Papa León—patient, objective, meticulous, scientific, responsible—intensified his exploration, tried this and that (choirs, choral ensembles, symphonic music, operas), but the results were totally unsuccessful, from which he deduced that the child's epidermis was affected solely by military music and, though minimally and weakly, out of pure sympathetic reaction, by very vigorous male choruses whose virility might suggest martial qualities. As a windup to every session the grandfather would place a cylinder of old marches on the phonograph, simply to enjoy his grandson's capillary display and take a close look at the unruly hairs; he would place the palm of his trembling hand on them and say to himself, "They're stiff and sharp as pins." But those interminable sessions bored Florita, who paid almost no attention, convinced that her brother was producing the phenomenon deliberately, though she did not know by what means.

On Thursdays Papa León would receive a visit from his old comrades Lucio Viana and Trifón de la Huerta, and they would play cards in the study for hours, so that on those days the experiments with Gervasio had to take place early; but one day, when the grandfather had taken a little too much time, Don Trifón surprised the boy in the middle of a performance, and Papa León, unable to go on hiding the secret from his old friend, timidly remarked, "Well, there's a sample of what my grandson can do, Trifón. What do you think of him?"

And Don Trifón de la Huerta, a man with a beard as wide as it was long ("Marxist whiskers," said Uncle Vidal), who had hunted woodcock with Mikel Lecuona and Gervasio's grandfather in the deep woods of Durango, came closer to the boy, inspected him from head to foot as if he were some strange little animal, and pronounced in his deep voice, "He certainly does remind me of Don when he pointed. The hairs used to stand up along his backbone too, d'you remember?"

Mama Zita, who after her initial fright had cared for the child from a nervous distance, like something either holy or diabolical, did not dare to caress his head; if she happened to touch it as she was bathing him in the mornings in the zinc bathtub, she felt a sort of electrical charge that increased her respect and led her to place a sponge between her hand and the boy's thatch of hair. And so that her son would not interpret what was really homage as lack of affection, she would ask him trivial questions during his bath, without expecting a reply, as if to say, "Don't answer me if you don't want to; all I want is for you to know that I'm with you." And when she saw him running down the hall or fighting about nothing with his sister Flora, she would tell herself tremulously, "When you see him like that, he seems like just an ordinary boy." But every time she remembered the performance of February 11, the way his hair stood up, the individual hairs like little rockets as he listened to "Red Berets," she shuddered and the tears would gently well up in her eyes. Mama Zita, a woman of rudimentary religious ideas, identified heroism with sanctity and tended to see religious devotion rather than bravery in her son, a viewpoint that her sister Cruz carried to extremes, and that in her mournful daydreams led to dramatic visual images: Gervasito decapitated, with his bristling head in a bucket, and around him a chorus of infidels (she was almost sure that they were Negroes) dancing before the witch doctor to the sound of the tom-tom. The visual quality of the scene was so vivid, and she recounted it with such a wealth of detail, that both sisters would look at each other and burst into disconsolate sobs, holding hands, staring into each other's eyes, asking themselves the only questions yet to be answered, "Where, when, how?" And then Aunt Cruz, rising to the loftiest mystical heights, would ramble on about the love of God and his inscrutable designs and end by asking Mama Zita about Papa Telmo, if he knew anything about it yet, to which Mama Zita would reply in alarm that that was the last thing that must happen, she hoped to die first, that she found Telmo particularly distant just now; for there was no question that naturopathic medicine, in addition to decreasing social standing, also led a man to materialism.

One afternoon when the two sisters were chatting over the mending basket, Papa León burst into the room in disarray, his bedroom slippers falling off his heels, the pajama showing at the neck of his bathrobe and under its hem a pair of hairless, skinny

14

white calves like two sticks. With his glasses perched on the tip of his nose, the boyish spark of conspiracy that the two sisters knew so well was shining in his eyes. He shut the door carefully, put a finger to his lips, tiptoed over to them, sat down on the edge of the sofa, and began to talk ingenuously about his experiments with Gervasio, explaining that the child was not attracted to the idea of martyrdom but to military heroism. Unaware of Mama Zita's reproving, almost indignant glances, he added that after a month of research he could conclude that the little boy's sensibility vibrated only to military marches, and that if in exceptional cases he reacted to other stimuli, these were very vital male choruses which in some way evoked a parade of soldiers.

Mama Zita had risen involuntarily to her feet, rigid and furious, and was looking at him as if to say, "So we've had experiments, have we? So it's been military marches, has it? And other stimuli, eh?" with the result that, as she advanced resolutely upon the sofa, Papa León got to his feet, hunched over like a beaten cur, and closed his eyes against the avalanche that was descending upon him. Mama Zita yelled at him that the experiments were over, that Gervasio was a child and not a guinea pig, and that if he continued with them she would grab that piece of junk (Mama Zita was referring to the phonograph) and throw it in the garbage pail. Papa León, who had opened his eyes little by little and was protecting his glasses with his forearm, retreated defensively. His red lips, among the scanty hairs of his beard, murmured justifications, but Mama Zita continued to threaten him, and giving him no respite, warned him *for the last time* to leave Gervasio alone, to keep out of the matter, because if someday the Lord wanted to show his preference for the boy, the child was at the Lord's disposal, without any need for his mediation. In the face of this attack Papa León turned and fled like a frightened puppy, shuffling his feet, through the door that Mama Zita was holding open, while his daughter closed it again and sat down opposite her sister, the mending basket between them, her double chin drawn down like that of the sleeping angel in Giotto's *Resurrection*.

"Excuse me, Cruz," she said in a trembling voice. "Perhaps I went too far with Papa, but I'm very nervous just now. I can't bear to have him treat the child like a laboratory rat. That's all over for the time being."

CHAPTER 2

A slanting ray of sunshine filtered through the panes of the glassed-in balcony and projected the children's moving heads against the flowered paper on the walls. On the lower panes, protected by brass railings, a big blue fly flew from one to another so rapidly that it seemed to be bouncing.

"The men only come at night; nobody comes at this time of day," said the little girl in a disappointed tone.

The panes were open a crack, and in the light of the dusty ray that found its way into the drawing room, the heavy mahogany furniture, the sconces, and the pictures in their gilded frames seemed to be taking a long nap. Opposite the balcony, in a house with a cut-off corner at the angle formed by two narrow streets, was Friné's, a cabaret that in winter opened only at night, except on Saturdays and Sundays, and the two children were fascinated by its multicolored doors, like those of a carnival wagon, flanked by two red lanterns which, as darkness fell, shed a ghostly reddish glow on the dreary shadows of the street. Mama Zita had forbidden them to look out of the balcony, but they did it secretly, escaping her vigilance and Señora Zoa's watchful eye, because they were entranced by the men who came to Friné's; surreptitiously, like thieves, trying to make sure that no one saw them, their overcoat collars turned up, their hatbrims pulled down over their eyes, impatient when they arrived, furtive and distrustful when they left. At noontime on blue-tinged Sundays in spring, with no men prowling about, the women of Friné's, in their heavy makeup, their hair loose (many of them dyed blond), and wearing wrappers in garish colors, appeared on the balconies over the café and chattered tirelessly to one another, laughing and fluttering like birds, smoking cigarettes in long bone holders banded with gold. The children were drawn to this spectacle, but if Mama Zita or Señora Zoa happened to catch them at it, they raised a tremendous fuss and pushed them away from the balcony, scolding them and not letting up until the children were shut into the playroom. Every time this happened Gervasio and Florita, desperate at having nothing to do, would sit on the balcony that overlooked the street where the Santa Brígida convent was, and looping back the curtains, would play at funerals for hours on end.

One morning Papa Telmo caught Mama Zita scolding the children, and from the bathroom doorway, his face lathered and his feet bare as was his custom, jovially asked what was going on; but Mama Zita lowered her voice so much that Gervasio could catch only two words ("bad women"), and then Papa Telmo burst out laughing with that big laugh of his that was half caustic and half mocking, and inquired if it wouldn't be more useful from a didactic point of view to teach them rather than hide them away, to which Mama Zita replied so quickly and crossly that neither of the children could hear her answer.

All the same, on the following Saturday Florita asked Aunt Cruz about that house with the brightly colored door across from the glassed-in balcony, and without batting an eye her aunt said, "Ah, it's a school." And Florita said, "A school for such big girls?" But Uncle Felipe Neri, who was coughing and grimacing because of his stomach acids, came to his wife's rescue and, after carefully folding his raincoat on the brass rail of the halltree, turned toward the children and asked, "Where's Crucita?"

"She's having tea with Mama."

"Doesn't it make her hands red any more?"

"Yes, but she says that at home it doesn't matter."

Uncle Felipe Neri, his ash-colored hair divided into two halves by a part and wearing his gold-mounted glasses, tried to smile, but the bitter twist of his mouth won out. Aunt Cruz and Uncle Felipe Neri had been Crucita's godparents at her baptism and she was their favorite niece; in good weather, before they went off to Fuenterrabía for the summer, they would invite her to Simón Beade's orgeat parlor to drink orgeat, and in winter when school was in session to the Blue Room at the club to have tea and cakes (though lately Crucita was trying to avoid drinking tea because it made her hands red). In any case, they admitted to Mama Zita that they were entranced by the tall girl with the green eyes and proud bearing, and that she possessed all the qualities they would have wished in the daughter they had never had. Even Crucita's contemptuous poutings, her stuck-up attitudes, her rudeness toward the humbler sort of people appealed to Uncle Felipe Neri, who would remark, "She carries herself like a princess. She doesn't like the common herd." And it was true that Crucita, who hadn't inherited Mama Zita's heavy figure, carried herself majestically, and her bold green eyes shone with aristocracy. Straight, slender, and willowy as she was, Crucita suffered nonetheless from a defect that prevented her from being the archetype of the perfect fifteen-year-old: she had no breasts, a defect that to her brother Gervasio, a careful observer of the scene around him, was a serious motive for concern.

"Why doesn't Crucita have titties?"

And Flora, who harbored a very original notion of cause and effect, answered unhesitatingly, "All her growth has gone into being tall. She's too thin."

Crucita's lack of breasts was one of the habitual subjects of conversation in the kitchen, though the same conclusion was always reached even after the lengthiest discussions: as far as Señora Zoa was concerned Crucita was too tough to have tits, while in Amalia's opinion she did not have them because she was rich and tits were the privilege of the poor; other things maybe not, but she had never known a single poor woman who didn't have them. However, this defect was not a serious obstacle for Aunt Cruz and Uncle Felipe Neri, not something that detracted from their goddaughter's dazzling beauty.

Uncle Felipe Neri, accustomed to the tyrannical discipline imposed by his ulcer, was a methodical and tidy person, to the point that every time a significant novelty arose in his life, he would start a notebook in which he wrote down everything concerning it. And so he had in his desk, properly catalogued, a professional notebook (joining the Army, service academy, posts where he had served, promotions, income, clothing allowance, triennial terms of service, uniforms, and so forth), a matrimonial one (engagement, request for his wife's hand, wedding, wedding trip, events of interest, menstrual periods and sexual relations, gynecologist, and so on), a third for his illness (first symptoms of ulcer, doctors, diagnoses, treatment, periods of remission, relapses, spring outbreaks, and so forth), and another relating to Crucita (birth weight, development, navel, first word, measles, and so on). By means of these conscientiously dated notebooks, it was not hard to reconstruct the rails along which their author's life had run. And now suddenly at forty-six, when he no longer expected surprises, at a mature point in his life more appropriate for finishing notebooks than beginning them, the episode of Gervasito had turned up: those strange capillary displays which had had such a strong emotional effect on him. No sooner had he returned home on Saturday, February 11, 1927, than Uncle Felipe Neri took a black notebook with oilcloth covers out of the lowest drawer of his desk, opened it, and in accordance with his invariable custom drew a cross at the top of the page lined into little squares. He wrote underneath in carefully executed letters: NOTEBOOK ON GERVASIO. The tip of his pen hesitated for a while, making little circles in the air, before it alighted on the paper to write the following: "I am starting this notebook, devoted to my nephew Gervasio, owing to a profound impression I have received, for it appears from certain indications that the child is predestined for a very lofty destiny. Tonight, during the family gathering at the home of my father-in-law, Don León de la Lastra, the boy went into a trance while listening to a military march; his skin bristled and the hairs on his head stood on end. Because of its extreme pallor and the blond hair in an aureole around it, the child's face reminded me of the Sacred Host inside a gold Gothic monstrance. My brother-in-law Vidal, who is prone to materialism, attributes the seizure to mere electrical phenomena, but I know that for a man of religious faith the phenomenon offers some aspects that are disturbing to say the least . . . " Some time later, when he was fully and fervently convinced, Uncle Felipe Neri added, "My sister-in-law Zita, always sensible and level-headed, has refused to allow Don León, my father-in-law, to make my nephew Gervasio into a guinea pig. We must let him live a normal life, and the Lord, if he thinks it advisable, will take it on himself to show him the way at the proper time. The latest tests seem to confirm the fact that the boy's trances respond to martial stimuli, which goes to prove, in contrast to the original belief of myself and Cruz, that what is prefigured here is not a saint but a hero. Praise be to God!"

As a result of this unexpected novelty Uncle Felipe Neri's affective inclinations were divided, and although his civilian side remained faithful to his niece Crucita, his military side shifted to Gervasio, the object of such great hopes on his part in those days. In any case his nieces and nephews (including Aunt Macrina's two little ones) exhausted his capacity for love, in accordance with the succinctly expressed maxim that he had written into Crucita's notebook on the night of her birth: "Childless aunts and uncles are the grandparents of their nieces and nephews." Faithful to this dictum, he and his wife viewed the world through the children; they took them out walking, cared for them when they were ill, guided their behavior, provided treats for them, saved for their futures; on Sundays and holidays, by strict turns, one of them shared their lunch, and after the meal, in an unchanging ritual, played cards for stakes of a penny, a game that Uncle Felipe Neri invariably won and just as invariably, in an oft-repeated act of generosity (which formed part of his austere system of education), gave his winnings to the niece or nephew who had been invited that day.

"Take it, for whatever you want to spend it on."

Gervasio was proud of his remarkable display, but in preference to Uncle Felipe Neri's grimaces he was intrigued by the harsh whiteness of Aunt Cruz's face, which Mama Zita and Aunt Macrina so much envied. Besides being put off by its naked look, he was troubled as to why those cheeks, so plasterlike in coloring and texture, should prickle like nettles when he kissed them. The first time he noticed it he had gone disconsolately to Florita in search of an explanation, and his sister's forthright reply had left him open-mouthed.

"Aunt Cruz shaves, and she's smelled like an old woman ever since the year one. Hadn't you noticed?"

"What do old women smell like?"

"Like dead water."

"And what's dead water, Flora?"

"Standing water; water that doesn't run."

Now, on the glassed-in balcony, Gervasio watched the blue fly's crazy parabolas above their heads. A middle-aged woman with a pink ribbon in her hair and jangling cheap bracelets on her arms had appeared on the balcony of Friné's, above the F of the sign; with her back turned to them, she looked up and addressed one Raquel in a hoarse, worn-out sort of voice, but Raquel did not appear. Gervasio sluggishly swiveled his head in her direction. A certain stiffness of the neck made the boy turn his head very slowly, as if he had problems with physical movement. The presence of his sister stimulated his imagination.

"Why does Aunt Cruz shave if she's a woman?"

"Because as women get old they get more and more like men, and men like women. Didn't you know that?"

Gervasio's gray eyes, with catlike yellow rims around the pupils, expressed distrust.

"Is that true or are you making it up?"

The little girl formed a cross with two of her fingers and kissed it.

"Just look at Papa León," she said, as incontrovertible proof.

Gervasio continued to be astonished.

"You mean Papa León's a woman?"

"Not yet, but he's gradually getting to be one. Haven't you noticed his voice?"

Gervasio admitted that his grandfather's voice was as high-pitched as a woman's and that his hands, which were small, translucent, and hairless (also like a woman's), had bluish lines on their backs because of the veins, like the rivers on Sister Luciana's maps at school. Still, he objected, "But Papa León has a beard!"

"Yes, but his beard hairs are soft and they're falling out."

Papa León's beard was certainly scraggly and thin, and you could see his chin through its lank hairs; it was hardly more than a jutting bone covered with skin, and when he laughed, in cackling identical spasms, his yellowish whiskers waved as if disturbed by a wind. And when he ate, especially on solemn family occasions when, according to Aunt Cruz, he succumbed to gluttony, his beard became as greasy as a sable's pelt.

Several days after their clandestine visit to the glassed-in balcony, Florita went to bed with flu. In addition to her embarrassing remarks, the little girl had another quality uncharacteristic of her age: she was patient, knew how to wait things out. And so, when Aunt Cruz visited her in the afternoon and sat down at the foot of the bed, knitting in her hands, and prepared to tell Florita a story, the child took up the conversation that had been interrupted several days before as if no time at all had passed.

"Auntie," she said, "why do those grown-up women go to school?"

"What women are you talking about, Florita?"

"Those young ladies from across the street, Auntie."

"Ah! The young ladies from across the street. I can see that you're very concerned about the ladies from across the street. You see, the fact is that it's a special sort of school"—here she coughed—"a school for young ladies who've lost their way."

"Have I lost my way, Auntie?"

"Heavens, what a thing to say!"

On this afternoon a pinkish tinge rose into Aunt Cruz's white powdered cheeks.

"What does it mean to lose your way, Auntie?"

"Look, Florita"—her voice took on a sugary tone to make the subject seem less important—"there are young ladies who were abandoned when they were little girls, and since they weren't educated when they were small, they have to be educated when they're older. That's why they go to school. Understand?"

The children tried to fill out these and other unsatisfactory pieces of information in the kitchen, their favorite place of refuge, especially in winter when the firewood crackled in the stove and Señora Zoa opened the draft, and the stove top and burners began to turn red like the lanterns outside Friné's. Amalia, seated on her high stool, hummed to herself in a corner as she polished the family's shoes. In that cozy redoubt conversations tended to revolve around knotty or confidential subjects. And so Florita, almost as soon as she felt better but while she was still convalescent, asked Amalia about the young ladies at Friné's. But Amalia didn't really answer her, only looked slyly at Señora Zoa and tossed her head meaningfully. But, as the little girl persisted, she said, "Why don't you ask your mama?"

"I already asked Aunt Cruz, and she said it was a school."

Amalia giggled.

"A school, eh? Did you hear that, Señora Zoa? Fine education those girls are going to get in that school!"

Amalia, with her thin, straight, plucked eyebrows that rose toward her temples, had been with the family for barely three years, but Señora Zoa, who had just passed her seventy-third birthday, had worked for Papa León since she was twenty and had stayed on with him after Mama Obdulia died and Mama Zita took charge of the house. And as a result of one of those unfathomable inclinations so characteristic of unmarried virgins when they reach a certain age, she had a burning passion for the boy, for the male child; it was a pure passion, asexual but exclusive, which was not content with loving and being loved but also demanded the repudiation of others.

"Who loves you, my treasure?"

"You do, Zoa."

The child would snuggle into the old woman's narrow lap against the hard curve of her ribs, as spare as a greyhound's but warmed by a special odor: sour, stagnant, domestic.

"Your mama doesn't have eyes for anyone but Crucita, so now you know it."

"And how about my papa, Zoa?"

23

"Your papa, your papa. Your papa's crazy about Florita, don't you know that?"

The world seemed to collapse under his feet, and the child would press his face against her, against her black skirt, clinging to that vague smell composed of mingled smoke, cookstove, and red floor tiles; and he would also take refuge in that loving lap every time that he quarreled with his sister and his mother scolded him. Then the old woman would take him in her arms and rub her snake-cold cheek against his as if seeking its warmth, and would repeat, "Mama doesn't love you, my treasure. Mama doesn't have eyes for anyone but Crucita."

This was how Gervasio, from the time he was a very small boy, grew accustomed to seeking security in Señora Zoa's always ready arms; he deposited both his joys and his troubles in her as in a confessional. It was why, as soon as he had left the gathering on the night of February 11, still dazed by Uncle Vidal's stentorian shouts, Aunt Cruz's tears, and the superstitious climate in the room, he started to run down the long hall and didn't stop until he could feel himself protected by Señora Zoa's bony arms.

"Zoa, I'm going to tell you a secret."

"Tell me, lovey, tell me."

He brought his lips close to the woman's transparent ear, almost invisible under her white hair pulled back in a bun, and whispered, "I'm going to be a hero."

"Aren't you the fool? One of those heroes that get killed?"

On the defensive, Señora Zoa instinctively raised her voice.

"No, Zoa, I'm going to be a hero without dying. Papa León said so. But Mama doesn't want Papa Telmo to know; it's a secret."

Amalia came in with her white cap and apron on and stood looking at them derisively, hands on hips.

"Just look at them, like two turtledoves. Anselmo Llorente's going to laugh his head off tomorrow when I tell him about it."

Amalia—dark, nervous, lively, limping a little on her right leg— always referred to her sweetheart by both his Christian name and his surname as a mark of deference and distinction, but in spite of her pretensions Anselmo Llorente was a poor figure of a man, leathery and lean, with a lascivious flat-cheeked face and rimless glasses whose lenses were always spotless. In both winter and summer he wore dark suits with a knife crease in the trousers and a little gray felt hat whose brim shaded his right eye. Until spring was well under way he never shed his navy blue overcoat, which almost reached his ankles, or the checkered scarf that protected his skinny throat so thoroughly that, between the hat and the muffler, a small, enigmatic, Oriental-looking face could barely be glimpsed. Sometimes Crucita would tell Amalia that Anselmo Llorente was quite the little gentleman, and she would smile with pleasure over what she took to be a compliment. But Amalia felt that she was ennobling him by referring to him by his Christian name and surname.

"I'm leaving. Anselmo Llorente must be waiting for me downstairs."

Gervasio didn't really like Anselmo Llorente, so colorless, so angular, so distant, striding to and fro in the vestibule of the old palace with long steps, his eyes furtive, his upper body bent forward, his hands in his pockets; and if the children spoke to him as they went by, he would answer with a grunt, not even noticing who they were except when Señora Zoa was with them, in which case he would raise his hat ceremoniously, exchange a few words with her, and shower her with flattery. And then he always said the same thing:

"If you're going upstairs, Señora Zoa, please tell Amalia to come down. I'm damn sick and tired of waiting."

Señora Felipa, the laundress, also thought that Anselmo Llorente was a remarkable catch.

"Heavens, that's some sweetheart you've found for yourself, my girl! He must have an awfully good job."

"He's a clerk," Amalia replied proudly.

"You can tell that a mile off; some clothes he wears."

On Mondays and Thursdays Señora Felipa came to the palace to do the family wash in the big zinc-lined trough on the gallery off the kitchen, overlooking the garden, where Clemente the deaf-mute, son of Pedro the doorman, pruned the rosebushes and loosened the dirt in the flowerbeds in preparation for spring planting. Señora Felipa and Señora Agustina, Señora Zoa's widowed sister-in-law who sewed for the household, lived in the outlying working-class districts where the city petered out and became

country—a squalid countryside (two rows of poplars fringing a
diffident brook) of stones, garbage, and garden plots surrounded
with wire. But while in the northern suburb where Señora Felipa
lived the brook formed a backbone for the huddle of adobe houses,
with walls of decaying thatch protecting the barnyards, in the
south, where Señora Agustina lived, the railway line was what
divided the group of houses scattered over the slopes of the hill,
sordid as a nomad encampment, pierced at all hours by the locomo-
tives' whistles.

At Señora Felipa's house in the northern suburb there was a
garden plot enclosed with barbed wire where she cultivated
potatoes, onions, and red cabbage, and behind the house, kept in
with wire screening, she raised a dozen white rabbits with red
eyelids, another dozen timid hens, and a grunting pig shut in a sty
made of badly joined boards through whose chinks the children
would tickle him with long reeds. The large and energetic figure of
Señora Felipa, bringer of healthful country air, attracted the children and enchanted them with the small events of her world.

"Yesterday the doe dropped a litter."

"Really, Felipa?"

"She had fourteen little rabbits."

"As many as that?"

"That's nothing. The year of the flu epidemic I had one that
dropped twenty-two."

Señora Felipa scrubbed the clothes against the rippled, soapy
washboard with her enormous swollen hands, and Florita observed
her livid fingers, puffed like toads, the tips wrinkled like dried
chestnuts, the nails white.

"Did you notice? Señora Felipa has hands like a drowned person's."

"What are a drowned person's hands like?"

Florita explained to him that at first drowned people got red,
then yellow, and later purplish, like Señora Felipa's hands, and
their fingers wrinkled because water made people older faster than
air did.

In good weather Zoa would take the children out for a long walk
on Thursdays, because Papa Telmo didn't want to see them in the
house or shut up in the little garden.

"They've got to have a walk, Zita; they have to exercise. If the muscles don't tire themselves out, they get poisoned."

The choice never varied.

"Where do you want to go, to Señora Felipa's or my sister-in-law Agustina's?"

The children did not hesitate.

"Let's go to Señora Felipa's."

But Señora Zoa would go to the northern suburb or the southern suburb according to the way she felt.

Her sister-in-law, Señora Agustina, had two children: Daniel, who was sallow, muscular, and surly and worked at his carpenter's bench on the ground floor of the house, following the course of the hours by the whistles of the trains heading to and from the capital, and Felisilla, the girl, who wasn't quite all there and drooled, and who despite having passed her seventeenth birthday knew no other pastime than to roll around in the pile of shavings that fell from the plane, laughing for no reason. But in that house, even apart from Daniel's obvious hostility, there were no animals except for a cock partridge in a cage near the door who never stopped turning round and round, pecking at the wires of the cage as if looking for a hole to escape through, and a frightened yellow canary which couldn't sing because it was a female. Since Señora Agustina wouldn't let them go a step into the garden plot, the children's only entertainment was to scramble up the fig tree as soon as the early figs began to ripen. But in the end Daniel, the carpenter, also got angry with them for eating the ripe fruit, and so Gervasio and Florita, whose last resort was to sit on the edge of the bank to watch the trains go by and wave at the passengers, never hesitated about the option offered by Señora Zoa every spring Thurday.

"Let's go to Señora Felipa's, Zoa; we get bored at your sister-in-law's house."

No matter whether they were coming from the northern or the southern suburb, Florita and Gervasio would return home at nightfall with cramped legs and faces burned by the first sun of spring. When they were close to home at dusk, on the street where the Santa Brígida convent was, they often met Amalia and Anselmo Llorente, very close together, very lovestruck, taking advantage of

the darkness. Sometimes Amalia was so carried away that she
didn't even see them, and at those times Gervasio would innocently
plant a slap on her tight buttocks and yell, "Hello there, Amalia!"

And she would whirl around, startled.

"Did you ever see such a thing! This kid is an imp of Satan."

At the street corner, opposite the arch of the palace entrance
with its wedge-shaped stones, men were starting to come to Friné's,
cautiously and mistrustfully, hiding their eyes under their hatbrims, except for the young recruits who went into the place
openly, laughing and shouting unreservedly, with youthful high-
handedness. A few meters farther on, the children would stop in
front of the street stand that offered them a whole world of stimuli:
comic books, rubber balls, many-colored marbles, cutouts, licorice
sticks, groundnuts, lupine seeds . . . After Florita reached the age
of eight Señora Zoa did not wait for them, but hastily disappeared
into the vestibule, confining herself to grumbling, "You'll come up
right away, eh? You know what a fuss Mama makes."

But they took their time over their acquisitions and exchanges,
doing their best to get the greatest possible return for Papa Telmo's
allowance and Uncle Felipe Neri's penny, if they had one; and
when they had finished they climbed the broad staircase of well-
waxed wood with the red carpet down the middle, chatting, planning what to play until suppertime, trading trinkets.

One night six weeks after Florita's illness, either because Amalia
was delayed or because she had made a date with Anselmo Llorente
at a later hour than usual, they saw him come along looking very
excited, whispering to one of the blond girls from Friné's, who
walked briskly on her high heels without paying any attention to
him; but because the sidewalk was narrow, Anselmo Llorente trot-
ted a little way behind her, stepping on and off the curb, hopping,
stretching his thin, wrinkled turtle's neck until his little pointed
nose almost got entangled in the blond woman's hair. But she
continued to walk imperturbably, as if Anselmo Llorente did not
exist. Gervasio nudged Florita and the two of them stopped on the
corner, and when the pair passed close by them they said in unison,
"Hello there, Anselmo Llorente."

Anselmo Llorente turned pale and the waxy tone of his skin
became almost green. He stopped, adjusted the knot of his tie as

if he had nothing better to do, and finally leaned toward them.

"What the devil are you kids doing here?"

"We've been at the candy stand."

"And where's Señora Zoa gone to?"

"She's upstairs, why?"

"Never mind. You oughtn't to be out on the street by your-selves."

"Who was that blond lady who was with you?"

Anselmo Llorente adjusted his glasses on his nose with one finger, buttoned his jacket, shrugged his fragile shoulders, hesi-tated, and finally pointed at the blond girl who was just going into the café, and said peevishly, "That girl, just like all the rest of them in there, she's nothing but a vixen, a . . . " He made pliers with two fingers, took Gervasio by the neck, and bent over him. "But you're not going to go to Amalia with the story, have you got that?" And he squeezed the boy's neck as if to warn him that he was quite ready to strangle him. "Now go upstairs and tell Amalia to come down. I've been standing here for half an hour and I'm damn sick and tired of waiting."

CHAPTER 3

On Sunday, April 28, 1928, as soon as Gervasio García de la Lastra had gone skipping out of the house with his penny in his pocket, Uncle Felipe Neri sat down at his desk before his notebook with the oilcloth covers, pulled out the piece of pink blotting paper that separated two pages, drew a cross at the top of the page, and wrote in his round, delicate, elaborate hand:

"I have just made a gift to my little nephew Gervasio of my military clothing, gear, and equipment from the time I was a cadet. Naturally it pained me to let it go, for the clothing of thirty years is an inexhaustible vein of memories; but it seems fitting and wise that the hero begin to familiarize himself with his attire. I hope that my sister-in-law Zita will not misinterpret my generosity, which has no intention of inciting him to violence but aims merely to clothe his vocation. First of all I asked the child, looking straight into his eyes, what it was that he felt when his hair stood on end, and he answered me very thoughtfully, 'Like courage, Uncle; like wanting to kill lots of bad people.' That was why I was surprised by his lukewarm reaction when he saw the capes, jackets, dress coats, caps, belts, and boots spread out on the rug in the Oratory. His first movement was childish: he stuck his little feet into some campaign boots that came halfway up his thighs and took two turns around the room, stamping his heels awkwardly. Then he put the sky-blue dress cape over his small shoulders and said quietly, 'Can I look at myself in a mirror, Uncle?' I went into the bedroom first, and he stood motionless before the mirror of the armoire, looking at himself for a long time, after which he turned to me and in his childish way, as if accusing me, gave me to understand that he couldn't imagine how anyone could live a whole life inside that clothing without feeling the desire to be a hero. I was taken aback, but because this child has inspired a solemn feeling of respect in me ever since the fateful night of his remarkable demonstration, I experienced a very strange sensation, as if I were facing a judgment of God. And then I confided in him and humbly confessed that at my age I could well be fighting in Morocco against the Moors, but that my fragile health prevented me from doing so. He raised his head, and with that adult gravity of which he is capable, looked into my eyes with such aplomb that I felt diminished, as if I were stranded and naked, and was barely able to say, 'For the love of God, don't regard me as a coward, Gervasio; your uncle isn't a coward but a sick man.' But he continued to scrutinize me with that touch of the supernatural and unbearable that sometimes shines in his eyes, to the point that a lump rose in my throat and I very nearly burst into tears. It was a devastating experience. When we returned to the Oratory he went back to being the same child as always: he made a pile of the jackets, spun the rowels on the spurs, pulled the caps down to his eyes, buckled on the belts, and finally asked me ingenuously whether, now that he was the owner of that clothing

and equipment, he only needed to be brave in order to be a hero.
His question surprised me anew, but because I believe in this
child's destiny with the same faith as if an angel had announced
it to me, God himself must have inspired my reply: 'The first thing
a person needs to be a hero,' I told him, 'is a good cause. You can
perform the greatest deeds, even sacrifice your life, but if you don't
do it for a noble cause it will be a useless sacrifice.' The boy listened
to me with his head a little on one side and assented, and from the
discerning expression in his yellowish eyes I guessed that he had
understood my words and that from now on he would be able to
differentiate a good cause from an unjust one with the same clarity
with which today he distinguishes the colors of his marbles."

Several days later, as they drove in Papa León's green Buick
along the narrow streets of the city's old quarter on the way to his
school, Gervasio, dressed in his white sailor suit, sitting on the
jump seat between his two sisters, was observing the back of
Benigno the chauffeur's neck, his strong, inscrutable profile, his
new cap, his gray uniform (also new) with three gilt buttons on
each sleeve. By an association of ideas he thought about his own
uniforms, and immediately took his eyes off Benigno and exchanged an understanding smile with Señora Zoa, who was sitting
next to Benigno; and as he smiled at her he felt a strange tightness
in his head. Mama Zita, who was sharing the back seat with Aunt
Cruz and Papa Telmo, had had a troubling presentiment an hour
earlier while combing his hair; she feared that the child would be
excited by the ceremony, and moved by the notes of the organ and
the nuns' sentimental motets might have a new outbreak and cause
a spectacle. Burdened by this fear, she did her best to flatten his hair
after plastering it down with sugar-water and a bottle of fixative
that she had sent Amalia to buy.

"Mama, why are you combing me so hard?"

"Today's an important day, Gervasio. You're still too young to
understand."

Mama Zita had never talked to her son about his remarkable
performance; indeed, she had never discussed it with anyone except her sister Cruz. She was naturally pliable and accepted everything except Papa León's insistence on instilling into that tender
head the duty of being a hero. If it came to pass she would have

no objection, but neither did she wish to help it along. More than the future, more than what might happen, she was tormented by the physical change the child had undergone, the pallor of his complexion, his skin prickling, his hair out of control and standing straight up. She confided to her sister when the two of them were alone, "I don't like these experiences, Cruz, they can't be healthy. During one of them my son might stay that way for the rest of his life. Can you imagine anything more horrible?" That was why she had made no objection to her brother-in-law's gift; those uniforms were a plaything, something to amuse him with, but on the other hand she was very cross about her father's obstinacy in putting the child through psychological experiments day and night. The image of that manelike little head, with the hair spread out like a porcupine's quills, had been engraved on Mama Zita's mind, along with the very vivid fear of its happening again: "If it comes from God," she said to her sister Cruz, "he has already played his part by revealing it to us. All we can do is wait." She felt that the appropriate thing was to surround Gervasio with a neutral, padded, protective atmosphere that would allow him to develop without traumas until, at the proper moment, the Lord or time, or time or the Lord, would unveil the mystery and make it plain whether those strange phenomena of the epidermis responded to pure tricks of physics, as Vidal believed, or whether they were due to supernatural causes.

Side by side in the pew after communion, Mama Zita bent over Gervasio's sticky head and suggested to him, between sobs, the petitions he must formulate to the Most High, "because today" (she had told him as she lovingly adjusted the collar of his sailor suit) "God can't deny you anything you ask of him." And Gervasio obediently repeated what Mama Zita suggested to him, while the nuns' nasal, stickily sentimental motets soaked into his spirit, raising it above everyday banality. Suddenly Mama Zita rested her forehead on the boy's slicked-down hair and whispered to him, as if it had just occurred to her, that he must pray very hard for Papa Telmo too. When she said that, Gervasio slowly raised his head as if rejecting the accusation implied in those words.

"Is it because Papa Telmo's bad?"

"It's not that at all, dear. Right now it's not a question of Papa Telmo's being good or bad. Today you have to pray to God for everyone, for bad people to be good and for good people to be better. Understand?"

Despite his mother's explanation, the boy continued to rack his brains: maybe Papa Telmo wasn't bad, but there had to be something about him that wasn't right, something that needed correcting, since Mama Zita had told him to pray for his father "very hard." Was it because he hadn't taken communion, perhaps? But neither had Uncle Vidal, nor had other men among the people in the chapel, so that couldn't be a sufficient reason. Huddled apprehensively on the kneeler, he stole glances at his father's robust figure standing next to him, very erect in his striped brown suit, his unfathomable gaze lost in the arch of the apse, waiting for him, his son, to finish giving thanks. A strange idea struck him: would it be a good cause to fight against Papa Telmo? He shook his over-combed head, but the idea pursued him insidiously. Could a struggle between a father and a son ever be a good cause? He buried his face in his forearm and muttered fervently, "God, God, make Papa good," but the communicants had already risen to their feet as they heard the sharp clap of Sister Luciana's hands from the side pew, and up above in the choir two dozen treble voices, formed into unison by the organ, were singing:

> Let my eyes behold thee,
> Jesus sweet and mild,
> Let my eyes behold thee
> And then let me die.

Gervasio, presiding over the big oval table at the club with its centerpiece of white flowers, a steaming cup of chocolate before him, innocently inquired about his uncles Norberto and Adrián, but Papa Telmo turned away as if he hadn't heard, while Mama Zita tied the spotless white napkin around his neck and whispered, "Eat and be quiet; your uncles can't come because they have to work."

But as the boy insisted, his sister Crucita stretched out her long neck from the other side of the table and added an explanation:

"They have to clerk in the store, you know that," and she pronounced the word "clerk" reluctantly, as if referring to some inferior activity.

Uncle Norberto and Uncle Adrián, Papa Telmo's brothers, were twins. They were snub-nosed, with prominent teeth and long stiff necks, and there was hardly any difference between them except for their height. Uncle Norberto, who had been born first, was a good foot taller than his brother Adrián, a whole head taller. Inseparable (both in the shop and in the street), solitary (they had neither friends nor wives), and untalkative, the few words they did pronounce (usually monosyllables) were thick and nasal, as if previously kneaded inside their noses. Neither of them had had anything to do with their brother's getting married, and yet the De la Lastra family harbored a deep-seated resentment against them, a resentment, as it were, against everything that might in any way recall that lamentable episode. Mama Obdulia's mean-spirited opinion, when she learned of Papa Telmo's matrimonial ambitions ("Those Garcías are shopkeepers, aren't they? They don't seem like persons of consequence"), was transmitted to the following generation, and Aunt Cruz as well as Uncle Vidal took special care to cultivate it in the children (making an exception of Papa Telmo) in the person of Crucita, the most reliable of the nieces and nephews, as soon as she reached the age of discernment. Actually, the Garcías' lack of consequence stemmed from the small notions shop they owned in the Calle de la Palma ("the most ordinary part of the city"), behind the main square. Mama Obdulia's insulting outbursts merely strengthened Mama Zita's incipient romance, which was just beginning to feed on glances, furtive appearances on the glassed-in balcony, and endless disappointments on Papa Telmo's part, who spent hour after hour lurking in the street when she failed to appear. Her mother's harassment, her studied scorn for the suitor, did not succeed in undermining Mama Zita's morale; nor did Aunt Cruz's acerbic remarks ("This morning your future mother-in-law was watering the plants on the balcony with a blue satin robe on"), or Uncle Vidal's rude comments ("I saw your future mother-in-law with a watermelon under her arm that was bigger than her bottom"). Mama Zita's huge, vague eyes with their meek gaze did not change, and she would either say nothing or reply quietly, without getting angry, to the coarse insinuations of her brother, who among other things, accused her suitor of "smelling of the kind of wine workmen drink." "Better a workman smelling of wine than a do-nothing smelling of cologne." Mama Obdulia's stubborn opposition crumbled unexpectedly on the day Papa Telmo received his degree in medicine with highest honors. Mama Obdulia's profound respect for the printed word and academic degrees was stronger than her class convictions. Mama Zita and Papa Telmo were married in the church of Santa Brígida with all sorts of favorable auguries. That was the only family event that Uncle Norberto and Uncle Adrián attended; they paid little attention to the succulent luncheon (despite their long, hungry-looking teeth), and when the dancing began took ceremonious leave, according to Aunt Cruz, "because they had to open the store."

After their parents died the two brothers continued the life of routine they had always led: from the notions shop to home, from home to the shop, with a ritual halt at the Correos bar on the main square to have a few glasses of white wine and one olive. After they had closed the shop in the afternoon they repeated the visit, though with a change of diet: one potato chip instead of the olive. According to Señor Josué, the druggist on the corner, the two uncles kept themselves alive on this frugal meal ("that's all they eat"), a possible opinion because both had no more flesh on them than a skeleton, though to tell the truth no one ever saw them drunk, as they had never been seen separately or with women. But though they hardly spoke to each other, they displayed a sort of synchronization of movements, an identity of facial expressions and gestures which Señor Josué pedantically described as "the dynamic analogy between twins." Neither of them ever smiled, despite the fact that their large, prominent teeth seemed to invite such a gesture, but neither did they appear to be bored: their little round eyes, like those of some night bird, attentively observed the world around them with a curiosity that turned to avidity as they watched the automobiles and motorcycles that were beginning to proliferate in the city. Uncle Norberto and Uncle Adrián were capable of spending hours in front of a motor, no matter how simple, without speaking or changing their position, simply observing, which led Señor Josué to remark, "the Mutes look at cars the way the rest of us look at women."

Florita and Gervasio surreptitiously visited their uncles Norberto and Adrián in the shop on spring Thursdays, when the long walks began. The uncles would receive them imperturbably, showing neither irritation nor pleasure, without the least expenditure of words except for very frequently calling them rascals, as Papa Telmo also did on solemn occasions; but they let the children play with the yardstick, the boxes of metal tips, the big scissors, and the hooks for picking up dropped stitches, while Señora Zoa, who appeared to have become infected with the family's chilliness toward the uncles, waited outside, chatting with Señor Josué or the janitor's wife in the next building. When the children emerged from the shop she always said the same thing no matter whom she had been talking to.

"Heavens, I wouldn't face your uncles if I was to be paid my weight in gold."

"Why not, Zoa? They're nice."

"They don't talk, lovey; all they do is look. And the man who doesn't do anything but look can't harbor good intentions."

In spite of Señora Zoa's negative opinion Uncle Norberto and Uncle Adrián were generous with the children, and every afternoon, when the visit was over, both men would simultaneously unbutton their jackets (as if one were the mirror image of the other), insert a thumb and index finger into the bottom pocket of their vests, and give each child a silver peseta. Uncle Adrián, the short one, gave it to Florita and Uncle Norberto, the tall one, to Gervasio; then they would administer a few pats on the backs of the children's necks, and making a visible effort, would say goodbye in their synchronized voices:

"So long, rascals."

Well aware of the aversion inspired by their uncles at home, Florita and Gervasio concealed their visits; from a very early age that rite formed part of their secret life. This was no bar to their missing the uncles on great family occasions, nor to Crucita's explaining their absence with cruel barbs that the simplicity of the children's minds found unacceptable.

"We can't ever be on good terms with Uncle Norberto and Uncle Adrián, little ones. We speak two different languages."

Gervasio accepted that explanation in the belief that Crucita was referring to the fact that they never talked; but he tried to get them to do so repeatedly, seeking some convincing reason underneath it all, an answer that was never forthcoming. And that was why now, at the club, he was pretending to concentrate on his cup of chocolate but was really looking at Papa Telmo's smooth face, trying his best to make out what was hidden behind those dark brown eyebrows, under that tanned skin, which had caused his mother to pray "very hard" for him. Sometimes, when his inquisitive glance had been particularly intense, he thought that he could glimpse a sort of melancholy cloud in his father's eyes, a hint of impatience or a shade of sorrow, glimpses that vanished like smoke in the wind as soon as Papa Telmo began to talk or laugh. But more often he listened, his head on one side, looking down, especially when Uncle Vidal started barking (that was the way he had described her brother's style of argument to Mama Zita one night), for Uncle Vidal was his antithesis. Even physically they were opposites, since Papa Telmo's swarthy complexion, full head of hair, his thick dark eyebrows sprinkled with a white hair or two, contrasted with Uncle Vidal's rosy diabetic skin, his slippery, shiny bald spot, his almost invisible albino brows and lashes. And so when Uncle Vidal proclaimed for the second time that morning that the demonstration at the Patriotic Union in Madrid had been a true plebiscite, even though he was pretending to address the table at large he had a particular target in mind, Papa Telmo; but Papa Telmo smiled, a neutral smile that had the effect of unleashing Uncle Felipe Neri's voice. He had just dissolved some white powders in water, and with the glass held high (as if he were about to propose a toast), he interposed, trying to keep the peace, that perhaps the term "plebiscite" was a bit of an exaggeration, but that it certainly revealed a very noisy state of opinion. Gervasio looked first toward one and then the other, studying the reactions of both sides, asking himself what the Patriotic Union might be and whether it had anything to do with Mama Zita's prayers for Papa Telmo. But unexpectedly Aunt Macrina, who because she was the youngest adult member of the family always liked to strike a gloomy note, performed a maneuver to change the subject and led the conversation toward the catastrophic fire in the Novedades theater in Madrid, emphasizing the blood-curdling detail that some of the victims were found clutching bloody knives in their hands, with which they had tried to force their way through the frantic crowd, an example to which Uncle Vidal, always avid for controversy, replied that it was perfectly consistent, for the Spanish people were "a nation of hysterics and savages." And when Aunt Cruz and Mama Zita made a faint effort to protest he repeated, "hysterics and savages," a remark which Papa Telmo seized upon to ask ironically whom he thought of as most representative of the national temperament, the demonstrators at the Patriotic Union or the knife-wielders of the Novedades theater. This objection infuriated Uncle Vidal, who shouted to the point of hoarseness that when he spoke of a plebiscite he wasn't talking about the common herd but the healthy sector of society. At this point Mama Zita intervened to show her disagreement and say that the Spanish people were a brave people, and that as a recent example they had the exploit of the "Plus Ultra"; but Uncle Vidal, an incorrigible nay-sayer, smiled sarcastically and shouted that his sister had just put her finger on the problem, since in fact Spaniards, to avoid working, were capable of discovering America or crossing the Atlantic in a sardine can, "the point was not to do a lick of work," a piece of effrontery to which Uncle Felipe Neri (whose face was still screwed up from drinking the white powder in his glass) replied in a scandalized tone that it wasn't true, that Spain might not manufacture airplanes but it did make brave men to fly them, and that Franco, Rada, Durán, and Ruiz de Alda were imperishable heroes; and as Uncle Vidal smiled, shaking his bald head in negation, he talked louder and louder, until Aunt Cruz, concerned for her husband's ulcer, stuck her powdered face between them and calmed them down, suggesting that instead of arguing like fanatics during a family occasion as beautiful as Gervasio's first communion, they might well organize an expedition to La Granja de San Ildefonso, taking advantage of the spring weather, to see the fountains play. Aunt Cruz's suggestion was so opportune that it had the virtue of reconciling viewpoints and dispersing the last clouds of disagreement: the whole family would go to La Granja in two cars, all except the two younger children and Papa León, getting up very early because the fountains played only until midday, and according to their friends the Bustillos, the spectacle was a lavish display of water, light, and color. Gervasio was no longer listening to the adults' conversation. With a glass of sugar-water in his hand, he was meditating on the mysteries of heroism, wondering why an adventure as enjoyable as the flight of the "Plus Ultra" could be considered heroic, and what seemed all the more incomprehensible to him, where the good cause was to be found in an action that was mere sport and so ordinary.

Back at home, tired of being on his best behavior, he watched Florita pull aside the curtains of the balcony in the playroom and peer at the street.

"Look, here comes a funeral," said the little girl.

"White or black?"

"Black."

He joined her. Four young men dressed in mourning, their eyelids red from crying, hats in their hands, were leaning against the cold walls of Santa Brígida, while a long line of men, looking more relaxed and with a suitably grave expression on their faces, passed by them making courteous bows.

"It must be a woman."

"Who?"

"The one who's dead. Don't you see how small the coffin is?"

Gervasio turned his head, pleasurably excited.

"Do you want to play?"

"All right, I'll start."

The little girl opened the balcony window and the requiem of Don Urbano, the parish priest, floated through the aperture as a mere hum, the words indistinguishable. When he had finished, the mourners began to disperse, while the family members on foot could hardly keep up with the horses' languid trot, hoofs ringing on the pavement; and on the upper balconies of Friné's an invisible hand pulled back the curtains and the curious blond heads of two of its inhabitants appeared.

Playing funerals was one of the children's favorite games, and they would bet the chocolate of their afternoon snack or a candy from the street stand on the number and color of the carriages that would stop at Santa Brígida that afternoon.

"Five black ones."

"Three black ones and a white one."

And if by any chance four black carriages had gone by, and at the corner of the cobbled street the fifth appeared, towering high and making a great racket, Florita or Gervasio, whichever was the lucky one, would be unable to control his or her glee, clapping jubilantly and cheering before the shocked eyes of the members of the procession. Sometimes Señora Zoa, who would be sorting underwear in the playroom, would join the childish contest, for like all old folks she enjoyed watching dead people go by (probably younger than she and certainly far better off financially) between the railings of the balcony, and feeling like a survivor. When a prominent person in the city died, Crucita would sometimes join the group, not to compete but to ascertain from behind the thin curtains whether the hearse, the crowd, the coachman's outfit, and the number of horses were in consonance with the deceased's status in life. In those cases Florita and Gervasio counted the carriages on their fingers, under their breaths, for Crucita thought that their taste for funerals was a macabre, coarse, and vulgar display, "the sort of thing lower-class people do," and wouldn't let them play.

At nightfall on that same day Papa León, with an air of mystery, shut himself into the study with Gervasio and, as he always did during these last few weeks, looked up and down the hall before closing the door to make sure that no one was spying on him.

"Do you remember what I promised you on the day you made your first communion?"

The boy hesitated.

"I don't remember," he said at last.

"Do you mean to tell me you have such a poor opinion of the General's memory?" He raised his right eyebrow, and three deep wrinkles copied the eyebrow on that side of his face.

"Don Cástor?"

"Don Cástor of course, what other general could it be?"

"Now I remember," the boy said suddenly. "You promised to show me the bullet that wounded the General and the beret he was wearing when he was killed."

Papa León squatted and opened the bottom drawer of the chest of drawers.

"I told you more than that," he added with the greatest solemnity. "I told you that that bullet and that beret were to be yours when I died. That is what I want, and it will be noted in my will; but just in case, now you know about it too."

He took out a little box of a pure blue color, like a jeweler's box, and opened it with reverent unction. A shapeless piece of grayish, flattened lead, like a dull lump, lay inside between layers of cotton.

"Is that what bullets are like, Papa León?"

"See, they're like that after they kill someone; before, they're thinner and sharper."

"But there's no blood on it."

Papa León shook his head in annoyance.

"Arresti, the field surgeon, washed it like a fool before he gave it to me as a souvenir."

He placed the blue box on the chest of drawers, squatted again, and brought out a big round, flat box with a marzipan eel pictured on the cover. He opened it and inside, along with half a dozen mothballs, a worn beret of a faded red color appeared. It had a gilded plaque in the center, covering the tab, that said "God, Fatherland, King."

"This is the General's beret, my boy. Now you know where it is."

"Did Don Cástor have it on when they killed him?"

"That's right. The General never took it off even to sleep."

The old man's cheeks were covered with a network of broken veins and, as happened every time he examined something closely, his glasses had slipped down to the tip of his nose and he was looking over the tops of the lenses. With his little wrinkled hands he turned the beret over and showed a hole, like a moth hole.

"Look, the bullet went in here."

Gervasio slowly turned his head.

"Was Don Cástor a hero, then?"

"Why, naturally he was a hero, what did you think? The General died before Burceña while he was directing the counterattack. We were five hundred men against four thousand, and when he fell, and Trifón and I ran to help him, he waved us aside and said, 'This is the time to fight.' Then, when the battle was over and we went back to him, Don Cástor was already dead."

The boy leaned back on the sofa, thinking.

"Do you mind telling me about it more slowly, Papa León?"

The old man consulted his ancient watch.

"Some other day," he said with a sidelong glance at the door. "It's suppertime and your mother will be angry with me if she finds us together. You know what a fuss she makes."

CHAPTER
4

Señora Zoa crossed the park every morning with a child holding either hand, on the way to school, and during the long winters (which were very severe in the city) the fog would twine among the skeletons of the trees so that the woman and the children, like ghostly shadows, seemed to be the last inhabitants of an inanimate world. In the faded crepuscular light enormous gray rats would run across the paths, and among the foliage near the frozen pond they could hear the peacocks' peremptory cries. Gervasio, with his fuzzy scarf pulled up to his eyes, liked the season's half-light, the deserted gardens, Señora Zoa's white breath preceding her red nose as if she herself were a fog factory. On rainy days, in spring and fall, big puddles swarming with earthworms formed on the paths, and Señora Zoa, her black umbrella open like a trapeze artist's, would jump from one side to another so as not to step on them, for she hated nothing so much as mice and creeping things.

On extremely cold days they used to meet "La Enana"—the Dwarf—on the main path: Señorita Candelaria Alonso, a middle-aged blonde with long curls falling on her shoulders and her poor little body, smaller than Gervasio's, mounted on a tiny bicycle with wide tires and security wheels at the sides. And it was not unusual, as they watched her, to have Señorita Aurora Burgos, "La Madruga"—the Early Riser—appear from the other side. She was a woman made in one straight line, nearly seven feet tall and very round-shouldered, whose little head nearly disappeared up there, its features blurred by the fog. Crucita said that both La Enana and La Madruga were "ladies of good family" and that they were distinguished and well educated, but that because of their physical appearance they had to stay shut up at home.

"Zoa, why do La Enana and La Madruga go out walking so early?"

"It's their looks; can't you see what they look like? If they went out at any other time people would make fun of them."

She speeded up her pace and added, as if to herself, "What I say is, why can't they cut a piece off one and add it to the other? Then both of them would be just fine."

"Can they do that, Zoa?"

"That's what I said, lovey, if they could."

On some days Señora Zoa, taking advantage of the absence of Florita, who was in bed with one of her periodic attacks of tonsillitis, would enact tender love scenes with Gervasio in the deep solitude of the park.

"What would become of you, my treasure, if it weren't for Zoa? Eh? Can you tell me that?"

The boy would look at her over the top of his woolen scarf with his unmoving grayish-yellow irises.

"Nobody loves you."

"Why doesn't anybody love me, Zoa?"

"Why, why? Who knows? But Mama is crazy about Crucita, and

as for your papa, nobody can tear him away from Florita. For them, it's as if you'd never been born."

Gervasio, familiar with these confidences from a very early age, would feel sorry for himself, would deplore his orphan state and feel the pressing need of something emotional to cling to.

"But you love me, don't you, Zoa?"

The old woman would crouch down and press the child to her breast.

"More than the apple of my eye."

The two would hug each other in silence, kiss each other frantically, and cry in unison with their cheeks pressed together, under the brooding frost-covered chestnut trees.

Mama Zita didn't get along with Señora Zoa.

"She has all the defects of maids who grow old in a household," she would say to her sister Cruz. "I simply can't get her to call Crucita 'Señorita,' and really I think the girl's old enough for her to do so."

For one reason or another, Mama Zita and Señora Zoa were in a permanent state of disagreement. And every time they had an argument Señora Zoa, believing herself the offended party, would begin to sob, shut herself in her room, and start to pack her suitcase. Gervasio, as witness of the offense, would cry right along with her, clinging to her skirts and begging her not to leave; and despite the fact that the scene had been played out a hundred times and was never more than a sham, the child never quite learned from experience. Between sighs, the old woman would be packing the suitcase with her seashell (which Gervasio had given her one summer in Fuenterrabía, and which held the roar of the sea), her churchgoing veil, her hair combs, her garters, the photograph of her sister-in-law with her children Daniel and Felisilla, and her black clothes, and finally, when he heard the click of the latch, Gervasio sobbed as if his heart would break.

"Will you remember me?"

"Yes, Zoa."

"Always, always?"

"Always, Zoa."

"Even if I die?"

In the face of this macabre possibility the child, like his grandmother Obdulia, hadn't the courage to reply, and would sob all the louder. The old woman would change her tactics.

"D'you know who's to blame for all this?"

"Who, Zoa?"

"Crucita, for your information."

"My sister?"

"Which Crucita do you think?"

Señora Zoa would pick up the suitcase to leave, and then the child would cling madly to her black-clad legs and yell, in full romantic spate:

"If you go away, Zoa, then I want to die!"

And when the old woman heard that, she would set the suitcase on the floor with great dignity, bend down, and press Gervasio against her ribcage and mercilessly kiss his cheeks over and over, with hard, wet, noisy, smacking, all-encompassing kisses, and at last she would straighten up, place the suitcase on the high iron bed, and without a word slowly start to unpack it, arranging on the dresser the articles of clothing and souvenirs she had removed a few moments before. When she had finished she would take Gervasio by the hand and the two of them would go out into the hall where Crucita was waiting for them, her full lips tightly shut and her green eyes sparkling.

"I knew that was going to happen."

"What did you know, tell me?"

"That you weren't leaving."

"Well, if I stay, don't think for a minute that it's because of you."

"You needn't think I'm going to die the day you do go, Zoa."

After each of these feints the old woman would mope around the house for a week, silent, gloomy, and sulky, while Crucita, the cause of her misfortune, would hum under her breath, come and go triumphantly, and look at her disdainfully, because Crucita, according to her godfather, was the one in whom, more than in any other member of the clan, the pride of caste was deepest. She was haughty, beautiful, clever, a good student; she knew how to manage fish knives and forks with confidence, had judicious opinions about important questions, knew how to play tennis, walk, glance, wear a long dress, and get a few reasonably harmonious notes out of the drawing-room piano. In short, despite the flatness of her chest (which she took to be an additional proof of her distinction), Crucita set the standard, lived with the adults, while the two younger children were relegated to the subordinate world of the playroom and kitchen. But suddenly, on the night of February 11, Gervasio had been revealed as a different sort of being with special gifts and automatically rose in rank, though all the family members were so startled that they concealed not only their feelings but the reasons for their change of attitude toward him. Gervasio was well aware of the change. He was conscious of the respect he inspired, of the fact that behind the everyday words spoken in his presence other hidden words were avoided for fear that something would be produced in his body, and that they were not sure whether this was an affliction or something to be desired. They observed him with concealed curiosity, as a little sorcerer with magical powers, as perhaps predestined for something; and proudly and gratefully the child accepted their homage. Nor was the change in Gervasio lost on Señora Zoa; but since she had not seen his metamorphosis at first hand she put it down to his age and accepted it resignedly, for it was a well-known fact that in those transports of love that old virgins have for the children placed in their care, everything is fragile and ephemeral. But the rupture had not yet taken place, had not passed the stage of finickiness and affectation, of mutually showing off their sore places to make the other feel pity; that is, the break was not yet definite.

"What are you crying about, Zoa?"

"About you, my treasure; you don't love me any more."

"Yes I do, Zoa."

"Then why didn't you come to see me yesterday, tell me that?"

"I was in the drawing room with my uncle and aunt, Zoa."

The date of February 11 had brought a change in Gervasio's life. After his first communion Mama Zita incorporated him into the group formed by his sisters, who went every Sunday to the nine o'clock mass said by Don Urbano in the parish church. The boy would step forward cheerfully to offer the holy water, and sometimes would put his hand in it until he could feel its coolness on his wrist; but one day Mama Zita told him that to do that was a sin, that holy water wasn't there to wash his hands in but to wash away his sins, and to use it for something it wasn't intended for was an offense against the Lord. Gervasio mended his ways, but sometimes, when fat old Severo the sacristan was filling the font, Gervasio would accidentally wet his fingers up to the knuckles; and then in bed at night he would be unable to sleep, gnawed by scruples, and would fight off sleep for fear of not waking up, of turning up dead in bed in the morning without having confessed.

On the feast day of Santa Brígida Mama Zita made a sponge cake for the parish priest, which she and Cruz had devotedly mixed the evening before. Don Urbano, long-faced and astigmatic, with one drooping eye shrouded in a bluish eyelid, stared greedily out of the other at the tender sponge cake, and after thanking Mama Zita for the gift began to chat with her about neighborhood problems and, clearly in allusion to the young ladies at Friné's, admitted how difficult it was in the city, and even more so in its historic district, to separate the wheat from the chaff, and how painful it was that palaces with coats of arms over their doors, inhabited by families of the highest principle, had to overlook houses of perdition.

When the priest had left Florita inquired, "Is our house a house of perdition?"

Mama Zita got angry.

"Don't be stupid! Our house is the old palace of the Count of Pradoluengo, and Papa León is his direct descendant. If your grandfather isn't a count himself, it's out of false modesty."

Next day Gervasio tried to impress Sister Luciana by telling her that he lived in a palace, but she replied that that was public knowledge and that no one in the city was unaware of his grandfather's house, because the coat of arms over the door was heraldically the most interesting one in the old quarter of the city. That night in the kitchen Gervasio asked what a coat of arms was, but Señora Zoa and Amalia were unable to answer him, and Florita ventured a guess that "maybe it was a breed of dog"; but Crucita, who was hanging about waiting to put her oar in, said that it was a shield like the one on the archway over the door, on the corner under the glassed-in balcony, and that only people who in olden times had a squire—that is, "people of lineage and position"— possessed one.

After that day Gervasio began to think well of his house, which until then he had looked upon as a big, gloomy, rundown sort of place. And so the big vestibule with its carved wooden ceiling and the shiny copper brazier in the middle, which he had always despised, suddenly became an appropriate spot for the count to take his leisure and warm his feet when he returned from his forays. Likewise, the inconspicuous perforation that Mama Zita had had drilled in the kitchen wall so that whoever called at the street door could be seen, now struck the child as an elementary precaution on the count's part to discover his enemies in time. He attributed a less definite but no less mysterious purpose to the secret doors, decorated with the same flowered wallpaper as the walls, in the green room and his grandfather's study, and even to the great mantelpiece in the drawing room, under whose hood a dozen people could easily be accommodated.

However, at Sunday mass his family pride tottered every time that Mama Zita, kneeling beside him with bowed head after communion, whispered fervently into his ear, "Don't forget to pray for Papa Telmo," a recommendation that distressed the child very much and made him think that his father must be descended from some terribly shame-making people. After his return home this suspicion caused him to look askance at his father and observe him closely; but he never discovered anything in him to find fault with except for some unusual action (possibly "in bad taste," as Crucita said), such as shaving barefoot on the wet tiles of the bathroom floor with the door half open, humming to himself. Unable to find the solution, one day he unburdened himself to Florita.

"Why does Mama make me pray for Papa Telmo after communion?"

"Don't you know why?"

"No."

Florita lowered her voice.

"Papa Telmo is a quack."

"And what's a quack?"

"Sister Caridad says that quacks are witches."

Despite Florita's confidential and even admiring tone, her statement left him feeling miserable, and with his extremely vivid sensibility he imagined Papa Telmo, naked from the waist up and with his face covered with lather, casting spells in front of the fire in the fireplace, under Giotto's *Resurrection* (with Mama Zita below it dressed in the helmet and breastplate of the sleeping guards), invoking the spirit of the last Count of Pradoluengo. This was the way in which Gervasio came to feel his first fears: fear of the dark, of ghosts, of the mournful creaking of the oak floors, the furniture's vague shapes, the great empty spaces of the old house. Some nights he called for water without being really thirsty, solely for the comfort of seeing Amalia or Señora Zoa appear; but most of the time he resisted, scolding himself for such weakness, and at those times his mouth would go dry, anxiety would settle in his stomach, and he would have to cover his head with the top of the sheet in order to get to sleep. He watched Papa Telmo apprehensively, and the mere fact of seeing him lather his face in the bathroom in his bare feet, something Gervasio had been witnessing ever since he could remember, seemed in the light of recent discoveries to be part of a magic ritual whose ultimate consequences he could not fathom. One night in the kitchen, alone with Zoa, he asked her about that mysterious rite of Papa Telmo's.

"They're just things your papa does to move his insides."

"To move his insides, Zoa?" His yellowish eyes stared.

"To move his bowels, lovey; your papa's one of those doctors they call naturopaths."

Those cryptic words (moving the insides, naturopath, which were in some way connected with witchcraft and the occult sciences) increased Gervasio's suspicions, so that his incipient mistrust turned into fear. But it was true that Papa Telmo, after practicing for several months in a pretty little town in the Basque country, had felt himself called to naturopathic medicine, installed himself in the capital city of the province, and had the name of his specialty printed on his prescription pads and visiting cards (to which Gervasio, perhaps because he was without curiosity about them, lacked access), so that he wouldn't be confused with allopathic doctors.

"And what's the difference?" asked Uncle Vidal sarcastically.

"The allopath puts out poison for flies; the naturopath removes the pie and the flies go away," answered Papa Telmo with the certainty entailed in explaining the obvious.

On the very few occasions when Papa Telmo attended the Saturday evening gatherings, Uncle Vidal would draw him out and his brother-in-law would go along willingly, pretending to a proselytizing ardor which he may really have felt, though usually he concealed it.

"The sun is my cook and the earth my pantry," he would say, smiling.

And indeed, his diet was mostly vegetarian and always moderate, but he refrained from imposing it on the children (perhaps to avoid a confrontation with Mama Zita) and was tolerant with them, as he said, because of their age.

"Albumin is necessary while the organism is still being built. Later there's too much of it."

Early on Sunday mornings he would walk at a rapid pace to some pine grove or lonely oak-covered hill, and once there would undress (even in winter, at temperatures of below freezing), do a few minutes of breathing exercises, and then rove around barefoot for a couple of hours among the thickets, taking the sun. He rejected sunbaths on principle and recommended baths of light, though never lying still but walking, and before the sun had reached the zenith.

"You have to take advantage of the chemical rays; by noon they're destroyed by the caloric rays."

After he had dressed he would practice a quarter of an hour of "optical nourishment," by means of which, according to his theories, the brain and bone marrow received reinforcement from the sun through the optic nerve.

"Light makes us feel splendid; shadows make us sad."

Uncle Vidal would make fun of him as he listened, and would remark that the great sportsmen were meat-eaters and did their resting in bed, to which Papa Telmo would reply that maybe the great ones did, but not the "chosen," those who followed the elementary maxim that "muscles don't tire, they get poisoned." When these subjects came up in the Saturday gatherings, Papa Telmo would say, half jokingly and half seriously, that during his stay in the Basque country he had carried out experiments with jai-alai players and that those who restricted themselves to a diet of dried fruits, almonds, and other oily products "would walk off the court as if they'd just come from an invigorating bath, fresh and relaxed, while their adversaries were so exhausted they could hardly walk." On very rare occasions Uncle Felipe Neri would take part in the conversation, wrinkling up his face as usual because of the acids, a circumstance that Papa Telmo would seize upon to offer him his services:

"If you'd make up your mind to it someday, Felipe, in a couple of months I'd leave your stomach as good as new."

While these conversations were going on Mama Zita would shrink into her chair, feeling terribly ashamed; she would have done anything to make him stop talking or disappear from the room, not because she thought his arguments scientifically unfounded, but because she considered them plebeian and felt that by expressing them Telmo was displaying the unworthiest aspect of his social extraction. Papa León and the uncles would listen to him, however, with open curiosity, as if to some eccentric person; and in Uncle Vidal's opinion "the three or four lunatics who came to his office every day" were eccentric too. By Mama Zita's orders he received them in the shabbiest rooms at the back of the house.

When Papa Telmo was not there the uncles would discuss his medical views. And although Aunt Cruz believed that Papa Telmo was nothing but a self-important quack who prided himself on being in the vanguard, Uncle Vidal (who laughed in great exaggerated bursts, and whose voice when he talked vibrated like a hammer on an anvil) thought that his brother-in-law didn't lack for brains but that he was crazier than a loon. And for Aunt Macrina, his wife, who would aim both her close-set eyes at Mama Zita like the barrels of a shotgun ("eyes too pretty for there to be two of them," said Don Trifón de la Huerta, who thus gallantly avoided any reference to their excessive proximity), Papa Telmo was a misfortune like any other.

"Poor Zita, you've really had bad luck."

And Mama Zita, vexed and upset, would defend herself and try to justify him in every way she could.

"He wasn't like this when we were married. Telmo was a doctor like all the rest of them. It was later he turned strange, at the time Mama died, when he took the notion of reading those big books and corresponding with foreign doctors."

However, Mama Zita's confusion reached a climax on the night when Uncle Felipe Neri, taking upon himself the wrath of God, raised his index finger over his ash-colored head and uttered the tremendous imprecation:

"The worst of it is that if he goes on like this, Telmo can't wind up anywhere but in pantheism."

A glacial silence enveloped the gathering. Aunt Macrina shrugged her shoulders, pursed her lips, and looked at Aunt Cruz, who stuck out the tip of her tongue, a blood-red tongue that contrasted with the plaster white of her face, and passed it over her upper lip; Papa León hung his head and coughed tentatively, and lastly Mama Zita, uncertain of which side to take, not knowing whether they were accusing her husband of being a Communist or a Freemason or both at once, puckered her face three times and burst into tears. Only Uncle Vidal, disdaining the others' opinion of his ignorance and plucking up his courage, asked, "What do you mean by pantheism?"

In the face of his schoolboy question Uncle Felipe Neri flushed ever so slightly (his ulcer used up so much blood that he couldn't really blush), took several seconds to think it over, and replied, "I mean that if Telmo keeps on running around naked among the pine trees, he'll wind up adoring the pine trees; in the end Nature will take control of him."

This was more than Mama Zita could bear, and so, after heaving a huge sigh, she collapsed against the back of the sofa while Aunt Macrina, all solicitude, blew gently on her forehead and Aunt Cruz fanned her with an ivory-ribbed fan that she had picked up from the table.

"Darling, you knew already that Telmo was a bit cool about religion."

Mama Zita rolled up her eyes again (imitating the attitude of the Lord's guardian angel in the copy of Giotto over the mantelpiece), flared her nostrils as if she were either going to die or sneeze, and breathed, "But I didn't know he was going to adore trees, like the monkeys."

Florita, the little girl, was not aware of all these details. She only knew, because she had heard Aunt Cruz say so, that Papa Telmo was a quack. And it was not until she asked Sister Caridad what a quack was, and the nun crossed herself and said "a kind of

witch," that she realized the extent of Papa Telmo's deviation from
the norm. Gervasio, however, once his sister had enlightened him,
got upset every time Mama Zita urged him to pray for Papa Telmo,
and within himself begged God to make his father stop being a
witch; but on the following day, when he caught his father humming with lathered face (red smile above the white foam), standing
barefoot on the wet tiles of the bathroom floor, he observed with
sorrow that so far the Lord hadn't listened to him.

Florita never let him alone and kept her brother in a perpetual
state of alarm; every afternoon she would come out with something
unexpected.

"I know what a vixen is, Gervasio."

"What?"

"A woman who commits sins for money."

"What kind of sins?"

"They haven't told me that yet."

A flash of illumination lighted Gervasio's brain.

"Maybe they wash their hands with soap in the holy-water
font."

Florita shrugged her shoulders.

"Maybe."

The boy began to think. Ever since the afternoon when Anselmo
Llorente had called one of the young ladies from Friné's a vixen,
his brain hadn't stopped working on the problem. What had Anselmo Llorente meant? That that lady was as free as a wild animal?
That she was as cautious and cunning as a vixen? That she was a
deceiver like the fox in the fable? Now, after what his sister had
told him, he had a pretty good idea of what she was, and imagined
the house across the street with a holy-water font behind every
door and the blond girls soaping their hands in them up to their
armpits and exploding into irreverent laughter right in the impassive face of Don Minervino, the owner. One day, connecting this
image with the conversations he had with Uncle Felipe Neri from
time to time, the idea came to him that to destroy those sinful
women and purify the house of the many-colored doors by fire
might well be a good cause.

"You mean make a hell for them, so they can purge their sins?"
asked his sister Flora.

"That's right."

Seeing his sister interested in one of his ideas excited Gervasio so much that, without a moment's hesitation, they began to plan to burn down Friné's.

"It'll be like defending God," said Flora. "As if the Archangel Michael were to come down from heaven with his flaming sword."

"Right," said Gervasio enthusiastically.

"Like the crusaders during the Crusades, aren't we?"

"Right."

And on the following Thursday, as soon as Mama Zita and Papa Telmo had gone out with Benigno in Papa León's Buick, Florita and Gervasio piled some old newspapers and kindling that they had stolen from Señora Zoa's kitchen in the narrow street behind the house. But scarcely had the flame caught the papers than "El Cigüeña"—the Stork—the former city policeman, appeared without a sound and, as he stamped on the smoldering newspapers, caught each of them by one ear.

"Can't you think of anything better to do, you little scamps?"

The policeman's squinty eyes bored right through them.

"It was only a bonfire," protested Florita.

"I can see it was a bonfire, but if I hadn't arrived in time you could have set fire to the house and burned the tail off the girls at Friné's. Does Don León know anything about this?"

The little girl shook her head, and as they climbed the broad flight of stairs with its red carpet, El Cigüeña between them, both of them were trembling. But when Papa León, who in the first decade of the century had been mayor of the city for a long time, came out to the vestibule and called El Cigüeña "Gerardo" and lifted his arms and said familiarly, "How are things?" and had him go into the study and sit down, and offered him a glass of anisette and a Havana cigar, and between glasses they began to talk about Don Segismundo Moret and "Poli el Patatero," and the prompt action El Cigüeña had taken that night, Flora and Gervasio began to feel easier. And later, when El Cigüeña left, his face puffy from the alcohol, giving them friendly little pats on the head and saying these little devils, with the abortive auto-da-fé forgotten forever, Florita asked Papa León, "Who was Poli el Patatero?"

"Ah, Poli," said Papa León with a little smile that reflected thirty-five years of nostalgia playing among his scanty yellowish whiskers. "He was a potato seller on the Calle de la Cárcava who went out of his head one night and shut himself up in his stall with a kitchen knife in one hand and a revolver in the other, and all he'd say was 'Here I am, you brave men. The first one comes in, I'll slit his throat.' I was mayor then, and I remember that the people from the insane asylum were so scared that they didn't dare try to put a straitjacket on him, and then in went Gerardo, without anyone having to tell him to, and jumped through the window and leaped on him and overpowered him. That was an act of courage, and on the day of the city's patron saint, with the police corps drawn up in the courtyard of City Hall, we gave him a medal." Papa León's eyes softened.

Gervasio slowly turned his head toward his grandfather.

"Does that mean that El Cigüeña is a hero?"

"Oh, so you call Gerardo 'Cigüeña,' do you? Why, of course he's a hero. What did you think? Did you think a policeman with a nightstick couldn't be a hero?"

CHAPTER

5

Even in his sleep Gervasio kept hearing Papa Telmo's rumbling shouts and immediately afterward, without a pause and mixed with sobs, Mama Zita's pleas, and then Papa Telmo again, his big voice drowning out hers, and again Mama Zita's earnest pleadings in a confused murmur, so that when he opened his eyes for good and heard the silence he was not sure whether that muffled argument had really happened or whether he had dreamed it. He went to the kitchen.

"Where are Mama and Papa?"

"They went on a trip, my treasure."

"Where to, Zoa?"

"To La Granja with your aunt and uncle, to see the fountains play."

"And why were they quarreling this morning?"

"They were fighting over you."

"Over me, Zoa?"

"Your papa didn't like the costumes your uncle gave you. He told Clemente to burn them."

Clemente the deaf-mute, son of Señor Pedro the doorman, took great care of the little garden behind the palace. He had white hair and eyebrows, hair that looked as if it had been spun out of cotton, a sign of albinism which in Señora Zoa's opinion came from a fright he had had. But on one occasion, when Gervasio reminded her that his brother was also white-haired, Señora Zoa argued that maybe the fright had happened to their grandfather, because by some turn of fate those things came to the surface every two or three generations. Patient, exquisitely careful, with rare manual skill, Clemente pruned rosebushes, grafted shrubs, scattered peat moss on the flowerbeds, and in general did his job with slow efficiency and a pleased, stupid smile always dancing on his face. That green redoubt, nestled among the galleries of the Giralda houses (which had once caused a lawsuit because according to Don Vicente Colino, the city chronicler, they spoiled the historic character of the neighborhood), the back of the Civil Government building, and the walls of the Santa Brígida convent garden, had profound significance for Gervasio. His earliest childhood had been spent along its paths, and there was no corner, tree, stone, or shrub that was unfamiliar to him. In the little central circle surrounded by a box hedge (which Clemente, in a excess of zeal, kept even by unnecessary weekly trimmings), Gervasio had learned to walk and to ride a bicycle. Later he had played hide-and-seek in the garden with the Bidegaín brothers (Fefa and Arturo) before Don Arturo's sawmill went into bankruptcy and they had to return to Toulouse to live with their paternal grandfather. Another point of reference was the old mulberry tree that shaded the drive leading to the coach houses (in which Papa León killed starlings with a nine-millimeter carbine, and where Papa Telmo liked to read after dinner in good weather, seated in a wicker armchair), whose leaves served to feed the silk-worms when spring came. And the round pool, with dead leaves floating on its surface, that Clemente used for watering and where Flora and Gervasio would catch tadpoles which they then kept in a glass jar until their legs grew and they turned into frogs. Or the little rocky grotto, under the arch of green leaves, with the blue-and-white statue of the Virgin of Lourdes, to whom they devoutly prayed a rosary on luminous May afternoons, kneeling on the grass.

Now, propped on his elbows on the balcony of the storage room, Gervasio regarded all this with indifference, keeping his eyes on Clemente, who was heaping Uncle Felipe Neri's military clothing underneath the balcony. And after he had finished piling up the jackets and capes the gardener, as though performing a funeral ceremony, laid on top of it all the sky-blue cape with the stiff braid clasps on the collar, took a can out of the garage, sprinkled the pile with gasoline, and set fire to it. Gervasio did not protest. He watched the bonfire with the same passive curiosity with which he had observed Uncle Felipe Neri's gift two weeks earlier, enjoying the flames, oblivious of the reason for them. He was fascinated by their glow, their capricious writhings, the smoke forming mon-strous shapes in the air, the way the braid and trimmings resisted the fire, and finally, after it had flamed up furiously, by the circle of white cinders to which everything had been reduced except for the campaign boots, stiff and black in the center with the spurs still on them. As if the deaf-mute had felt the intensity of Gervasio's gaze, he raised his eyes to the balcony and saw the child, his chin resting on the iron railing, watching motionless. He smiled at him.

"Why are you burning that, tell me?" asked Gervasio.

Without ceasing to smile, Clemente emitted a few inarticulate sounds accompanied by expressive gestures.

"Did Papa Telmo tell you to?"

The deaf-mute assented with awkward movements of his arms. He was barely twenty, but his white hair and freckled face made him look older. He continued to smile as he collected the ashes with a shovel, and when he looked up again Gervasio had disappeared. Señora Zoa and Amalia were chatting in the kitchen and took no notice when the children burst in.

"And is that Rodolfo Francisco from around here?"

"Born and bred in the San Juan district, Señora Zoa, I should say so. You just ought to see him, so good-looking! He's been dancing for more than three days and you'd never know it."

The old woman was beginning to catch the other's enthusiasm. In a few seconds she had worked out a plan for the afternoon: they would leave a glass of milk and some cookies on the sideboard for the grandfather, who was indulgent, telling him they were going to her sister-in-law's so that he wouldn't wait for them. That way they could stay at the Novelty until nine at night and no one would miss them.

"Well, do you mind telling us what you're talking about?" put in Florita, tired of listening to such meaningless talk.

"It's a dance contest, sweetie," explained Amalia, making no effort to hide her exhilaration. "Rodolfo Francisco, he's a boy from here, has challenged Breslau, the champion of Europe, to see which one can hold out the longest. They've been spinning like tops since Wednesday and Rodolfo Francisco hasn't given up yet. What do you think of that?"

The little girl began to show some interest.

"Do they dance by themselves?"

"Either by themselves or with somebody, see. If you want, you only have to go up on the stage and they'll dance one with you."

Gervasio watched both of them without fully understanding.

"Doesn't Rodolfo Francisco eat?"

"He has to! But he doesn't stop dancing; he eats while he's dancing because the one that stops, loses."

"And . . . and . . . and doesn't Rodolfo Francisco go to the toilet?"

Amalia started to laugh, with that hearty, jovial, impudent laugh of hers.

"The one that goes to the toilet loses too, sweetheart. They have to do it in a can. But since they don't eat much and sweat a lot, see, they hardly ever need to."

The working-class neighborhoods were buzzing that afternoon; they were experiencing Rodolfo Francisco's challenge as something of their own, and the streets around the theater were crowded at all hours. It was a restless, fluid, multicolored crowd, always the same and always different, like the water in a river. Some groups went into the theater to cheer their idol on, while others came out to the street for a breath of air, describing his stamina, trying to gauge his chances for victory. The fact that a hollow-eyed, shabby young charity boy, Rodolfo Francisco, had challenged the European champion, a hulking blond brute, made their breasts swell with patriotic pride. Actually Rodolfo Francisco, despite a few spells of weakness, was standing up gallantly to the champion; he managed a rather feeble smile and from time to time slowed his rhythm to recover his strength. As for Breslau, he jumped and turned and pirouetted and lifted his partner off the floor in a boastful show of physical strength. In little groups, people whispered their opinions.

"Physically the foreigner's better prepared, truth to tell. Rodolfo Francisco can hardly stand up by now."

But Señora Zoa, Amalia, and the children did not lose faith in their representative. They had managed to push through the crowd at the door and were standing in the center aisle, unblinkingly watching the dancers as they turned this way and that on the stage. Indeed, the German seemed to be fresher, but nothing had been decided yet, everything was still to be hoped for from Rodolfo Francisco's sense of honor. The theater was like an oven. Pennants and streamers hung from the baroque chandelier in the middle of the ceiling, and Spanish and German flags waved from the light fixtures on the side walls. Through the cigarette smoke and the dust hanging in the air they could just make out the stage, decorated with flags and colored ribbons, closed off at the back with a curtain and illuminated by four brilliant spotlights. In the pit half a dozen musicians, replacing one another at short intervals, wearily played sentimental dance tunes, and part of the audience sang along with them enthusiastically. Gervasio, standing in the aisle, squinted through smarting eyes.

"Which one is Rodolfo Francisco, Amalia?"

"He's the one with the black vest and the sandals on, the dark one, the thinner one, can't you see him? Gee, he's so cute!"

A group left and they seized the opportunity to sit down. The superiority of Breslau, his blond mane bare, dancing with authority and arrogance, was perfectly obvious. Rodolfo Francisco, very pale and thin, imitated him, following the rhythm in a minor key, fighting his fatigue, though sometimes, when he managed to overcome his weariness, he would twirl around and elicit howls of enthusiasm from the crowd. At the moment both of them were dancing a tango; the dancing couples moved toward the footlights, stopping on the very edge of the stage and then retreating, emphasizing their steps, making the cadence of the piece more exciting with lascivious movements, the boys looking disdainful, the girls with tousled hair, all of them sweating, damp half-moons under their armpits. And the ever-changing, frenzied audience shouted, roared, applauded, cried syllable by syllable the name of their fellow townsman:

"Ro-dol-fo, Ro-dol-fo, Ro-dol-fo!"

From time to time one of them, still more carried away, would throw some object onto the stage (caps, hats, wineskins, tobacco pouches), and emphasize the action by yelling in a stentorian voice, "Long live the mother that bore you!"

A young woman with a chubby-cheeked baby sleeping in her arms was sitting next to Amalia, and did nothing but nod her head and say, "My heavens, four days and four nights of this, it's so easy to say."

Seated between the two women, Gervasio watched Rodolfo Francisco's turns on the stage, his pallid face, the big bags under his eyes that made them look hollow.

"Rodolfo Francisco is very tired, Zoa; I think he's going to lose."

A heavy-set workingman in a torn beret turned around from the front row.

"Just you wait, kid; what the Spaniard lacks in style he's got in pure guts. We'll see who loses."

A skinny man in shirtsleeves, wearing brown pants and red suspenders, rushed out from backstage, raised to his lips a green megaphone bigger than the horn on Papa León's gramophone, and shouted, "Attention, ladies! Those of you who wish to have one dance with either of our great champions, please come up to the stage. The first hundred hours of competition are about to end."

Amalia did not hesitate.

"Keep an eye on my purse, Señora Zoa. I'm not going to pass up a schottische with Rodolfo Francisco." She got to her feet.

"How about Anselmo Llorente?"

"He can go jump in the lake."

"And what happens if you and he get fixed up?"

But Amalia was already in the aisle, starting to cover the distance between the floor and the stage, where new couples were spurring the dancers to further efforts with such success that, when Rodolfo Francisco put his arm around Amalia's narrow waist and the girl, dragging her right foot ever so slightly, flung her head back and raised her diabolical eyebrows, parting her red lips (so provocative in her low-necked dress and tight belt), smiling at the audience, a loud voice yelled from the topmost balcony, "You dance better with the lame one! Eh, Rodolfo?"

The young woman with the baby in her arms turned toward Señora Zoa, blinked several times as if her eyes itched, and asked, jerking her head toward the stage, "Do you two work together?"

"Yes, we work in the same house."

"Well, she sure is laying it on thick. You can see that being lame doesn't hold her back a bit."

The shouts grew louder and Rodolfo Francisco, with Amalia in his arms, spun round and round, sometimes standing tiptoe on one foot; but under the curly mop of hair the light in his eyes was weaker and weaker. But when Amalia returned to her seat, very proud of herself, she said that Rodolfo Francisco was in perfect shape, that he was every inch a man, and that the result of the challenge was still in doubt. Very agitated and nervous, she straightened her hair and the neck of her dress, powdered her sweaty cheeks, smiled as if to herself with secret pleasure, and said to the children, "Not a word about this to Mama, did you hear me?"

And over the children's heads she warned Señora Zoa, "And if I do happen to get fixed up with Anselmo Llorente, don't you go to him with the tale. He makes such a fuss about things!"

After the dances with the volunteers were over, the little man in the red suspenders consulted the jury, at one side of the stage, whispered briefly to each of its five members, and again stepped up to the footlights with his megaphone.

"Distinguished audience," he announced, "I have the honor to inform you that both champions have passed the hundred-hour mark established by the jury, and in view of the fact that both are

still in the contest the jury has decided to end the competition with
a tie. One hundred hours for the European champion, Herman
Breslau, and one hundred hours for the Spanish representative,
Rodolfo Francisco. A big hand, ladies and gentlemen, for both
champions!"

Something resembling an enormous, interminable roll of thun-
der burst out in the theater; a unanimous, deafening ovation punc-
tuated by voices hoarse from shouting (Ro-dol-fo, Ro-dol-fo,
Ro-dol-fo!) and the flourishing of handkerchiefs, scarves, and
coats, while the dancers moved to the front of the stage, smiling
and waving, and the woman with the baby in her arms, pleased
with the outcome, admitted to Señora Zoa, "They've given a little
bit of a hand to the local boy, as they ought to, don't you think?"

But the little man in red suspenders, believing that he saw a
certain shade of disappointment in the German's face, put the green
megaphone to Breslau's lips, an action which he utilized to address
the crowd.

"The decision of jury I agsept and my adwersary, Godolfo, gon-
gratulade. But for spezial favor to this audienz, I vill one hour
gontinue valtzing."

And then, without warning, everything started to happen.

After the courteous applause that greeted the German's words,
a completely exhausted Rodolfo Francisco grabbed the megaphone
in his turn and in a gasping voice declared that he too would keep
dancing for another hour as a tribute to the audience, "because,"
he ended, raising his voice with an effort, "anything a German
does, a Spaniard can do too." A thunderous ovation followed his
words, the orchestra struck up the quickstep "Gypsy Spain," and
in the balconies, with bravos and cheers for Spain, the spectators
began grabbing the flags that decorated the light fixtures and waving them in the air, in an atmosphere of mad patriotic exaltation.
And amid the noise, the hurrahs, the waving flags, and the stirring
music, Gervasio rose to his feet, beside himself; he began to ap-
plaud, to join enthusiastically in the shouts for Spain, until without
warning he felt a sort of shudder go down the back of his neck, and
at the same time felt something like the edge of a barber's blade
descend his spine, while his skin began to produce a cold, erectile
energy of its own and he felt a strange sensation in his head, as if

someone were baring it, removing a hat that was too tight and pulling his hair straight up. Gervasio stood motionless, clutching the seat in front of him, thoroughly frightened, with each individual hair standing up like a rocket; but the audience was concentrating on the dancers and didn't notice him, until the baby of the woman next to them, when it saw his bristling mane, let out an adult scream, buried its little face in its mother's lap, and broke into convulsive howls. This caused her to follow his gaze and also encounter Gervasio's enormous, swollen head. The young mother screamed, eyes bulging, and without a moment's hesitation was on her feet in terror, protecting the baby with her arms and screeching, fleeing out the other end of the row. But before she reached the aisle an astonished Señora Zoa was shaking Gervasio and giving him careful little slaps on the cheeks, trying to bring him to himself.

"Did you ever see such a thing! Do you mind telling me what's going on? Why are you acting like that?"

For her part Amalia, huddled in the seat with her hands to her cheeks, was sobbing, "Just look at the head that's gone and grown on him, Señora Zoa! Now what'll we tell the mistress?"

Meanwhile Gervasio, his grayish-yellow eyes fixed on the stage, was subsiding as the audience's enthusiasm diminished; the cold force that was prickling his skin lessened and with it the pull on his hair, which gradually began to settle down, returning his head to its normal proportions. The woman next to them was already escaping down the side aisle, muttering to herself, cradling the baby (which never stopped howling) and casting sidelong, hostile glances at Gervasio. Upstairs they could still hear a few sporadic exclamations, even some last cries of "Long live Spain!" But the paroxysm was diminishing and with it Gervasio's seizure, which went along with the exhausted and overwrought atmosphere. Señora Zoa, in a effort to protect him, had caught him in her arms.

"Come on, my treasure, go to sleep," and as soon as the boy's eyes started to close, she turned authoritatively to Florita.

"What happened to your brother's head, tell me that?"

"How do I know, Zoa? Maybe it's that thing about being a hero that Papa León talks about."

"You mean that's the way heroes look?"

"I don't know, Zoa; what makes you think I can tell you?"

An hour later, with cries of "Ro-dol-fo, Ro-dol-fo, Ro-dol-fo," the audience assaulted the stage, settled the weary champion on the shoulders of a robust, short-legged fellow, and followed by a vociferous group of last-ditch supporters, carried him out of the auditorium in this posture amid fervent cheers which followed him down the street and did not end until Rodolfo Francisco, riding on someone's shoulders and surrounded by a youthful and enthusiastic mob, made his triumphal entrance into his home district.

CHAPTER 6

In the dark house they could just hear the creaking of the floor under the heavy furniture, and far away, muffled by the closed panes of the balcony windows, the slurred voice of a drunkard singing in the narrow street in front of the church of Santa Brígida. Amalia switched on the light in the vestibule and stood for a moment, listening.

"I can't even hear your grandfather. He wouldn't have gone to bed, would he?"

Amalia was trying to make up with the boy. Still excited by the afternoon's events, she had scolded him in the streetcar on the way home.

"What in the world do you do those silly things for? A person can't take you anywhere."

"I don't do silly things, Amalia."

"Well, isn't that just great; I suppose I'm the one who does them."

"I don't do them, Amalia," the child repeated. "They just happen to me."

Now the maid was briskly tapping her high heels down the hall to let the old gentleman know that they were home; but when she reached the dining room and saw that his afternoon snack was untouched on the silver tray, just as she had left it, and when she didn't hear his voice, a sort of gloomy presentiment passed through her mind. She retraced her steps and said to Gervasio, "Go on, run and find Grandfather and ask him why he didn't drink his milk, whether he doesn't feel well."

When the boy pressed the light switch, he found him sprawled on the carpet with the General's red beret on his head, his broken eyeglasses lying beside the table leg, his left arm bent under his chest. Gervasio lacked the courage to step over the threshold and cried loudly for help.

"Zoa, Amalia, Flora, come, Papa León's dead!"

As they all knelt beside him, the old woman was the first to discover that he was still breathing.

"Go on, Amalia, run as fast as you can to let Don Justino know."

The beret had fallen off and Gervasio put it back on his forehead, and Señora Zoa scolded him nervously, telling him not to play with those things, and Florita began to cry and said she was scared, and while Gervasio tried to console her, Papa León scratched his chin with his left hand, making the paralysis of his right hand obvious, and then the little girl covered her eyes with her hands and turned her back on the others, screaming, "Half of Papa León's dead!"

At that instant Don Justino, Mama Zita, and the rest of the travelers burst into the bedroom pell-mell, having met at the front door, and the doctor's first action was to remove the patient's beret. But Gervasio told him that his grandfather wanted to die wearing it and Mama Zita, a prey to superstitious fear, tried to put it on his head again, so awkwardly that it covered his nostrils, and then Papa León stretched his left leg twice and the doctor warned her, "Be careful, señora, you could asphyxiate him." With one knee on the floor, he raised his eyes to the uncles and aunts, who were watching his every move, and added, "Can you leave me alone with the patient for a few minutes?"

A quarter of an hour later Mama Zita appeared with tear-filled eyes in the drawing room, where the aunts and uncles had gathered.

"It's a hemiplegia," she explained. "In view of his age, Don Justino doesn't think he'll come out of it, but if he did it would be in a wheelchair."

The aunts and Crucita started to cry, the men stopped arguing under the fireplace hood, and Uncle Felipe Neri wrinkled his nose as if he felt nausea coming on and collapsed, muttering, onto the divan with the lenses of his glasses fogged over; and while Papa Telmo looked after him, loosening the collar of his jacket and the waistband of his trousers, Uncle Vidal walked round and round the room, brushing past the furniture, raising his eyes to the ceiling, now and then passing his white hand with the diamond ring on it over his rosy bald spot. Uncle Felipe Neri sighed and said feebly, "Thanks, Telmo."

Papa Telmo straightened up and addressed the group of women. He said with professional dignity, "These episodes can last a long time. It's not a question of a day or two." He looked toward Uncle Felipe Neri and added, "It would be a good idea to organize a schedule for sitting up with him before we all wind up unnecessarily exhausted."

And then and there they established turns for sitting up in pairs, trying to match them as to age and sense of responsibility: Aunt Cruz and Uncle Felipe Neri, Aunt Macrina and Uncle Vidal, Mama Zita and Señora Zoa, and Crucita and Papa Telmo. One pair watched over the patient day and night, and the others dozed or wandered around the house like shadows, waiting their turn, anxious to learn of anything new coming out of the bedroom, generally futile and insignificant things.

"Papa has moved one eyelid."

"Grandfather has broken wind."

"Sometimes he gives the impression of wanting to write something with his left hand. Why don't we give him pencil and paper?"

Only trifles, no fundamental change. Papa León lay motionless on his right side, and from time to time raised his left hand to his beard and stroked it from top to bottom. No one took off the beret again. ("It's his last wish, and we ought to respect it," Mama Zita had decreed), but when the pressure of the pillow or the weight of the gilded plaque ("God, Fatherland, King") shifted it, the watcher on duty would straighten it. But the patient's lack of cooperation would cause it to go crooked again and slip down over his eyes like a visor, so that Papa León on his deathbed reminded Gervasio of the black-smudged pinecone seller who walked the streets of the old quarter on Saturdays, crying his wares. Don Justino, who visited Papa León morning and evening, suggested one day putting the beret on the night table, over the water pitcher, so that he could see it if he opened his eyes; but Mama Zita argued that her father had put it on his head before the attack, which indicated his wishes. Don Justino did not consider this argument valid, since these circulatory accidents happened so quickly that they didn't give time to put on or take off anything, and therefore the most likely thing was that the grandfather had had it in his hands when the thrombosis occurred. Mama Zita didn't give an inch, and only agreed to take it off for a few minutes "out of respect for the Lord," when Don Urbano came over from the church to administer Extreme Unction.

Outside school hours, with the family concerned only for the grandfather, Gervasio wandered around the house like a fugitive. Florita was very much affected and wept, ate little, and couldn't sleep at night, but he experienced the process like something repeated, as if he had lived through it before. On the other hand, he had not completely recovered from the impression caused by his new seizure in the Novelty. Though after the first time that the sign had appeared he had felt proud of his peculiarity, to the point of preening himself before his family like a reincarnation of the medieval hero Guzmán el Bueno, this time, after the experience in the theater, he felt ashamed. It was humiliating that his external appearance could make babies cry and adults take flight. Every time he referred to it Amalia would comment, "Like a cat facing a dog, that's the way you looked, sweetie. My word, what hair!"

In addition, the fact that the second attack had occurred during a dance contest and had been activated by a quickstep led him to doubt the importance of the seizure. After they had left the Novelty, when Amalia scolded him in the streetcar, he had thought that perhaps Papa León could settle his doubts. But when he found him dying, sprawled at the foot of the bed, the child for no particular reason established a relationship of cause and effect between the two happenings. During the days that followed he continued to be bothered by the fact that his hair had stood on end during a frivolous spectacle, though his childish mind did not fail to recognize that in the theater there had been waving flags, the sound of applause, cries of adhesion to Spain, all accompanied by a rollicking, stirring kind of music that had undoubtedly aroused patriotic feelings in his breast. Uncle Felipe Neri forgot the sick man for a few minutes on the afternoon that Gervasio told him that "that" had happened to him again and asked him whether, by any chance, Spain in itself was a good cause. He became very excited, took the white handkerchief out of his pocket, used it to rub the lenses of his spectacles, placed the palm of his hand on the upper part of his stomach as if to placate his nausea, and said, "After God, my boy, Spain is the highest cause."

"Is Spain the fatherland?"

"That's right, Gervasio, Spain and the fatherland are one and the same."

"For everybody?"

"Let's make sure we understand each other. Spain is the fatherland of Spaniards; for a Frenchman, his fatherland would be France, and for a German, Germany."

"Does that mean everyone has a fatherland?"

"Naturally; it depends on the place where he was born."

The child thought of Breslau.

"And if a German does something for Spain, does that mean he isn't a hero any more?"

"It depends," said Uncle Felipe Neri, choosing his words with great care. "If he did it for Spain but against Germany, he could even be a traitor."

"A traitor?"

"Listen to me, my boy," he argued, trying to soften the disappointment that his words were producing in the child, "there are times in life when the line between heroism and treachery is as thin as a sheet of cigarette paper."

"But can you be a hero and a traitor at the same time, Uncle?"

Uncle Felipe Neri's fluttering, hairless hand gradually rose from his stomach to his chin and caressed it two or three times, mechanically and meditatively. He found Gervasio's belligerent gaze unnerving.

"Well, maybe you're still too much of a child to understand it, but it is possible for the apparent contradiction that you mention to take place: to be a hero to some and a traitor to others, depending on which side of the action you're looking at," explained Uncle Felipe Neri. And he added in a weak voice, "In fact, the history of the world is full of such contradictions."

Liquid rose into his mouth so quickly that he had to put his hand to his lips to keep it from spilling out. After supper that night he spoke frankly to his oilcloth-covered notebook. "I'm in a tight spot. This afternoon, when I tried to clarify some ideas for him, I confused my little nephew Gervasio. Trying to shape the concept of a 'good cause' entails problems for the little fellow. In the first place, he is disappointed by the fact that nationality, the chance of having been born in one place or another, determines each person's fatherland. A few days ago he had another of his seizures when he heard Spain being cheered, and he can't accept the idea that Frenchmen and Germans would be unaffected by such acclaim. On the other hand, he rejects the ambiguity of the heroic act according to whether it is viewed from the right or the wrong side of the cloth. What he wants is both the heroic act in a pure state and pure treason; black and white, with no in-betweens. He prefers to shut his eyes to the problem's complexity. How to guide him? Lord, illumine me!"

Next day, during Mama Zita's turn to watch, Papa León opened his left eye for a moment, looked at her slyly, as if he were winking the other at her, and spoke only one word, but with the avidity of a thirsty man demanding water:

"Music!"

He closed his eye again and stayed in the same peaceful fetal position that he usually adopted. Mama Zita ran through the house in triumph, spreading the good word.

72

"Papa opened one eye! Papa opened one eye!"

But then Aunt Cruz, hopes high, asked her the necessary question, "And so?" Mama Zita stopped in her tracks, hesitated, stammered, and eventually admitted, "Why, yes, he opened one eye, asked for music, and shut it again."

"Papa asked for music? But he must have said something else."

"He only said music, Cruz, but as fervently as though his life depended on it."

In that tense and routine atmosphere made up of little novelties, the dying man's voice demanding music became an order. Within a few seconds Papa León had the phonograph at hand on the dresser, with its big brass horn and boxes of cylinders. You would have thought that his relatives believed that blind obedience was an indispensable starting point for a possible recovery. But Papa Telmo told them not to get their hopes up, that the sick man was still in a coma and that the music episode was merely a reflex action of no significance for the illness. Nevertheless, Mama Zita insisted that there was lucidity in his eye when he asked for music, and that therefore he would have music. And in accordance with her words, a few seconds later the rasping strains of "Red Berets" sounded in the hall and the neighboring rooms. The familiar chill surprised Gervasio at the door of the bedroom, and as soon as he felt the hair trying to rise on the top of his head he hastened to take refuge in the playroom, where the sound of the phonograph did not reach. It was the first time that he had felt a lack of confidence in himself. Why was he hiding? Was it because Papa Telmo might discover him, or out of fear of his metamorphosis? Out of instinctive repugnance toward his physical change, or so as not to distract the general attention that was concentrated on the sick man? Gervasio didn't know. But he stayed shut in the playroom for hours (because Mama Zita was playing one cylinder after another without a break), and after that, every time that the prickling symptoms returned, he adopted the same precaution.

Ten days after he had fallen ill, Papa León died. In the small hours of the morning Uncle Felipe Neri went from one bedroom to another, calling all of them to his bedside, but by the time the first one (Mama Zita) arrived he was already dead. As a sign of mourning Aunt Cruz lifted the phonograph needle, and the silence became so profound that the red color of the beret, in contrast to the whiteness of the bedclothes (which Señora Felipa scrubbed daily in the zinc tub on the gallery), acquired an almost audible tone. At dawn Papa León's old comrade-in-arms Don Trifón de la Huerta appeared, with his provocative Marxist beard, his greenish-gray suede spats, his starched white collar, and his derby hat; and without greeting anyone, he placed the roll of "Oriamendi" in the phonograph case, snapped to attention at the dead man's feet, between two tapers (his left elbow at his waist and the black derby in his hand), hawked, tried out the note twice in his throat, and at last sang in a low voice, following the music of the Requeté Band of Navarre:

> Forward, brave battalions,
> Victory is near;
> We'll defend our banners
> Fighting without fear.
> Whatever be the effort,
> But one aim we own:
> Return the rightful monarch
> To his royal throne.
> For God, for king, for country
> Did our fathers fall,
> For God, for king, for country:
> One fate awaits us all.

When he had finished he went over to Mama Zita and warmly pressed her right hand between his two hands, as he clicked his heels and sketched out a profound bow.

"Excuse me, señora," he said. "It was an old pact the two of us had made. Your father and I had agreed that the survivor would honor the dead comrade, as in the heroic times, with the strains of our hymn. Alas, I will not have that good fortune now. I am at your feet, señora. I mourn with you."

One by one, he offered greetings to all present and left the bedroom. Gervasio watched Papa León's face, its flinty features, its ashen color, looking as if it had turned to stone; but neither then nor the next day, in Santa Brígida during the funeral, nor at the door of the church afterward when half the city, deeply moved, filed by the family, did he shed a single tear. He merely followed the cortège like an automaton (with the same skepticism as the old men from the asylum did, carrying torches in their gnarled hands), as if the person who lay in the coffin had never had any connection with him. Uncle Felipe Neri, who did not take his eyes off the boy, thought that he was unemotional and self-contained but not grief-stricken, and that if he did feel sorrow he controlled it, was successful in his efforts not to show it. Aunt Cruz had also noticed the boy's impassivity and his rigid control of his feelings, and after they returned home she confided to her husband, "Did you notice, Felipe? Gervasito hasn't shed a single tear for his grandfather." Uncle Felipe Neri thoughtfully agreed, and as soon as he had eaten supper he sat down at his desk, opened the oilcloth-covered note-book, drew a cross at the top of the page, and wrote: "Last night Papa León died, and his grandson Gervasio, despite the great affection, the cordial relationship that always existed between them, has not shed a tear. Passive, dry, almost hieratic, he attended the ceremonies like an outsider. His mother is grieved by what she thinks of as insensitivity, but what reason does she have to make such an imputation? The chosen (precisely because they are chosen) scorn the passing show, even life itself. Heroes and martyrs are detached beings, apparently indifferent to death. This detachment affects, with still greater reason, what we might call terrestrial possessions, including those we love. Why not think of Gervasio as one of the chosen? Let us not forget that the child accepted the burning of the military uniforms I gave him with Spartan resignation . . . It is a sign . . ." and so on.

Without warning, on the following Sunday after communion, when Mama Zita whispered to him, "Pray especially for Papa León today, because he loved you so much when he was alive and wasn't able to confess," for a few seconds Gervasio had a glimpse of his grandfather naked, writhing in the flames of hell (his beard, like the burning bush in the Bible, burned but was not consumed), gesticulating, crying out to him; and the vision was so horrifying that a strangled sob rose in his throat. He closed his eyes and buried his face in the forearm that rested on the pew, and continued to cry (according to Mama Zita's impartial version) "until the twelve o'clock mass was over and fat old Severo came out of the sacristy with the snuffer, ready to close the church." When Uncle Felipe Neri was informed of this news he hastened to bring the jottings in his notebook up to date: "Six days after the grandfather's death, Gervasio has wept for him; he sobbed bitterly, till all his tears were spent, for more than three hours. Therefore the detachment that his mother attributed to him is not justified, even for mystical reasons. The boy shows an unmistakable duality, but it is obvious that the sign he has received has not dehumanized him. Perhaps he is still too much of a child, but it is surely illogical that death in itself should not affect him and yet its recollection, a week later, should cause him to weep."

CHAPTER
7

Papa León's death produced a void in the old mansion of the counts of Pradoluengo, a void that Gervasio sensed, as he also vaguely sensed the open conflict among Mama Zita, Aunt Cruz, and Uncle Vidal over which of the three was to inherit it. After his father's death Uncle Vidal started to refer to the house as a palace, no doubt to justify the handsome compensation that would have to be paid to the person not awarded it. That person, in view of Mama Zita's attachment to the house, might very well be himself.

"The city keeps growing, Sister, and Pérez Mínguez the contractor would pay a million this very day for the land it stands on."

But Mama Zita drew herself up and said that the house had been her cradle, and that even if she died in indigence she wanted it to be her tomb as well. Uncle Vidal's reaction to her eschatological aspiration was to prod his sisters with talk of estate taxes and the demands of the public treasury, though Aunt Cruz and Mama Zita argued that that was what the treasury certificates and the portfolio of investments (a very well-balanced one in the opinion of Don Trifón de la Huerta, the executor) were for, to satisfy those demands, a claim that Uncle Vidal rejected in his booming lay preacher's voice.

"If we dispose of assets to pay the Treasury, then the distribution won't be fair; Cruz and I will be left unprotected."

Uncle Vidal enjoyed putting on an act in front of his sisters, exclaiming with outflung arms that they were victims of an all-absorbing State and that, though it might seem irrational, they were poorer now than when their father was alive. Mama Zita whimpered, sighed, asked how such a cruel thing could be possible, to lose one's father and one's fortune at the same time, and in view of her inability to understand, Uncle Vidal put the situation to her in different terms.

"You can choose between the palace and the securities, Zita, but if you decide for the palace you'll have to pay symbolic rent, and if we set a rent, no matter how symbolic it is, can you tell me how you intend to live? On Telmo's income?"

He said this ironically, since there were few adherents of naturopathy in the city and most of them enjoyed good health; but one night, when Uncle Vidal was pressing his sisters hard and Uncle Felipe Neri attempted to come to their defense, Uncle Vidal focused his glacial blue glare upon him and said acridly, "Second parties keep out!"

Uncle Felipe Neri held his tongue, convinced that brothers-in-law had no part to play in the dispute. Aunt Macrina, however, in view of the deadlock the negotiations had reached, suggested one night the possibility of consulting her brother Jairo, who had obtained a doctorate *cum laude* at the University of Madrid and was an aspirant to a judgeship and very well versed in testamentary law. Aunt Macrina, the only girl among four siblings, venerated her brothers, and at every opportunity would refer to them with limitless admiration. Hence, if Crucita complained about her problems with backhand in tennis ("If I use one hand it's not strong enough, and if I use two the ball doesn't go where I want it to"), Aunt Macrina would lower her eyelids, eclipsing her beautiful close-set eyes, and say, "What a pity that your Uncle Jairo doesn't live here!"

But if the question under discussion had to do with the medical area or with horseback riding, then it was her brother David, a famous cardiologist and equestrian, who would have offered a solution without delay, just as her brother Fadrique, an executive of the Library of Christian Authors, would have done if the problem had had to do with economics or literature. Nor did the fraternal gifts end there, for if the conversation turned upon masculine presence, elegance, easy manners, or ability to get along with others, her brothers Jairo, David, and Fadrique had no rivals in the world. That was why, in view of the intricate matter of Papa León's heirs and despite her husband's cold, abrupt decision to leave second parties out of it, one evening she dared to suggest, "Why don't we put the matter in my brother Jairo's hands?"

And she asked the question with pride, not in a tone of asking but of offering, the tone that she was accustomed to use because she thought it the right one, appropriate to a Madrilenian conversing with provincials. But despite her suggestion the arguments became more and more bitter and Uncle Vidal's shouts grew so loud that the foundations of the old house trembled, and, penetrating partitions and walls, filtered into the little sanctuary of the playroom.

"Why are the grownups fighting, Flora?"

"Because Uncle Vidal wants to keep this house for himself and be a count."

"You mean the person who keeps this house will be a count?"

"That's what Amalia says."

However, what Uncle Vidal had in mind with respect to the palace was what he succeeded in achieving after more than six months of shouts, threats, and delays: dividing it. Aunt Cruz and Uncle Felipe Neri were installed in the west wing, over the garage, in the rooms that Papa Telmo had used as an office, the ironing room, and three large storerooms that had been closed off years before; and, to facilitate their independence, a private entrance was built with access through the garden. The rest of the mansion was left to Mama Zita, and as if that weren't enough, Uncle Vidal made the generous gesture of giving each sister eighty thousand duros in securities, keeping the rest for himself and undertaking to pay the taxes connected with settling the estate to the Treasury. Mama Zita and Aunt Cruz let themselves be persuaded without resistance, for they had always dreamed of living together again just as they had as girls ("together but separately, you know what I mean," explained Mama Zita), and on the other hand Uncle Felipe Neri, by now resigned to the sterility of his marriage, was consoled by proximity to his goddaughter Crucita, and (as he noted in his oilcloth-covered notebook) "by having Gervasio closer to me and trying to keep him from his father's malign influence." The nearness of their uncle and aunt also pleased the children, for they enjoyed novelty, and as far as Gervasio was concerned the rehabilitation of those gloomy closed rooms filled with shadows and junk, which had fed his earliest fears, represented the coming of peace. The dragon had died; light had killed it.

But what Uncle Vidal had not counted on when he awarded himself the generous portfolio of securities of his inheritance was the disaster of the Fenedosa Company a few weeks after the divisions had been made. Fenedosa ("an investment offering a guarantee of high returns") sank like a stone, underwent a well-publicized bankruptcy, and the trial and subsequent imprisonment of Don Teodoro Blanco, its managing director, did not result in any sort of compensation for him. The bankruptcy converted his shares into worthless paper and reduced Uncle Vidal's fat portfolio to one more name on a problematical list of creditors. Those were stormy months in the old palace of the counts of Pradoluengo.

Uncle Vidal, always given to farcical performances, would sit on the edge of the divan, unbutton his jacket, cover his bald spot with his hands, and shamelessly proclaim himself a "poor, wretched fellow," and encouraged by the effect on his sensitive sisters of his shouts and gestures, would refer to his children as "those innocent little victims who someday will parade their indigence through the soup kitchens of Saint Vincent de Paul." Aunt Cruz and Mama Zita would sniffle as they listened to him and then, during their dull sewing afternoons, sitting next to the balcony and looking out over the garden where Clemente the deaf-mute was pruning rosebushes and transplanting bulbs, they would confer about how to help their brother, even, if need be, by redistributing the inheritance as if Papa León's death had taken place after the Fenedosa catastrophe. But Uncle Felipe Neri, with his spotless eyeglasses, his churning stomach juices, and his ash-colored hair parted into two halves, scolded them with gentle irony, called them a pair of innocents, and told them that, even admitting the fact that Uncle Vidal had lost his investment in Fenedosa, he had ample resources to live like a prince for a hundred years without lifting a finger. Papa Telmo kept out of the quarrel, but one night when he found Mama Zita sitting at her dressing table, unhappy to the point of tears, he vigorously supported Uncle Felipe Neri's opinion.

"You mustn't lose sleep over your brother Vidal, Zita; he knows how to look out for himself," he said with his broad, snub-nosed smile, like the smile of a retired boxer.

For months the Fenedosa affair was the chief subject of the Saturday evening gatherings in the palace. According to Uncle Vidal, the victim most affected by the bankruptcy, "Fenedosa would bring hunger and despair to distinguished families in the city." And since Uncle Vidal had that resounding tone of voice which, when he spoke of Fenedosa, took on a mournful prophetic tinge, his economic difficulties filtered down to the least important members of the household.

"Your uncle's been left without a cent, sweetie."

"I know; it's Uncle Vidal, I bet."

Amalia mischievously winked one eye under her vertical eyebrow.

"And do you know whose fault it was?"

"No, I don't, Amalia."

The girl exchanged a knowing look with Señora Zoa.

"A lizard that slipped in."

On the following Saturday, before Uncle Vidal and Aunt Macrina arrived, Mama Zita shut herself in the playroom with the children for a few minutes.

"I want to warn you about something: don't ever think of mentioning the word 'Fenedosa' in front of Uncle Vidal. Do you hear what I'm saying?"

"Yes."

As soon as Mama Zita was out of the room, Gervasio went running to the kitchen.

"I know who the lizard is, Amalia," he said, panting.

"Who, let's see?"

"A lizard called Fenedosa."

Amalia let out a cackling giggle.

"What a kid this one is, he's an imp of Satan!"

Gervasio didn't know what that word was, or still less its significance, but after Mama Zita's warning it rose automatically to his mouth every time he saw Uncle Vidal or Aunt Macrina, like the water to Uncle Felipe Neri's, and he had to compress his lips as hard as he could to keep it from escaping. There were times when the temptation was so irresistible that he would shut himself in the bathroom and, sitting on the bidet, repeat over and over that enigmatic word, which stuck to his palate like a dry cookie, until he got tired. But he would hardly be out of the bathroom, if he happened to meet Uncle Vidal or Aunt Macrina, than he would again be assailed by an immoderate desire to say the word. As for his sister Florita, she thought that "Fenedosa" was a succulent, delicious word, so that every time they played funerals, if the carriages were late in arriving, she would repeat "Fenedosa, Fenedosa, Fenedosa" under her breath until she got bored.

At the end of March the subject of Fenedosa was superseded when Uncle Jairo won the competitive examinations for a judgeship in the city. The children, excited by Aunt Macrina's comments, expected to meet a different sort of man, something like a copy of the Archangel Gabriel statue that presided over the holy-water font in the chapel at school, but merely life-size and dressed in a jacket and tie.

"Aunt Macrina says he's tall, tall, really tall."

"Like La Madruga?"

"I don't know if that tall."

But Uncle Jairo arrived and struck them as a normal man, with thick graying hair, a square jaw, and a well-cut gray suit. He had sad eyes that were a bit screwed up as if the light dazzled him. He was middle-aged and a bachelor, and had no friends in the city; on Thursdays he went with Crucita to play tennis, and on Saturdays attended the family soirées, though he was by nature taciturn and spoke very little, only what was indispensable and only when he was addressed. But if he did take the floor Aunt Macrina listened to him enraptured, for he had a doughy, hoarse, and very manly voice, and his features, especially his eyes when he warmed to a subject, were even milder and more attractive than in repose. Uncle Jairo, though he didn't admit it, accepted those gatherings because he had nothing better to do.

"Uncle Jairo gets bored at our house."

"How do you know that, Flora?"

"He doesn't like the things that Uncle Vidal talks about. The only thing he likes in the whole house is Crucita."

"Really, Flora?"

"Don't you have eyes in your head?"

Uncle Jairo's appointment to the Superior Court revolutionized not only the mansion but the whole city. In a matter of a few days he became the fashionable man, object of all eyes and subject of all conversations. On mending afternoons Aunt Cruz and Mama Zita also referred to him as a paradigm of masculine good looks.

"There's absolutely nothing wrong with his looks."

"A teeny bit on the dull side, don't you think?"

"Maybe, but I'm not sure whether that's not just what's attractive about him."

Amalia, in the kitchen, was more explicit.

"My heavens, what a man, Señora Zoa. With a good-looker like that I could lose my head, mind what I say. What a way he has of looking at a person!"

Apparently the children did not amuse him, but if one of them came to his attention for one reason or another, he would give them generous gifts of money and even play with them for a while; it could even be said that their presence in the drawing room during the Saturday evening sessions helped to dispel his boredom. One night Papa Telmo appeared at the gathering, and to the general surprise Uncle Jairo, undoubtedly sick and tired of the usual restricted subjects, acquired a sudden passion for naturopathy and agreed enthusiastically when Papa Telmo, referring to his vegetarian diet, succinctly expressed his creed: "The sun is my cook and the earth my pantry."

Aunt Cruz exchanged conspiratorial glances with Mama Zita

and Aunt Macrina with Uncle Vidal, because for the first time since
his arrival Jairo was interested in something besides Crucita. The
elementary remedy against constipation, consisting in shaving
barefoot before breakfast on wet floor tiles, literally dazzled him,
and when Papa Telmo declared that "constipation isn't a problem
of the intestines but of the mind," his joy knew no bounds; and
when minutes later Papa Telmo referred to "the succulent pleasure
of walking barefoot, feeling the earth's magnetism under the soles
of one's feet," Jairo had become a fervent convert to naturopathy.

On the following day, Sunday, he went to the country with his
brother-in-law and the two of them took a light bath together, then
walked naked among the oak trees and drew up a schedule of
gymnastic exercises, a procedure that they repeated regularly. This
unusual comradeship between the two men caused anxiety in the
city and occasioned an increase in the amount of gossip (both
covert and malicious) about the new judge and his habits. Mama
Zita, less imaginative and relatively ill-educated, was convinced of
her husband's eccentricity and thought of his brother-in-law as
simply another eccentric, an opinion that Uncle Felipe Neri supported by pointing out the possibility that Uncle Jairo might also
be a pantheist. One afternoon Aunt Cruz, her face crimson despite
the white powder, enriched the repertory of anecdotes about Uncle
Jairo with a stunning revelation.

"Macrina has told me that in Madrid he used to meet every
Tuesday with young Protestants."

"Good heavens!"

Uncle Felipe Neri cut in.

"I'm not surprised. Luther's followers in Madrid are increasing
in number."

"Who did you say?"

"Luther, the first to raise the banner of revolt against the Pope."

"Ah!"

Within a few weeks Uncle Jairo had become the target of scandal
and the object of slander. Now and then Aunt Macrina would visit
his room in the Hotel Vieja Castilla to tidy it up a bit, "for you
know that men have no sense of space and pile everything up so."
One morning Aunt Cruz went with her and returned saying that
the room was as austere as a monk's cell, but there was no crucifix

over the head of the bed and instead there were engravings of flagellated saints and naked boys on the walls, and a strange sort of Bible on the bookshelves.

Unaware of these speculations, Uncle Jairo continued to play tennis with Crucita on Thursdays and go with Papa Telmo on Sundays to take bare-skin baths in the pine woods. One day he met the children and Señora Zoa in front of the ticket office of the Lux movie theater, which specialized in Westerns, and in a free-spending gesture asked for a box and stayed with them. Flora and Gervasio, absorbed by the incidents of the picture, warmly applauded the Indians' defeats. During the intermission Uncle Jairo bought them sourballs and chocolate bars and asked why they were applauding.

"Because Indians are bad."

"Who told you that?"

"Because they're bad in all the pictures."

"Well, I'm sure that when you're older you'll think differently."

Gervasio did not quite understand Uncle Jairo's words, but guessed that his sympathies were on the side of the Indians, which troubled him so much that it took him two hours to go to sleep that night, and when he finally managed to do so he dreamed of Uncle Jairo on horseback, bare-chested and with feathers in his hair, galloping over a plain at the head of a group of redskins. The images were so vivid that when he woke up he could hardly distinguish reality from what he had dreamed; but his obsession continued to disturb him, and when Señora Zoa served him his breakfast he asked her, "Is it true that Indians are good, Zoa?"

"Aren't you the foolish one! How can you think that those filthy savages are good?"

"Well, Uncle Jairo says so."

"You leave your Uncle Jairo alone and thank God you were born a Christian."

But the boy continued to be dissatisfied, and when he came home from school he went in through the garden and up to his uncle and aunt's part of the house.

"Uncle, are Indians good?"

"Well, I suppose there must be all kinds."

"Then are cowboys bad?"

Uncle Felipe Neri coughed twice, invited him to sit down, and wiped his eyeglasses with an immaculate white handkerchief.

"Look, my boy, bringing faith and civilization to unbelievers is a meritorious action in itself."

"And is it good to kill them for that?"

"Kill, kill, that's a very hard word, Gervasio. There are times when a little force has to be exercised, I'm not saying there aren't. Unbelievers tend to be like babies, they yell and kick when you wash their faces. Is that reason enough to leave them dirty?"

During the nine o'clock mass at Santa Brígida on Sunday, kneeling between Flora and Gervasio, Mama Zita told them with unusual warmth, "Today, offer your communion for Uncle Jairo."

Gervasio slowly turned his head toward her.

"Is Uncle Jairo bad?"

Mama Zita shook her head nervously.

"It's not a question of his being good or bad. Pray to the Baby Jesus for him and don't ask so many questions."

When they came out of church his sister Flora told him that Mama Zita was making them pray for Uncle Jairo because he was a friend of Papa Telmo's and both of them went together on Sundays to run around naked in the pine woods, and that was a grave sin. But for once Gervasio rebutted his sister's arguments, holding that if Mama Zita made the children pray for them, it was because neither one of them liked heroes, and that was why Papa Telmo had told Clemente to burn Uncle Felipe Neri's uniforms and why Uncle Jairo was on the Indians' side against the cowboys. From then on the figure of Uncle Jairo was surrounded by a mythical and contradictory aura. Amalia too, after her fashion, expressed the surprise that his ambiguity caused in her.

"That uncle of yours, what good does it do him to be so handsome when he's never been seen with a woman in his life?"

"Well, he goes out with Crucita, Amalia, and plays tennis with her."

"Sure, sure, Crucita; d'you think Crucita's a woman? Why, she doesn't even have breasts."

Despite this deficiency, Uncle Jairo had showed his preference for her ever since his arrival. They chattered and laughed about nothing, and her uncle added frequent theoretical explanations to his practical tennis lessons, which made it necessary to take Crucita by the shoulders, or the waist, or under the arms, and make her bend or twist her supple body. The girl accepted this instruction with delight and treated Uncle Jairo with the greatest affection and intimacy: she would nuzzle him, hang around his neck, sit on his lap. Aunt Cruz witnessed this process with alarm and warned her sister, "Don't you think Crucita goes too far with Jairo? Crucita isn't a little girl any longer, Zita."

For the moment Mama Zita saw nothing unseemly in her daughter's behavior.

"In lots of ways Crucita hasn't matured yet."

When the girl was not present Jairo extolled her figure, her slenderness, the way she carried herself, and then Mama Zita, rather flustered by his praises, referred to "her slow physical development," to which Uncle Jairo replied firmly, "May she never develop! That's her greatest charm."

The family had been conscious for some years of Crucita's breasts (the lack of them, that is), and waited for Uncle Jairo to offer some justification for so gratuitous an opinion; but he was a little embarrassed by his hasty expression of enthusiasm, and aware that the atmosphere was not favorable for going into details, merely said, "It's an androgynous beauty. She has the grace of a Greek ephebe."

Aunts and uncles exchanged glances, shrugged their shoulders, and ended by accepting what seemed to be praise, thinking that perhaps Uncle Jairo, being a Madrilenian, was more a man of the world and up-to-date, and might be in a position to state that there was nothing so ugly as a prominent bust on a woman.

Amalia, however, thought that this defect was substantial enough to annul femininity. Uncle Jairo's periodic presence in the house, the smell of his cigarettes, the discreet masculine perfume he used, made her more headstrong than usual. She still went out with Anselmo Llorente three times a week, but would come in with her hair tousled, her clothes torn, and an occasional pink mark on her face and neck. Señora Zoa would shake her head knowingly.

"You be careful, now. In spring the blood's up."

"You go to the devil, Señora Zoa!"

Her moods had become unpredictable; she did her daily tasks

lazily, and gave the impression of waiting for something. One night when she came home early, Gervasio opened the door for her. Her cheeks looked swollen and her eyes sparkled.

"Have your papa and mama come home yet?" she asked the boy point-blank.

"Not yet, Amalia."

"Well, then, come along with me for a little while, sweetie."

She went down the hall in front of him, limping a little on her right leg, to the very last storeroom, the one next to Aunt Cruz's part of the house. Once inside she shot the bolt on the door, sat down on the couch covered with an old piece of cretonne, and began to take off her shoes and stockings. Then she pulled her dress and slip over her head, and in the faint light that came through the transom Gervasio saw the black fuzz in her armpits.

"You have hairs on your arms, Amalia."

"I've got more hairs than that, baby. Amalia has lots of hairs, you'll see what a lot of hairs Amalia has!"

The shifting protuberances of her breasts, the white flesh shining in the half-light, the mysterious nest of her pubic region, the strange circumstances around him, frightened Gervasio. But she hastily undressed him with hot, nimble fingers, lay down, put the child on top of her and began to contort her body wildly.

"I'm a little horsie and you're Uncle Jairo, all right?"

The child was sweating, his face hidden between those overflowing breasts, trying to escape from the girl's cruel embrace, the painful pressure of her thighs. But she held him tighter and tighter, groaned, touched him again and again, murmured gloating, obscene words, and at last squeezed him so tightly that she almost cut off his breath, gave a couple of muffled cries, and was still. Gervasio could hear her ragged breathing beside him; he slid off onto the floor and then the breathing stopped and he heard her hoarse, languid voice.

"Did you like that, baby?"

"No, Amalia."

"Scared you, did it?"

"Yes, Amalia."

"Your uncle wouldn't have been so scared, that's for sure."

"Which uncle, Amalia?"

"Your Uncle Jairo, which uncle did you think?" She broke into provocative laughter. "Wow, what a man!" The child was trying to put his bare feet through the leg-holes of his underpants. "Hold on, sweetie, I'll dress you right away."

Before they left the storeroom Amalia tugged at his jersey and warned, "Not a word to Mama, understand? Or Señora Zoa or Florita or anybody . . . This is a secret between Amalia and you."

A strange association of ideas inspired Gervasio to say, "And how about Anselmo Llorente?"

"Him less than anybody, d'you hear? Don't you even think about doing that."

The child felt pervaded by a smutty excitement. He was possessed by the vague knowledge that he had done something nasty; but at the same time he sensed that the secret of life turned on those viscous intimacies, and that ignorance of such actions was what justified the thing that grownups called "childish innocence." Suddenly he stopped feeling innocent, understood the existence of Friné's, the existence of those men with pulled-down hatbrims who prowled around its doors, Anselmo Llorente's bad temper every time Amalia was late, and the excitement of the girls who went up on the stage of the Novelty to dance with Breslau or Rodolfo Francisco. He began to see things in a new light. Still upset by Amalia's lewd spasms, he trembled at the thought of a sensual adolescence. The impression went so deep that he did not dare to discuss it with Florita. What sealed his lips was not fear of revealing a secret, but an inner shame. As for Señora Zoa, he suspected that if he told her she would feel jealous and would go for Amalia's eyes like a panther. And so he kept the secret to himself, though from time to time Amalia managed to remind him of his complicity with fleeting winks and evasive smiles.

As Holy Week approached Uncle Jairo showed an interest in the ritual and the processions, and Aunt Macrina informed him that most of them passed under the balcony of his hotel, where the whole family could watch them together in all their splendor. This was why, though in Uncle Jairo's opinion the room was uncomfortable and inadequate for the purpose, everyone in the family congregated there to watch the Good Friday procession. Aunt Macrina's little ones played among the furniture, while Papa

Telmo, Uncle Vidal, and Uncle Jairo, standing behind the group of women seated on the balcony, chatted briskly. Gervasio, leaning on the arm of a chair, stared as if hypnotized at Uncle Jairo's tanned, vigorous hand holding a cigarette, and without knowing why felt a chaste desire to have that hand caress his head. But Uncle Jairo paid no attention to him, absorbed in what Papa Telmo was saying and wholeheartedly agreeing with his two fundamental conclusions: first, that gluttony leads men to dig their graves with their own teeth, and second, that responsible people ought to begin to look out for their old age at thirty. He smoked the cigarette down to the holder, turned around, and squashed the butt into an ashtray on the night table.

On the dark street, preceded by a drum corps, the float depicting the prayer in Gethsemane had appeared between two lines of hooded figures, and Mama Zita and Aunt Cruz crossed themselves. Aunt Macrina turned her head toward her brother.

"There you have the most famous sculptures of Juan de Juni, Berruguete, and Gregorio Fernández," she said for the third time, with the pride of a professional guide.

Uncle Jairo smiled at her again, while below them the confraternities and floats passed by one after another, the flames of the tapers wavered, the tunics and hoods changed from one color to another. Mama Zita and Aunt Cruz waxed fervent over the presence of the barefoot penitents, while Crucita's great desire was to identify them. And every time she discovered someone she knew, she would address Uncle Jairo with a little grimace of superiority.

"Just imagine how ridiculous, Uncle; Lola Alvarez Puga, barefoot in the procession."

Having been forewarned, Uncle Jairo nodded indulgently, but when the procession was half over and the lacerated, bleeding Christ figures began to appear, his gentle eyes ceased to blink, while his right hand, afflicted with a strange agitation, seemed to find no place to rest. It wandered from the chair arm to his pocket, from his pocket to his chin, until at last he clenched his fist and sank the well-kept nails into his flesh. Gervasio stealthily observed his pale, contorted face, the violet smudges under his eyes, his tight lips, while at the same time he began to be conscious of the gloomy strains of the band that brought up the rear of the procession (notes muffled by the mutes on the trumpets, the slow, hollow, funereal beating of the drums) which was slowly approaching. The child could not have said what it was that set him off, whether the bloody Christ statues, the fierce figures representing the "Christ-killers," Uncle Jairo's pained expression, or the strangled music of the band that ended the parade. ("Surely," as Uncle Felipe Neri was to write hours later in the oilcloth-covered notebook, "the combination of two or three factors was necessary for Gervasio to go into a seizure this afternoon, a strange, profound one that frightened me, for at a given moment I feared an attack of convulsions.") The fact is that the child felt on his neck something resembling an electric shock which, finding no outlet, stayed imprisoned inside him and snaked through his body, putting such pressure on his skin from inside that his head gradually fanned out like a peacock's tail (the hairs standing up as stiff as sabers), his face twitched, and his arms and legs became covered with granular skin, a little blond hair crowning each point.

Papa Telmo was the first to discover his uncouth metamorphosis.

"That child! Holy God, that child! Zita, please!"

He shouldered Uncle Jairo out of the way, dragged up an armchair and bent over the child, while the women pushed their chairs aside in alarm, making spaces between them, and Vidalín, in Aunt Macrina's lap, repeated over and over, "My cousin's playing tricks, isn't he, Mama?"

Papa Telmo caught Gervasio in his arms and laid him on Uncle Jairo's bed, shouting orders.

"Close the balcony doors! This child is having a horripilation!"

He bent over him and lifted one eyelid, felt his pulse.

Uncle Jairo closed the balcony, Mama Zita grabbed one of the boy's hands, Uncle Felipe Neri tried to fluff up the pillow.

"Better take it away," said Papa Telmo.

Uncle Felipe Neri removed it. Aunt Macrina took her children out into the hall. Mama Zita caressed the child's limp hand. His eyelids were closed, and he was trembling and seemed unconscious.

"My God, Telmo!"

Papa Telmo was not listening to her. His bloodless lips released a torrent of abuse against the hooded marchers, the sinister figures, the bloody statues, and the funeral march. He kept saying, pointing at Gervasio's manelike head of hair, "It's a horripilation! Never in my life have I seen a case like it," and he pressed the pale little face between his big hands. "Don't be afraid, son; Papa Telmo's with you. Those bad men won't hurt you."

Gervasio's hair slowly settled down again, his skin flattened out and assumed a vegetable smoothness. He half opened his eyes.

"He's coming around," said Uncle Vidal.

The first things that Gervasio saw when he opened his eyes were the blurred, anguished faces of Mama Zita, Papa Telmo, Aunt Cruz, Uncle Felipe Neri, Crucita, Flora, Uncle Jairo, and Uncle Vidal around the bed.

"Are you feeling better, my darling?" Mama Zita put her hand on his forehead.

Papa Telmo brushed her aside with an authoritative gesture.

"Leave him alone now; leave him in peace." He turned to Uncle Felipe Neri. "Open the balcony, Felipe, let him have some air. Would you like a little water, son?"

Gervasio felt flooded with tranquil happiness. Again, he was proud that people felt anxious for him; he knew himself to be the center of general attention. Uncle Jairo bent over the bed and patted him on the head. The child shut his eyes and smiled quietly. Papa Telmo sat down beside him and again squeezed Gervasio's face between his big hands.

"You were frightened, weren't you, you rascal?" He smiled.

"Yes."

"You were scared of those hooded men and those bad fellows who wanted to kill Christ, isn't that right, son?"

The boy nodded. Papa Telmo asked him two or three other unimportant questions before looking into his eyes with professional curiosity.

"Has anything like that ever happened to you before?" he asked.

Several clearings of the throat were audible, and Uncle Vidal's dry, splintered, warning cough. Mama Zita shut her eyes. Aunt Cruz bowed her head. Wordlessly, Uncle Felipe Neri took off his glasses. The child's eyes passed over the flustered faces of his relatives one by one, then he turned them languidly toward his father and lied with edifying self-possession:

"Never: This was the first time."

PART
TWO

CHAPTER 8

Gervasio's enrollment in the Colegio de Todos los Santos to begin his secondary studies represented a break with the past, a breach with a warm childhood rich in experiences, though it had been excessively restricted and protected. He left behind a world of fantasy which at one time had seemed fundamental and which now, from his new perspective, struck him as very fragile. In a matter of a few months the principles that informed his life had matured and become more rational, so that the habits and persons that had sustained his early childhood gradually faded, losing significance for him: the funeral game, Sister Luciana, Amalia, Anselmo Llorente, the long walks with Señora Zoa, El Cigüeña, Benigno the chauffeur, Clemente the gardener; those phantoms of the early morning light, La Enana and La Madruga; Don Minervino and the ladies of Friné's; Felipa the laundress, Severo the fat sacristan of Santa Brígida, Sunday movies at the Lux cinema, Señora Agustina and her children Daniel and Felisilla . . . From the vantage point of his ten years Gervasio looked upon his little history as a seamless whole, without analyzing it, with a mixture of irony and confusion. Sometimes he thought that the dividing line between his carefree past and his responsible present was marked by the afternoon when he experienced hate. It was on his last long walk with Señora Zoa, when he had scrambled into Señora Agustina's fig tree, and while he was enjoying a tender, sweet early fig, Daniel the carpenter had shot him a long, festering look of reproof. It was so devastating and intense that the child turned his head, believing that he could not possibly be its only target. But when he realized that he was alone, that he was the exclusive object of that look, he threw the fig to the ground and slid down from the tree in fright, slipped up behind Señora Zoa, and said to her under his breath, "Zoa, let's go. I don't want to stay here any more."

After that day Gervasio searched in vain for a guarantee against hate; he wanted only to be loved. He was used to a cushioned and problem-free existence, and Daniel the carpenter's look had revealed to him that not everyone was on his side and also that he might involuntarily do himself harm. He began to sense that the supports that he had always thought firm were not lasting. Señora Zoa's lap, for example, was no longer a refuge; it did not give him a sense of security. The old servant shrank, became more wrinkled, and he began to see her as what she was: a frail little black bundle, slow-witted and crippled with arthritis. The discovery, though gradual, was shattering. And yet he had to pretend to some affection and accept her effusions in order not to disappoint her; but his love for her had withered some time ago, and now (he felt ashamed to recognize it) it became more and more urgent to place an emotional distance between the old woman and himself. Mama Zita came to his aid on the day that Florita turned eleven, by notifying the servants that from that date onward the children had ceased to be children and had begun to be the young master and mistress. For Gervasio it was an unexpected rise in rank. Florentina, the new maid, accepted the change as quite natural, and said "Señorito Gervasio" with indrawn breath, as she might have said "Your Highness," or "Mr. President." Señora Zoa, however, sticking to habit, weakened by old age and inadequate circulation, could not entirely take in the new situation, and in a confused attempt to please everyone, beginning with herself, combined words with completely different meanings, like "treasure" and "señorito," in referring to Gervasio, which caused him increasing discomfort. Often Señora Zoa, forgetting what she was supposed to call him and giving way to her impulses, even in the knowledge that there was no longer a link between them, would hug Gervasio to her breast. Although she could feel him squirming in her arms, she would not let him go until she had planted her customary kisses on his cheeks. These demonstrations caused revulsion in Gervasio, for he had noticed that the old woman, as Florita had pointed out to him some time before, smelled of stagnant water (especially the bun at the back of her head, stuck through with hairpins), and her once smooth skin was more and more wrinkled and was turning cold and rough, like the hide of turtles. But his irritation reached a peak on the day that his schoolmate, Pedro María de la Vega, witnessed one of these overwrought transports. In reaction to the old woman's effusive demonstration, Gervasio wriggled out of her embrace and yelled at her that no blood relationship gave her the right to hug him like that, while his friend Pedro, or Peter, as they called him, watched the scene half embarrassed and half amused, and Señora Zoa murmured something that was no less true for being laughable: that her treasure, her baby, had stopped loving her.

This scene put an end to a long idyll, and Mama Zita, in view of Señora Zoa's inability to do her work and Gervasio's rejection of her emotional outbursts, suggested to her one day that she retire to her sister-in-law Agustina's house; but as her nephew Daniel refused to shelter "a lackey of the bourgeois class" under his roof, Señora Zoa at last agreed to enter the Little Sisters of the Poor, an institution of which Mama Zita was a patroness. And as she collected her poor belongings, sobbing, Mama Zita consoled her by telling her that the house would always be open to her and that she was expected for lunch "as often as she felt like it." Señora Zoa put away the photograph of her niece and nephew, the seashell, and her clothes in the cardboard suitcase, no doubt remembering the sweet pretenses of years past when her baby, her treasure, would clutch frantically at her legs and stop her from leaving. Now Gervasio didn't even make an appearance until Mama Zita opened the street door. Then he appeared in the vestibule and held out a distant and expressionless hand which she bathed in kisses and tears, as she said over and over, "Good-bye, good-bye, Señorito Gervasio, my treasure."

After her departure Señora Zoa would visit the family on an occasional Sunday and, though Gervasio tried to escape, she would lurk behind half-open doors solely for the pleasure of seeing him, resigned by now to not mixing in his affairs, and when it was time to leave (Gervasio was never on hand to say good-bye) she would stare at Mama Zita with her bleary eyes and say complacently, "Well, señora, Señorito Gervasio's turning out to be quite the little peacock. You must be proud of him."

But Señora Zoa melted into the background of Gervasio's history, as did Amalia, who fell victim to her springtime lusts and wound up pregnant; and Anselmo Llorente, the man responsible for her condition, disappeared without a trace. Mama Zita gave her a scolding in the green room, making it clear that her bulging belly was not only a grave sin but a source of scandal for the children, and that therefore she could not stay in the house. Amalia, despite her haughty eyebrows, begged, pleaded, humbled herself in vain, and at last, with no other person close to her in the city except for the deserter, Anselmo Llorente, inexorably played out her fate: she threw herself under a train, that old resort of the city's desperate folk. Mama Zita, when she learned of her horrible end, had Don Urbino say a novena of masses for the girl; but one day when she tried to persuade her husband to accompany her, Papa Telmo refused with one of his irrational, Voltairian sentences:

"Sorry, Zita, I refuse to share your remarkable Christianity that excludes your fellow man."

But even within their apparently unhappy aspect, these events turned out to be providential for Flora and Gervasio. After having lived with them for so long, it was doubtful that Señora Zoa and Amalia would have taken them seriously, would have maintained the deference due to their age and station—would, in a word, have paid heed to a social hierarchy. But now Florentina, the new maid, with her little white cuffs and piqué collar, and fat Ani in the kitchen, referred to them as "señorito" and "señorita" as naturally as they called Mama Zita or Papa Telmo "señora" and "señor."

And Florita, too, ceased to be a fixture in Gervasio's life. Her fascinating power of seduction faded, and with the change of schools Florita became an adolescent girl in a school uniform who would start to whisper to her friend Manena Abad as soon as Gervasio came into the room, and then they would laugh foolishly. Flora had a personal world of her own now, into which her faraway past hardly entered.

"Do you know, when my brother was a little boy he wanted to be a hero, and every time he heard music his hair would stand on end?"

Manena Abad, of the blond locks, would laugh heartily with that muffled, husky laugh of hers, and Gervasio would lower his eyes in confusion, because though he had not renounced heroism, he was embarrassed by the memory of those phenomena that had accompanied his early childhood. He had reached the age at which the human ideal is ordinariness, not to be different from anyone else, not to exceed the norm, and the very mention of his display made him feel ashamed. However, after almost three years without a sign of it, he thought that that episode was closed. His seizures might well respond, as Uncle Vidal had speculated on several occasions, to pure electrical phenomena and had been superseded as he matured. For Uncle Felipe Neri, however, the realization that those years had gone by without the appearance of an external sign was a disappointment. He was reluctant to admit that Gervasio, having been a remarkable child in his early years, should now sink into anonymous commonplaceness and become a boy without any fineness of perception. What had become of those movements of the hair, that sensitivity, those edifying trances? Troubled by the boy's lack of reaction, one Sunday in October he took him out for a walk when the regimental band of San Quintín was giving a morning concert in the bandstand in the park. He knew that he was acting against Mama Zita's wishes, as surreptitiously as Papa León had done in times past, but hope was stronger than prudence in his case. The attempt turned out to be a failure, because though he stopped several times in front of the bandstand where the noise of the brasses was almost unbearable (positively maddening during the more florid strains of "The Siege of Zaragoza"), no change occurred in Gervasio; he seemed oblivious to what was happening on the bandstand. His passivity in the face of stimuli that had been infallible in the past plunged Uncle Felipe Neri into a profound crisis: "The presumed heroism of my nephew Gervasio" (he confided that afternoon to his oilcloth-covered notebook, lying dusty and forgotten in the top drawer of the desk) "has faded like those precocious inclinations which, at certain points in a child's life, make youngsters want to be policemen or firemen. After not writing in this book for two and a half years, I renew the contact today only to register my disenchantment, for this morning my nephew, during a concert of military music, did not react despite the martial quality of the compositions. He underwent no seizure nor any change at all. He wandered aimlessly around the bandstand where the music was being played, kicking at chestnuts or staring vaguely into the distance. Neither the hymns nor the quicksteps caused the slightest emotion in him; he said nothing; nothing occurred. The same would have happened if I had taken Clemente, that poor retarded boy who tends the garden, with me instead of Gervasio. This makes me think that what at the time I considered to be a sign from on high was perhaps nothing but a reflex action, like a sneeze when one's nose tickles. May the Lord hold us all in his hand."

Although for other reasons, Papa Telmo also kept the boy under observation for a time after the Good Friday horripilation. He started by observing him from a distance, testing his nervous reactions as if in a game; but at times, stimulated by some comment that the child made, he would ask him questions without seeming to give them importance.

"You haven't felt afraid again, the way you did that afternoon at the procession?"

"No."

"And can you tell me what happened to you that afternoon, son?"

The boy would shrug his shoulders, stick his lower lip over the upper one, and decline to answer. Papa Telmo resigned himself. He didn't want to harass him, but if Gervasio occasionally asked for water or the urinal at night, he would go into his bedroom as if he had just happened to pass by the door.

"You're scared, aren't you, Gervasio?" he would say, staring obsessively at his head.

"No."

"Do you want me to leave the door open?" He kept on looking at his head. "Shall I stay with you for a while?"

"No."

"Are you all right, then? Nothing hurts?"

"No."

Little by little the incident was forgotten, as "an epileptic type of attack produced by any sort of excess," explained Papa Telmo, "because the child isn't fearful, that is, not abnormally fearful." Uncle Jairo, who at that moment was standing next to a bush taking off his trousers, commented, "What a scare he gave us! I'll never be able to forget that head of his, bristling like a trapped animal's."

Uncle Jairo continued to go to the country with Papa Telmo, though with ever more frequent lapses. The demands of the naturopathic life had begun to annoy him. And besides, after the Sunday exercises his appetite increased, just when he was trying to lose weight.

"Today I'd give a year of my life for a good paella. I'm dying of hunger."

Papa Telmo reproached him for his weakness, and on the following Saturday Aunt Macrina remarked, "My brothers are so impressionable. They pick up passionately on anything new, but in the end they don't follow through. Almost the same thing happens to them with politics, especially David."

Mama Zita, when she was alone with Aunt Cruz, offered the opinion that "as for being handsome, Jairo certainly was that, but he was also a regular weathervane." As for Gervasio, she worried about him a good deal less. And though her sister persisted in interpreting his attacks as proof of celestial favor, she preferred God's silence. One afternoon she confided to Cruz, "In April it will be three years since Gervasio had the last of those attacks. I don't want to tempt God, but I do so hope that those horrible things are over for good."

Aunt Cruz turned her powdered face away in annoyance. She couldn't understand her sister. She failed to comprehend how she could describe as "horrible things" and "those attacks of his" something that she and her husband thought of as marks of distinction from on high. But Mama Zita's faith was not composed of such daydreams.

"And who told you that they were signs from on high and not mere physical phenomena, as Vidal insists?"

Mama Zita, her fears assuaged, watched Gervasio grow, observed his new relationships. She liked Pedro María de la Vega—Peter—because the Vegas were "a local family all their lives; an institution." Peter's parents were Don Belarmino de la Vega, member of a distinguished family, and his wife and first cousin Genoveva Serrada. An eagerly awaited only child, Peter was intelligent, thoughtful, and, moreover, sedentary, much given to reading, board games, and quiet pastimes. Peter taught Gervasio how to make model ships inside bottles and to play chess and stage mock naval battles. Peter's maternal grandfather, Don Alvaro Serrada, had been a naval officer, and it seemed (in the opinion of Don Belarmino, a high-ranking civil servant in the Treasury Department) that his grandson had come into the world with the exclusive aim of emulating him. At the age of seven he knew from memory the plans of the Spanish warships *Oquendo* and *Reina Cristina,* and arranged naval units, represented by matchboxes, to illustrate the tactics followed by the fleets in the battles of Lepanto, Trafalgar, or Jutland, and could explain with remarkable lucidity the victors' strategic successes and the losers' mistakes. He was a bookish child who, with his little slanted eyes, his clean freckled hands, and his mop of curly hair, impressed Gervasio to the point that it became an obsession to win praise from him; but this did not prevent him from occasionally tiring of Peter's sedentary ways and joining more active friends like Lucinio Orejón, who pinned paper dolls to the soutane of Father Dictinio, a recent arrival from the seminary, or placed percussion caps along the edge of the blackboard so that they would go off in bunches, with a horrible noise, every time that Father Sacristán got angry and pounded on it with his fist. Along with this, the fact that he had a girl friend (who was still in bobby socks), his precocious mustache, and his baggy pants made him immediately assume for Gervasio (though for reasons different from Peter's) a prestige that increased on the day that Father Dictinio ran down the hall after him, and Lucinio, realizing that he was losing ground, managed to place a glass-paned door between them, against which the Father crashed with a deafening noise of broken glass. The courage with which Lucinio faced rumors of expulsion, his arrogance while his parents abased themselves in the principal's office, begging indulgence for their son, increased his influence and authority.

Gervasio's sister Crucita didn't like Lucinio ("Orejón, Big-Ears, you tell me, how far can a boy go with a name like that?"). She thought of him as a yokel, a boy without any distinction whatever, as demonstrated by "those huge great pants of his, a ridiculous caricature of English knickerbockers." Sometimes Lucinio, tired of his escapades, would sit down and listen to Peter, and then he was capable of spending whole hours listening to him describe a naval battle or watching him glue a match inside a bottle to make a sprit for a frigate. Without meaning to do so Gervasio found himself serving as a hinge, reconciling two completely opposite characters, as on the day that he brought the naval battle of Jutland to life in the bathtub of his house (with ships made of pine bark and paper, which were subsequently burned). As Florita had done in former times, Lucinio offered him the stimulus of the unexpected, of surprise; he knew how to work out an appropriate plan for every circumstance. Hence in the month of January, when the river froze over, they skated as far as the Isla del Vado, where they hid a treasure (a top, a stone marble, and a penny), so that now, every time that Gervasio crossed the suspension bridge and glimpsed the island where they had had their adventure, he felt an indescribable emotion. Peter, though he was more cautious, gladly participated in these adventures, which he would then ennoble by lending his friends some book connected with them (in that case Stevenson's *Treasure Island*), which bestowed epic embellishments, celebrated by important intellectuals, on their innocent exploit. Gervasio was very happy with these two friends, who represented talent and action; and though it was to Lucinio, every time he talked about

his girl friend, that Gervasio recounted his lewd experience with
Amalia (bringing it up to date and attributing the initiative to
himself in order to shock his friend), it was Peter, an admirer of the
military life, to whom he showed the red beret that Papa León had
left him and the shapeless bullet that had cut down General Don
Cástor Arrázola.

So Gervasio's personality was gradually enriched and divided,
for if, on the one hand, when he was with Lucinio Orejón, he
seemed to be a restless, reckless, and active boy, on the other, in
his relationship with Peter, he would have been called a quiet,
busy, and tranquil youngster. There were certain occasions when
the two currents joined and Lucinio, Peter, and he were happy
together at the point where their interests coincided, as happened
one day when they saw the Norton motorcycle belonging to uncles
Norberto and Adrián, which Lucinio had just discovered and
praised highly at school. For Lucinio the two Mutes were unreal
beings, paradoxical but admirable: they had long teeth and didn't
eat, tongues and didn't speak, and they could take off on a motorcycle at a hundred and twenty kilometers an hour without having
the wind so much as snatch the hats off their heads. The day that
Gervasio revealed to Lucinio that the Mutes were his uncles, Lucinio thought he was joking. But Peter was also fascinated by the
diabolical machine that Lucinio had described so lovingly, and one
afternoon when they came out of school Gervasio, swelling with
pride and trying to surprise them, took his friends to the notions
shop. The black Norton, with its brilliant nickel trim and all its
equipment, rested silently at the edge of the curb like a sleeping
monster. Uncle Norberto and Uncle Adrián did not change expression when they saw him come in and greeted him with the usual
phrase, as if they had been together the day before.

"So what does the rascal have to say?"

By hints and insinuations Gervasio gave them to understand
that he and his friends would like to have a ride on that piece of
machinery; and then Uncle Adrián, the shorter one, smiled his
cannibal smile and without a moment's hesitation set him on the
back seat, gave two kicks to the starting pedal, seated himself in
the saddle, settled his hat more firmly on his head, and said, with
his head turned a little to one side, "Hang on tight."

And he set off like a madman, engine popping, along the street called Perdón de Dios, zigzagging among the farm carts, automobiles, and streetcars and finally reaching the old bridge at a hundred kilometers an hour. Buffeted by the wind, Gervasio stuck like a leech to Uncle Adrián's narrow waist, cheek resting against his back. Uncle Adrián, as usual, kept his impassive face raised, his hands on the handlebar grips, his hat stuck on the back of his head. On the unpaved highway between the two bridges he speeded up the machine still more, so that on the back the boy heard the whispering of the trees as they passed, interspersed with the regular explosions of the exhaust.

"Careful, Uncle!"

But Uncle Adrián did not apply the brakes until they reached the crossroads where the suspension bridge was, only to turn at right angles and plunge into the city again. Back at the shop, silently, as if performing a rite, Uncle Norberto placed Peter on the gas tank and Lucinio on the rack and immediately went over the same route. And though Peter, who was in front, felt that his breath was being cut off and waved his arms like a drowning man, Uncle Norberto did not slacken speed or make any comment until the trip was over. That was an unforgettable experience which Lucinio took delight in remembering, suggesting the possibility of repeating it.

They often saw the uncles riding on the motorcycle, straight as beanpoles, stuck as close to each other as they must have been in their mother's womb, with Uncle Adrián, the thinner one, in front driving and Uncle Norberto behind him with his yellow teeth showing and his hat on the back of his head. When they saw them going by, the humbler people in the neighborhood would say in a knowledgeable tone, "There go the Garcías; what a pair of nuts they are," or would comment ironically, "Since they don't talk, the Mutes have bought a motorcycle so they can make some noise."

About the middle of March Father Sacristán (broad forehead covered with wrinkles, as if his sole task were to think) spoke to them for the first time, in religion class, of the Republic as a synonym for chaos and atheism. This caused Gervasio to be suspicious of it and exclude it from a presumed list of "noble causes," a decision that was later corroborated when he heard Mama Zita's and Uncle Felipe Neri's negative comments at home. The Saturday evening gatherings had not been interrupted, and Flora and Gervasio participated in them to some degree. All was the same as in years past except for one thing: the main subject of conversation was no longer money but politics, which meant that the discussions were incomprehensible to the children, to the point that Gervasio often had to employ all five senses in the attempt to understand, and rack his brains trying to find out what to believe. For instance, the person who for Papa Telmo (on the rare occasions when he attended the family soirées) was "the dictator" became "the general" for Uncle Felipe Neri, "Primo" for Uncle Vidal, and "the Marquis of Estella" for Aunt Macrina and Crucita, shades of meaning that one had to keep in mind so as not to get lost in the labyrinth. And the day that the press announced "the Berenguer solution" and the calling of new elections, Uncle Felipe Neri remarked that "this is a time-serving compromise, not a solution," and Aunt Cruz, who had previously talked the matter over with her husband, stretched out her white throat with the black ribbon around it, like a dying swan, and predicted, "Here we go again. May God have us in his keeping."

It was in those days and in connection with those events that Mama Zita appropriated a popular expression that was destined to be used very often: "The big one's going to break out," an ambiguous phrase that predicted some catastrophic event, though within an indeterminate lapse of time. This vagueness of expression caused "the big one" to threaten on the day that Primo de Rivera died in exile in Paris, as well as at the time of the Cuatro Vientos mutiny and the arrival of the highly charged spring of 1931. For Gervasio, who liked categorical definitions, "the big one" meant something temporary, though undoubtedly bloody, and hence he did not exclude the idea that perhaps "the big one" would make clear once and for all whether his bent for heroism was a fact or a thing of no importance, forged by his family's fanaticism. And so the boy, though he feared "the big one," also awaited it with a certain degree of impatience.

One Thursday when he came out of school with his friends, he found his uncles Norberto and Adrián distributing leaflets from their motorcycle on the Avenida de los Tilos. Uncle Adrián was driving as usual and Uncle Norberto, much taller, sitting stiffly on the rack with an impassive face, was strewing the street with papers which, owing to the machine's speed, fluttered about for a time before settling on the pavement at the feet of passersby. Gervasio caught a sheet in midair and stopped to read it: "If you want freedom and justice, vote for the Republic." He swallowed, greatly upset, as he watched the motorcycle move away. He refused to recognize the evidence. It wasn't that he had thought of his uncles as monarchists, but with their silence and their Norton he had supposed them to be indifferent to the question. Suddenly his uncles (those uncles for whom he felt veneration, perhaps because at home they were thought of as "those damned uncles") had come out against everything that constituted his world and that he thought of as worthy of respect: Mama Zita, Uncle Felipe Neri, Don Urbano, priests, churches, school . . . Uncle Norberto and Uncle Adrián astride the Norton, riding like mad devils, were becoming harbingers of an evil cause, detonators of "the big one." He sensed that Peter was standing near him.

"Did you know your uncles were Republicans?"

"I had no idea," he excused himself.

A week later, at nightfall, he and Lucinio discovered the Norton parked in front of Friné's. Gervasio's heart beat so hard that his chest hurt. Lucinio made an angry gesture.

"Fuck your uncles! Besides being Republicans they're whore-chasers."

The mysterious attraction that the motorcycle and its owners exercised on Gervasio was stronger than his disillusionment.

"Why don't we wait till they come out?"

They huddled in the shadows of the narrow street where the church of Santa Brígida stood. Gervasio, choking with emotion, alternately watched the balcony of his house and the door of Friné's. Impatience made the wait seem like an eternity. Lucinio kept grumbling away, and both of them were almost ready to give up when the brightly painted door of the cabaret opened and the girls' boisterous laughter spilled into the street. In the midst of the group, held by their arms or shoulders, smiling at the night with their yellow teeth, were Uncle Norberto and Uncle Adrián. One of the girls stepped forward, planted a loud kiss on Uncle Adrián's forehead, and asked him to "do some acrobatics for a send-off."

"Are your uncles acrobats?"

"Shut up!"

Uncle Adrián was willing; he had taken off his jacket, and in his vest went to the place where the sidewalk widened, set the palms of his hands on the ground, and somersaulted his skinny body until his head was down and his shoe soles up on the wall, on the façade of the building. From inside the house came Don Minervino's angry voice, but the girls laughed and applauded enthusiastically, paying no attention to him, and after Uncle Adrián had recovered his vertical posture he made an elaborate bow with his hat in his hand, took his jacket in the other, and with fleet agility scrambled onto the shoulders of his brother, who had started the Norton. He waved the two articles of clothing in his outstretched arms and shouted two cheers for the Republic as they disappeared down the street.

That Sunday Mama Zita told the children not to leave the house after mass. On the previous night Gervasio had heard Marcial, the taxi driver from the corner stand, say as he rubbed one hand over the other, "Now comes the good part for the ones who're going to lose." He supposed that "the good part" must be "the big one" and made no comment, but thought to himself that if some people wanted "the big one" to break out, there must be some advantage for them in "the big one." Next morning, except for the silent lines that twined in front of the polling places, the streets were deserted and the few pedestrians who passed under the balcony did so hastily, as if they were cold, as if escaping from some danger. Mama Zita and Aunt Cruz took Señora Zoa in the car to vote, and Papa Telmo left the house immediately after dinner. On a small scale, the same tension reigned within the family as in the city. They had eaten dinner in silence, looking at each other over the tops of the glasses, and only Florita asked, when it was time for dessert, "Is the Republic the big one?"

Mama Zita and Papa Telmo exchanged a long glance, but neither of them answered. In the afternoon Aunt Cruz and Uncle Felipe Neri came over to their sister's house through the garden and shut themselves up with her in the sewing room. At nightfall Uncle Vidal appeared, greatly upset. His bald spot, usually so rosy, had become gray and dull as ashes.

"The king is leaving. The anti-dynasts have won. They've proclaimed the Republic in Madrid."

Mama Zita also turned pale when she heard him, raised her cold hands to her bloodless cheeks, and said in a pathetic tone, "The big one! This time the big one has broken out for sure!"

Hours later, after it was fully dark, they could hear outside the noise of a crowd singing the Republican hymn and some scattered cheers for the Republic. Mama Zita screamed hysterically, "Turn out the lights! Nobody look out of the balconies! Let's act as if we'd all died!"

But Flora and Gervasio were already in the playroom, in the dark, watching the silent, ragged multitude pass by behind the band, most of them wearing black espadrilles, with an occasional more enthusiastic person shouting "up withs" and "down withs" in a stentorian voice. Three of the ladies from Friné's were applauding, and behind them on the glassed-in balcony stood Don Minervino, raising his arms and gesticulating as if in a silent film. Suddenly Señora Zoa's nephew Daniel appeared among the demonstrators, skipping and jumping, and made a mocking sign to them as he passed under the balcony.

"What's the matter with Daniel?"

"I don't know; he must still be mad at me because of the fig."

At the end of the parade came the Norton at a funereal pace, with Uncle Adrián driving, and motionless behind him, with a big tricolor flag over his shoulder, Uncle Norberto. When he saw them Uncle Adrián took one hand off the handlebars and gave them a sort of salute, but Flora and Gervasio, who were watching the parade with their hearts in their mouths, did not return it.

Papa Telmo showed up late, while they were having supper, and Mama Zita greeted him gravely, her face turned to one side, refusing him a kiss of welcome as she did every time they had a quarrel. Papa Telmo placed his blue cheek within reach of her lips a second time, but she refused him again. She said irritably, "I hope you're satisfied."

Papa Telmo turned his hands palms upward as if to say that he wasn't hiding anything; let them search him.

"All right," he said, seating himself at the table. "It's a new start. Let's see if this time we get somewhere." He untied the knot of the napkin and spread it in his lap as Florentina, with her cap on her head, offered the soup tureen for him to serve himself.

CHAPTER 9

Carlos Centeno—thin, bony, nervous—raised his malevolent black eyes to the lighted balconies where the poster was fastened and dug his neighbor, Paco Criado, in the ribs, saying in a voice loud enough for Gervasio to hear, "That's where García's father must be, getting ready for the revolution."

Behind him, walking with Pedro María de la Vega, Gervasio pretended that he hadn't heard and looked toward the opposite sidewalk in the hope that he could draw the others' attention there; but at that moment, to make his embarrassment complete, Imanol

Solavarrieta gave a lazy little cough from one of the last places in the file and Carlos Centeno answered it like an echo, with the same forced cough, and then, to reinforce the signal, jerked his head at the big sign that occupied three balconies on the third floor of the building: Republican Left.

Ever since Papa Telmo's political affiliations had become known at school, Gervasio had felt diminished, in the difficult position of sailing against the current. Everyone in the class knew, for Father Sacristán had taken care to disclose it, that the Republic meant atheism and chaos, so that in view of Papa Telmo's political connections Gervasio, the direct descendant of evil, was in a certain sense responsible for the outrages that were daily being committed in the country. Only Peter's steadfastness and Lucinio Orejón's rough, unbreakable loyalty made his existence at school bearable. The priests wandered about the halls in fear, pretending to a calm they did not feel, and on Saturdays Father Sacristán, after handing out the week's grades, would inform them of the situation and attempt to keep up his spirits. But one morning, when he told them about the burning of some convents in Chamartín de la Rosa, his voice stuck in his throat, he began to stammer, and to the astonishment of his youthful audience covered his eyes with his hands and burst into tears. In view of Father Sacristán's failure Father Nestares, the director, delegated the task of information to Father Unzueta, who was colder and more imaginative; instead of specific events he gave them rambling talks about militant atheism, sacrilegious ceremonies that were "the order of the day," thefts of communion wafers, or savage mutilations of religious statues. But in any case, no matter whether Father Sacristán or Father Unzueta was speaking, behind their words Gervasio always saw Papa Telmo's brown hand holding the incendiary firebrand, or breaking into the sanctuary of Santa Brígida and then stabbing the Host at the club (as, according to Father Dictinio, the Freemasons did in their conclaves) to the approval of his accomplices, who, when they saw blood spurting from the Sacred Bread, smiled wickedly because their associate Telmo had sacrificed the Lamb again. The cause-and-effect relationship between Papa Telmo's ideology and the mob's excesses seemed obvious to Gervasio, but when he caught sight of him every morning in the bathroom, with lathered face and bare feet, saying good morning to him as if nothing at all were happening, he seemed such an innocuous and well-intentioned man, so incapable of those excesses, that it was difficult for Gervasio to assume a hostile attitude toward him. On the other hand he had accepted Papa Telmo's Republicanism quietly, for in Peter's opinion, despite Father Sacristán's explicit condemnation of the Republic, republic and monarchy alike were human choices, and in consequence the fact of placing an uncrowned head before a crowned head did not represent an error. So it was the word "left" that troubled him now, for according to the words of the Gospel only those whom Christ had rejected could gather under its banner. On the day of the Last Judgment the good people would be on the Lord's right and the bad ones on his left, no two ways about it. And yet men, blinded by pride and in anticipation of the final judgment, simplified God's task by adopting positions in advance. In view of Papa Telmo's recalcitrant attitude, Gervasio had no other choice than to pray for him, to try to recover him and reconcile him with God. After communion on Sundays, at the school mass, he missed Mama Zita's piercing voice exhorting him to pray for his father; but he tried spontaneously to make up for her absence, and with his eyes pressed against the sleeve of his jersey would importune divinity over and over:

"God, God, make my father be converted; make my father join the Right."

A lump swelled in his throat, for (just as had happened a few days after Papa León's death) he glimpsed Papa Telmo writhing naked in the flames of hell, vainly crying out to him. This nightmare of Papa Telmo purging his error stayed with him for a long time and was hard to shake off, and naturally it was when the awful vision assailed him that his prayers were most fervent. During recess he would often go to the chapel and, kneeling in the front pew under the warm breath of its many-colored windows, would implore the Most Holy Virgin to remove the blindfold from Papa Telmo's eyes. With the fervor of burning mysticism, he made extravagant vows in exchange for his father's conversion: he would carry a hundred-pound cross in the Good Friday procession, would pray the fifteen mysteries of the rosary every day for ten consecutive years or go on his knees as a pilgrim to the tomb of the Apostle in Compostela. But Papa Telmo, unaware of Gervasio's tormented fantasies, ate, drank, laughed, read the newspapers, went to the country on Sundays, and joked with Uncle Jairo, as if nothing that went on around him had anything to do with him. On Saturdays he usually skipped the family gatherings, a circumstance that the uncles and aunts made use of to criticize his behavior. Only Uncle Jairo came timidly to his defense by saying that to interfere in the ideas of others was an attack on freedom of conscience, to which Mama Zita replied that she agreed as long as those ideas had nothing to do with the supernatural element, threatening the beloved person's eternal fate, in which case love justified interference. Uncle Jairo tried to answer, but Crucita, who was sitting on his lap, wouldn't let him; she put her hand over his mouth, straightened the knot of his tie, made faces at him, took his spectacle case out of the inside pocket of his jacket and started to play with the glasses, putting them on and taking them off like a little girl, while Aunt Cruz fumed, thinking that Crucita was too old for such silly behavior. And one autumn afternoon, while the sycamores were shedding their yellow leaves on the flowerbeds and garden paths, she expressed her concern to her sister Zita. A blush rose to Aunt Cruz's powdered face as she said that her goddaughter's behavior with Jairo was unacceptable, that her blandishments were out of place, that even the most courteous man ought to be on his guard, and, to make a long story short, that a serious warning to the girl was in order "before it was too late." Mama Zita, who was beginning to worry about her daughter's show of affection to someone who was "after all, a person outside the family," one afternoon called her daughter to the green room in the most remote part of the palace, in an attempt to talk to her. But no sooner had she mentioned Jairo's name than Crucita crossed her arms over her chest and began to yell that in that miserable house they were all dirty-minded, and when Mama Zita made a slight movement to take her hand and calm her down the girl snatched it away, sobbing, and ran out of the room banging the door behind her. That scene was the beginning of an unexpected train of events. Uncle Jairo, who had already given up the Sunday walks with Papa Telmo, also stopped coming to the Saturday gatherings; and one evening, to the general astonishment, Aunt Macrina announced to the assembled

group that the air of the city didn't agree with her brother Jairo and
that he had decided to request a transfer to Madrid. Gervasio
sensed that Aunt Macrina knew more than she was telling, but he
too, when a week later he happened to see Uncle Jairo with Crucita
and Manolito Finat, the best tennis player in the city, on a park
bench at twilight, said nothing about the encounter and contented
himself with spying on his sister, along with his friend Lucinio,
until he could establish that Crucita, Uncle Jairo, and Manolito
Finat met in the public gardens every day. Lucinio commented
excitedly, "It's logical, isn't it? Even if your sister doesn't have
titties, she's quite a dish. What I don't understand is what the other
one's doing there, mounting guard."

At the end of January Uncle Jairo appeared at the house to say
good-bye. He was leaving for Madrid. Crucita, standing beside
him, looked like an abandoned child, but contrary to expectations
she did not make a scene, limiting herself to a sidelong kiss and
saying boldly, for everyone to hear, "Uncle, as soon as I can I'll go
to Madrid to see you."

Uncle Jairo tried to explain the reasons for his transfer, the
advantages that the capital had for a judge, and Aunt Macrina, who
was obviously pained and annoyed with her in-laws, agreed that
in any case life in Madrid was different from life in the provinces.
Gervasio watched Papa Telmo closely, imagining a warm farewell
embrace, but to his surprise Uncle Jairo put forth a languid hand
to Papa Telmo and said something startling to him:

"Telmo, don't let your faith flag."

Mama Zita and Aunt Cruz exchanged a look of astonishment,
while Gervasio asked himself what faith it could be that Uncle Jairo
didn't want to see flag in Papa Telmo. For him the word "faith" had
a strictly religious application, so that any interpretation connected
with naturopathy and politics was frivolous to the point of not
making sense. Uncle Jairo left him immersed in these thoughts,
picked up his pigskin suitcase, and went out to the stair landing
without saying good-bye to him.

In accordance with Father Sacristán's predictions, "every day the
calendar brought some new and diabolical event to add to the
already long catalogue of iniquities" that Father Unzueta under-
took to pass on to them every Saturday. After the establishment of

freedom of worship and the secularization of cemeteries came the expulsion of the Jesuits and the transformation of all other religious institutions into mere civil associations. One day the fathers turned up without their soutanes, the older ones wearing dark suits with oversized jackets and baggy trousers and the young ones, trying to avoid uniformity, in loud electric-blue or flame-colored jackets, so that in the case of the first group as well as the second, they could be identified at a distance.

"Here comes a priest in civvies," Gervasio would say to Peter.

And as they watched him come closer with his stiff walk, uncertain where to put his hands, his cap sitting on his head like a cowpat, its sole function that of hiding his tonsure, Peter would burst out laughing.

"So who told you?"

Crucita, who after Uncle Jairo's departure laughed and talked volubly, commented sarcastically that she didn't think that the government's order obliged priests to have their suits made by their own enemies. For his part Lucinio Orejón, insensitive to any degree of subtlety, celebrated the new order with a noisy string of firecrackers in a class given by Father Dictinio (pale, beardless face over the thick knot of his loud necktie), which helped to dispel the tension of the past few weeks.

Though many pupils followed their teachers to Portugal, the expulsion of the Jesuits caused an increase in the number of students at the Colegio de Todos los Santos, a novelty that relegated Papa Telmo's defection to a secondary plane in Gervasio's mind. Meanwhile, the aggressive attitude of the street urchins who daily attacked the students at the school, throwing stones and stealing their afternoon snacks and other possessions, made them decide to organize resistance. This meant that Gervasio often witnessed, in the Plaza de las Tazas, stone-throwing sessions or bloody fights between uniformed schoolboys and ragged street children ten to fourteen years old. Peter tried his best to adopt a suitable defensive strategy, but it was hard to resist in a disciplined way the constantly increasing waves of ragged youngsters who attacked them at the doors of the school every day, greeting the files of boys as they emerged by singing a version of the Republican hymn adapted to the circumstances:

> If priests and friars only knew
> The thrashing that's in store,
> They'd sing their hearts out in the choir,
> "More freedom, give us more!"

Stones and blows fell like rain, and in the belief that they were the cause of the attack the fathers would relinquish their custody of the students, telling them to break ranks.

"Go straight home, and please, make sure that the bigger boys look out for the smaller ones."

But Gervasio had the music of that hymn printed on his brain, and every time that his enemies sang the words he had a vivid mental image of Papa Telmo with a bullwhip in his hand, pursuing the seraphic figure of Father Dictinio up the steps of the choir and lashing away at him with every step. This was one of his weaknesses: he automatically transferred every one of the great national events to the level of his family. It was why, perhaps, he responded so fervently to the street children's verses, joining the chorus led by Lucinio, replying to the same tune:

> If there's really no hereafter,
> As the unbelievers say,
> How come they're eager to confess
> Before they pass away?

This desire to confess, which they somewhat gratuitously attributed to unbelievers, reminded Gervasio that Papa León had not enjoyed this privilege and that perhaps in the near future the same thing would happen to Papa Telmo, and that at the last hour the Lord in his majesty would find him drawn up on his left, of his own free will. This idea grieved him to the point that on some evenings, while Mama Zita and the uncles and aunts were commenting on the week's events in the drawing room, the boy would curl up in the chimney corner under Giotto's *Resurrection* (Mama Zita, helmet on head, placidly sleeping at the Lord's feet) and watch the crackling flames in the fireplace with horror in his heart.

"Lord, make Papa Telmo be converted; make him good, like Uncle Felipe Neri," he would say to himself.

Occasionally Papa Telmo, to avoid the appearance of a complete break, would drop in on one of the palace evenings, and when this happened Uncle Vidal and Uncle Felipe Neri would blame him for the Republicans' excesses and accuse him as if he were personally responsible, and Papa Telmo would listen to them in silence without offering excuses, without the slightest acrimony. But one night Mama Zita, flanked by her family, got up her courage with Papa Telmo and recited one after another the list of complaints against the Republic, a list that she had not dared to recite in the privacy of their bedroom: burning of convents, sacrilegious attacks, removal of the Cross from schoolrooms, expulsion of the Jesuits, the exiling of Cardinal Segura, humiliation of the Army, secularization of the religious orders, and so on, and when she had finished Uncle Felipe Neri added sternly, "Not even Diocletian, Telmo, not even Diocletian!" But instead of getting angry Papa Telmo assumed a conciliatory smile and let them talk it all out, even admitting that perhaps mistakes had been made in building the new system, but that, as the head man said, the worst days were certainly over by now. Despite the moderation of his words, Uncle Felipe Neri, his lips raw from stomach acids, exclaimed furiously that he refused to hear described as "the head man" the person who had reduced him in rank, and who had stated in the Congress that Spain had ceased to be Catholic. But even then Papa Telmo did not lose his composure: he smiled again in a kindly way, as if presiding over a children's class in religion, and in a cautious, nasal, and slightly satirical tone observed that he did not think it was Christian to take a sentence out of context, for really, what Azaña had said in Congress was that "though it was certainly true that Spain was a country of millions of believers, it was no less true that the creative power of the Catholic mind had been null for centuries." When he heard this Uncle Felipe Neri started to spit out famous names of Spaniards of recent times (Menéndez Pelayo, Vázquez de Mella, José María de Pereda, Father Coloma), and Mama Zita added that how were Catholic minds to create anything in Spain, my boy, if your head man threw the Catholics out, while Uncle Vidal repeated insinuatingly something that he had read somewhere, that "Señor Azaña was a man capable of constructing, with admirable skill, the feeblest and most horrendous pieces of nonsense." But Papa Telmo continued to smile, placating those who contradicted him with soft answers, and Gervasio stared at him so hard that he saw Papa

Telmo red all over—hair, skin, clothes, all red—and shut his eyes in fear and begged the Lord to help Papa Telmo see the light and not to let him be dazzled by the brilliance of the Evil One.

Days later Mama Zita, convinced of the value of symbols in such dreadful circumstances, pinned a tiny silver cross on the right breast of Flora and Gervasio's jerseys. A week later Gervasio and Lucinio were attacked by a gang of little fanatics as they left a soccer game. It was an epic and unequal fight, from which Gervasio emerged with a gash and huge bruise on his head and a wound from a thrown brick on his lower back. After he had been given five stitches at the first-aid station, Lucinio took him home. Papa Telmo lost his composure, laid him on the divan, and went over him with expert fingers.

"Does it hurt, son, does it hurt?"

He was very upset, and when he heard Mama Zita's high heels coming he turned gruffly toward the door.

"You have to avoid provocations, Zita." He flexed the boy's knees, bent his body, tested one by one the bumps between each vertebra. "They've given the child a terrible beating because of that cross."

Mama Zita, her bulging cowlike eyes brimming with tears, kissed the boy's forehead and turned to face her husband.

"Do you really think, Telmo, that to wear that cross on his breast is a provocation?"

Papa Telmo hesitated.

"Well, maybe not, Zita, maybe you're right. Maybe this isn't the result of a provocation but simply the heat of the times." He shook his head in distaste and added sadly, "We're all making serious mistakes these days."

The attack on Gervasio, and his decided reaction in defense of the Cross, aroused a new germ of hope on Uncle Felipe Neri's part. He looked upon the boy as a martyr, the lenses of his glasses clouded over with tears, and he couldn't wait to unbosom himself to the oilcloth-covered notebook. Moments later, seated at his desk, he wrote, "My nephew Gervasio moved me deeply today, shedding his blood in defense of the Cross in the face of a merciless enemy greatly superior in numbers. Either instinctively or deliberately, my little nephew Gervasio is a crusader now.

Perhaps the period of mere symbols has been left behind."

The boy was rather proud of the episode, the blood, his bandaged head, the memory of what he had done. He got together with Peter over and over, told him the adventure in detail, but no praise came from his friend's lips—at most, a cautionary word or two.

"In these times a person has to be careful."

Desperately, in an attack of vanity, he told Peter that in the opinion of his uncle the military man, a person who shed his blood for the Cross was a crusader; but Peter, even though he accepted this, did not offer the slightest sign of admiration for Gervasio's feat of arms. He squinted his slanted eyes still more as he said, "That may be true from a semantic viewpoint, but you can be sure that things would go better for all of us if we organized."

By one of those chance decisions of fate (for Uncle Felipe Neri, chance was God; nothing occurred by hazard here below), a few days later Father Nestares, the director, went from class to class encouraging the students to enroll in the Eucharistic Crusade, a religious organization that interceded before the Most High, with prayer and sacrifice, for him to take "this unhappy nation" under his protection. Gervasio, as if responding to an inner demand, was the first to sign up. He was moved to do so not only by his blood (already shed in defense of the Cross) but by a visceral sympathy toward the medieval movement of the Crusades, which were so knightly and edifying. His adhesion was so zealous, his ardor so strong, that during the old priest's first talk on the subject he discerned in his ascetic and catarrh-ridden face something of Peter the Hermit's proselytizing fervor. It was in this state of mind that he accepted the investiture (an oath, offering, and pinning on of insignias), and when, absorbed in the ritual, he promised to be faithful to the doctrine of Christ, to defend it and disseminate it to the best of his ability, Father Nestares (who, crammed into a worn blue jacket shiny at the elbows, received the oath) was gradually transfigured. His faded appearance turned elegant and his shabby outfit became a suit of shining silver armor. During the minutes that followed, while the old priest was speaking, Gervasio saw himself riding on a white steed, brandishing the sword that Florita's blond friend Manena Abad had given him when he departed, decapitating infidels at the side of Father Nestares, whose armor shone on the field of battle; and at the cry of *Dieu le veult!* he attacked the walls of Damietta with a pennant flying at the end of his lance. Wave after wave of the infidel lay between him and the city, but Gervasio, indomitable, infused with grace, wiped out all resistance, battled mightily, and his fighting spirit increased when he saw Papa Telmo as a captive, shouting to him with a great voice. When he heard him he dug in his spurs, lance fixed, at the precise instant when Father Bernabé, the music teacher, raised his baton and the school chorus in the choir above began to sing the crusaders' hymn. Still immersed in his warlike fantasies, Gervasio instinctively and fervently joined in.

> To arms, to arms, Crusaders,
> Fight fiercely, fight with faith.
> May Christ be king of all,
> All people here on earth.

This time he felt the electrical charge in the first vertebra of his neck, a sharp discharge that seemed to becloud his mind and then, in successive waves, left his body stiff and electrified. A strange force seemed to pull at his head as if pulling a cork, and simultaneously his nerves tensed and his skin rose in bumps. He felt as though he were starting to levitate and, seized with vertigo, clutched with both hands at the back of the pew in front of him. He felt weightless, outside himself, and when Peter scolded from beside him, "Stop fooling around," he heard him from very far off, from above, as if he were sunk in a dark swamp from which he was trying to emerge by terrible effort. And when he succeeded in coming to the surface he had a sensation of relief, like that of a swimmer who has thrashed desperately under water and manages to get his head out into the air and light. He took a deep breath, and as he did so could hear whisperings behind him and an exchange of stolid coughs between Carlos Centeno and Imanol Solavarrieta. Once he had recovered he noticed that his hair was settling down (in spite of Father Pentecostés's irritated movement in the side pew), and the blood began to circulate through his numb arms and legs again.

Outside in the courtyard a group of his friends, half awed and half amused, asked him to repeat the performance. But Gervasio, trying to gain some advantage from the situation, had eyes only for Peter and for his reproving attitude. When they were back in the classroom the ill-tempered Father Pentecostés made him kneel by the window as a punishment, and before he left for home made him write on the blackboard a hundred times, "I must not play tricks in the Lord's house."

When he left school an hour later, alone and feeling like a laughingstock, thinking about the fact that he had repeated the display after a four-year interval, he didn't know whether to be sorry for himself or to congratulate himself. He felt pride in the possibility of a heroic future (especially in the present circumstances, when he might possibly become a protagonist in "the big one"), but on the other hand the change in him, which was both shocking and ugly, made him ashamed. It was doubtful that anyone could interpret that erection of his hair as a sign of courage. To begin with, his classmates' reaction had been ambiguous; they hadn't cried, like the baby in the Novelty, but neither had they made up their minds to laugh; they had simply showed surprise, attributing the metamorphosis (as had Father Pentecostés and, unfortunately, his friend Peter) to megalomania, to his well-known desire to stand out from the crowd. On the stairs Imanol Solavarrieta had called him "Porcupine," and Carlos Centeno, more wittily, had placed himself under his command, dubbing him "Gervasio Lion-Head, Paladin of the Third Crusade." In short, even though the prospect of heroism appealed to him, the prelude to it struck him as undesirable.

Uncle Felipe Neri was more irritable day by day, his stomach acids constantly active, and was unable to understand Gervasio when, after his return home, the boy told him that "that thing, the thing about my head," had happened to him again. He stared at him in confusion from behind his spotless eyeglasses, twisting his lips; but after four years of silence on God's part he was so distracted by the Republican ignominy that he simply failed to understand him. Only when Gervasio alluded to the day of the Good Friday procession in Uncle Jairo's hotel did light dawn, and then, moved to the marrow of his being, he dragged him off to the storeroom, fearful that Aunt Cruz or one of the servants might disturb them; and as Gervasio told the circumstances of the new display, his short-sighted eyes grew soft, he smiled, broke out in

gentle perspiration, his lenses fogged over, he interrupted to ask
about new and revelatory details. Two points were now defined:
first, the Lord had broken his years-long silence. Second, the music
in itself had not sufficed to bring on the display (for Gervasio, by
his own account, was already in a trance, engaged in fierce battle
with a Seljuk Turk, when the crusaders' hymn began and his hair
began to rise). Uncle Felipe Neri's flat-set eyes shone as he listened
to his nephew's mature explanations.

"It isn't only the music now, Uncle. Now I have to be thinking
about something for it to happen."

"Something great? A heroic action?"

"That's right, Uncle."

"What were you thinking about this morning, my boy?"

"About the Crusades."

"About the Crusades to the Holy Land?"

"About the Crusades and about Papa Telmo."

Uncle Felipe Neri curled up like a snail, crossed his arms over his
stomach protectively and asked, consumed with jealousy, "And
what was Papa Telmo doing in the Holy Land, can you tell me
that?"

"He was a captive of the Turks and was calling to me."

"Your father a captive of the infidel?"

"Yes, Uncle, a captive. I raised my lance and went to help him,
but before I got there the crusaders' hymn started, the two things
got mixed together, and then it all happened."

"And tell me, didn't you think anything else about your father?"

"I didn't have time. But if *that* happened to me, it was because
of the crusaders and Papa Telmo, because of both things, I'm sure
of it. We'd practiced the hymn lots of times and nothing had ever
happened."

Suddenly the door of the storeroom opened and a tall, blue-
cheeked man (his dark beard close-shaved), mild of eye and wearing a black beret, appeared in the doorway. The knot of his tie was
loose and his trousers were too long and very baggy. Gervasio
thought "a priest," but the man, surprised to see the boy there,
fingered his chin and did not move, standing in the doorway, until
Uncle Felipe Neri said in a flustered tone, "Excuse me. I was discussing something with my nephew. I'll be with you in a moment."

The man turned around and left. He had a stealthy way of walking and a cautious air about him, and from behind Gervasio could see that his jacket was too big, that it swung out in the back. Gervasio slowly raised his head toward his uncle.

"Who is that man?"

"A friend. He's going to have supper with Cruz and me tonight," said Uncle Felipe Neri without much conviction. "Tomorrow we'll go on with our talk."

Alone again, before going to meet his guest and fearing that his initial impression would be diluted, Uncle Felipe Neri went to his room, sat down at his desk, opened the oilcloth-covered notebook, and at the top of an untouched page did not draw a cross as was his custom, but wrote in his careful script, "Who but God?" He had been doing this, in letters and other documents, ever since the arrival of the Republic (a mere cross, in the present circumstances, struck him as cowardly and not very eloquent). Under it he wrote, "My nephew Gervasio, now an adolescent, had a fresh transport today and, as was to be expected, his explanation of the event is more reasonable and coherent than before. He believes that his trance on this occasion was the result of a special state of mind rather than of music. The music in itself, without this previous state, would not have traumatized him. What caused the seizure was the convergence of the two things. The trance occurred at school, during the initiation ceremony of the Eucharistic Crusade, an old and pious organization which has been revived. According to what he himself says, the boy associated the Crusade with the historical event that bears this name and imagined himself fighting against the infidel. Curiously, before the walls of Damietta he saw his father among the captives (it must be borne in mind that my brother-in-law, the boy's father, is a confirmed Republican who has left the Church, something which has been upsetting my nephew for a long time). The boy argues, however, that throughout his trance his father made no resistance to the crusaders; rather, he shouted for their help in being freed and joining the crusader army. The boy feels that this is symptomatic, for just as he was going to his rescue the congregation's hymn (which certainly has words, and some high notes, that are distinctly military) sounded in the chapel where the ceremony was taking place, and it was at this moment that the horripilation occurred and the vision that had made it possible (the battle, the Turkish horde, his father a prisoner, and all the rest), vanished. The boy told me about it with such fervor that anyone who hears him (in this case myself) can have no doubt that he has been marked from on high to carry out some glorious mission. Unable to contain my emotion, I asked whether he had received some revelation apart from the trance; but, very sure of himself, he replied that he had not. I also asked him if he had a vision, and he said that, apart from seeing Papa Telmo (as he has called his father since earliest childhood) as a captive, and Father Nestares on horseback in silver armor, he saw no other person in the battle whom he recognized, but insists (and he gives much importance to this fact) that in his fantasy dream his father was not a member of the enemy ranks but a captive of the enemy, *anxious to be rescued.* The Lord has spoken again. Let us confide in Him."

CHAPTER 10

With an air of mystery, Flora informed Gervasio that Uncle Felipe Neri had a priest hidden in his house, a Jesuit, Father Rivero, who said mass very early in the morning in the family chapel and after breakfast walked in the garden until Clemente arrived. As in old times, Flora and Gervasio agreed to watch for him from the balcony of the ironing room, behind the curtains, before they went off to their respective schools. Father Rivero walked slowly among the shrubbery reading his breviary, but on some mornings, perhaps nervous over what was going on or unable to concentrate, he would put the book away in the pocket of his jacket and make signs in the air with one finger or say his rosary, moving his lips a great deal and pushing the black beads with the thumb of his right hand. When he had finished he would put the rosary away in a little leather case, kneel on the gray gravel before the sky-blue image in the grotto, and pray the Litany, the Credo, and the Salve with his arms held out in the shape of a cross, lifting his chaste eyes to the Virgin. One morning while he was praying, Uncle Felipe Neri appeared in the garden accompanied by Don Urbano, the parish priest of Santa Brígida, and after introducing the two priests discreetly retired. Then Father Rivero took Don Urbano to the far end of the garden and invited him to sit down on the slatted wooden bench under the pergola, while he knelt on the other side of the box hedge and confessed his sins to him through it. Gervasio could see Don Urbano, with his cheek very close to the hedge, listening, while Father Rivero talked and talked on the other side, hands clasped, until at last Don Urbano raised his head and imparted absolution to Father Rivero, who received it humbly, his body bent forward, giving himself little blows on the chest.

Two weeks later the scene was repeated, but on this occasion it was Father Rivero who sat on the bench while Don Urbano confessed his sins to him through the hedge, and when he had finished absolved him by tracing, slowly and ceremoniously, a large cross over his head. A month later each confessed the other, so piously and quietly that you would have said that both of them had been sentenced to death. Flora clapped her hands together.

"I'd never seen a priest confess to another priest, had you?"

"Ssh! I hadn't either."

The presence of Father Rivero in Uncle Felipe Neri's house was an obvious fact on which no one dared to offer an opinion. What was a Jesuit doing there? Why hadn't he gone to Portugal with the rest of the order? Had he ceased to be a priest, perhaps? Gervasio didn't know, but one afternoon, some time later, Lucinio Orejón informed him that "the priest who was hidden in your house," was director of an academy in the crypt of Santa Brígida, where his brother Felices and other university students went, and which was called "The Scholastic Center of Mary Immaculate and Saint Aloysius Gonzaga." Gervasio denied this roundly at first ("There aren't any priests in my house; there never have been"), but Lucinio Orejón answered drily, "Save your breath; my brother Felices walks him home every day after class." In view of this evidence Gervasio told him that Father Rivero had taken refuge in his uncle's house, not his own, more than four months ago, but that he did not know the reason. Then he wanted to hear more about the academy, but Lucinio only knew that it belonged to the Luises, because Father Rivero had been director of that congregation before he was exiled. Confident of Don Urbano's good relations with his family, Gervasio proposed to Lucinio to go and visit that scholastic center, and Peter, though ordinarily he didn't like to get mixed up in things, joined the expedition. Hidden in the doorway of the old building, they watched the tardiest pupils arrive, walking briskly, the lapels of their trenchcoats turned up, their hatbrims pulled down over their eyes, just as the clients of Friné's used to walk. After a while Gervasio, Lucinio, and Peter left the doorway, crossed the street, and went into the church. A small, weak candle in front of the sanctuary was the only living note in the shadowy temple. Gervasio signaled to his friends to follow him, but in the dark ambulatory, by the entrance to the crypt, the figure of Don Urbano suddenly rose up before them.

"Where are you boys going?"

Gervasio told him who he was.

"And what are you doing here at this time of day?"

"Going to Father Rivero's class."

"Who told you about those classes? The academy is only for university students." He looked each one of them up and down. "You're still little boys. How old are you?"

"Thirteen."

"You see; you'd better go and play."

"I'm fifteen already," interrupted Lucinio.

"Even so." Don Urbano clutched one hand with the other. From the bottom of the spiral staircase they could hear the murmur of a slow, disciplined voice. "When you enter the university you can come back here."

They accepted their failure resignedly. At any other time it would have meant frustration, but since the Republic had been proclaimed the city offered any number of opportunities for amusement and adventure. Things were very relaxed at school and the students lived in a state of high excitement. After what had happened during the crusader ceremony, Gervasio was surrounded by a certain aura. The little boys called him "Porcupine," and the older ones, the students in the fifth and sixth years of secondary studies, adopted Carlos Centeno's nickname for him verbatim: "Gervasio Lion-head, Paladin of the Third Year." In any case, his hair-raising performance had left an enigmatic wake in the school. There had been few witnesses, but rumors spread, and most of them attributed it to a special gift like that of Evencio Gredilla, who could wiggle his ears at will, or that of Javier del Río, a recent arrival from the Jesuit school, who could bend his fingers back until they touched his wrist, as if they were made of rubber. Gervasio neither affirmed nor denied; he let himself be admired. His own attitude toward the phenomenon was indecisive, for though it led people to laugh at him, it also made him stand out from the rest, gave him a mysterious prestige within the confines of the school; and Gervasio, having passed the stage of wanting to be like everyone else, began to find a certain enjoyment in knowing that he was different. What he really wanted with all his heart was Peter's admiring recognition, but Peter said nothing, stood firm. In the face of his indifference, one afternoon after he had beaten Peter in a naval battle, in accordance with the innovations introduced into the game by Lucinio Orejón (Greek fire, rockets, gunpowder, and matches as projectiles against the paper squadrons drawn up in the bathtub), Gervasio became inflamed with patriotism and revealed his secret to his friend, whose approbation he so unsuccessfully sought: according to his grandfather, who had been in the war, and his uncle Felipe Neri, the army officer, he was made of the stuff of heroes, had been born to perform great deeds. Once again, Peter showed his characteristic prudence.

"How does it feel?"

"Didn't you see my hair the day the crusaders swore the oath?"

"And that's all?"

"My hair standing up, that's only the signal. When my hair stands up my strength grows and then nobody could defeat me."

Peter continued to take the scorched boats out of the tub, and when he had finished opened the drain.

"Don't you believe it," he said. "That happens to everybody in one way or another. Haven't you noticed that at bullfights, when people want the bullfighter to fight closer to the bull, they play a march? They say that music has that effect."

Gervasio did not give up, and two days later at home he tried a demonstration. Alone in his room, with his jersey sleeves rolled up to the elbows, before the phonograph that he had inherited from Papa León, listening to "Oriamendi," he closed his eyes and tried hard to concentrate, but his very zeal undermined his attempts. He disconnected the machine in disappointment.

"It's no good; I can't manage to concentrate."

In view of this new setback Gervasio concluded that Peter needed proof, a demonstration of courage. Words did no good with him. Neither did signs. Maybe if he could show a certain amount of fearlessness in one of the adventures proposed by Lucinio, Peter might change his mind.

In those days the gang gained two new members, also leftovers from the Jesuits' departure: Dámaso Valentín and Eduardo Custodio. Dámaso wore his hair in a brush cut; his thin, elastic lips and the open, smiling expression of his light brown eyes brought an enormous joie de vivre to the group. The youngest of five brothers, all of whom had left home, he lived with his widowed mother and two old servants in the most aristocratic part of town. Perhaps because life was easy for him and his weekly allowance double that of his friends, Dámaso was always smiling, and when he did so he displayed a notched front tooth (souvenir of a childhood fall) which he daintily caressed with the tip of his active red tongue. An adaptable and generous boy, he accepted enthusiastically any plan suggested by his friends, and his prosperity even allowed him to place his small personal properties at the group's disposal. This was the case of the hard rubber ball with which, shortly after they had met him, they began to play after school on the sidewalk that ran alongside the park, defying the zeal of the municipal guards. But one day, when they were caught by the park policeman, they wound up in the barracks, and while the sergeant was taking their names in walked Gerardo, El Cigüeña, all hairy and shabby, coughing into a dirty handkerchief. Gervasio went up to him.

"Don't you remember me, Señor Gerardo? I'm Don León's grandson."

Gerardo looked at him sidewise with his shifty eye, the handker-

chief at his mouth, smothering his cough, and after a long pause
he asked in his thin little voice, "The late Don León de la Lastra?"

"Yes, he's the one. Don't you remember that one day, when we
were children, you caught my sister and me lighting a bonfire
behind Friné's?"

Gerardo's cough vanished; his squinty eye lighted up.

"Your grandfather gave me the Medal of Municipal Merit the
day I overpowered Poli."

"I remember. My grandfather always used to tell us about it. He
said you were a hero."

Gerardo, El Cigüeña, greatly impressed by the lofty idea of him
that was held in high places, used his good offices, and the sergeant
tore up the charge and gave them back the ball. Then he went with
them to the door of the barracks.

"Go with God, my boy. If you show up next month you won't
find me here; I'm going to retire around San Ubaldo's day."

Eduardo Custodio was the other; pale, slow and roundabout in
speech, with a touch of humor, he suffered from a premature aging
that showed in his nearsightedness, his heavy eyelids, his limpness,
and a certain stiffness of the legs for which he tried to compensate
with tenacity and pride when he played soccer, his great passion.
He did not use glasses, and usually combatted his myopia by pulling at the outside corner of his eye to make images clearer, and
when he went to the movies or some other kind of show he used
opera glasses that had belonged to his great-grandmother. The
second of eight brothers, Eduardo made them free of his house on
the first day they met, and his elderly parents, Doña Loreto and
Don Colomán, took part in the young folks' cheerful gatherings.
Don Colomán was the third generation of the dynasty founded in
Salamanca by his great-great-grandfather Colman MacGregor, a
seminarian who had left the Irish College there. Along with his
desertion he lost not only his habit but his surname, for he had no
male issue; but Colomán II's grandson not only recovered the pa-
tronymic but passed it on to his descendants, so that Colomán IV,
Eduardo's older brother, was for the moment the last representative
of the McGregor dynasty, though the surname had been displaced
by the addition of Custodio, the name of the Salamancan grandfather. In their relations with their sons Don Colomán III and his wife

displayed a British style of liberalism that aroused the envy of Gervasio and his group. For Don Colomán III and his clan there were no taboos or forbidden subjects. Eduardo himself, conscious of his parents' permissiveness, made a boast of it before his new friends:

"Mama, you're so anxious to have a grandchild that you wouldn't care if I gave you an illegitimate one."

And Doña Loreto would laugh ("the things this boy says!") and her audience would imitate her and laugh too, all except Gervasio, who blushed at the mere thought of the García de la Lastras' reaction if he took the notion to make a joke of that kind to Aunt Cruz or Mama Zita. In their fights with the street youngsters Eduardo Custodio replaced Lucinio's brusque, straightforward bellicosity with a cerebral element: he agreed that one had to fight, but not against the blind masses, rather against the instigators of those masses. And with a strange idea of instigation they began to throw stones at the house of Doña Jovita, the most fashionable brothel in the city, the Protestant chapel, and the People's Club. And on the day that the government abolished the clergy's financial support and collections were organized in the different churches to help them out, Eduardo Custodio suggested that out of the monthly duro his parents gave him for the purpose (and which in any case would get lost among the thousands of others), they could take three pesetas "to arm themselves." This was not a bad thing to do, quite the contrary, for it meant that the clergy would be protected in two different ways: mere subsistence, and physical security properly speaking. At Eduardo's urging they also acquired some slingshots provided with metal forks, square black chunks of rubber, and strips of sheepskin to hold the ammunition, whose efficacy was quickly put to the test: when their three forays were over not an unbroken window remained on Doña Jovita's balconies, the Protestant chapel, or the front windows of the People's Club.

The friendship of Damasito Valentín and Eduardo Custodio strengthened the group against the hostile maneuvers of Carlos Centeno and Imanol Solavarrieta and also entranced Gervasio, who daily felt more removed from the family atmosphere. Almost none of his outside activity reached the house. They were two different worlds. If he occasionally told Florita and Manena Abad about his adventures, and if he observed a touch of concern in Manena's questions, he preened himself as if he had come back from a war. But Mama Zita, who was growing more and more disturbed about the imminence of "the big one," did not interfere. Sometimes she scolded Papa Telmo for his guilty silence, but he would answer her patiently, in the temporizing tone of a person who knows himself to be in the right, that "in this country where everyone blabbers, keeping quiet is a reasonable attitude." And so Mama Zita was terribly startled on the afternoon that Papa Telmo, shock showing in his face, burst into the sewing room with a letter in his hand and made the following sensational revelation to the two sisters:

"Jairo has had the gall to ask me for Crucita's hand."

Mama Zita rolled up her eyes and crossed herself.

"Why, she's still a child, for heaven's sake."

Then Papa Telmo, utterly disconsolate, collapsed into an arm-chair and said reluctantly that Jairo was not only a mature man but a shopworn one, which was worse. Mama Zita, totally at sea, asked him what he meant by "shopworn," to which Papa Telmo replied evasively that he was "a forty-year-old with a lot of mileage on him," and that under those circumstances Crucita could hardly be happy with him.

When she came home from playing tennis at teatime, before her parents had decided what strategy to adopt to solve the problem, Crucita confronted Papa Telmo and asked him point-blank, "Can you let a person know what you've decided about Uncle Jairo's letter?"

Papa Telmo lost his temper.

"So you were in cahoots, were you?"

Crucita shrugged her shoulders insolently.

"A man and a woman who're in love are always in cahoots. Weren't you and Mama when Mama Obdulia didn't want you to have anything to do with each other?"

Aunt Cruz whimpered, "You're barely twenty, darling, and Jairo is over forty."

Crucita was unyielding (well drilled by her partner, as Papa Telmo was to say later), and especially hard on her godmother's objections.

"What do you know about that, Auntie! The world is full of

happy couples with husbands who are twice as old as their wives, and vice versa."

The arguments increased, and when Saturday came Aunt Macrina also showed her lack of agreement with the proposed marriage, though from a different viewpoint.

"I'm sorry, Cruz, but as far as I'm concerned you haven't the necessary maturity to run my brother's house."

Uncle Vidal, caught between two fires, had nothing to say, but when asked for an opinion he went off on a tangent.

"That's all we needed: Jairo and Crucita! Why don't you ask your precious Father Rivero if these aren't signs of the end of the world?"

But the stubbornest resistance came from Papa Telmo, which was what especially worried Mama Zita.

"Telmo knows the world better than we do, Cruz. There's something besides his age that isn't right for the child."

Convinced of the triteness of her own arguments, she let her husband do the talking until one day Crucita, sick and tired of so much opposition, with her arms crossed on her breast (as if she wanted to avoid a final argument: her incomplete development), confronted her father with a hard green stare and asked him flatly if he had forgotten the grandparents' opposition to his marrying Mama Zita and their contempt for him. And if at that time he had thought of the arguments they put forward as mere bourgeois prejudices, then what couldn't she say about his present behavior, a man with pretensions to being modern who turned into a reactionary at the idea of his daughter's marrying a mature man. Crucita's arguments, hurled into Papa Telmo's face like so many blobs of spit, left him defenseless, and although he had pretended to accept the explanation that Father Rivero had been invited to Uncle Felipe Neri's house as a former fellow student, on the afternoon of his defeat he unveiled the deception.

"I'd like to talk it over with the Jesuit you've got hidden in your house, Cruz."

Everyone was startled, but Uncle Felipe Neri hastened to arrange the interview, which added nothing new. Father Rivero declined to take responsibility.

"Certainly a marriage under these conditions is risky, but we have no canonical impediments to raise. Don't forget that the ministers of this sacrament are the contracting parties themselves."

Papa Telmo fumed at the priest, confronted Crucita again, and maintained a stiff correspondence with Uncle Jairo which no one ever saw; but in the second half of April, María Cruz García de la Lastra, dressed in white with a long veil of illusion tulle, and Jairo Jaraiz Blanco, member of the Territorial Tribunal of Madrid, contracted matrimony in the family chapel of Aunt Cruz and Uncle Felipe Neri, in private, for, according to *El Correo de Castilla,* "circumstances were not propitious for endowing the union with the luster it deserved, in view of the distinction of the contracting parties' families." Uncle Jairo, standing before the altar, looked like Crucita's father going with her to take her First Communion, but the poise and good manners of his brothers David and Fadrique, their courteous attentions to their respective wives, led Mama Zita to the conviction that perhaps she had opposed the match too much and that Crucita would be happy with Jairo, for, mileage or no, he was manifestly a very well-mannered man.

However, Crucita's departure, along with the threat of "the big one," sufficed to plunge Mama Zita into deep depression. Every day she would shut herself into her room to "cry to her heart's content," as she said, or spend whole afternoons confabulating with her sister Cruz. As usual they had joined forces to curb the increasing animosity of their sister-in-law Macrina during the Saturday night gatherings. Sometimes she went to confess with Father Rivero and took a walk in the garden, returning home comforted, but her relief was short-lived, lasting only a few hours. Crucita sent no news. Two postcards had arrived from the Canary Islands containing love and kisses for everyone. That was all they said, but Jairo had not signed them. After they were installed in Madrid she usually wrote once a week, and her letters were pure routine, uninformative, without reference to her new situation. After a month Mama Zita began to telephone her on Saturdays. She needed to hear her voice. She knew her daughter, and her voice was enough to let her know how things were going. The first telephone call disconcerted her; Crucita's voice was the merest thread, barely audible. Subsequent calls surprised her by their total lack of enthusiasm, their long, inexorable silences. She complained of nothing, accused no one, but her pauses were sad and haughty. Every week Mama Zita was more discouraged when she hung up the phone.

"That girl isn't happy, Cruz, something is happening to her."

And she would weep inconsolably, unsure of just what was happening to her. Early in September Crucita telephoned to say that she would arrive on the fast train to Irún to spend a few days with them. Mama Zita and Papa Telmo braced themselves. Cruz, who since childhood had been extremely thin, had lost still more weight; her smile was weak and the look in her green eyes dull. Though she resisted confidences, problems came to the surface in bunches, like cherries ("she was a bit lonely, Jairo didn't go with her to play tennis, he didn't always have time to lunch at home, the friends he saw the most of were very young and rather frivolous, her husband was kind to her but when he got together with his nephew Luisito he was unbearable, the two of them listened to music and talked about abstruse things in a joking tone"). She nobly recognized that Mama Zita and Papa Telmo had been partly right: Jairo was a bit old for her, he was "like an old man," and if she accused him of it he would smile at her, take her by the hand, and say, "You're still too young to understand me." These subjects were avoided during the Saturday gathering and Crucita, wanting to say something nice to Aunt Macrina, made reference to "how good-humored her nephew Luisito was," to which Macrina replied, to general consternation, that they had never had a nephew of that name and that it was obviously an imposture or a joke on her brother Jairo's part. Papa Telmo tried in every way he could to get something out of Crucita when he was alone with her, but succeeded in nothing but vague, brief smiles and the ready-made phrases that increased his irritation: "Have to let time pass," "Rome wasn't built in a day," "The first year is the hardest," "We'll gradually get used to each other."

Two weeks later Mama Zita and Papa Telmo went to visit her in Madrid. They had to stay at a hotel, because although Crucita had quite a large house, "Jairo didn't look very pleased when she asked him about it." Otherwise their son-in-law behaved very correctly and courteously to them, invited them to the theater and the horse races, but privately their daughter admitted that "Jairo's age was certainly a drawback, and worse than his age the cold

loneliness of that big old house." Papa Telmo, who when he saw
the apartment had commented that it was a "numbing, lawyerlike
place, a house for a bearded prosecuting attorney," urged her to
make women friends, go out, play tennis; and when Mama Zita
returned home, by arrangement with Aunt Cruz, she suggested to
her by telephone the desirability of visiting Inesita Pons, daughter
of a childhood friend of hers, whose address she sent. This contact
improved things a little. Crucita began to get her bearings. Inesita
was spontaneous, vital, practical; she went shopping with her, got
membership for her in the Royal Tennis Club at Puerta de Hierro,
and the two of them went there together every afternoon on their
bicycles. But the pleasanter Crucita's expansions were, the
gloomier her returns home. Dorotea, the old servant, scarcely spoke
to her, and Jairo's friends, especially his "nephew Luisito," paid her
no attention. Her attempts to form a quartet with Inesita Pons and
her husband Juan Manuel were unsuccessful. Jairo opposed them
from the first moment.

"If you want to, I can go out once a year with that boy, but please
don't ask anything more of me. I'm too old to start new social
contacts."

For the first time Crucita lost her temper.

"Well, I don't like your friends either. I don't think they're
interesting."

That was when the first quarrel broke out, and Crucita's first
unconcealed tears. Mama Zita sobbed, too, to hear her feeble, tormented voice on the telephone, and three days later, after receiving
a letter from her, she shut herself up in her room and didn't even
come out for dinner. Next day Gervasio found the letter in the
secret drawer of his mother's dresser, and in addition to her usual
complaints Crucita said in it, "There are days when Jairo bursts out
in kisses and bites and calls me 'his exciting ephebe,' and he must
do it to mortify me because he knows all too well what a complex
I have about my breasts, and an ephebe, according to the diction-
ary, is an adolescent boy." After Papa Telmo read this letter he lost
his head completely and talked of nothing but Rome and the
Tribunal of the Rota, said that he had "indisputable arguments for
annulling that monstrous union," and talked to his daughter at
night on the telephone, urged her to have patience, assured her that

everything would be arranged, and sent her kisses. Mama Zita, now in complete agreement with Papa Telmo, remarked, "That nuisance of a Jairo, besides being old he's very strange."

"Of course, it's a complex case of sexual inversion."

"Inversion, what's that?"

"Never mind. Just foolishness of mine."

Despite pressure, Crucita was aware of her responsibilities and unwilling to annul the marriage. Now and then her letters displayed some hope. Inesita Pons had lots of friends and she was becoming a member of the group. The negative side of her new friendships was that every day she felt farther away from her husband and there were nights when she was already in bed by the time Jairo returned home, and then he went and slept elsewhere, in the guest room, "with his nephew Luisito." Gervasio observed his parents, scrutinized their faces, listened in on their conversations, and over and above his disenchantment, noticed that there was something positive about Crucita's marriage: Mama Zita and Papa Telmo had found a point of agreement on a subject outside the realm of politics. He was so used to his mother's tears that they did not bother him, but he did suffer over his father's collapse, his despair, the way he had of pressing his head between his hands when he was alone, as if he were about to crush it. Usually, when Gervasio came home from school, he would find his father listening to the radio, to that sepulchral, clear though gloomy, dehumanized voice that broke portentously into the room by the mere turning of a knob. It was through that voice that the family learned of the revolutionary strike in Asturias and the occupation of Oviedo by the miners. The drawing room of the house again became a very noisy place. Uncle Felipe Neri, dressed in a pearl-gray suit that made the others long for his uniform, placed the responsibility on his brother-in-law.

"The revolution's here, Telmo, is this what you and your kind want? The masses have taken power."

And Uncle Vidal turned his fear into grumbling.

"If they don't allow three cabinet members from the conservative party into the government, you tell me where democracy lies."

Papa Telmo, defeated by Crucita's misfortune, perhaps rendered defenseless or disagreeably surprised by the revolutionary strike, fended off the attack as best he could, sprawled on the divan opposite the fireplace under Giotto's *Resurrection*. But the two uncles pursued him, needled him, as if the miners' retreat depended on his orders or as if he had a private line to the president of the government.

The city was also paralyzed by the revolutionary strike, and Gervasio, ignoring Mama Zita's recommendations, rushed out on the street along with his friends. A very strange atmosphere hung over it. The deserted avenues and plazas, the shop shutters closed and locked, the cafés empty, the street doors of the apartment houses open only a crack, reflected misgiving and fear and gave the impression of a city under siege. They walked together along several streets until they came to the Avenida de la Constitución, where they could hear the forlorn sounds of distant music. The demonstration caught up with them on the corner, a few hundred shabby men in visored caps and black espadrilles, preceded at a funereal pace by Gervasio's uncles on their Norton, with an improvised band bringing up the rear playing the "Internationale." Lucinio nudged Gervasio with his shoulder.

"Some comrades your uncles have turned into!"

Uncle Adrián, his balding head bare, his chin sunk on his chest, his yellow teeth biting his lower lip, drove the motorcycle in loops so as not to lose contact with the group, while Uncle Norberto, bareheaded too, very straight on the rear seat, carried a faded tricolor flag over his shoulder and gave it an occasional languid wave. The procession went by in silence, and the only sound was the backfiring of the motorcycle amid the ragged notes of the music.

The revolt broke out that afternoon. Gervasio, Lucinio, and Eduardo Custodio wandered from one place to another, guided by shouts and groups of running men. The rebels, after assaulting the Pablo Esteban Armory in the main square, surged toward the outskirts of the city, waving shotguns and pistols, and besieged the Lepanto Civil Guard barracks in the Alameda district. Sheltered behind trees, they fired at random, and a few civil guards in their fatigue caps, protected by the banks of the canal at the edge of the little garden, responded with their carbines, defending the barracks. Gervasio and his friends witnessed the confrontation from a street corner, and when they saw a guard spin around and fall backward on the cement with a bloody head, he took his slingshot out of his pocket and began to assail the attackers' flank; but Lucinio Orejón shoved him aside irritably and said, referring to the slingshot, "Leave it to me; that's kid stuff."

In his right hand shone a newly greased black pistol, which he aimed at the trees and fired again and again until the chamber was empty, at the very moment when an open truck filled with Assault Guards, armed with rifles, parked along one wall of the barracks. Its members, scattering into the culvert alongside the street, opened fire on the attackers who, surprised by their arrival, turned tail and fled toward the Plaza del Haro. The commanding officer of the reinforcements stood up, pointed toward the corner where the boys were crouching, and barked two words. Without previous agreement the boys started to run along the street toward downtown, hastily turning corners, panting, until they reached the deserted arcades of the Glorieta del Angel. Lucinio pushed open a door that was standing ajar and wiped his forehead with his arm, smiling.

"We made them run," he said.

"Who gave you that pistol?"

The boy took it out of his pocket again—black, shiny, intimidating—with courteous respect. He patted the butt and smiled again.

"It belongs to my brother Felices; he has three."

"Your brother Felices has three pistols?"

Historic pride swelled Gervasio's breast. For the first time in his life (the fight with the toughs in the stadium had been a mere skirmish), he felt that he had taken part in a virile action, with risks, with casualties. Back at home Mama Zita and Cruz, pale and shaken, were huddled over the radio, listening in dramatic silence to the latest news. Gervasio went over to them, but Mama Zita hardly gave him time to sit down.

"Let's go; your father's coming."

They had agreed to listen to the radio by turns. Their positions, so often contradictory in the face of the opinions it emitted, had made the room a hell. An elementary notion of democracy, of mere coexistence, made this the only feasible course. In any case, it was quite unbearable to have Papa Telmo exulting while they suffered, and vice versa. Domestic foundations trembled as a result of their verbal confrontations.

Next morning Gervasio snatched up the newspaper before Papa

Telmo had finished shaving. As his eyes skimmed the headlines on the first page an empty space seemed to open in his stomach. His hands and his knees shook.

> REBELS ASSAULT LEPANTO BARRACKS. ONE CIVIL GUARD SERGEANT DEAD AND TWO OTHER MEMBERS WOUNDED.
>
> Yesterday lamentable events took place in our city which, as they became known, produced a deep impression. During the early hours of the afternoon, unrest began to be observed among members of the working class, who tried to prevent the departure of trains from our city. The forces of order, who went to the station in considerable strength, were informed that groups of rioters were attempting to assault the Don Pablo Esteban Armory, located in the Plaza Mayor. A busload of Assault Guards went there to prevent it, but when they reached the Charity Schools they were surprised by firing from groups who had stationed themselves on the corners of neighboring streets. Guard Heliodoro Navafría received a gunshot wound in the leg while repelling the attack of the rioters, who then immediately went to the Lepanto Civil Guard Barracks in the Alameda district, where after intensive gunfire Sergeant Salustiano Arias was killed by a bullet in the head and Guard Gregorio Peña was wounded and remains in guarded condition. From the corner of Calle de Huertas, a small group of boys threw stones and fired several pistol shots at the attackers, but a short time later the arrival of Major Aldecoa at the head of reinforcements from the Assault Guards dispersed them and put the rebels, who scattered into the Alameda park, to flight, thus controlling the situation and arresting two of the chief instigators. By early evening calm had returned completely to our historic city, shaken for several long hours by the tragic and lamentable events of the afternoon.

Gervasio's heart pounded in his breast. He realized that he had had his baptism of fire, and even though he was unnamed, enveloped in *El Correo's* concise but eloquent phrase ("a small group of boys threw stones and fired several pistol shots at the attackers"), he had just entered history; almost unawares, he had begun his career as a hero.

During the next few days the radio brought more soothing news. Ochoa and Yagüe had entered Oviedo, reestablishing order, while Batet forced surrender of the Generalitat, which had just proclaimed the Independent Catalonian Republic. But—a strange thing—on this occasion the news that satisfied the rest did not seem to displease Papa Telmo either. Stupefied, Gervasio observed his relieved smile. What did it mean? For the moment, Gervasio told himself, it meant that what Carlos Centeno and Imanol Solavarrieta said, that "Papa Telmo was in the club preparing the revolution," was untrue. One of two things: either his father was going back on his old convictions or he didn't want the revolution, at least not in Asturias or Barcelona. What did Papa Telmo want, then?

Unexpectedly, two days later at lunchtime, Crucita appeared at home. A porter from the station piled trunks, suitcases, hatboxes, and other gear in the vestibule. Her green eyes were red with crying and her pale cheeks sunken. Mama Zita hugged her so frenziedly that the girl couldn't help bursting into tears.

"It's over, Mama. I'll never go back to him."

Once she had recovered from the first emotional shock, Crucita expressed her fear of confronting Aunt Macrina, Jairo's sister, but Mama Zita took her by the waist and gently led her to her old girlhood bedroom.

"Don't worry, darling. Uncle Vidal and Aunt Macrina went to Portugal yesterday with the children. They won't come back until there's a bit of light showing in Spain or until 'the big one' breaks out once and for all."

CHAPTER

■■

"Sit here," said Mama Zita, pointing to a chair beside hers. "I sent for you because you're old enough to face up to certain responsibilities. And Spain is gambling its future on tomorrow's elections. All we good Spaniards have to put our shoulders to the wheel."

It was late in the afternoon. A languid ray of sunshine, filtering through the curtains on the balcony windows, lighted the scene: Mama Zita, Aunt Cruz, Uncle Felipe Neri, and Father Rivero, gathered around a table, were checking off long lists, adding, subtracting, stuffing pamphlets into envelopes, distributing ballots and

identity cards into improvised paper folders. Gervasio, seated next
to his mother and proud of knowing he was needed, watched his
Uncle Felipe Neri, busy as a schoolboy, his glasses pushed up on
his forehead and a pencil in his hand. He lifted his lusterless eyes
to Father Rivero with a grimace that was meant to be a smile.

"Sixty-four," he said. "You were right, Father."

"That is, sixty-four votes," said Mama Zita.

"Except for error or omission," finished Father Rivero.

And when Mama Zita turned toward Gervasio and began to give
him instructions about what he would have to do next morning, the
Jesuit lifted one finger, smiled, apologized with unctuous tact, and
then Mama Zita realized that she had gone too far, put her hands
to her cheeks, and excused herself in embarrassment.

"Oh, excuse me, Father! I hadn't realized."

"You needn't apologize; often our desires outrun our discretion.
But it's better for only one person to have the responsibility for this
matter in his hands."

Father Rivero paused, put his head on one side, and looked
fixedly at Gervasio, with the same intense look he gave to the
statue in the grotto every time that he prayed the Litany in the
garden. The boy blinked.

"Very well, my lad, let's take things in order; what this family
wants is for everyone to vote tomorrow, or rather, everyone who
wants to have order, peace, and justice prevail in Spain. That is why
we're going to have to try to have crippled and sick people participate, and if necessary (here he smiled again), even dead ones. With
this in mind we've divided the city into sectors which we have
entrusted to different persons, one of them yourself" (he handed
him, over the table, a red pencil and a few sheets of paper). "Take
note, please. Your beat includes the following centers: Convents of
Adoration and Servants of Jesus, Domestic Service, Little Sisters of
the Poor, and Charity . . . have you written that down? Now then,
your mission is as follows, though we may ask you to do some
other jobs too: you're to take a taxi driven by someone we can trust
at nine in the morning, and you will visit the convents on that list
one by one. After you arrive you must ask for the Mother Superior,
to whom you are simply to say, 'I've been sent by Father Rivero';
they already know. Then," (he took five envelopes with the diffe-

rent addresses on them from the table and gave them to Gervasio)
"you will give each one the envelope that has her address, and the
nuns will tell you which persons among those in their charge you
are to take to the respective polling places, at what hour and in
what order." (Father Rivero's voice buzzed like a horsefly, a slow,
monotonous, disciplined voice with a noticeable ecclesiastical
pitch. He placed his white hand on the boy's forearm.) "There is
an essential point that must be kept in mind: the rhythm of the dual
or false vote. I'll try to explain. We must see to it that the nun or
woman who is going to vote in place of someone else as well as vote
herself does so discreetly, without calling attention to herself on
the part of the election officials. That is why you must try to leave
some time between votes, and if possible have the person change
her clothing so as to make it difficult to identify her. If it's a
question of old women you don't have to be so careful; all old
women look alike. But in any case, before going into the polling
place you had better instruct them. Don't talk too much, you'll
confuse them; simple people need few and clear words. And as for
those voting for others who are either not here or dead, get it into
their heads that their identification card is the one they're carrying,
and that the Christian name and surnames on the card are theirs.
The Mother Superiors already know about this and will send the
clearest-headed ones." (He smiled again, pleased with his explanation.) "Let's hope there will be no trouble. Your mother will give
you final instructions first thing tomorrow morning."

Señora Zoa, by now a mere shadow, a little black bundle in the
back seat of the Chevrolet belonging to Tadeo Crespo, the taxi
driver at the Casino, wrapped in a shabby old shawl, kept looking
at him and smiling her denuded, toothless smile.

"And where do you say I have to mail this letter, Señorito Gervasio?"

"Don't worry, Zoa, don't be nervous. You've got to mail the
letter where I tell you, but without explaining anything to anyone.
The only thing you have to do is give your name when the gentleman at the table asks for it."

He spent morning and afternoon transporting voters to the polls
(nuns, old folks, cripples, housemaids), and at the door, before they
went in, he would give them instructions and encourage them, and

when they came out the old women would ask ingenuously, with a touch of pride, "Did I do it all right, señorito?"

At nightfall, just after the polling places closed, Gervasio appeared at Uncle Felipe Neri's house to give his report to Father Rivero, who rubbed his hands confidently.

"We're going to win, my lad; we're going to win easily."

But they did not win, and a few hours later Father Rivero disappeared without a trace from Uncle Felipe Neri's house.

"He's gone to Portugal with the Society," said Mama Zita and Aunt Cruz by way of explanation when someone asked about him, though no one knew exactly where he was.

After the defeat at the polls Mama Zita received an urgent letter from her brother Vidal, exhorting her to emigrate to Portugal with the whole family. "You're perfectly free to do as you wish with your own person, Sister, but you have no right to expose your children to the risks of an uprising like the one in Asturias." Uncle Vidal, with nothing else to do, wrote long, flowery, academic letters from his place of golden exile, hearing the sound of the sea from his desk in the hotel. But, like a general hearing the suggestion to surrender a place he is committed to defending, Mama Zita replied without hesitation, "I think it's unworthy to leave the field before giving battle."

Since Crucita's return Mama Zita had been edgy and irritable, not only toward her son-in-law Jairo, but with everyone who might remind her of him in some way, beginning with Aunt Macrina and Uncle Vidal, whose expatriation she considered an act of cowardice. For many weeks Mama Zita and Aunt Cruz tirelessly discussed the girl's situation; Crucita, still frightened by her decision, imputed all sorts of terrible things to her husband (selfishness, disdain, sadism, petulant demands), though neither she nor Mama Zita nor Aunt Cruz, all cast in the same prudish mold, knew exactly what his weak point was. Only Papa Telmo knew how to handle the matter, and as soon as Crucita was feeling better he went to the Chancellery and on the following day to Madrid, came home, and went again. His naturopathic office was neglected for several days. He personally filled out the documents which his daughter signed submissively, without reading them. "It's for the annulment," was the only thing he told her. And she put her name to the paper willingly. Only on one occasion did she ask him, "What reasons do I allege, Papa?" "Incompatibility of temperament," answered Papa Telmo, and shook his head as if to say, "and everything else that has nothing to do with the case."

Crucita had changed. Her fatuousness, her arrogance, hardly showed now. By her thoughtless marriage she had meant to defy the city, defy its stupid pretensions, its provincialism, its bad taste; but abruptly, after her fiasco with Jairo, she had to undergo the humiliation of defeat: commiserating glances, smothered smiles, hints of words, awkward questions. She went out very little; she had given up tennis, her former refuge, and neither went out with friends nor to the theater or the movies. Politics as such did not interest her, perhaps because she had never really tried to understand it. However, she was terribly upset by the possibility that someday crowds of ragged people would get out of control and burn the old palace of the counts of Pradoluengo with the same savagery with which they burned convents and churches. This was the only trait that the new Crucita had retained from her former self: her scorn for the common people. But since her unfortunate marriage, her rejection of society was absolute: she despised the upper class for its conventionalism, the middle class for its hypocrisy, and the lower class, as always, for its vulgarity. And so Crucita, without really understanding why, very much wanted a change, something that would turn things upside down, though she had no specific plan about the way things ought to be afterward. What she really wanted was for the city to forget her and let her go back to living "as if nothing had happened." That was why the daily tension, the explosions, the shots, the disturbances, did not affect her. She began to sense an opportunity for freedom in "the big one" that Mama Zita feared so much. After all, for her "the big one" might mean wiping out a whole heap of errors once and for all. In this frame of mind Crucita was constantly listening to the radio. You would have thought she was expecting "the big one" to come through the receiver, as ingenuously as children wait for the arrival of the Wise Men and their gifts through an open balcony window. And indeed, one morning she heard it come, through the sepulchral voice of Radio Madrid. She heard that Don José Calvo Sotelo, head of the opposition, had been assassinated in the Eastern

Cemetery by a squad of Assault Guards, and she ran through the house spreading the news. A few days later she and Gervasio caught an excited voice, which faded out at intervals, talking about General Franco, the Canary Islands, and troop movements in North Africa. They tuned in Union Radio, which specifically announced a military uprising against the Republic. Aunt Cruz and Mama Zita hugged each other, weeping, and said, "Spain is saved!" But Gervasio found Papa Telmo, who had been given the news by Crucita, with his elbows on the desk in his office, his head between his hands, murmuring, "It's Pavía all over again: this country is hopeless." His concentration was such that he muttered his words as if he were praying. Gervasio did not dare try to bring him out of his absorption and went out into the street.

It was late in the afternoon and silence and confusion hung over the city; a sort of heavy stupor, like the dog days of summer, the dead calm that comes before major storms. He walked the streets alone, aimlessly, until he came to the Avenida de la Constitución; there he saw two young men coming along the deserted street, the sleeves of their blue shirts rolled up, holding pistols high and yelling "Hurrah for Spain!" Hiding behind a treetrunk, he watched them with a mixture of fear and admiration. Behind them came three more, and then larger groups appeared with carbines and red-and-black flags, coming from the direction of the Glorieta del Angel. They too were yelling "Hurrah for Spain!" and waving their rifles, and from time to time a balcony window creaked and some timid clapping could be heard. An open bus filled with Assault Guards, armed with carbines and a large bicolored flag, whizzed by him. Minutes later, after some shrill notes on a bugle, a cavalry battalion took positions in every quarter of the city. Some balconies and windows began to be decorated with sheets and bunting, and ovations for the soldiers grew more enthusiastic and more frequent. Almost immediately the first shots began to sound, spaced-out bursts differing in intensity and coming from different directions. A stout older man dressed in a good suit and wearing a Panama hat, the only civilian in Gervasio's field of vision, warned, "Look out! Here come the Pacos!"

The groups of militiamen scattered. Gervasio looked to one side and the other uncomprehendingly. A car filled with armed youths

from the "Spanish Renovation" group, flags at its windows, passed
by him at high speed and stopped on the corner of the avenue. Its
occupants, in civilian clothes and wearing green berets, tumbled
out of its four doors and without warning began to fire their rifles
at the rooftops. The same thing was happening in other streets,
where the only traffic consisted of militia and soldiers. Sometimes
there was a timid detonation, like a challenge, from rooftops and
attics, and then the military forces would scatter and answer the
rash action with sustained fire aimed at random. When Gervasio
reached home Mama Zita hugged him in the vestibule.

"They've captured Army headquarters, son. The city is ours.
Now we can cry 'Long live Spain!' "

In the drawing room Aunt Cruz, Crucita, Florita, Aniceta, and
Florentina were still gathered closely around the radio, smiling and
triumphant. Papa Telmo was not there. Gervasio looked for him
everywhere. He felt a vague fear for him. He had not understood
his father when he muttered something about Pavía, as if speaking
of danger, nor did he understand what that glorious Spanish victory had to do with all this. Papa Telmo wasn't in his office or the
waiting room or in the out-of-the-way ironing room. For a moment
Gervasio thought that he might have gone crazy. He crossed the
garden and went into Uncle Felipe Neri's house. Through the partly
open door he could hear the sound of conversation, and before
going into the living room recognized his father's voice. He looked
through the crack in the door and saw him sunk into an armchair
facing his uncle, who was again dressed in uniform, with his old
decorations on his hollow chest. They were talking fast, as if someone were making them hurry, and it was some time before Gervasio
realized that his uncle was offering to hide him ("the house of a
lieutenant colonel who's one of them is a guarantee, Telmo"), but
his father rejected this measure because it might compromise Uncle
Felipe Neri, and also brought up the point that he "had a moral
duty to face up to the situation." Even though Gervasio was aware
of how wrong his behavior was, he kept on looking and listening
through the crack in the door. Papa Telmo expressed a desire to
entrust some business matters to Uncle Felipe Neri, who consented
with a catch in his voice; he spoke to him about Crucita's situation,
her mistake, about Jairo's sexual perversion and the status of the

annulment suit at the moment. Uncle Felipe Neri wrinkled up his face as if his stomach acids were acting up, as if that delicate problem repelled him, and nodded; and after Papa Telmo had told him that if anything happened to him he must take up the affair and carry on the negotiations with Rome, Uncle Felipe Neri sat up very straight in his chair to promise that he would. Then, when Papa Telmo said unexpectedly, in a different tone of voice, "As for Gervasio's problem . . . ," the boy felt weak in the knees, an astonishment that was also mirrored on the withered face of his uncle, who leaned forward to say, "I didn't know that the lad had problems."

Papa Telmo said that he referred to Gervasio's horripilation. "It'll be an ugly business," he explained, "if these things get worse and shootings and atrocities start." He looked up at his brother-in-law from his subordinate position and added, overcome with emotion, "I'm afraid that my son's extreme sensitivity isn't built to withstand that kind of violence."

When he heard his father's candid interpretation of his seizures Gervasio felt the blood rush to his face, and his embarrassment increased when he saw that Uncle Felipe Neri was in agreement and promised "to do everything he possibly could for the boy." When the conversation was over Papa Telmo stood up, thanked Uncle Felipe Neri, who had stood up too, and the two of them looked into each others' eyes for a long time, the tips of their noses almost touching, and at last they hugged one another and pounded each other on the back several times as if to seal the agreement.

A few shouts, confused voices, men running, stray explosions came in from the street, followed by thundering barrages and, about midnight, the roar of a cannon and shouted orders of "Halt!" in the street outside, with prolonged intervals of silence which were broken anew by snipers and the thunderous replies of the riflemen. By dawn, soldiers and members of the Falangist party circulated victoriously through the quiet streets, and people offered them wine, cigarettes, and sandwiches. That afternoon Uncle Felipe Neri presented himself to the new Captain-General, warning Mama Zita not to open the door to anyone she didn't know. Forty-eight hours later a terrifying group armed with carbines burst into the palace asking for Papa Telmo and, when they saw Uncle Felipe

Neri appear with his stars and medals, were disconcerted and tried
to explain that they had been entrusted by the authorities with
"cleaning up the city," and that they had orders to arrest Telmo
García. Uncle Felipe Neri, very calm, praised their discipline but
persuaded them that home arrests had to be carried out legally, by
judicial order and the approval of the Auditor-General, in accordance with the state of war that had been declared in the country.

In each others' arms in the old playroom, Mama Zita and Papa
Telmo heard the squad leave, but when two days later another
squad turned up with the papers in order they hugged again, this
time in the vestibule, Papa Telmo kissed each of his three children
one by one, quickly picked up the suitcase with a few books and
toilet articles he had prepared, told Mama Zita, "Don't worry; this
can't last long," and turned to the young fellows with the carbines.

"Whenever you like," he said.

He was wearing a tweedy sweater and gray flannel trousers, and
Uncle Felipe Neri, scrupulously dressed in uniform, went with him
and came back two hours later with the latest news; for the moment Papa Telmo was in no danger. He had been confined in the
bullring, down by the river, along with hundreds of others, friends
and men of the same political persuasion, and he, Uncle Felipe Neri,
had received permission to visit him once a week and take him
news, food, and everything he might need. Mama Zita sighed with
relief. Papa Telmo's imprisonment, with Uncle Felipe Neri as guar-
antor, was a sort of tax she had to pay, resignedly, to the Cause.

But for Gervasio his father's arrest was a hard blow in which
feelings of complicity, commiseration, and shame were mingled.
The first day that he went out on the street he happened to meet
his schoolmates Carlos Centeno and Imanol Solavarrieta, who
made fun of him and ridiculed him. Damasito Valentín was with
him, and the ensuing fight with the other boys did not make him
feel any better. He soon forgot the punches, but the insults, the
ugly words, Papa Telmo's irritating stubbornness, stayed floating
in the air. Dámaso Valentín shrugged his shoulders, passed his
active red tongue over the notch in his tooth, and tried to console
him.

"Nobody needs to give up his ideas just because someone else
doesn't like them," he said. Then he steered the conversation in a

different direction. Lucinio Orejón had gone to Madrid; he had seen him, along with his brother Felices and Colomán IV, in a truck, waving their rifles, calling out "long lives" and "down withs," in the Glorieta del Angel. Gervasio, wishing to blot out the evil picture of Papa Telmo arrested, suggested the idea of going too, but Mama Zita convinced him that Lucinio was older than he was, and that the war was not child's play. The word "war" was mentioned in the palace for the first time, and Crucita, her eyes round, asked Uncle Felipe Neri, "Does that mean this is a war, Uncle?"

Uncle Felipe Neri smothered a belch, pursed his pale lips, and admitted that the Glorious Uprising had failed in Madrid, Barcelona, and the Basque country and other key points, and that according to the latest news trenches were being dug and parapets raised in half of Spain, with a view to a long campaign. Then Gervasio looked at him imploringly and Uncle Felipe Neri stroked the back of his neck with his sickly hand and added, raising his eyes to the ceiling through his spotless eyeglasses, "May God help us, but it's still possible that you'll have your chance."

From that moment onward Gervasio was encouraged by the conviction that "the greatest occasion known to the centuries," as Cervantes had put it, awaited him, and that the whole disturbing process of horripilation that he had experienced since childhood had only been a preparation for facing it. Peter talked to him about the Navy, about the Cartagena mutiny, about the massacre of petty officers and officers, of the need for well-trained youth to offset the superiority of the "Red" navy; and Gervasio, humbled by Papa Telmo's desertion, listened to him open-mouthed, avid and tense, until one night when he couldn't sleep, when his friend's words and thoughts of his father were torturing him, mingled in an intricate nightmare, he reached a clear conclusion: the name of García de la Lastra had been stained, and it was his duty to wash it clean. By an association of ideas he thought about his uncles Norberto and Adrián, "the ones furthest from the truth," and asked himself what had become of them; and this was enough to make him imagine them astride the Norton, crossing towns, sticking close to the banked curves, Uncle Adrián bent over the handlebars with his hat on the back of his head and Uncle Norberto sitting stiffly behind with his long teeth showing, a tricolor flag waving wildly over his shoulder, in flight. Gervasio was sure that they had escaped on the motorcycle at top speed, skimming over valleys and mountains at a hundred kilometers an hour until they reached the frontier. He couldn't help finding a certain grandeur in their action, though after thinking about it for a little while he concluded that they had stained the family name too. And so the idea of washing it clean began to be an obsession.

The boy waited impatiently for Uncle Felipe Neri's first visit to Papa Telmo. He felt sure that the latest events to occur, and such remarkable ones, might have made a change in his convictions. The experience had been a hard one, and shut up in the bullring along with other miscreants, he must have had a chance to think. But for the time being, in the first batch of mail carried by Uncle Felipe Neri, Gervasio did not write to him. His indignation was still too keen. His father had betrayed them before the whole city. Mama Zita, more conciliatory, had said to him several times, "Write a few words to Papa," but he had avoided doing so, pretended he hadn't heard. Then he waited nervously for his uncle's return, counting the minutes, and when he saw him with his tentative smile, his dull eyes round behind the lenses of his glasses, he thought, "Papa Telmo must have repented." But Uncle Felipe Neri unbuttoned the pocket of his uniform jacket without a word, took out a sheet of paper folded into four, and said, "Telmo's well and in good spirits. He gave me this note for you all."

He held out the letter to Mama Zita and Gervasio read it along with her, over her shoulder.

"Dear Zita and children: It has been a week since we parted and I miss you, as I miss some of the comforts of home, but I can't complain. My life is filled with routine and is methodical. I don't eat too much, but I do get vitamins, in accordance with my personal philosophy, by the type of nourishment through the skin that I practice daily. I do exercises with a group of friends, walk, read, talk, and time passes without my being conscious of it. Don't worry about me. This will soon be over, and in a few weeks we'll be back together again. The thing that worries me most is that there is no news of my brothers. They are not here in the bullring, and Angel Alvaro, the druggist next door, has told me that the shop hasn't been open since the eighteenth, and that he heard very strange noises there that night, in the small hours of the morning. God willing, they have been able to escape. In any case, you'll find the key to the back room of the shop in the top right-hand drawer of the desk in my office. Would it be too much to ask you to go there, to see if there's some information?

"Dear Zita, you are constantly in my thoughts. I hope that the process of annulment of Crucita's marriage is progressing, and that the two younger ones are well. I don't like to abuse my brother-in-law's good offices, but if it's not too much trouble, have him bring me the plaid traveling blanket that I use to cover my legs when I read in the garden. For the moment it's not cold here, but one does feel the chill by morning. For Cruz and all the rest of you, love from your Telmo."

Mama Zita furtively dried her eyes and handed the paper to Crucita. Gervasio coughed stupidly, trying to show indifference, though a sharp-pointed lump rose in his throat as a dull irritation consumed him internally. Why wasn't there a single reference in Papa Telmo's letter to the new situation? He had only said "when this is over." Did that mean that for him "this" was only a passing nuisance, like a hailstorm or a windstorm?

Next day he went to the notions shop with Uncle Felipe Neri. There was a strange odor in the back room, rather sweet, like perfumed chemical fertilizer, but the cardboard boxes were in order and apparently the shelves too. But when they opened the door into the shop that vague odor, now decidedly nauseating, grew stronger, and as soon as Gervasio switched on the light he saw his uncles' silhouettes above the counter, naked, astride the motorcycle, in the same sporting attitude in which he was accustomed to seeing them on the city's streets. Uncle Adrián (his hands strapped to the rubber handlebar grips with strips of adhesive tape, a wedge of cardboard holding up his head, his hat pushed back on his head like a skullcap, and a bullet hole in the middle of his forehead) was leaning over the handlebars, and behind him, unmoving (with a black hole between his eyebrows and his yellow teeth showing) was Uncle Norberto, with a bicolored Nationalist flag over his shoulder. He heard Uncle Felipe Neri's anguished voice saying "My God!" but he had already gone around the counter and was looking at the macabre spectacle with no obstacles in the way. Contrary to his first impression, the bodies were not naked. Uncle Adrián was wearing some light-blue knitted panties with a matching brassiere clasping his skinny chest, and Uncle Norberto the same outfit but in pink. Together they made a picture like something in a wax museum; two yellow mummies whose prominent teeth showed in a grimace of futile ferocity. Gervasio looked at his uncles' bodies in terror, so overcome with horror that when he heard Uncle Felipe Neri's scarcely whispered lament of "My God!" again, he felt as if he were waking from a nightmare. But when he realized that it was no dream, that the profaned bodies were still there, provocative and silent, and that the awful odor continued, he was assailed with nausea and vomited violently on the floor under the counter.

In the little yard at the back, he and his uncle stared at one another without recognition. Uncle Felipe Neri's cheekbones were stiff, green, and his chin had turned a glaring, waxy white. And the bags under his eyes, always so prominent, looked as if they had been painted on under his blank pupils. The expression had been wiped out of Gervasio's eyes and his yellowish irises had a vacant expression; his mouth, whose shape could hardly be discerned around his bloodless lips, hung open as if he refused to recognize the evidence, or were getting ready to vomit again. Uncle Felipe Neri's blank, forlorn eyes vainly sought support in him, looked at him as if to say, "Forget this horror. Refuse to believe that you've seen it. Wipe it out of your memory, and attribute it to mere natural phenomena." But after he had closed the door and they were back on the street, a new, active, dynamic Uncle Felipe Neri emerged.

"Come on, hurry; come with me."

"Where are we going, Uncle?"

"To militia headquarters."

Gervasio looked admiringly upon his uncle's weak, clenched jaws, his courage. But the muscular young man who received them, his bare forearms on the table, paid little heed to their accusation. Death was the order of the day in the city, it could not be otherwise. "Suicide, Lieutenant Colonel, that's the easiest way to escape responsibility." Uncle Felipe Neri did not give in, stood up to him; nobody committed suicide and then tied his hands to the handlebars of a motorcycle. The young man with the rolled-up sleeves persisted, without showing any concern.

"Maybe it was a mutual elimination, Lieutenant Colonel."

"Then where are the pistols?"

The young man smiled, hesitated; it didn't seem to matter to him that his arguments were so easily demolished. He referred to the hundred-man squad charged with "cleaning up" the city as "an unselfish act of service." They were aware of their obligation to bring arrested persons before their superiors, if possible at headquarters, but that was not always possible.

"Uncontrolled elements, Lieutenant Colonel, often get ahead of our men. They take justice into their own hands, what can we do about it?" Uncle Felipe Neri pounded on the untidy table and demanded control, and, beside himself, shouted that a state of war did not justify murder. For his part the militiaman tried to calm him down, mentioned how hard his superiors worked not to leave any loose ends, referred to internal orders about these matters which were unmistakable and severe. But when Uncle Felipe Neri, in a burst of energy such as Gervasio had never imagined in him, demanded the filing of an accusation, the young man with the muscular forearms pointed out to him, "With respect, Lieutenant Colonel, such an action is not advisable at the moment."

"File the accusation!" repeated Uncle Felipe Neri.

Two weeks later, after Uncle Norberto and Uncle Adrián had been buried in the civil cemetery, Uncle Felipe Neri received a courteous message from the National Chief of Militias in which he said that, apart from the savage actions of uncontrolled elements in the rearguard, a known and lamentable fact, "Our information service had detected, days after the Glorious Uprising occurred, the existence of a clandestine Red organization whose object was the physical elimination of their own comrades, with the aim of preventing the activity of informers and the capture of compromising documents, in view of which this office has considered it more prudent not to pursue the accusation which you presented, and to file it along with others, of which fact I am now apprising you."

"God be praised," muttered Uncle Felipe Neri, waving the paper as if fanning himself. But the way he pursed his lips, and the convulsive movements of his Adam's apple, showed that stomach acids were rising into his mouth again.

CHAPTER 12

About the middle of August Uncle Felipe Neri received a letter from Señora Agustina informing him of the disappearance of her son Daniel and begging him to try to find out where he was. Mama Zita confirmed that Señora Agustina had a son named Daniel and a retarded daughter named Felisa, that the family's precarious livelihood rested on the young man's shoulders, and that Señora Agustina and her children were "good people," though she did not exclude the possibility that Daniel, led astray by Marxist propaganda, might have done something foolish "contrary to the spirit

of the Uprising." In addition, the missing man's mother was the
sister-in-law of Señora Zoa, whom Uncle Felipe Neri knew very
well indeed, and to whom Mama Zita and the rest of the family
owed so much, for she had served unselfishly in the house for
fifty-seven years. (Gervasio, who was present during the conversation, thought of Daniel at his saw, beret powdered with sawdust,
and his long glare of hate on that faraway afternoon when he had
surprised him in the fig tree eating a fig; but he held his tongue.)
Nevertheless, Uncle Felipe Neri needed specific information (day,
hour, place from which he had disappeared, clothing, shoes, physical description, and so on), and wrote a detailed letter to Señora
Agustina in order to procure them. In accordance with his new
custom he headed the letter, as a devout and strident profession
of faith, with the defiant question "Who but God?" without realizing that in view of its recipient's circumstances it might seem inap-
propriate. By return mail he received an abject reply from Señora
Agustina, who wrote in her wretched handwriting, terribly discouraged, "No one but God, Señorito Felipe, I should say not, but
please try to find my son." Uncle Felipe Neri, whose ulcer grew
more active with every passing day, took a diligent interest in
Señora Agustina's problem. He sent a lieutenant to her house to
draw up a complete report, which then served as a basis for writing
a circular to the municipal secretaries of all the towns in the province. He very soon received a reply from the mayor of Valdepuente
de Rubiales informing him that a week before, at kilometer four,
hectometer three of the provincial highway to Acevedo, the body
of a young man whose description matched that described in the
circular had been found in a ditch, full of bullet holes. In view of
the fact that no one had claimed the body, he had given orders to
bury it "at the edge of a field, where it is at your disposal." Uncle
Felipe Neri appeared with a doctor in Valdepuente de Rubiales,
where they proceeded to exhume the corpse and perform an au-
topsy. It showed that there were two perfectly healed fractures of
the femur in the right leg, corresponding to those the boy had
suffered at the age of five when he was kicked by a mule. Uncle
Felipe Neri, grieved to the point of tears, deposited the corpse in
the city's municipal hospital, notified Señora Agustina of the discovery, and expressed his condolences to her, imploring her "not

to judge the spirit of the new Spain by such vile acts." As was becoming customary for him, he headed his letter with the well-known "Who but God?" But Señora Agustina's succinct response left him in a state of consternation: "Dear Señorito Felipe, I already told you no one but God, I should say not, but there's nobody as wicked as those bastards who shot my son."

For several days he was greatly perturbed. Lofty aims were not to be achieved by unworthy means, and fearing that the latest events might undermine Gervasio's patriotic morale, he summoned him to the ironing room one afternoon for a confidential chat. He found his nephew "disoriented," as he wrote later in the oilcloth-covered notebook. "He is distressed by the contradictory acts that he sees around him and that prevent him from distinguishing good from evil. The fact that we have mercifully concealed his brothers' deaths from his father has done no good, for we cannot deceive the boy, who was a witness of the fact. Hence, though he understands the arrest of his father, an enemy of the Uprising, he detests the murders of his uncles and Daniel Ovejero, nephew of an old servant for whom he felt veneration in the past. I fear that his patriotism may be choked off by so much bloodshed. He admits that he hears the march 'The Volunteers' in the Café Avenida every day ('a kind of music, Uncle, that would have lifted me right off the ground before') without feeling any emotion, for he is unable to concentrate his mind, and every time he tries to do so 'the ghosts of Uncle Norberto and Uncle Adrián appear' and confuse him. The boy needs an incentive that will neutralize the depression caused by the recent murders."

The return of Aunt Macrina and Uncle Vidal infused new life into the flagging Saturday evenings, formerly so cheerful and noisy. Uncle Vidal turned out to be a leading figure in the new situation, for he had been involved with organizing the uprising from his place of exile; and every time that he referred to his mysterious participation his bald spot turned pink and shiny, in contrast to the livid, opaque tone it assumed when there was mention of the murders committed in the city, which he considered, along general lines, to have been "appropriate and inevitable." When this point was touched upon he would turn to his sister Zita and say in his rumbling voice, "What Felipe has done for Telmo is a life-insurance policy, Sister. I don't know whether you've thanked him enough, because if it hadn't been for him your husband would have been taken for a ride like so many others."

Aunt Macrina, however, was silent and apprehensive. The last news of her brothers dated from early July; she had heard nothing about them since then, but feared for their lives, especially Fadrique's, for he was an ex-candidate of the Spanish Confederation of the Independent Right and an active member of the National Association of Catholic Propagandists. Two weeks later, without warning, David's wife Esperanza appeared at the gathering on her way to Seville. She was dressed in mourning, her abundant blond hair gathered into a knot and a three-strand pearl necklace decorating her generous décolletage. She had escaped from the Red zone through an embassy, by way of Valencia, and despite her sufferings appeared even younger than she had seemed at Crucita and Jairo's wedding. In the presence of the assembled family she reported the news she had brought, without mincing words.

"The Red horde showed no mercy. David and his brothers have been murdered."

She was a tall, stately woman, a little overweight but still beautiful—a Valkyrie, as Uncle Vidal used to remark in happier times. As she told her dramatic stories she did not cry; she stated them coldly, not omitting the most brutal details. David, her husband, had been denounced by a stable boy at the Hippodrome with whom he had had some minor altercations in the past. They had tied him to his own horse's tail, and in that position he had run his last race with Lucho Martín, a former Spanish high-jumping champion.

"It was horrible. They stuck flaming darts into the horses' croups and set them off at full speed. David and Lucho were dragged to the end of the track, bumping along, and were destroyed, unrecognizable"—her gold bracelets tinkled as she raised her hands to her eyes—"but at least I was able to recover my husband's body and give it proper burial in the Almudena Cemetery. Fidela, poor thing, didn't even have that consolation."

Tears ran from Aunt Macrina's beautiful, close-set eyes and rolled simultaneously down the side of her nose till they reached its tip, where she dried them with a little lace handkerchief that she took from the sleeve of her dress. Despite her self-possession,

Esperanza's voice also shook when she told about Fadrique. With ten fellow members of the National Association of Catholic Propagandists, he had been taken in a truck to the Cerro de los Angeles with its heroic-sized statue of Christ, to witness "the shooting of God." And after they had fired on the statue they turned to them and said, "God is dead. Long live the Republic!" But because none of the eleven would submit, they lined them up at the foot of the monument and the squad leader said, "If there's no God, then there's no use for altar boys." And they shot them right there, at the foot of the sacred statue (Elena and Uncle Fadrique's children were safe in San Sebastián).

At this point in her tale the watchful eyes of everyone present converged on the girl Crucita, for if the horde had liquidated all three brothers it was obvious that only Jairo's death remained to be recounted. Esperanza looked at her too, feet curled under her in a wing chair beneath the copy of Giotto's *Resurrection,* her hair cut short like a boy's, head held high, hands clenched. Esperanza paused, but she had warmed to her tale and in view of the prevailing suspense it was impossible not to speak. She took two steps toward the armchair where the girl was sitting and ran a hand over her defenseless nape.

"As for your husband, my dear, he was no luckier. The horde murdered him in his house (in your house), in his bed (in your bed); they stabbed him"—she grasped a few pearls in her three-strand necklace and played with them for a few seconds—"then they mutilated his body horribly, but it's better not to go into details."

Crucita shuddered. Mama Zita, seated on the chair arm, put her arm around the fragile shoulders, drew her close, and shot a withering look at Esperanza.

"You could have been more tactful."

Taken by surprise, Esperanza looked one way and then the other as if seeking support, but no one except Mama Zita seemed to have noticed her blunder. Aunt Macrina was crying gently, chin sunk on her breast, and Uncle Vidal was leaning over her solicitously; Uncle Felipe Neri, his right hand on his stomach, nodded wordlessly, his dull eyes looking at nothing, while Aunt Cruz, red-eyed in a corner, kept repeating, "They're wild beasts; they're wild beasts."

Esperanza's revelation caused a serious crisis in Mama Zita's heart. Should she dress Cruz in mourning? Publish a funeral notice for Jairo in the newspaper? Have funeral masses said for him? Was all this consistent with the fact that the marriage was in process of annulment? When Jairo died, was he not still her daughter's husband? Through Uncle Felipe Neri, Papa Telmo advised her to do so, to organize the rites and also to destroy the papers pertaining to the suit because there was nothing left to annul. Mama Zita dictated the notices, stating the circumstances of Jairo's death: "Vilely murdered in Madrid by the Marxist rabble." Tall, expressionless, never wavering, Crucita presided over the funeral mass, and outside the church kissed hundred of feminine cheeks, pressed hundreds of masculine hands belonging to worthy fellow citizens who looked sympathetic but a little later, gathered in groups, commented, "She really has a nerve; first she leaves him and then she has a funeral mass said for him."

Though she did not realize it, this was the change in her life that Crucita was waiting for. And so, after a few months, she resumed her sports activities, her walks along the Avenida de la Constitución with her girl friends, and her attendance at performances and demonstrations. From time to time she even allowed some wounded officer, or one on leave from the front, to invite her for a glass of beer in a café or walk home with her.

Some time later Mama Zita received a long letter from Inesita Pons, writing from Pau, whose ambiguous contents she was unable to decipher fully. Only two points were clear to her: the murder of Inés's husband Juan Manuel ("One night they put him in a car and filled him full of bullets on the Cuesta de las Perdices"), and the fact that Jairo's murder had had nothing to do with politics; it was "the revenge of a rejected sadist who, not content with killing him, then mutilated him and stuffed his parts into his mouth." Mama Zita read and reread the paragraphs referring to Jairo's death. Rejected sadist? Revenge? Parts? At last she shook her head and murmured under her breath, "These Catalan girls, always using such fancy words." The postscript, however, was uncompromising: "It's better for Crucita never to learn the circumstances of her husband's death." Mama Zita, terribly upset, sent the letter on to Papa Telmo; to her brother and sister she merely said, "Inesita Pons wrote. The horde killed her husband too. It seems that they put him in a car and filled him full of bullets on the Cuesta de las Perdices."

Lucinio Orejón, though, died at the front from a bullet in the chest as his battle group was advancing on Madrid. The death notice was only one of many published by *El Correo* during those days: "Lucinio Orejón Díez fell for God and for Spain, at the age of seventeen years, on the Madrid front." Gervasio read it over and over, shivering. There were so many dead that he sometimes thought that no witnesses of the horrible butchery were going to be left alive. But those open deaths, facing the foe, revived his spirits and were a help and a consolation. Alone in his bedroom, he repeated the word "Lucinio" hundreds of times, as he had done with the word "Fenedosa" until, like that one, it was worn thin and had no meaning. He remembered his friend at school, his incipient hirsuteness, his badly cut, baggy trousers, his robust red neck, enthusiastically throwing stones at the Protestant chapel or Doña Jovita's brothel, always ready for action. But no one—not his parents or his brother Felices, who came from the front for the funeral—knew any details about his death. When the sentries were changed they had found him dead on the parapet with a bullet in his heart, probably a stray. Gervasio asked himself whether Lucinio was a hero, and Uncle Felipe Neri, who had been waiting for just this favorable opportunity, agreed that he was "a real hero, for the true heroes were the anonymous ones, those who offered their blood for a cause, without boasting of it or seeking a reward." And, as he still seemed to see a shadow of doubt in his nephew's eyes, he added sententiously, alluding to the murders that had taken place behind the lines, "The cowardly behavior of ruffians takes nothing away from sublime actions."

His friend Peter, though temperamentally not as close to Lucinio, supported Uncle Felipe Neri's verdict: "Lucinio was a hero because he had offered his life without expecting anything in return." Gervasio could not quite match his friend's passive action with the deeds of Guzmán el Bueno and the Drummer Boy of Bruch, those heroic archetypes, and said so to Peter. But Peter, whose lucid opinions always astonished Gervasio, blinked his little eyes and explained that those cases were different because they were symbols rather than heroes, and that if history were not based on symbols it would crumble like a body without a skeleton. Gervasio cut Lucinio's death notice out of the newspaper, framed it, and put it in a prominent place on the second shelf of his bookcase as an example to imitate.

One morning Peter, Dámaso Valentín, and he, in their wanderings through the city, came close to the bullring. Gervasio, who had not been near it since before the Uprising, was impressed by the precautionary measures, the forces stationed around it, the sentry boxes at the doors, the four machine guns mounted up above on the rim of the stands. Behind the closely guarded bullpens the flood-swollen, turbulent river ran among green vegetation, making eddies near the banks, and Gervasio thought how difficult things would be for Papa Telmo should he try to escape. A few weeks before he had begun to write to him, at first a few conventional lines and gradually more affectionate ones, slipping into his letters some piece of news, such as Lucinio's death, that might cause him to reflect. But in this particular case his father's reply had filled him with astonishment: "Don't let Gervasio even think about joining up for this war. And if by any chance it lasts for a long time and he receives orders to enlist, you must appeal to Felipe's kindness once again, to try to find him a relatively safe job." Gervasio, saddened and disenchanted by the failure of his subtle hints, had let two more weeks pass without writing to him.

Now he was there, facing his father's jailers, a stone's throw from him, so near that if he called his name Papa Telmo might hear him. That evening at nightfall, all alone, he stayed for an hour in front of the orchestra in the Café Avenida, waiting for it to play "The Volunteers" (a tune so exciting that he often went to the café simply to raise his low spirits). That very night he dreamed that he was attacking the bullring, pistol in hand, that he overpowered the guard at the door of the bullpen and fled with his father through the thicket to the river, where his friend Lucinio Orejón was waiting for them with a boat (even in his dream Gervasio realized the inconsistency, and kept saying, "Lucinio can't be helping me; Lucinio's dead"), and rowed with all his might. But as soon as the sirens started to howl and the searchlights in the bullring went on, investigating the grass like shining fingers, the machine guns began to fire on the river. In the background came the stirring strains (God knows from where!) of "The Volunteers," and Lucinio matched his oar-strokes to the rhythm of the march, so strongly that each stroke made the oarlocks creak. It was such a vivid dream that Gervasio awoke in the middle of a seizure, tense and soaked with sweat, still gasping from the running he had done. He lay motionless for a few seconds, face up, gasping, crushed by the darkness, asking himself whether Papa Telmo was really free and Lucinio alive, while the attack passed and his hair, which had stood up like a halo, subsided onto the pillow.

Next morning he told Uncle Felipe Neri about the experience, assuring him that it was the first time in his life that the seizure had happened when he was asleep, while he dreamed about freeing Papa Telmo. Unable to suppress his jubilation, Uncle Felipe Neri smiled and gave him little pats on the back of his neck; awake or asleep, Gervasio continued to be one of the chosen. He would have liked to be alone to meditate on his joy, but Gervasio kept pressing him.

"Would it be a heroic action to free Papa Telmo?"

"Of course! Nothing can compare with accepting a risk for one's father."

"In spite of his being an enemy of the Cause, Uncle?"

"In spite of that, my son. There is a hierarchy of values in life, and after God nothing is as important as the ties of blood."

Gervasio listened to his uncle's arguments. He raised his eyes sluggishly to his uncle's face and narrowed his question.

"And if it wasn't my father but someone I didn't know?"

Uncle Felipe Neri hesitated, pursed his dry lips; but forced to it by his nephew's expectant look, he added in a less convincing tone, "In that case it would lend itself to interpretation. To free an enemy of a noble cause, placing that very cause in danger, could even be a crime."

"But Father Dictinio said that we're all brothers, Uncle."

Defeated, Uncle Felipe Neri took refuge in his oilcloth-covered notebook the moment he was alone. Christ had indeed said that we were all brothers, but when Christ said that, he couldn't have been thinking about this crusade, which was organized specifically to defend him. And so, after noting that for the first time Gervasio's seizure had taken place while he was asleep (brought on by a bold dream whose background was a stirring musical accompaniment),

Uncle Felipe Neri wrote, "My nephew insists on discovering what the ultimate meaning of heroism is; that is, whether or not heroism responds to an ethical incentive. As I have done each time that he has presented the question in these terms, I have diverted my reply toward the legal aspect. But I fear that, even despite his extreme youth, my arguments have not convinced him. The question is a complex one. There are obvious cases which do not lend themselves to doubt, but others are hard to define, which leads me to reduce heroism to a problem of good intentions. I think that it is hard to go further than that. The man who sacrifices himself knowingly, with honest intentions and clear eyes, is a hero. We can add little more." He closed the notebook with an irritable bang, adjusted his glasses with one finger, and heard his intestines twisting in a sort of interminable groan.

At nightfall Gervasio went back to the Café Avenida. The lively strains of "The Volunteers" carried him back to his still latent dream, so that the members of the orchestra were blotted out and Lucinio came to life before his eyes, rowing in the bow of the boat, while Papa Telmo regarded him gratefully and the craft slipped downstream among the machine-gun bullets. The music sounded more stirringly than in his dream, and yet the shock was minor, the erection of his hair only partial (no more than the crown and nape). It rose lazily and softly, like a faint stirring of wings, rising and settling again, and during this phase of indecision a husky little voice drew him out of his self-absorption. Manena Abad, her blond locks caught into two braids, one on either side of her head, was regarding him, her blue eyes round with astonishment.

"What Florita said is true! Your hair stood on end." She stretched out her thin bare arm like a small child. "When I hear music I get gooseflesh too sometimes."

United by their musical emotion, they walked together along the central path in the park. For the first time Gervasio was walking alone with a girl, and the unusual situation led him to imagine that the two of them were the center of attention on the path. But stronger than his suspicion were the girl's all-enveloping voice, her shining blue eyes, the expressive movements of her slender hands.

"Is it true you want to be a hero?"

"Maybe. When I'm older."

"Do you think the war's going to last that long?"

This subject led him to speak of his father, a prisoner in the bullring, and Manena said that it was horrible and Gervasio admitted that it was a nightmare that pursued him night and day. But the girl asked him whether he felt bad for himself or for what people would say, and Gervasio concluded that actually it was as much one as the other, but that he wouldn't be satisfied "as long as he hadn't washed the family name clean." Their arms swung as they walked and sometimes their hands brushed together, a contact that gave Gervasio delicious pleasure and led him to seek it deliberately. The strange ease with which he could share with this girl concerns that he ordinarily reserved for his friends, or for himself, made him feel comforted. And after they separated he thought that now he had a person to whom he could talk about his heroism, and especially (an objective dreamed of in all his reveries) "a beautiful girl who would tremble for his safety." Without specific agreement, they met again on occasional afternoons among the small group of people who listened to the concert on the terrace of the Café Avenida, and each time they would walk together along the central path in the park, chatting. Gervasio was more pleased every day with the girl's graceful figure (the figure of an unfinished woman, a woman in transition), her blond-streaked hair, her blue eyes, her voice (a warm, comfortable, very feminine voice that grew husky when she referred to important matters), and especially her good sense, her sensitive ability to share his problems. For years after his disturbing contact with Amalia, he had made up his mind not to have anything to do with women, and yet he now realized that the viscous impression left on him by that experience was not a necessary part of communication with the opposite sex.

Gervasio gradually brought the girl into his Wednesday fantasies, the days on which the local radio station broadcast a program of military marches under the title "On the joyous path to peace," to which he listened in withdrawn solitude, eyes half closed, lying on the divan in the drawing room opposite the mantelpiece. The women were bustling about some distance away, at the other end of the house, which meant that he could absorb himself in the music without annoying interruptions. At first he listened to the marches with a certain feeling of remoteness, even allowing himself the frivolity of keeping time with his foot; but as the program grew more fervent Gervasio's heart was uplifted, his brain entered a creative phase, until he reached a point when the strident noise of cymbals, bugles, and drums became a vivid stimulus to his imagination rather than a mere accompaniment. Music and thought mingled together, and in the heat of their combination Gervasio would begin to build his exploits, passing the beads of his personal epic through his fingers, as it were: the attack on a strongly defended height to the sole accompaniment of a machine gun spitting fire; the bringing down of a big bomber by a tiny fighter plane flown by himself, or the sinking of a battleship with a torpedo, naturally fired by himself, from the unstable base of a fast launch. By the time he had reached this emotional level the music disappeared, or at least Gervasio ceased to notice it, just as the racing driver bent on the pursuit of his rival ceases to hear the motor of his speeding vehicle. The music acted as a stimulus to his subconscious. Then the seizure would take place: an icy little snake ran down his spine, his skin began to pucker (bubbling like soda water), and his bristling hair would stand up energetically, out of control. He would stay in this condition for a long time, excited by the music even though he did not hear it, heightening bold exploits which only his reverie made convincing. And after he had established a relationship with Manena Abad, he liked to put her into the story as an eyewitness of his deeds, and under her gaze the seizure would become even stronger and with it his fantasies, so that in his paroxysm he quite often went so far as to give his life for the Cause. The picture of the girl lamenting his death, in addition to moving him deeply, also provided a tortuous masochistic pleasure which Gervasio, recalling Father Sacristán's words (though they referred to different sorts of situations), began to call "my solitary Wednesday vice." Under the influence of this joyous ecstasy, he sometimes brought a mirror which, when it gave him back the image of his upstanding hair, strengthened and prolonged the display, making the tickling sensation in his neck even pleasanter and more sensual.

Now he had frequent conversations with Peter about the nature of heroism, for Gervasio had become convinced that, in modern times, there could be no heroism outside of individual action. How to reconcile heroism with the anonymous concentration of a regi-

ment, or the disciplined crew of a battleship? Peter argued that that
was exactly where heroism lay, in subordination, in anonymity, in
a refusal to be conspicuous, but Gervasio did not share his view;
submission was one thing and heroism another. And so the dozens
of dead who were daily brought from the front were unselfish
beings, heroes perhaps, but by no stretch of the imagination the
proverbial hero, the hero of the medieval *gestes,* that he wanted to
be. Nowadays the company of a machine (tank, machine gun,
airplane, torpedo launch, anything) was essential in order to excel,
to stand out from the crowd. Without it a person could never be
anything but one more sheep in the flock, an infinitely small piece
in vast military actions. According to Napoleon, each soldier carried a marshal's baton in his pack, but in Gervasio's opinion, if a
person wanted to be somebody in combat he would have to seize
that baton and use it. The hero of legend even demanded the
support of a witness who could transmit all the details of the
exploit to the world, and thus inspire others to follow his example.
Peter, still unaware of his friend's incipient relationship with
Manena Abad, smiled.

"That is, every soldier has to have a troubadour with him to sing
his praises later on? Isn't that what you mean?"

Gervasio found his pretensions laughable when he heard them
expressed by his friend; he got flustered.

"Oh, that's not it! You're not even trying to understand me.
You're making fun of me."

In the end Peter laughed at Gervasio's strange conclusions.

"I suspect that what you want isn't to be a hero, but an exhibitionist."

CHAPTER 13

Even more than by the risk of war, Doña Guadalupe Rueda, widow of Valentín, was troubled by the thought that if her lazy and irresponsible son Damasito spent months wandering around the city streets he might fall victim to depravity. Her second marriage and its consequences had opened Doña Guadalupe's eyes and made her adult, foresighted, and suspicious. She would never understand why what she thought of as a supremely favorable day in the life of a family in financial straits should have become the immediate cause of its dissolution. But that was what had happened. The four sons of her first husband, Don Jerónimo Prado, though they were still very young, left her as soon as her second, Don Dámaso Valentín, had married her. Hence, after his death and with the other children independent, Doña Guadalupe's only consolation was the late fruit of her second marriage, Damasito, on whom she concentrated all her capacity for affection, her tenderness, and her preoccupations. But now suddenly, with his secondary studies finished, the university closed, and the country at war, how could she keep an eye on her boy's movements? What advantage could there be for her adolescent son in this blameless but endless indolence? The result of her anxieties was the decision to fix up the attic of her house for Damasito and his friends; it was a cubbyhole hardly ten meters square with a slanting ceiling and a double skylight, which when sparsely furnished could serve as a meeting place and a tactful way of maintaining control over the boys. And so one day Doña Guadalupe, accompanied by her old servants, removed all the dusty junk from the attic, cleaned the ceilings, scrubbed the floor, and with the place still smelling of disinfectant, offered it to her son, stressing the fact that the gift was to last "for the duration." The boy and his friends joyously took possession of the attic, for despite its discomforts that little room represented for them the first sign of independence.

The modest furnishings which Doña Guadalupe provided for the room (an iron garden table and half a dozen crude pine stools) was soon enriched by the boys' contributions, for they were daily more delighted with their club. Gervasio, the most enthusiastic of all, contributed a worm-eaten rack for hanging coats on, a clock whose striking mechanism was broken, an Annunciation that had been crudely carved by a shepherd in soft stone, a washstand, and the old phonograph he had inherited from his grandfather with all its cylinders. Peter decorated the attic with a series of English engravings of ships and naval battles and a figurehead representing an opulent mermaid holding in her arms a galley on the point of shipwreck, as well as the inspired work of his own hands: models of corvettes, frigates, brigantines, and half a dozen bottles and flasks of different sizes with ships inside. In addition to the clubhouse, Dámaso Valentín contributed a blue liqueur decanter and matching glasses, an old desk with its rolltop missing, and a wooden bookcase to keep books and souvenirs in. Finally, Eduardo Custodio, whose house had up to that time been the group's meeting place, wheedled out of Don Colomán III and Doña Loreto, who viewed his change of allegiance with consternation, an old pine plate rack, a walnut chest, and a five-place bench. Doña Loreto and Don Colomán III celebrated the establishment of the club (as the attic was called from the very first), with an afternoon party that allowed Eduardo to bring off one of his usual pranks, giving his mother a pair of trousers with a torn fly. Doña Loreto pretended to be scandalized: "Just look where that boy has torn his trousers." And she held up the garment, showing it to everyone. Then Eduardo, very seriously and carefully, his fleshy eyelids half shut, answered in a resigned tone, "It's the size of it, Mama. What do you expect me to do about it?" Eduardo Custodio deliberately played this game of boldness and familiarity with his parents, for he felt that because of his physical slowness it was the only thing that gave him a certain preeminence in the group, a preeminence that he shared with Peter and which in the course of time gradually passed to Fortunato Delgado, Tato, the latest member of the club. He was an athletic boy from the public high school, swimming champion of the province and introducer of water polo into the city; he played it with a red ribbon around his head to keep his blond, almost white hair, which he wore combed back, out of his eyes. His impressive stature, his robust shoulders, his belligerent chin and powerful jaws gave him a deceptively aggressive appearance, but Tato Delgado was the least violent boy in town, a soft, angelic youngster who was frightened of girls and, at the club, spent hour after hour playing solitaire and singing familiar snatches of comic opera under his breath.

Peter's intelligence and Tato's strength complemented each other from the first day of their acquaintance. Peter found agility and physical power in Tato, and Tato found skill and good judgment in Peter. Peter had transferred his cabinetwork to the club, and there, under the skylight, accompanied by the phonograph's scratchy tunes (*Aida* or Beethoven's symphonies), he built corvettes and cruisers with his little freckled hands, using no model other than a drawing or photograph, while his friends played interminable games of poker. Sometimes, when they tired of cards, they would gather around him to enjoy his careful work, his skillful manipulation of the tiny pieces (filaments, threads, pins, matches, toothpicks) that he combined so cleverly until he had reproduced the model. Little by little Gervasio and his friends familiarized themselves with naval techniques and added seagoing terms to their small vocabulary (bow, stern, port, starboard, top, forecastle, overall length, gangway, waist, rigging, stanchion), almost unconsciously entering a new, distant, and fascinating world. But the one who showed the most interest in Peter's work was their new friend Tato Delgado, the swimming champion and fine water-polo player, for whom Peter's unswerving vocation for the Navy was a motive for admiration.

"As soon as I'm seventeen I'm going to enlist in the Navy. And then when the war's over I'll enter the Naval Academy. I want to be a sailor like my grandfather."

Without trying to, Peter was doing a work of proselytism which gradually captivated his fellow members at the club. Tato Delgado was the first convert, at least the first to say so. Open to any new idea, he found in Peter's chosen profession a sporting and adventurous quality that was very congenial to his temperament. He began his collaboration with Peter in the little shipyard, and even did simple things on his own under Peter's direction. He showed disciplined patience as well as youthful fervor. The slow development of a brigantine inside a bottle, made of tiny pieces of cork and wood, using long silver-plated tweezers that moved inside the bottle with the skill of a hand, fascinated him. At the same time he listened open-mouthed to Peter's stories of naval battles, so that Peter, aware of his friend's increasing passion for seafaring subjects, brought collections of books on marine subjects, ranging from Salgari to Conrad, to the club.

Three months after meeting Peter, Tato Delgado was his best friend, building ships his favorite pastime, *Mutiny on the Bounty* his best-loved book, and his vocation was decided: the sea. Tato Delgado and Eduardo Custodio, who were a few months older than their other friends, were the first to apply to the Naval Command in El Ferrol, requesting enlistment in the Navy as volunteers. Filling out the applications—a simple bureaucratic procedure—was, however, a joint activity, the most glorious event in the history of the club up to that time.

One bright, chilly afternoon, with a red sunset showing above the rustling trees of the park, Gervasio told Manena Abad about his plans.

"I'm going to enlist in the Navy, you know? My friends and I are going to crew a torpedo boat, and when the war is over we'll exhibit the medals we've won in a glass case in the club."

For Gervasio, inclined toward action that was either individual or in small groups, a place in a speedy launch was the only condition that he placed on requesting enlistment in the Navy. It was unanimously accepted, not only because the others wanted to please their friend, but because the torpedo boat represented better than anything else the spirit of adventure that motivated them all. After a year and a half of war Gervasio continued to escape into abstraction every week with the program "On the joyous path to peace," enjoying the stirring of his hair, though the scene inspired by the music varied each time. Since his recent decision the sea was what prevailed, the attack of a small launch with himself and his friends as crew against a gigantic battleship, the *Jaime I* to be exact. In his daydreams everything was methodically organized: Eduardo at the helm, Damasito as navigator, Tato and he at the launching tubes, Peter at the bow directing the operation. Dodging bursts of machine-gun fire, sheltered by darkness, the boat drove straight for the battleship, and thirty meters away Eduardo veered to port, a maneuver which Tato and he employed to launch the two torpedoes against the monster's waterline. He experienced intensely each phase of the offensive (bold approach, violent turn to port, launching of the torpedoes, ear-splitting explosion, retreat), and after the mission was over, their return to base before an enthusiastic crowd, with Manena Abad in the first row, warmly applauding the heroes. After Tato and Eduardo had sent in their applications, this was the action that Gervasio imagined most intimately on Wednesday mornings.

"Are you really going to be a hero?"

"I want to be one so you can see me."

"But that's impossible! They don't let us girls go to war."

The girl's astonished, virginal gaze caught his, and Gervasio held her eyes with his own and, with nothing more to say, squeezed her little hand hard, until she protested.

"Stop it. You're hurting me."

The long, bitter winter often made him think of Papa Telmo, because of his frequent requests for warm clothing to combat the cold. In the course of time Gervasio had come to think of his father's lack of freedom as a natural thing, but he was infuriated by the pretentious stubbornness with which he clung to outmoded ideas, ideas in which, according to Gervasio's sister Crucita, no family of any importance in the city believed any more.

"I don't love him any more, I swear. I don't care what happens to him. If I write a few words to him it's only to keep my mother from being unhappy. 'I'm fine, I'm glad you're well.' That's all. I haven't anything else to say to him."

"You shouldn't do that; after all, he's your father."

Gervasio lazily turned his head toward her.

"Do you think it's better for me to deceive him? Invent a story every Saturday to soften him up?"

Gervasio was as much surprised by Papa Telmo's attitude toward the Cause as by the attitude of Mama Zita and the uncles toward Papa Telmo. All three felt that his imprisonment was not only acceptable but providential. His arrest, mitigated by the stars on Uncle Felipe Neri's uniform, was responsible for his survival. What more could they hope for? Gervasio's sisters Crucita and Flora, confused by the war's constantly changing circumstances, had forgotten the immediate past, but Mama Zita and her brothers were still too close to the deaths of Uncle Norberto and Uncle Adrián, Daniel Ovejero, and many others in the city not to feel fortunate. Aunt Macrina, however, had hardly opened her mouth since her sister-in-law's visit; only now and then would she let fall, as if by accident and staring insolently at Uncle Felipe Neri, that "Telmo, despite being more prominent, had been luckier in this zone than her brothers had in the Red zone." Gervasio felt ashamed when he heard her, for it was obvious that as long as Uncle Felipe Neri stayed near them Papa Telmo's life was guaranteed. But the fact that his father used this advantage not only to stay alive but to criticize the Crusade, arguing that someday the rebels would pay for their crime, or that the country would soon return to what he called normality, made Gervasio boil with indignation.

One February morning the wail of the siren on the railway station announced an attack on the city by enemy airplanes. The crash of the bombs' explosions surprised Gervasio on the stairs, on his way to the palace cellar (his great-grandfather Lucio's wine cellar some fifty years earlier), which had been made into an air-raid shelter. He could hear the ragged, heavy explosions, and in the pauses between them, the high-pitched chatter of the machine guns mounted on the cathedral and the barrage from the four cannon that the artillery regiment had placed on the city's out-skirts. It was a deafening duel, like a summer thunderstorm, which when it ended left the streets and squares empty, sunk into a dusty silence broken by the nervous hooting of improvised ambulances. A black column of smoke, which Gervasio used as a point of reference, rose from the Glorieta del Angel. In the main square groups of people talked about the attack, tried to estimate the number of victims, spoke of the deaths of five children in a school, and demanded a scapegoat. An elderly man, with a blue shirt and black tie on under his overcoat, waved his cane and shouted at the top of his voice, "To the bullring!"

People flowed into the circle along its six radial streets, and in a few seconds had become a crowd shouting wildly, "To the bull-ring! To the bullring!"

The word spread, became general, and the column of smoke off to one side began to dissolve and grow shorter, assuming the shape of a dense gray mushroom. Standing on the hood of an automobile parked in the center of the circle, the city's second most prominent Falangist was haranguing the crowd and waving his walking stick, suggesting the possibility of shooting five prisoners for every inno-cent victim, an offer that the crowd accepted enthusiastically, re-peating, "To the bullring! To the bullring!" in a paroxysm of hate.

As soon as the anger-maddened mass began to move, Gervasio realized that the threat might come to pass and that the wild crowd was perfectly capable of disarming the guards in the bullring, tak-ing it over, and killing the prisoners. Then he elbowed his way through the crowd, succeeded in reaching the park, and started to run, trying to arrive before the demonstration, idiotically con-vinced that his father's life depended on his getting there first. "God, don't let them kill him; don't let them kill him," he said to himself as he ran. And the image of Papa Telmo appeared in his mind, not in his white doctor's coat or with jacket and tie, but in his invariably striped pajamas ("like a jailbird," he thought now), with his snub-nosed face lathered, his bunioned feet on the wet tiles of the bathroom floor, just as he had seen him every morning since earliest childhood. And superimposed on this vision he saw the spectral forms of Uncle Norberto and Uncle Adrián, their long yellow teeth, panties and brassieres trimmed with delicate lace and covering their skinny nudity, astride the Norton. The demonstrators' intermittent howls, the hooting horns of the automobiles at their head, assailed his ears; and as if that noise were a spur he ran even faster until, after he turned the last corner and saw the bullring at the end of the avenue, he felt a sharp pain in his side and halted, started to walk, breathing hard. Two trucks filled with Assault Guards passed him; they tumbled out in front of the prison and with linked arms formed a cordon around it, near the sentry boxes, with their carbines obviously loaded. Up above, on the rim of the ring, the machine-gun crews hastily took up positions. The noise of the demonstration grew louder, and when he saw the two automobiles that headed it turning the corner, Gervasio began to tremble, fearful that no force in the world would be able to contain it. The distance between the crowd, which advanced yelling and waving flags, and the double row of guards grew visibly smaller, and when the first demonstrators reached them a stubborn struggle began, with that theatrical zeal that marks every confrontation where both attackers and defenders know that fundamentally they belong to the same cause. Still, Gervasio watched the confrontation in anguish from a nearby rise, fearing that guards and sentries would eventually give way, and kept repeating to himself, "Don't let them kill him, God; don't let them kill him."

The defenders' dissuasive attitude, displaying a certain amount of exhibitionism, with their carbines crossed over their chests, caused the attackers to retreat slightly. But when from the top of the bullring a machine gun fired several intimidating bursts and the officer on duty, from one of the openings on the top tier, asked for quiet through a megaphone, the huddle fell back and the crowd stopped and waited, a circumstance that the officer used to promise the citizens, "justly indignant over the execrable crime," that it would not go unpunished and that the innocent victims would be avenged; but while the high command was deciding about the how and the when, they should show signs of patriotism, fall back, and cease their attempts at lynching or taking justice into their own hands. The demonstrators, their enthusiasm dampened by the long walk, flattered by the torrent of oratory that had been unleashed on their behalf, and in a word conscious of their strength (now delegated to the gallant officer who had spoken to them), applauded at first timidly and then warmly. They burst out into "up withs" and "down withs" until they gradually began to disperse, stepping back, initiating the retreat toward the city in small groups, their homicidal impulse appeased.

During the months that followed, the bombardments continued, futile bombardments with no apparent aim except to frighten the civilian population and remind it that the country was at war and that from time to time the enemy had been found there. People's reactions were increasingly less defiant, milder, as if they had at last accepted the fact that bombardments were a normal risk, and though talk of acts of revenge and reprisals continued to circulate, there was no way either to confirm or deny them. Store owners resignedly took their precautions, piling sandbags around their establishments, fastening strips of adhesive tape across the show windows to prevent the panes from shattering, while Civil Defense set up air-raid shelters in the basements of the city's tallest or most solidly constructed buildings. On his occasional visits to the palace cellar Gervasio had witnessed scenes of collective panic which, in his opinion, undermined the morale of the home front. And to reduce it, as well as to control his own fear, he decided to inaugurate a system to frighten off the devils that had been haunting his mind for some time: it consisted of singing, singing at the top of one's lungs, loud enough to drown out the noise from outside, the crash of the bombs and cannon, and in consequence calming the spirits of those who had taken refuge in the shelter. Gervasio, aware of how frightened the group was, would begin the hymns himself and would stand up with his arms raised, directing the chorus, demanding louder and louder voices, until the cavelike cellar was filled with ardent patriotic cries:

> A legionnaire am I, so brave and loyal,
> Soldier of the Legion is my name.

> The soul must suffer as on Calvary,
> And seek redemption in the flame . . .

Terrified, and ashamed of their terror, the people in the shelter joined the chorus, overcoming their initial embarrassment, and tried to blot out the crash of the bombs with their voices.

"Louder, louder!" Gervasio would insist. The cellar became a clamor:

> "Long live Spain!" will be our motto,
> For Spain we'll gladly give our lives.
> "Long live Spain!" will be the virile cry
> Of the patriotic youth who bravely strives . . .

The tendons in their necks standing out, throats tense, they grew hoarse in their proud show of defiance of the attackers. Their fear forgotten, it was as if by their very songs they were actively participating in repelling the attack. The result was that during the bombings Gervasio became an indispensable presence in the palace cellar among his humbler neighbors. There was one skinny old woman who walked leaning on a stick, with a heavy black shawl wrapped around her even in summer, who would beg him impatiently even before the noise of the bombs, cannon, and machine guns began, "Come on, Gervasio, my gallant; sing, before the fear gets into us and we all dirty ourselves in the corners."

They would form a close, solid, fraternal circle around him, singing with one voice. Gervasio, with his hands held high, would mention the title of the march and give them the note: "Faithful Infantry," "Death's Sweetheart," "Warrior's Fire"—any song would do, especially those that composed the repertory of the program "On the joyous path to peace." Whether they began with one hymn or another was unimportant. Within a few minutes a nucleus of resistance to the enemy that would be very difficult to silence had been created there, in that close, damp, low-ceilinged cavern, protected from the outside by hewn stones.

One night, when the alarm surprised him while he was asleep, Gervasio went down to the shelter in his pajamas, wrapped in a brightly colored blanket; and when he saw around him those poor people in their nightclothes, with a spark of hope in their eyes, his fertile imagination flew to the catacombs and he saw himself leading a group of converts who were being persecuted by the emperor, singing hymns to their God in the knowledge that almost immediately he and his followers were going to die in the circus, torn to pieces by lions. The emotion of the moment trembled on his lips; the chorus of singers, obedient to the movements of his hands, the voice in his own throat (which was gradually becoming more fervent), moved him deeply. And when he began the verse, "Going to your side to see you, my most faithful companion," he felt a violent shock on the back of his neck (that night the most sensitive part of his head). But far from compromising and moderating his tone he grew more defiant, his voice became a shout, while his skin began to prickle and his hair stood on end as though some invisible being were trying to pull at it and lift his light, insubstantial body off the ground. Tense, completely carried away, his head bristling like a giant thistle, his blue pajamas showing under the brightly colored plaid blanket, in full display, at first he did not notice how the circle of singers was falling back until the old woman in the shawl crossed her eyes, raised her gnarled hands to her toothless mouth, emitted a howl of terror, scrambled to her feet with extraordinary speed, and fled as fast as she could, muttering to herself, toward the cellar stairs. Four others escaped after her, then ten more, and immediately a great rout began; the terrified occupants of the shelter, pushing and shoving, casting furtive glances at Gervasio's head, jostled one another on the stairs in an attempt to reach the open air, despite the heavy explosions and the rhythmic chatter of the machine guns on the cathedral.

Mama Zita and Aunt Cruz, who had witnessed the trance, ignored the general defection and praised his patriotism, and Uncle Felipe Neri, who had also been present, wrote in his oilcloth-covered notebook with an unsteady hand, "Today my nephew Gervasio's hair rose of its own accord. He merely provided the words and music, which means that his emotional sensitivity is increasing. Tonight's trance in the air-raid shelter, while he was answering the enemy's criminal bombardment with song, has undoubtedly been the most intense, indescribable, touching, and emotionally moving of all those I have had the privilege of witnessing. It is obvious that the Lord has marked him for very lofty exploits." But Gervasio realized that his last display contained a warning rather than a prophetic indication; in times of patriotic enthusiasm like these, when any unexpected group fervor could

bring about his metamorphosis and the consequent collective
panic, it was risky to walk bareheaded on the street. It was then
that he decided to use the red beret he had inherited from Papa
León (a faded red, drained of color by the passage of time). In
addition its heavy metal plaque (God, Fatherland, King) was a
guarantee of safety. And as if that were not enough, the beret, so
gloriously displayed in a hundred battles, was a badge in harmony
with Mama Zita's vague store of political ideas, always distrustful
of the Fascists and the Blue Shirts. Gervasio was decidedly grateful
for that defense, which became (according to his own definition)
"like a turtle's shell," an aesthetic safeguard. This recourse did not
fail him even during the most exalted patriotic demonstrations of
the next few weeks; that is, the tickling sensation on his neck and
the crown of his head continued to occur, but the heavy beret
aborted any attempt at erection, kept his restless hair in check, and
this allowed him to take hitherto unthinkable risks and gave him
more freedom of movement. And, too, Manena Abad liked the new
style ("the red of the beret suits your face"), though at the club it
gave rise to scornful comments like those of Peter, who couldn't
understand how a man could use a traditionalist symbol if he didn't
share its ideals.

One blazing August morning the legionnaires arrived in the city.
The streets were hung with banners to receive them, and a large
crowd stationed on the sidewalks gave a warm ovation to the
soldiers' rather histrionic gallantry. Gervasio, with his grandfather's faded beret on his head, standing on tiptoe in a group of his
friends, was entranced by the green shirts open to hairy chests
tattooed in blue, the shirtsleeves rolled up above the elbows, the
flexible hemp boots on their light feet, the caps dashingly set to one
side, the perfect synchronization of their movements to the rhythm
of the band, the trained goat-mascot keeping pace with the soldiers
at the head of the rank . . . It was a thrilling spectacle to which the
music (the sharp notes of bugles, the incendiary thrum of kettle-
drums and snaredrums), struck the note of exaltation that the boy's
emotions required:

> No one in the ranks
> Knew that soldier's name,

So brave and so audacious,
Who enlisted seeking fame . . .

The hairs on his forearms stood straight up, he suddenly felt as though his body were being torn apart, and as those thrilling men passed in front of him (faces grave, chins jutting, gaze fixed on the infinite), he felt a shock in the middle of his stomach and simultaneously a fierce struggle between his hair, which was trying to rise, and the General's old red beret, firmly fixed between his forehead and his nape, which was trying to keep it from doing so. It was a tenacious battle that took place there, and had it been a question of a mere passing fervor, the beret and the plaque (God, Fatherland, King) would have smothered the capillary impulse; but the defiant parade continued, the soldiers ("Legionnaires to fight, legionnaires to die"), kept going by at a dizzying pace, advanced upon him, literally enslaved him, so that when the leaders of the rank passed by him his wire-stiff hair, after a tremendous struggle with the beret, succeeded in pushing it up, pushing it off, raising it above Gervasio's bristling head, until at last it hung from the longest hairs as if from the hook of a hatrack. Gervasio raised his hands to his head in alarm, trying to prevent his hair from getting out of control, but the phenomenon was so violent that the hairs slipped between his fingers, eluded them, and then stood up in the space between them, as stiff as reeds. Totally demoralized, he crammed the beret down on his skull (like someone applying the bell of a snuffer to a candle flame) and then seized it by the edges and pulled it down so violently that the embarrassing display began to subside, his emotion waned, the skin on his arms smoothed out again, and his hair settled down docilely just at the moment when the backs of the last legionnaires disappeared between the spectators' heads, on their way to the station.

After this unusual display (which fortunately no one had witnessed), Gervasio promised himself that he would "avoid the occasion" (in accordance with Father Sacristán's instructions about sin): no more parades, no more demonstrations, no more inflammatory meetings, no situations in which music was an essential ingredient. In short, no encouragement of his hyperaesthesia. The solution was apparently plausible, but suffered from a serious defect: now that the time was coming when he would go to war, the appropriate thing was to reinforce his fighting spirit, not to weaken it. At least this was Uncle Felipe Neri's opinion.

"If your soldier's morale requires music and imagination, listen to music and imagine things, Gervasio. Our fatherland needs soldiers with morale." In view of this difficult alternative, the boy made a splendidly generous decision: to sacrifice his hair, keep his head close-cropped (hair that was always standing up but which could not attract anyone's attention because it was so short). During this new phase he did have several attacks, but just as amputees sometimes feel pain in the amputated leg, he felt the prickling sensation a few inches above his scalp, at the ends of long, nonexistent hairs, without his friends becoming aware of it. On this occasion Manena Abad was less enthusiastic: "I don't think short hair suits you; it makes you look like a rookie." But Gervasio's chief concern at this time was not his rebellious hair but his father's permission, the hope that Papa Telmo would not object to his intended enlistment in the Navy. At first, as Uncle Felipe Neri had told him, Papa Telmo became furious, raged, rolled up his eyes, threatened to escape, to get himself killed by the guards or to throw himself off the top of the bullring; but after he had calmed down the uncle persuaded him that the boy was about to be drafted and that the risk would always be less in the Navy than in the infantry. Papa Telmo began to fuss again, but suddenly his broad boxer's features began to expand, his voice softened, and an expression of mild conformity arose in his eyes.

"Do whatever you think best, Felipe. You've had the upper hand since the beginning during this miserable time. When it comes right down to it, all of us are in your hands."

On that same afternoon, during the club's daily meeting, Gervasio, Peter, and Dámaso filled out their applications and sent them off the following morning. Ten days later Tato and Eduardo Custodio received notice to report to the training ship. In the farewells that followed Eduardo Custodio, his heavy eyelids over his nearsighted eyes, raised his glass at the last moment, unsteady on his feet, with two bright pink spots on his thin cheeks.

"For . . . for the club," he said. "May we all meet here again after the war's over."

The grandfather's old phonograph played military marches from the Carlist war. Beside him Tato Delgado, feeling sentimental, raised the blue glass from the liqueur set, filled with wine, and touched it to each of his friends' glasses one by one. At last he said, in a tone of voice that was meant to sound gruff, "For the club and for all of us. May God give us luck."

PART
THREE

CHAPTER 14

It was when Gervasio rubbed his nose against the khaki uniform and bumped into the row of medals that adorned the chest of Uncle Felipe Neri (who was embracing him in front of the hatstand mirror in the big vestibule of the house) that he fully realized that he was going to war. At first his uncle had given him a conventional, mechanical hug, but suddenly, as he released his hold, something made him pull Gervasio toward him so tightly that the boy was conscious of his painfully beating heart and the tender emotion that softened his eyes. "Do your duty," said the colonel into his ear.

And he said no more because he was choking. His eyes, ordinarily so dull, shone wetly and his lips curled in a senile grimace that could equally well have been a sign of impending tears or an effort to subdue his stomach acids. Standing a little way away, in front of the ebony chest with its ivory inlays, his friends Peter and Dámaso Valentín, who had come to pick him up, passively watched these farewell effusions, their bulging suitcases beside them. And when Señora Zoa, who had become a little, sighing, black bundle, stood on tiptoe, stretched as high as she could, and hung on the boy's neck, alternately calling him "my treasure" and "Señorito Gervasio," kissing him avidly, Dámaso Valentín, with the tip of his red tongue in the notch in his tooth, opened his thin lips in a sarcastic smile. Señora Zoa's noxious caresses brought memories of the past to Gervasio's mind: that mossy odor of stagnant water from his earliest childhood, the old woman's threats to leave, his frantic opposition as he clung to her skinny legs and cried hysterically, "Zoa, if you go away I want to die." When he pulled his face away from hers he looked at her for a moment, her ancient, wrinkled skin, her toothless mouth, her bleary eyes, her white hair dragged back in a bun, offering him a box of pastries in her trembling, almost transparent hands.

"Take it, my treasure, it's for the train."

The evening before, Gervasio had invited Manena Abad to the movies. He would have enjoyed it very much if she had wept on his shoulder, but the girl appeared to be calm and courageous. He had fumbled for her hand in the darkness and that little hand had not resisted, and then Gervasio had dared to ask her, "Will you be my sponsor while I'm at the war?"

"I don't know if they'll let me at home." She shrugged her frail shoulders doubtfully.

"You don't have to tell them. All you need to do is write to me and think about me a little."

She assented, and when they left the theater Gervasio, feeling extremely tender, gently squeezed her hand as if sealing a pact. He said nothing about Papa Telmo. Four days previously, when he had received the notice from the training ship, he had written him a few boastful lines: "I'm going to war, to save Spain, and will return either dead or victorious." The reply, on a miserable little piece of square-ruled paper, was humble, laconic, and pained. "I wish you luck, my son, may your sacrifice speed the end of this tragedy." For Gervasio the word "tragedy" didn't fit the context of what was going on. How to compare a crusade with a tragedy? The gloomy conclusion implied by a tragedy was the last thing he expected from this war. When Mama Zita saw how miserable he was, she had consoled him. "Pay no attention; don't be upset, dear. You know what a fuss your father makes about things. Behave like a Lastra, but don't run any more risks than you have to."

Mama Zita, after the inhumanity of the scenes she witnessed daily at the hospital, aspired to nothing but saving his dignity; she rejected heroism if it brought mutilation or death. Gervasio, proud of his mother's understanding attitude, stressed the need to wash the family name clean ("Papa Telmo has covered it with mud, and every day that he spends in the bullring makes it dirtier"). But Mama Zita's answer was that the De la Lastra name had never been stained, and as for the name García (she bit her lip, frightened by her own idea), the charity dining room that had been installed in the uncles' notions shop had redeemed it.

Now Mama Zita clung to him, weeping torrents, as if she could armor him with her kisses (smacking, nutritious, total kisses, like Señora Zoa's in times past), to the point that her daughter Cruz, dignity offended, scolded her for them without actually doing so ("Heavens, Mama"); but Mama Zita, deaf to her objections, kept on kissing Gervasio. And when at last she drew away from him, she gazed intensely into his eyes and told him resolutely, as if giving an order, "Come back."

Peter, Dámaso, and Gervasio ate Señora Zoa's pastries in the corridor of the train, sitting on their suitcases, hemmed in on all sides by hundreds of soldiers who were singing obscene songs to the accompaniment of any kind of musical instrument and trading bottles and wineskins. Gervasio was still embarrassed, and in an attempt to justify the old woman's unseemly show of affection swore and swore again that, though it might seem impossible, the dried-up little old woman, whom Peter already knew, had nursed his own mother at her breast. The train was dirty, crammed even to the lavatories, clattering, whistling, without a single woman on board; it smelled of war, sounded like war, was the color of war.

Gervasio looked from one group to another, trying to discover from
their uniforms, insignias, and emblems what the ranks, service
branches, and duties of his traveling companions were. At one end
of the next compartment a legionnaire with square sideburns, his
cap hanging improbably from one ear, asked about their blue pea
jackets. And when Gervasio proudly answered, "Navy," he shook
his head and murmured, "And meantime the infantry's out there
in the cold." Opposite him an artillery corporal with a bandage that
covered half his leg was cutting a big round loaf of bread, dividing
the potato omelet it contained with a knife, and spearing pieces on
the point of it to offer to everyone in the compartment. In the
corridor, in a confusion of badges and uniforms, all sorts of trades
and exchanges were going on (cognac for sausages, cigarettes for
candy), out of a common desire to instill a little human warmth into
that overcrowded, smoky, chilly train. Twilight trembled on the
windowpanes, and as the night progressed the coach grew shadowy, the soldiers fell asleep, the artilleryman rested his head
against the glass, and the legionnaire with the square sideburns
called for silence twice. But for a few minutes they could still hear
a guitar being played at the other end of the car before the coach
fell silent.

Gervasio, his head propped against the frame of the window
whose panes vibrated against his neck, was unable to fall asleep;
he watched the bodies lying around him, sleeping in sprawled
positions, pale faces smudged with soot, slack from lack of sleep,
arms or packs serving as pillows, mouths open, snores like death
rattles forming an accompaniment to the clatter of the wheels over
the tracks. "It's a train full of dead men," he thought, but then,
frightened by the macabre comparison, shook his head vigorously
to scare the idea away, doing his best to replace it with the image
of Manena Abad. From time to time the locomotive whistled or
labored up a slope. Little by little the noises (snores, heavy breathing, whistles, the glass rattling against his ear) dissolved, Manena
Abad's profile vanished, and he lost consciousness so thoroughly
that when he opened his eyes (he did not know whether minutes
or hours later), he saw the familiar glow of dawn on the clouded
glass, on the puffy, sleep-softened faces of the soldiers in the coach.
One buttock was asleep and Dámaso Valentín's elbow was shoved

into his thigh; he carefully removed it and managed to stand up. Hunched over, he endured the prickling sensation in his leg, screwing up his face, looking at the legionnaire who lay with his cap off, his gap-toothed mouth protected by the fringe of a thin mustache that at the ends almost touched his highwayman's sideburns. He was snoring in bursts, as if stammering as he breathed, and sometimes his head would fall on his chest and he would open his eyes in fright. Gervasio turned toward the window, cleaned the fog off the glass with his sleeve, and through the transparent space saw that the flat, brown, arid lands outside had changed into rolling meadows divided into plots, and the high, clear, blue sky into a low, heavy, lead-colored awning. A very fine rain was beating on the panes and soaking into the earth, while the green folds of the landscape, covered with heather and ferns, sloped ever more steeply until they became mountains, which the train was boldly piercing through a series of noisy tunnels. The foggy half-light seemed to make no progress, as if daybreak had stagnated, and when his friend Peter joined him at the window, rubbing his eyes, a blue triangle appeared between two somber hills. Peter pointed to it in astonishment with his soot-blackened nail and said, transfigured, accompanying his discovery with a sleepy smile, "The sea!"

Gervasio lived through the next few hours in a daze, completely exhausted, the torpor of sleep clinging to his eyes with the stickiness of cobwebs. From the damp, cobbled pavement, through the fence that stretched all the way down the street, he could see the navy yard with the commercial wharf to the right of it, the huge dry docks, and opposite him, standing out against the long gray line of repair sheds, the training ship, its Gothic rigging cutting through the fog. Seven uniformed sailors with their white sea bags on their backs and two young men in civilian clothes with their suitcases joined them near the sentry box at the gates of the navy yard. In a few minutes everything piled up on him. Vague, incoherent scenes joined onto others in a dreamlike flow, and in the center, like a cruel, ubiquitous god, stood Petty Officer Ortiguera with his bold lipless mouth like a sphincter, foul-spoken and loud. ("Landlubbers! Fine shipment they've sent me!") He preceded the little group through the different buildings, performing the preliminary proce-

dures: medical examination, vaccination, the storeroom for clothing and shoes, distribution by deck compartments, assignment of
lockers and storage boxes, and at last, before their final acceptance,
a shower on the poop deck near the mizzenmast, naked, with two
dozen idle or off-duty sailors standing around, yelling and applauding their awkward movements, while they soaped their
weary bodies in embarrassment and Petty Officer Ortiguera (olive-
skinned, heavy-browed, work uniform tightly belted, bottom
prominent) poured out a string of taunts.

"Come on now, your balls! Did you hear me, sailors? Soap your
balls! We don't want any crab lice on board!"

The sailors laughed and applauded, the circle drew closer, while
the unresisting and frightened boys soaped their genitals over and
over, tried to cover their pubic hair with soapsuds, hopped around
naked and grotesque under the streams of icy water, enveloped in
the music of bugles and drums coming from the quay.

On the other side of the wharf, half a mile away, the quiet,
languid city (buildings dissolved in the rain, shabby rooftops,
white glassed-in balconies) shone palely. Between them and it, in
the dockyard, a gunboat escorted by a band of chattering gulls was
returning from a patrol, while a dingy tug, looking as if suspended
from a black plume of smoke, strained to pull a heavy freighter
away from the pier. Gervasio, greatly depressed by the shower
episode, looked upon the city and the activity of the port as a
faraway lost world. He felt worse every moment. He had believed
that exchanging his civilian status for the military life meant exchanging freedom for discipline, but Petty Officer Ortiguera's gratuitous malevolence had opened his eyes. The close, solid group
(forge of heroes; all for one, one for all) that he had dreamed about
every time he visualized the training ship vanished, to be replaced
by a profound impression of overcrowding and hostility. A thousand men living together in a nutshell wiped out any hope of
privacy from the outset, made being alone impossible (lines for the
heads, for showers, for the galley, for the infirmary; noisy groups
in the waist of the ship, on deck, on the poop deck, everywhere).
Feeling oppressed, Gervasio enumerated the unexpected list of discomforts to his friends, but Peter, with his vast capacity for adapta-
tion, smiled out of his amused, slanting eyes.

"Don't worry; they won't leave us much time to think about it."

Indeed, Gervasio and Peter spent the afternoon rowing alongside the wharf, while in another group Dámaso was learning to make sailors' knots with a three-strand line on the poop deck. The boat held seven rowers on a side, and when the operation began Petty Officer Jorquera, standing on a thwart in the bow, gave the order "Out oars!" After they had pushed off from the side of the ship he lifted one oar in the air as easily as if it were a walking stick, and executed a series of didactic movements.

"Attention, sailors! This is rowing . . . this is backing . . . this is feathering . . . this is up oars . . ."

Gervasio watched the petty officer's thin little figure carefully, absorbed in his first practical lesson. Removed from the promiscuity of the training ship, numb to the rain (which was heavy and as sharp as pinpoints) that obscured the city's line of buildings and made the oily water of the bay even denser, he had eyes only for the undersized figure of the petty officer who, very upright on the thwart in the bow, was working hard at synchronizing their movements.

"One, two . . . one, two . . . one, two . . ."

The keel split the water and the boat slid over the oily surface in the direction of the dockyard. The training ship was left behind, its rigging hanging like lace in the fog, while the rowers industriously rowed, backed, and raised oars under the petty officer's reproving stare. Suddenly he leaned forward and half closed his eyes.

"Second seaman from the bow, starboard side, isn't feathering right!" he said.

Gervasio smiled to himself condescendingly. He was feeling ready to make peace with the Navy, and had concluded that the exercise (except for raising the oar, a movement that was almost too much for his physical strength), was useful, rhythmic, healthy, and intellectually accessible. Inwardly very pleased with himself, he wondered who that fool could be who hadn't learned the lesson after the petty officer's perfectly clear instructions.

"I'm going to throw the second seaman on the starboard side into the water!" said the petty officer in a threatening voice.

Gervasio winked at Peter and attempted to exchange a conspiratorial glance with him, but Peter did not meet his eyes, and a grimace of annoyance appeared on his lips. Simultaneously Gervasio heard whispering behind him, but before he had fully realized that the second seaman on the starboard side was himself, Petty Officer Jorquera was beside him, vastly annoyed, his work uniform soaked and his knotty arms akimbo.

"Do you want to go to the brig, sailor?"

When Gervasio raised his eyes to him there was such an innocent expression in them that Petty Officer Jorquera didn't say a word. He sat down in the center of the thwart, seized the oar, and feathered in the air half a dozen times, as he explained, "The blade of the oar has to turn inward, not outward. Do you understand, sailor?"

Gervasio nodded. As Petty Officer Jorquera got to his feet he looked at him with pious irony, and before moving back to the bow told him, "In the Navy you'd better say, 'Aye, aye, sir,' or 'No, sir,' as the regulations specify."

They returned to the ship under the fine rain.

"One, two . . . one, two . . . one, two . . ."

Gervasio, crouched in disenchantment, did his best to synchronize the movements of his wrists and the bending of his body to the proper rhythm. A long way off he could see some slender shapes tied up to the wharf, and behind them a vague tongue of green coast entering the sea. The training ship was coming visibly closer and Petty Officer Jorquera, his back to them, boathook in his hands, calculated the momentum to the gangway and ordered, "Up oars and aboard!"

Minutes later the three boys, in dry clothes, taking advantage of a pause in the rainfall, were watching the off-duty brigade drawn up on the starboard side in front of the duty officer (puffed-out chest, haughty stare, chin tucked on breast, gilded gorget at his neck), who was passing the formation in review. When he had finished he turned around and made a slight bow in the direction of Don Manuel Borau, the seamanship officer, who gave the order to break ranks. Like a flood-swollen river bursting its dikes, noisy groups of sailors spread along the cobblestoned quay, turned around the dry docks, and started to head for the city through the wide gates in the fence.

Dámaso Valentín, still concentrating on the rope in his hands, held out an intricate knot for his friends' inspection.

"Does anybody know what this knot is?" He smiled maliciously, his tongue in the notch in his tooth, but before Gervasio and Peter had time to react he answered himself as he tied another knot in the opposite end of the line.

"It's a clove hitch. And this one?"

He laughed at his friends' astonishment.

"Don't you have eyes in your heads, sailors? It's called a mouse. What else could it be?"

The fine, gentle rain started again, and Gervasio and his friends took refuge on the orlop deck, under the lockers. Peter and Gervasio watched Dámaso's incessant manipulations of the rope without much interest. They had had a sleepless night in the train, followed by a confused and depressing day in the training ship, but Gervasio said nothing, reluctant to show premature disappointment. But his exhaustion increased when he went to bed and unhooked his hammock only to see that someone had stolen its clews. He spread his pallet on the linoleum beside the hammock boxes, and used his boots, cap, and sailor's rope for a pillow; he wrapped himself in the blanket, closed his eyes, and tried to sleep, but his depression, the blanket's harsh contact with his face, the pallet's lumpy surface, the hammocks swaying over his head and reducing his living space, eventually woke him up. Peter and Dámaso, on his left, had laughed as they slung their hammocks on the hooks, which had caused the duty sailor to interfere, but now they were sleeping peacefully with their hammocks swinging in the shadows. The silence, his fatigue, the others' regular snores, seemed to invite sleep, but Gervasio was overexcited and opened his eyes in search of relief. He counted the sleeping figures above him, then the portholes on the port side, the tables and benches fastened to the ceiling with iron bands. He turned over several times, drew up his legs, stretched them out again; all in vain. Suddenly he saw it. It was coming along the side of a table, nervous, furtive, wrinkling its little muzzle, and when it reached the other end it turned around and ran along the surface of the table in the opposite direction, swung on the lines of the nearest hammock, and then slid onto the mats fastened along the rail. A little later it reappeared. It raised its twitching muzzle as if smelling something, its jet-black eyes fixed on him, wriggling, indifferent to the humans around it. Gervasio, terrified out of his wits, jumped up and grabbed a boot from under his bedroll and threw it violently. The duty sailor, knife in hand, came to stand beside him.

"Anything happening, sailor?"

Gervasio passed his hand over his lips.

"Nothing," he said. "A rat the size of a dog; it was coming at me."

The duty sailor laughed quietly and said in a sneering tone, "If you're afraid of rats, sailor, you'd better ask for a discharge."

And he went off again, humming and rhythmically hitting the palm of his left hand with the now-sheathed knife.

CHAPTER

15

After Gervasio put on his dress uniform and padlocked his locker, Dámaso Valentín, who was trying his best to fasten the wide trousers around his skinny waist, raised his head, saw him, and went off into a sudden gale of laughter. He laughed and laughed, pointing his index finger at his friend (dickey hanging, still untied at the back, trousers halfway up his legs), bending over at the waist in a storm of hilarity that made his bright eyes soft with tears. His laughter grew louder and louder, in one burst after another, while he slapped his right thigh and repeated, hiccuping, as if to justify

his giggles, "You look like a little kid dressed up for First Communion." A short time later, as soon as Dámaso was able to fasten the
dickey and trousers, knot the black taffeta tie, and set his cap at a
comical angle on the back of his head, the band with its gold letters
over one ear, the situation was reversed and it was Gervasio's turn
to laugh aloud as he looked at his friend, while he ostentatiously
fanned himself with his cap as if to avoid total collapse. And then
both of them mingled their bouts of laughter under Peter's prudent
gaze. Incapable of sharing the trifling reason for their good humor,
he urged them not to be late for formation.

But the farcical atmosphere continued half an hour later on the
Calle Real crowded with sailors, groups of girls walking hand in
hand, and married couples with small children in tow. Gervasio and
Dámaso, bareheaded, caps under their arms, kept laughing at every
move the other one made, squeezing between the passersby, using
Peter as a screen, pushing and shoving him. They laughed harder
than ever in the face of his increasingly irritable scolding, so that
when a colonel in Military Administration, Don Arsenio de la Cruz
Maello (who, for the sake of military efficiency, held discipline in
higher esteem than number of divisions and armament), passed by
and observed their leaps and caperings, the frivolous disregard with
which they wore the uniform, reprimanded them harshly, con-
demning them for lack of discipline. The colonel's shouts and
Peter's martial attitude (rigid, petrified, right hand at his temple),
taking the reproof upon himself, in contrast to his companions'
slackness (bodies resting on the left foot, caps under their arms, a
relaxed and purely civilian expression on their faces) made the
strollers crowd around, avid for a free show. This caused Don
Arsenio de la Cruz Maello, flattered by the attention he was getting
and always ready to improve military discipline, to order the in-
subordinate sailors to come to attention, and as he reminded them
of their duty to wear the military uniform properly and to salute
their superiors, stressed a point which was even more important
than forms, and which produced a great impression on the by-
standers: namely, that "the greatness of the fatherland was forged,
rather than on the battlefield, by upholding standards and making
them stick even behind the lines." Now the three boys were listening to him unblinkingly, stiff and tense, the tips of their fingers

grazing their right eyebrows, so that when the colonel finished his tirade and asked them how long they had been in the Navy, and Peter answered, almost without moving his lips, "Only one day, Colonel," a pitying stir ran through the crowd, giving the impression that the punishment would go no further. But for Don Arsenio de la Cruz Maello the act of insubordination was too demoralizing (especially in view of the fact that the complement of the training ship changed every day) to be left unpunished; and therefore, weighing the two factors—the seriousness of the offense on the one hand and his audience's compassionate attitude on the other—he chose a judgment of Solomon: to end the scene on the street, absolve the three recruits from personal responsibility, and continue his campaign against indiscipline at the highest levels. In a word, Colonel Don Arsenio de la Cruz Maello sent a message to his commanding general, Don Herminio Souto; and General Don Herminio Souto, in his turn, transmitted the complaint to Marine Command, and Marine Command, in the exercise of its authority, sent Captain Don Ildefonso Barbosa Belisario, commander-in-chief of the training ship, the following instruction:

TEXT

This Command having observed that sailors belonging to the crew of the training ship under its authority, during the evening promenade, flout the standards of decorum and behavior that must be demanded of them in view of the glorious uniform they wear, and that simultaneously, either out of carelessness, ignorance, or indolence, they often ignore the duty of saluting their superiors, or do so without the required degree of martial spirit, this Command wishes to remind you:

FIRST: that in future no sailor in the crew of the training ship may have shore privileges until one week after his arrival on board, and that throughout this period of time he must spend whatever sessions are deemed necessary for the instruction and formation of martial spirit in newly recruited volunteers, and

SECOND: that the traditional review of off-duty sailors carried out on this training ship, as in all Navy ships, by the duty officer and for the purpose of determining the condition of the uniform and degree of personal cleanliness, in future must end with a second scrupulous inspection to determine the level of martiality attained by the group of sailors, to avoid embarrassing episodes like the one alluded to above, and which have given rise to the present communication. El Ferrol del Caudillo, 22 January, 1938. Third Year of Triumph.

Captain Don Ildefonso Barbosa Belisario, commander-in-chief of the training ship, imparted this exhortation to all his officers; the officers, in turn, disclosed its contents to their subalterns and the subalterns to the sailors; and finally, in order to transmit it as thoroughly as possible, a copy of the aforesaid instruction was posted on the bulletin board with four thumbtacks and announced over the loudspeaker, so that no one on board could plead ignorance. Six days later, as Seaman Second Class Gervasio García de la Lastra, in dress uniform, chest puffed out, very pleased with himself, was resolutely treading the deck, doing his best to adopt a brisk step under the attentive gaze of the duty officer, Ensign Don Agustín Tarrega, and the seamanship instructor, Don Manuel Borau, at the moment when he brought his hand to his right temple, as regulations demanded, and turned his proud head toward his judges, the instructor's angry disapproval cracked like a whip.

"That neck! Out!"

Two days later Seaman Second Class Gervasio García de la Lastra, convicted of slovenliness and inspected in advance by his friend Pedro María de la Vega, tried to correct his faults, to put a little dash into his walk and suppleness into his neck; and with this aim in mind he led the parade in front of the duty officer, Lieutenant Don Gaspar Hungría, and the above-mentioned instructor, Don Manuel Borau. But before he got as far as the second of these, an irritated voice ("That neck! Out!"), which seemed to rise from the very bowels of the earth, sealed his confinement. Persevering to the point of obstinacy, Seaman Second Class Gervasio García de la Lastra made two more attempts to overcome this unexpected obstacle, but the yells of the instructor in seamanship, Don Manuel Borau, and his loud and peevish disapproval ("That neck! Out!") at the moment he raised his hand to his right temple, not only caused Gervasio to desist but gave him the devastating impression that he had not yet learned how to walk. Pedro María de la Vega's solicitude and words of comfort were of no use. Gervasio García de la Lastra's decision, in addition to being firm, was apparently entirely rational: the very fact that he had to think about the act of walking made it completely unnatural for him, and hence he believed that he should wait until the Naval Command's exhortation had expired and the old state of indiscipline was restored before he could satisfy his desire to go ashore. It was perfectly clear: God, who had marked him to do great deeds, had denied him the physical grace necessary to carry them out. And so he was condemned to stay aboard day after day, pondering his ineptitude, while his friends went off duty.

Under these circumstances a new factor soon intensified his inferiority complex: the indelible impression left in the training ship by his friend Tato Delgado (who had shipped on the *Baleares* a week before they arrived) and the admiring references to his person. When Petty Officer Rego, the mess chief, learned of Gervasio's friendship with Tato, he frowned with his thick eyebrows that were more white than black and said, "You're from Tato's home town? A good lad! The day he left us we should've flown the flag at half-mast as a sign of mourning."

Petty Officer Rego did not conceal the fact that in the course of his long military career he had never been so impressed with any other aspirant. And the others felt exactly the same: there was a rare unanimity in their opinions. Nobody could compare with Tato. Champion in rowing, swimming, water polo, rigging, signals, target practice, gymnastics: Petty Officers Ortiguera, Luque, and Mariño positively drooled when his name was mentioned. Conversations at the mess table often centered on him, and when Petty Officer Rego recalled him his heavy black-and-white eyebrows would draw together in emotion: "You had to see him on parade: fit, concentrated, martial, just like the rulebook. Tato wasn't a soldier, he was an artist." Paco Quesada, who had alopecia and ate with his cap on to hide his bald spots, was amused by the petty officer's devotion to Tato and enjoyed egging him on.

"Petty Officer, do you remember how he used to sing 'The Saucy Girl'?"

Petty Officer Rego would nod nostalgically.

"He even sang well. If singing had been part of the training on board, he would have been Number One."

The crew would tell the anecdote about Don Manuel Borau, the seamanship instructor (Gervasio's implacable foe), who was ordinarily cold and disdainful, after the big parade on Columbus Day. Tato's performance at the head of the rank had been so memorable that at the end of it Don Manuel couldn't help hugging him before the whole formation, and in full spate of admiration had told him with tears in his eyes, "You Castilians are a fucking good bunch!"

The high degree of admiration that Tato commanded on board increased Gervasio's feeling of incompetence, for he was constantly subjected to insidious comparisons.

"Even if you swear to it, I can't believe you're from the same town as Tato Delgado."

The mere fact that his sworn enemy and cause of his misery, Don Manuel Borau, had raised Tato to head of the rank made him feel even more discouraged. "Some get so much and others so little," he would say to himself during his periods of depression. Crushed by Tato's multiple perfections, Gervasio would take refuge behind the name of Eduardo Custodio, who was also from the same city. Petty Officer Rego would draw his pelican eyebrows together and say, "Now, Paleface was something else again." Paco Quesada, the bald one, would add, "Paleface couldn't see worth a damn. Without Tato's help he would never have passed the final inspection." Eduardo's physical ineptitude lightened Gervasio's depression momentarily, but the fact that it had been Tato who corrected it made his discouragement worse. It was unkind to set the standard so high. On the other hand, Tato's recognized mettle was no guarantee of how he would perform in action. A bowlegged man might get to be a hero before he did; indeed, saints and heroes often came from the refuse of humanity, from the humblest levels, even from the dregs of society. Gervasio, lying in the feeble winter sunlight or wandering around the decks, thought about these things. His failure had brought him closer to Antero Arias, who had also fallen behind. Round-shouldered, pigeon-breasted, awkward, Antero Arias, a fellow from Galapagar in the province of Madrid, did not hide his resentment.

"Ain't it a fucking shame? Now it turns out you have to be Robert Taylor to be in the Navy."

He too had stopped putting on his dress uniform and trying his

luck, because the "Out!" with which Don Manuel Borau had dis-
qualified him had been even sourer than the one he had used with
Gervasio. Antero was thin-skinned and superstitious and refused
to recognize his physical deficiencies, but attributed his failure to
the seamanship instructor's ill-will.

"That's what I said, if you're not a male model you're not good
enough to defend Spain."

He stuck close to Gervasio and led him into bad habits, and
Gervasio, with nothing else to cling to, followed along. He drew
comfort from Antero Arias's difficult personality, his fierce hatred,
just as Eduardo Custodio's mediocre performance compensated for
the glorification of Tato Delgado. On the other hand Antero Arias,
who was interested in the occult, initiated him into its mysteries
and helped him to pass the long, idle hours he spent on board. One
afternoon, to Gervasio's complete astonishment, he used his mental
energy and succeeded in lifting the four legs of a wooden table off
the floor, invoking the spirit of Don Manuel Borau's mother with
obscene epithets.

Antero Arias's coarse vocabulary was the norm rather than the
exception on board. At first Gervasio was put off by the vulgarity
and thievery that reigned on the training ship, but in that contagious climate he soon adapted to the new ethic. If he never replaced
the clews that had been stolen from him the first day, it was not
out of virtue but because having to look after them was too much
of an effort. He had got used to sleeping on the floor and didn't miss
them. However, he lost no time in replacing the cap and hammock
rope that disappeared every three or four days. To snatch the cap
off a recruit, who was carelessly walking along the deck, by reaching his hand out of the forecastle and then disappearing up the
ladder on the other side was lots of fun. It was even easier to
appropriate a rope and leave someone else's hammock sagging,
lying limply on the storage bin. These were simple finger exercises,
and although in the first weeks, under Peter's critical eye, he and
Dámaso felt slightly conscience-stricken, in time the "appropria-
tions" became a sporting custom whose ethics were not worth
discussing. Peter's bursts of anger didn't sink in, never got below
the surface.

"If you do the things they do, you'll wind up being like them."

Dámaso Valentín, tip of his tongue in the notch in his tooth, would explode.

"Shut up, for fuck's sake! Can you tell me what's different about us?"

Gervasio's forced imprisonment revived his taste for letter writing. On some afternoons he would avoid Antero Arias's company and sit down in a corner of the lower deck, folder on his knees, and write to Mama Zita, Uncle Felipe Neri, or Manena Abad. Antero Arias would search for him through passageways and decks, and if he found him writing would sit wordlessly beside him on the floor and spend hours in silence, cleaning his nails with a toothpick. The first letter to Mama Zita posed problems of salutation for Gervasio. The expression "Mama Zita," imposed by Mama Obdulia's stupid weakness, was meaningless at this stage in his life. The word "mama" by itself had a trite, soapy, puerile connotation that was unworthy of a seasoned combatant. At last he wrote:

Dear Mother,

We've been on the training ship for two weeks and I still haven't had time to write. We spend all our time hustling, as we say in sailor's slang.

Reveille at 6, while it's still dark: shower on deck even though it's freezing; breakfast (coffee and a piece of bread that you have to make last for the four times we eat); scrubbing the decks with brushes and swabs, while others polish the brass or clean toilets, "heads" as they call them here. At ten, two and a half hours of drill with rifles on our shoulders, on the shipyard quay (Tato Delgado, who shipped on the *Baleares* with Eduardo two weeks ago, got to lead the rank). We have dinner at 1, usually soup, ham and greens, or hash, and two hours later go back to work. The afternoon exercises are more varied and more interesting: gymnastics, rowing, signals, knots, Morse code, rigging . . . We only have to peel potatoes on alternate days. At 6 one of the two brigades, either the port or starboard one, half the crew, can go ashore. The city is small, not as cold as at home, but it does rain a lot. Señora Jacoba, the laundress, washes and irons our clothes quite cheaply. In my next letter I'll send you some pictures: one in work uniform, with my cap on, and the other in the dress uniform, wearing the "rag," as they call the middy blouse here. You know, Dámaso and I laughed so hard when we saw ourselves dressed like that on the first day that an officer had to call us down? Give me news of Papa. See that he gets this letter and tell him I think of him. Kisses to my sisters and the uncles and aunts and a great big hug for you from

Gervasio

Under the influence of a sort of filial modesty, he was perfecting the arts of pretense and evasion, learning to say things without saying them, writing half-truths. He told his mother, for instance, that he was rowing, but omitted the fact that he wasn't much good at feathering; he mentioned that every afternoon one brigade went ashore, but neglected to say that when it was his brigade's turn he had to stay on board because his appearance wasn't smart enough; and finally, he said that he climbed the rigging, but concealed the fact that he did everything he possibly could to avoid it and go no higher than the top of the lower mast because he got so dizzy.

However, the first time that he climbed to the main topgallant mast (with Peter behind, keeping a sharp lookout and covering his rear), he did so without hesitation. Ratlines and shrouds, though they hurt his tender city-boy's feet, did not intimidate him. It was the steep ladder to the main topsail (back turned to the deck, the first serious obstacle of the exercise) that made him beg Peter to stay behind him. His friend kept saying, "Go on up, on up, eyes on the tip of the mast, don't look down," but Gervasio felt the attraction of the abyss and couldn't help looking out of the corner of his eye at the deck. On the topgallant crosstrees he trembled. The water was lapping against the ship's hull, and from above it looked like a tiny bug. What he was expected to do was to move along the yard, bare feet on the foot-rope, hands clinging to the slender bar that stretched above the yard; but he did not dare to do it. The foot-rope, fastened to the ends of the yard, threaded through eyeholes placed at intervals, tightened or loosened under its user's weight, and Gervasio, fearful of being projected like an arrow from a bow, clutched the bar with white knuckles, stiff jaws, and trembling knees.

Beside him Peter urged him to relax, but his head swam up there, fifty meters in the air, with the ship's hull below him like a tiny fish. After they were spread-eagled on the yards Don Manuel Borau, ever watchful, reviewed the formation and blew his whistle.

His companions let go with their right hands when they heard the order and saluted military-fashion, but Gervasio didn't have the courage, and though he began the movement, he noticed that the foot-rope was giving way and grabbed the bar with both hands. The instructor's eagle eye noticed him in spite of the distance, and he took his whistle out of his pocket and yelled harshly, "Salutes at command apply to everyone! Do you hear me, fourth sailor on the topgallant, starboard side? Or do you want to go to the brig?" His tone was even shriller than the whistle's. Don Manuel Borau waited (broad, corpulent, hands behind his back, the nickel-plated whistle stuck in one corner of his mouth, his steely gaze fixed on the mast) and Gervasio hesitated; but the image of that man, whose eyes never left him, threatening him, was stronger than his fear. His left hand grabbed the bar and he slowly raised his right hand until it touched his temple. Pale, his eyelids squeezed shut, his jaws clenched convulsively, he repeated the salute three times until Don Manuel Borau was satisfied. "Inside and down!" he shouted, and ordered them to break formation with a series of shrill whistles.

After that, every time that the exercise of "saluting at command" was announced, Gervasio tried to avoid it or went through all sorts of maneuvers not to climb higher than the top of the lower mast. And yet he wrote to Mama Zita about climbing the rigging as if it were great fun, and preened himself to Manena Abad ("You can see the whole world at your feet, very small, unimportant, as Moses must have seen it from Mount Sinai"). And perhaps showing a bit of unconfessed eroticism, he spoke of "feet torn by the ratlines and shrouds, and flesh bruised by the halyards," but Manena Abad appeared unimpressed by these baroque exaggerations, did not hasten to reply, and was not at all enthusiastic.

Gervasio was obsessed by how to address her, and had awaited her first letter with great emotion. How would she begin it? "Dear, beloved, friend, unforgettable . . ."? But Manena Abad, with her usual skill, avoided the problem: "Hi there, sailor boy! What's going on up there . . . ?" He didn't care for the "sailor boy," which seemed an inadequate description of a warrior. Obviously the girl undervalued his situation, did not think that he was in danger, and he felt cheated by her indifference. He had borne everything with resignation (the crowding, the proximity of rats, dizziness, being shut up on board), imagining that far away, in his home town,

Mama Zita, Manena Abad, Aunt Cruz, Uncle Felipe Neri, his sisters, Señora Zoa, and even Papa Telmo himself, were trembling for his sake. Manena Abad's letter, with its frivolous salutation, had the effect of limiting his ambitions, of suggesting that his small initial failures, despite the fact that he had been marked out since childhood, might outweigh his military gifts. However, he could not bring himself to lie to Uncle Felipe Neri.

"My life here is a constant upheaval, Uncle," he wrote him, knowing that it wasn't true, that his sensitivity had become dulled, so that even the marches that accompanied the two and a half hours of drill had lost their compulsive qualities. "I can't concentrate," he told himself. "I'm not capable of concentrating." And there was something in this. During the *Salve* sung on board in the half-light of evening, another propitious moment, there was a chance for an imaginative daydream; but in this case the trivial, muted, pallid music was not a sufficiently strong stimulus to exalt his imagination.

Another short-lived enthusiasm was that of the torpedo boat the club had dreamed of for so long. A few days after their enlistment Petty Officer Rego had disillusioned them.

"The crews of those boats are never recruited from here."

Peter asked why.

"They have as many as they need. How much of a crew do you think a boat like that takes?"

Utopia receded; it remained a utopia. Gervasio told Uncle Felipe Neri about it: "As for the torpedo boat, it seems not to be viable, Uncle. There aren't many of them and the crews are all complete. In the best of cases they might possibly assign us to one, but never all five of us as we had hoped."

Dámaso Valentín nagged at him: "Think of something else, dammit; your uncle can get us assigned anywhere. I can't stand much more of this."

He complained about the training ship, "the brigantine of useless effort," as he called it.

"What kind of training is this?" he asked. "Can you tell me what you learn by standing in line buck-naked, out in the cold at six in the morning, soaking wet, waiting till the petty officer decides to cross you off the list?"

The question attracted all the recruits' attention to him, and then he would assume an affected voice and answer himself:

"You learn to fuck yourself in the training ship, that's what; that's what it's for."

His philosophy spread, gained proselytes. Every time he opened his mouth the recruits looked at him as if hypnotized. Dámaso would go on, "What good does it do you to scramble up the mast if there isn't any mast on a warship? What good is handling a rifle if sailors don't use rifles?" Using a preacher's technique, he would stop, lower his voice, and finish off his speech: "In the training ship they teach you to have a miserable time so that nothing that happens to you for the rest of your life can seem bad to you; that's what the training is for!"

Peter, officious and disciplined, scolded him.

"You're demoralizing the troops, and a war was never won with demoralized troops."

Usually they chatted on the orlop deck, sheltered from the drizzle, and when the sun came out on deck, at the bow, looking toward the shining city on the other side of the bay. Without their realizing it their vocabulary had become coarser, and Dámaso had started to smoke.

One afternoon Peter was struck by an idea and asked himself whether, since to be transferred to a torpedo boat was not viable, they couldn't enlist on the cruiser *Baleares,* the flagship, where Tato and Eduardo were already serving? In a ship whose crew numbered more than a thousand there would be no problem about adding three new sailors. And even apart from that, could they imagine how happy Tato and Eduardo would be on the day when they saw them appear through the gangway with their white sea bags on their shoulders? Peter's exultation was contagious. With the same enthusiasm with which he had planned the idea of the torpedo boat in the club, he now speculated about the cruiser *Baleares.* Peter described the ship to them (displacement, overall length, speed, turrets, fire control, and so on), arousing their desires, confirming their determination. At bottom this was what they had always wanted. Gervasio even began to suspect that in the *Baleares* there would be a possibility for heroic action. Dámaso Valentín's brisk slap on his back made him even more enthusiastic.

"Come on, dammit, write to your uncle!"

And that same night Gervasio, with a slight stirring at the back of his neck, wrote a fervent letter to Uncle Felipe Neri, imploring him to use his good offices until he could get them accepted on the flagship with their friends Tato and Eduardo.

On the afternoon of February 28, 1938, Don Manuel Borau, the seamanship instructor, unexpectedly cancelled the military appearance review that had been ordered by Naval Command in the month of January, and for the first time in five weeks the port-side brigade went ashore with no other requisite than the personal cleanliness review. However, on March 1, 2, and 3, Don Manuel Borau again held the military appearance review and on March 4 and 5 again omitted it, without any apparent reasons for the change. Hence, on March 6, the day that his brigade was off duty, Gervasio was prepared. He put on his shore uniform and awaited events (if Don Manuel Borau, after the personal cleanliness review, went to the gangplank to perform the military appearance review, he would return to the orlop deck and remain on board as usual; in the opposite case he could go ashore with his brigade for the second time since his arrival on the training ship). Gervasio feared that Don Manuel Borau might recognize him, but this did not happen; with a firm and mechanical step, his face puffy, his gray eyes cold, the instructor inspected the brigade without noticing him and immediately afterward, following Don Gaspar Hungría's imperceptible nod of approval, he gave the order to break ranks and Gervasio, almost without realizing it, was free (running with long strides down the cobblestones of the quay, turning around the dry docks, the shipyard, and at last passing through the big gate before the sentry's indifferent eyes), like a schoolboy on vacation. Peter and Dámaso vied with each other to orient him, to serve as his guide. They bought tickets for a movie and left when the picture was half over. They wandered through most of the city, and at nightfall went to the house of Señora Jacoba, the laundress in the upper part of town. After exchanging their laundry bags she stood looking at Gervasio maternally, her powerful arms with their thick reddened wrists crossed on her breast.

"So this is the missing one? He's a fine fellow, the naughty boy."
Back on the street they took a narrow alley to the Plaza Deschamps. Peter's fine intuition noticed an imperceptible change in the atmo-

sphere. "I don't know!" he explained. "More people on the street, tighter groups, a strange feeling. As if they all had somebody ill at home. Can't you see it?" Dámaso laughed, but Gervasio observed in the eyes of passersby an expression of connivance, of helplessness, that they had not had before; a sort of need to feel protected. Small groups chatted on the sidewalks in low voices, emphasizing their words with exaggerated gestures. From a second-floor balcony three girls applauded when half a dozen drunken sailors went by. A boy in a gray workman's blouse was closing the trapdoor in front of a hardware store. Some faces expressed a stony seriousness, like that of the people who used to attend the funerals at Santa Brígida. Peter looked around them. "Something's happened," he repeated. He took Gervasio by the arm and they went into a café. There the strange atmosphere in the street was accentuated by the pathetic emptiness of the tables, the idle waiters with white napkins over their shoulders, an engineering officer drinking alone, in silence, at one end of the bar. The skinny waiter, brows drooping, came toward them, while the officer turned toward the other five and said thickly, "If it hadn't been for the English there wouldn't have been any survivors." The waiter regarded them indifferently, frowning, his expression mournful. Peter said, "Has something happened?"

The waiter tried without success to raise his eyebrows.

"Don't you know? The Reds sank the *Baleares* last night, off Cartagena. National Radio has just announced it."

"My God!" exclaimed Gervasio, and looked at the shocked, speechless faces of his friends.

In the street discussions were going on in front of every doorway. They met a trembling old woman who was staggering along muttering to herself. The applause from the balconies became more frequent and broke out every time a small group of sailors or soldiers passed by. Two little girls were chasing each other in the crowd, screaming, unaware of the disaster. A naval captain passed by them, so absorbed in his thoughts that he didn't notice their salutes. Behind him two very young girls, almost children, walked along crying, each holding a handkerchief. Two silhouettes, a man's and a woman's, filtered through the curtains of a glassed-in balcony, were listening to the monotonous muttering of a radio.

The eyes of passersby seemed to reflect stupor rather than grief, as if rejecting something that could not be helped. An automobile carrying a vice-admiral passed them, sounding its horn. Gervasio was surprised when he heard himself saying, "Tato can't have been killed. He could swim better than Johnny Weismuller."

Dámaso looked at him. He was rolling a cigarette as he walked. He said laconically, as if he were condensing long and arduous thought into two words, "Those bastards."

A little boy who was running in the opposite direction shoved him, spilling the tobacco. He swore in annoyance. He was intensely pale, his thin lips taut and lusterless. The notes of an accordion came from the street corner, one muted military march after another. People were crowding around a ragged blind man who was sitting on the ground, his dirty beret full of coins. They stopped. A woman dressed in black was weeping beside him, others were tossing coins at him, while the vagabond forced mournful groans out of the accordion and then played the sunken cruiser's hymn. Gervasio felt his hair starting to rise under his cap, but a full display did not take place. The music and the blind man's tuneless voice were more funereal than martial. The boys started to walk again, aimlessly. On the square in front of Naval Command headquarters several hundred persons had gathered: stunned civilians, drunken sailors, tearful women giving voice to unintelligible laments. A hoarse voice demanded entrance and information. Peter said sententiously, as if to himself: "As far as the war's concerned this is a setback; for Galicia it's a catastrophe." A little girl with a bow in her hair and wearing a very short blue coat cried for her mother. The crowd stirred restlessly, demanded names and details of the tragedy. Dámaso turned to Peter.

"Why don't we go?" he asked.

Groups of sailors were walking disconsolately toward the dockyard fence. Peter took Dámaso Valentín by the arm.

"Let's go," he said.

His wide-set eyes were clouded and he had two pink spots on his cheekbones. Gervasio laid a soft hand on his shoulder. He felt lost, in need of comforting and being comforted. But where? How? By whom?

"Let's go," he said.

The paving stones rang under their boots. In the feeble light of the street lamps the dockyard's enormous quay did not seem like the same place where they received their daily instruction.

"It doesn't seem possible," Gervasio mused.

A sailor, holding his cap in his hand, was vomiting in the shadow of a repair shed while his companion supported his forehead. At the end of the gangplank a youngster dressed in work uniform, almost a child, was crying silently in a corner, waiting for someone. Little groups of sailors whispered on the deck. On the lower decks the tables were set up, but no one was sitting at them, and the off-duty sailors who had just come from shore formed into groups with those who had stayed on board, talking about the news. It was hard to get through the passageways, but when they reached the mess they saw, presiding over the empty table, Petty Officer Rego's noble grizzled head (right hand supporting his brow) in front of a bottle, as if he were pondering some complex problem. He raised his eyes when he heard them and looked at all three one after the other with his heavy, sleepy-looking eyes.

"They've told you, have they?" he said in a level, strangely dull voice. "They lay in wait for them at night, in ambush, without offering battle. Eight against one, and by treachery! Face to face they'd never have been able to sink them."

He picked up the bottle by its neck, but with a mature and responsible gesture Peter gently took it out of his hand and the petty officer did not protest, merely gazed at him out of his watery eyes before his head fell on his arm and he went to sleep.

CHAPTER 16

The sailors pressed around the bulletin board in silence, but as soon as Petty Officer Ortiguera (sleepy eyes, protruding ears, pursed mouth) appeared with the list in his hand and fastened it up the crowd began to churn, the sailors pushed and shoved in front of the glass, swore, standing on tiptoe, trying to ascertain the fate of relatives and friends once and for all after a thirty-six-hour wait. Then for a few seconds, until the nearest sailors could read the first names, the training ship stayed in suspense. The gloomiest rumors had circulated the day before (everyone had been lost; there were no survivors. The *Canarias* had been sunk too. The Red fleet, emboldened by its success, was preparing a landing on Mallorca), and now, though after delay, the official report gave the dimensions of the tragedy: the ship that sank in the small hours of March 6 had been the *Baleares,* and the number of sailors picked up by the British destroyers *Boreas* and *Kempenfelt* was 317 (of its 1,200-man complement); that is, the dead and missing reached the figure of 900, seventy-five percent of the ship's company. The training ship shuddered from deck to keel. Aboard it were fathers, sons, brothers, friends of the sunken cruiser's sailors, and the chances of finding that they were alive, now statistically established, were one in four. That was why the crew members, crowded between the gunwale and the upper works, were milling around impatiently in front of the lists of survivors, typed in alphabetical order, which Petty Officer Ortiguera had just posted on the bulletin board. The sailors shoved again, elbowed one another, pushed, shouted, swore, and from time to time someone who had learned the truth after a vain examination of the list pushed his way through the tumult and disappeared sobbing into the nearest hatchway, or leaned on the rail in the bow with his head in his hands, gazing at the city empty-eyed and stunned, while others—fewer of them—heedlessly jumped up and down in the front rows, laughing and crying, saying the beloved name over and over, shouting the good news to those who hadn't seen the list yet, making them share it: the man presumed dead was alive.

Gervasio, Peter, and Dámaso waited, leaning against the rail, until the crowd had decreased so that those most directly affected by the catastrophe could inform themselves, and as the crush lessened and the group began to thin out they started their slow progress toward the bulletin board, taking two steps forward and one back, magnetized by that implacable list which allowed no appeal and coldly decided who, among the cruiser's crew, had died and which others had had the good luck to survive. Gervasio's knees were weak and his heart raced, and he could feel the warm, intermittent gusts of Peter's breath on his neck. And as soon as his eyes made out the names on the list, he anxiously spelled under his breath those listed under the letter C: Cabo, Castillo, Coloma, Colomer, Cobo, Coronado . . . Custodio! There it was! Custodio

Maeso (Eduardo). He yelled something in exhilaration, he didn't know what, among the other voices, and behind him Dámaso's crowing voice repeated, "Paleface is immortal!" Something shook the back of his neck, perhaps Dámaso's jubilation, perhaps the imagined picture of Eduardo battling the waves in the dark of night while the cruiser sank. Certainly, the incipient prickling at his nape grew more pronounced as he read the surnames under the letter D and the name of Fortunato Delgado did not appear. He read the list again more slowly, and when he heard Peter's voice behind him ("It's not there. They've killed Tato"), his hair rose straight up as if paying homage to his dead friend. It stood up under his cap like the prickles on a thistle, obstinately pressing until the cap became detached from his head and rose like a rag. Merciful hands were laid on his head, aborting the phenomenon, and when he turned around he saw Peter with his hands still on his head in a sacramental attitude, as if anointing him, and their fleeting glances, veiled by tears, met for an instant. As they turned away, Damasito between them, with supporting arms around each other's shoulders, he repeated like a refrain, "They've killed Tato; those bastards."

The news of that unthinkable casualty spread through the training ship, and even though most of the ship's company had closer losses to mourn, they grieved with them and concluded that the very fact that that compendium of naval virtues had been lost was a sure sign of the explosion's violence.

"If somebody was to tell me that there'd been only one survivor, I would have answered without hesitation: 'Tato Delgado,'" said Petty Officer Rego, greatly moved. Don Manuel Borau himself, always so chilly and frugal of speech, referred in the laconic sentence with which he closed the military mass held on the quay, to "those who shared our tasks only a few days ago, making the name of this training ship proud, and today are on duty among the stars," a remark which in Peter's opinion referred specifically to their dead friend.

Tato's death aroused a dry anger in Gervasio rather than grief, a desire for revenge that had nothing to do with patriotism. On some nights when he went to bed he would remember Tato, the red ribbon tied around his blond head, playing water polo, twisting and turning in the water like a dolphin, and later, dressed in his checkered jacket, singing "Katiuska" at the top of his voice on the Paseo de las Piscinas. And then he would say to himself, "We have no alternative but to get out of here. We have to avenge Tato somehow." And, spurred by this desire, he wrote a feverish letter to Uncle Felipe Neri ("Heroics," his uncle wrote in the oilcloth-covered notebook) that was a devouring flame: "The *Baleares* has fallen gloriously, Uncle, and with it our friend Tato Delgado. We simply can't wait to get off this ship. I won't sleep soundly until I know that he's been avenged." He did not request, as he had done at other times, but rather demanded his uncle's mediation, and in the heat of creation adopted as his own the drunken words spoken by Petty Officer Rego on the night the news was received: "The enemy squadron didn't offer battle. In ambush in the dark, it set a trap for the *Baleares.* Face to face they'd never have been able to sink her." On Peter's advice he added, "The *Canarias* or the *Juan de Austria,* Uncle, sister ships of the *Baleares,* might be where we could serve." Seated on the deck, notebook on his knees, Peter was writing to Eduardo Custodio congratulating him (What was he congratulating him for? Because he'd saved his life? For his actions in combat, about which Peter knew nothing? For the cruiser's heroic end?), begging him to answer immediately (if the censorship would allow it) with details about the sinking, if the cruisers were sailing alone or under convoy, if there had been a bombardment or previous engagement, number of ships in the attacking force and their formation. The strategist underlying Peter's personality inevitably came to the surface, causing him to forget his grief. The last lines of his letter were devoted to Tato: "What were his duties on board? Did the explosion of the torpedoes get him? Or was it true that the magazine blew up and took all the ship's superstructure with it?"

Next morning, unexpectedly, Peter received a letter from Tato Delgado. The return address said, "Cruiser *Baleares,* Palma de Mallorca or wherever she may be." Gervasio's hand shook as he touched it. After his experiences with Antero Arias, surprising events with certain supernatural features had given him trembling fits. "Doesn't it scare you? It's like getting a letter from the other world," said Dámaso. But Gervasio thought about the return address, "Wherever she may be." Had Tato sensed, perhaps, that by the time the letter arrived the cruiser would be at the bottom of the sea? Damasito tried to force a smile but only succeeded in pressing his thin upper lip against the gum like a rabbit, showing the notched tooth. In his letter, dated March 5, the day before the sinking, after apologizing for the delay in writing, Tato told about his sudden transfer to the *Baleares,* his post in Turret One and Eduardo Custodio's in Station A, a surface fire control station. As if their thoughts had crossed, he suggested the possibility of all five of them meeting someday on the flagship ("maybe it's a utopian idea, but let's dream, and give wings to utopia"). Gervasio and Dámaso Valentín, heads together, were reading the letter along with Peter, over his shoulder.

"You'd think it was a last will and testament, for God's sake," said Damasito, taking a packet of tobacco out of his uniform pocket and spilling a little into the palm of his hand.

"He blew up inside the turret. That explains everything."

"What does it explain?"

"That he died. The seizings kept him from getting out. He didn't have a chance to hit the water."

Horrified, Gervasio pondered Tato's imprisonment, and unconsciously established a connection between the return address on his letter and the sinking of the *Baleares.* What tortuous paths had Tato's mind followed to intuit that by the time the letter reached its destination the cruiser might not *be* in Palma de Mallorca? A sharp uneasiness caused him to consult Antero Arias, who turned Tato's letter over and over in his clumsy hands while he told Gervasio in sibylline tones about morbid intuitions, states of divination, presages and premonitions. To settle the question he invited him to meet one day ("if that sonofabitch Borau doesn't reestablish the Inquisition") in the private room at the La Marina café to try to convoke Tato's spirit. Dámasito laughed about it, but Peter was angry.

"When are you going to send that idiot on his way?"

But though Gervasio docilely accepted his advice and had nothing more to do with Antero Arias, Tato's death continued to be a permanent source of reflection. Like all those who died on the *Baleares,* as popular opinion had it, his friend was a hero. But could one accept a hero who had no intention of being one, a hero because of some seizings? Could Tato, hermetically sealed in a steel

box as he was, have done anything but die? What did he really do
in there? Did he yell, cry, pray, implore, curse, despair, scrabble at
the bulkheads, beat his head against them, or did he serenely accept
the death that was approaching? Would not heroism lie precisely
in that detail? Ever since his solitary daydreams as he listened to
the program "On the joyous path to peace," Gervasio had scorned
secret, anonymous, silent death as useless. Concealed heroism
served for nothing when it lost its didactic character; it stopped
being heroism. If action could be captured by a hidden camera that
would demonstrate that the dead man had not died like a rat,
soiling his underwear, but firing against the enemy to the last
cartridge, it would assume a different meaning. But in the present
case, without witnesses, without documentation, nothing was left
but doubt, unless the man who died in war was a hero for the
simple reason that he had died. Did not the hero, like the saint,
need some champion to demonstrate his singularity against the
arguments of the devil's advocate? Sometimes he recalled, painfully, Peter's ironic comment of some months ago, when he had
said that Gervasio didn't want to be a hero but an exhibitionist.
Was that his unconfessed desire, perhaps?

Gervasio kept his ruminations to himself; he didn't want to share
them. He knew that as far as Peter was concerned Tato's heroism
was unquestionable, an obvious fact. Peter venerated his friend,
admired both his life and his death; he represented an example to
be imitated. This conviction led Gervasio to conclude that the only
way to make Peter admire him, to deserve Peter's applause, would
be to die in action. All the rest was excuses. From this viewpoint
it seemed natural for Peter not to be impressed by the raising of
Gervasio's hair (a trick of physics, or at most pure electrical phenomena, as Uncle Vidal said). His behavior during the most recent
episode, pityingly placing his hands on Gervasio's head to avoid
the laughable spectacle of his cap flying off, had been eloquent in
this regard.

One afternoon while they were peeling potatoes on deck,
Dámaso Valentín told him about Peter's plan, after the war was
over, to exchange the figurehead that presided over the club for a
big photograph of Tato, bordered with the colors of the flag. It was
a blow for Gervasio. He was jealous. He was jealous of a dead man,

and within himself he determined to die too, so that his photograph would preside over the club in the near future along with Tato Delgado's; and Peter, with Manena Abad (a grown-up, perpetually celibate Manena Abad, ever faithful to his memory) would place a bunch of carnations below it on every anniversary of his death, to commemorate his sacrifice.

Against all expectations, discipline on the training ship was not relaxed following the sinking of the *Baleares.* After a few days of a certain laxity strictness reappeared, more inflexible than ever, in accordance with a resolution that was no less evident for remaining unexpressed: the ship had to turn out such tough and experienced sailors that the tragedy could not happen again. Don Manuel Borau revived the military appearance reviews, with such strict standards that on some afternoons more than twenty-five percent of the off-duty brigade was rejected and returned to the lower deck. Antero Arias, with his skinny shoulders, shed his blouse in a rage, showing his thin, pigeon-breasted torso for a few moments, and cursed the Navy and its bulletin boards.

"What I say is, in this country you have to be a pretty-boy to enlist in the Navy."

Gervasio also returned to ostracism. He stopped putting on his dress uniform, stopped trying to pass review. But now a little flame of hope cheered him: the conviction that Uncle Felipe Neri must be operating at high levels, and that in consequence his days in the training ship were coming to an end. On the other hand, determined to rise above adversity, be prepared for any alternative, he chose the most difficult and dangerous exercises (he was trying to convince himself and convince his friend Peter that the sinking of the *Baleares* and Tato's death had changed him). He rowed enthusiastically, underwent instruction without flagging, became an expert signalman, and each time that Don Manuel Borau ordered "salute on command" with his piercing whistles, there was Gervasio, the first to volunteer, scrambling up the rigging to the topgallant, climbing imperturbably past the lower masts, spread-eagling himself on the foot-rope without hesitation, mastering his vertigo. But Peter did not seem to notice his progress and was passive, aloof from his efforts; and just as in the past he had never criticized his lack of courage, he did not praise his boldness now; as always, he said nothing and punctiliously did his duty.

One morning, during mail call on the waist, Gervasio received a bulky letter from Uncle Felipe Neri. The whole family had written in it, from Mama Zita to Florita; there was even a half sheet of square-ruled paper written in the bullring by Papa Telmo. Besides his challenging "Who but God?" and his paean of praise to the heroes of the *Baleares,* Uncle Felipe Neri informed him that the question of transfer "was under way," which implied (for Gervasio, who had supposed it settled) a new delay. To the depression brought on by this letter was added unfavorable news from Mama Zita about Eduardo Custodio. Eduardo's life had indeed been saved, but he was hospitalized, bandaged like a mummy, with third-degree burns and a serious eye infection that would require a slow process of recuperation. The doctors who were caring for him were not optimistic. "Your letter, which his mother read to him, comforted him very much. He wanted me to tell all of you that Tato, like everyone serving in Turret One, was blown up when the torpedoes exploded." Gervasio sighed deeply. Peter, sitting on the storage bin of a compartment on the orlop deck with his forehead resting on his bent knees, wondered which was the crueler fate for a boy of seventeen, blindness or death. Damasito, sitting cross-legged on the linoleum, folded the edges of a cigarette paper, tipped into it a few shreds of tobacco from which he had previously extracted the hard bits, and rolled a cigarette. After Gervasio had read his mother's letter he passed it to Peter and opened Papa Telmo's note. He never told his friends anything about his father's notes. He feared both their comments and their silences. In his opinion, his father had not responded to the claims of the Uprising. He was obstinate and ungrateful. At first Gervasio had been sure of his conversion, but as time passed he accepted his silence. His notes were usually short and elementary ("I'm well," "I feel down-hearted," "I'm warm," "I'm cold," "The package of sweets delighted the whole community"). They almost never referred to the war, perhaps to keep from compromising Uncle Felipe Neri, but on this occasion he made an ethical judgment about Gervasio's last letter: "War is the great ambuscade, my son. The one who prepares the best ambushes will be the victor. War means the end of clean sport, of 'fair play' as the English call it. But the important thing is to recognize this and not criticize the enemy for tricks that we ourselves will be willing to play tomorrow. Is your little head so sectarian that it's incapable of recognizing a meritorious action in your adversary? Good-bye, my dear son, may God go with you on the next part of your course." He crumpled the paper angrily and Peter raised his head in surprise.

"Is something wrong?"

"My father."

"What's the matter with him?"

"Same as always."

"Did you think he was going to change his ideas because they didn't agree with yours?"

Gervasio did not answer. There was a hidden challenge in Papa Telmo's letter. Only some courageous action on Gervasio's part could make him change his opinion. But where was an action that Papa Telmo would not consider a stratagem? He left the rail and lay down on the linoleum, his fingers interlaced behind his head. He was annoyed. Even Eduardo's lamentable situation seemed less meritorious after he had read his father's note. Was that some sort of Voltairian joke, to hope that God would go with him on the last part of his course? How did he dare to invoke the name of God? How make God compatible with the horde? If the horde, whose ideas Papa Telmo shared, had burned God in any number of convents, had fired on God before Uncle Fadrique's eyes on the Cerro de los Angeles, what significance could be assigned to his invocation? He closed his eyes and shook his head in discouragement: "I'll never write to him again. For me, it's the same as if he'd died."

On the following afternoon, when Peter and several other groups in the port-side brigade were climbing the rigging, others were rowing in the dirty waters of the port, and Dámaso and Gervasio were conversing with signal flags on the afterdeck, an unexpected voice yelled from the top of the topgallant mast, "The *Juan de Austria* is coming into the river!"

A huge commotion ensued. The signalmen hastened to communicate the news with their flags to the boats that were rowing in the bay, Dámaso shouted it down the hatchways, the news ran from mouth to mouth and group to group; it was received with such jubilation that within a few minutes all activity on board had ceased and the ship's company was crowded on deck or swarming into the shrouds, turning it into a blur of waving white handkerchiefs, while a lean, stylized, gray silhouette of enormous dimensions, flag waving on its stern, entered the port after coming around the last curve in the river's mouth. For no more reason than that, enthusiasm overflowed. The cruiser's sudden appearance offered an opportunity for satisfaction after the sinking of the *Baleares;* it was almost like revenge, or testimony of a resurrection. The ship was passing so close that they could see the sailors drawn up to port and to starboard, standing firm, heads high, while on the afterdeck the band played the march "The Trumpets Sound." Gervasio watched the ship's progress unblinkingly, its slow advance cleaving the oily waters, the slight smoking of its oblong funnel, its solid, resting turrets with their crews on the deck below . . . Without any previous symptoms he noticed a stirring at the back of his neck and a chill down his back, but in a quick reaction, fighting down the exciting pleasure of having his hair rise, he hastily buttoned the earflaps of his cap under his chin. The display had been exorcised.

"Hot damn, what a ship!"

He heard Dámaso's admiring exclamation beside him. The cruiser had just dropped anchor opposite them, bow turned to the dry dock. The harsh rattle of the anchor chain in the hawse-holes drowned out the music of the band. Paradoxically, the cruiser's coming to a stop loosened tongues, and the training ship, which had been silent during its maneuver, broke out in cheers, shouts, vague rumors, daring and contradictory guesses. For the most pessimistic the arrival of the *Juan de Austria* meant that it had been damaged in the battle of March 6, while petty officers and officers, zealous defenders of Navy morale, resistant to all dramatizing, insisted that it was a routine visit to clean the hull. No one could agree, but at last, after laborious maneuvers, by nightfall the cruiser was a prisoner in the dry dock, stranded on the ways under floodlights amid the frantic activity of pulleys, hanging platforms, soldering apparatus, cranes, and capstans. The hammering of rivets sounded in the shipyard day and night, like an automatic drum. During their free time Gervasio, Peter, and Dámaso, leaning on the rail, rapturously watched the workmen's activity, the diligence of the sailors on deck. Dámaso got very excited.

"Get in touch with your uncle, dammit. If we let it get away now, God knows when we'll have another chance."

"My uncle has it in mind."

"Yes, but does he know that the *Juan de Austria* is here?"

After heated debates they agreed that the quickest way to inform him would be a telegram, but the telegram was never sent. Next morning Don Ildefonso Barbosa, commander-in-chief of the training ship, called them to his cabin and told them to get ready to leave, for Don Ventura Escribá, commander-in-chief of the cruiser *Don Juan de Austria,* had put in a request for them.

CHAPTER
17

Off Cape St. Vincent the cruiser made a forty-five-degree turn to port (the violence of the turn was especially noticeable in the ship's list and the vibration of the bulkheads), and after the turn came the sea breeze, a southwest wind so strong that it shredded the flag and threatened to tear the cap from his head. The sea was rising, and whitecaps showed on the wave tops. The bow entered the waves with such force that what a few minutes before had been a gentle, sleep-inducing roll, like a rocking chair, became an abrupt pitching movement (the ship's bow alternately rose and fell, advanced in rotating, screwlike movements). Gervasio felt the change of course in the soles of his bare feet, but paid little attention to it. Face to the wind, holding on to the chain of the spar deck with both hands, he squinted his eyes, trying to assume a seamanly facial expression, proud of his first experience at sea. The night before he had written about it to Mama Zita and Uncle Felipe Neri, and though nothing in the world could diminish the joy of his debut, when he wrote the return address ("Cruiser *Juan de Austria.* Palma de Mallorca or wherever she may be") he had shuddered violently.

Before the ship left port the commander of Station H, Lieutenant Don Mario Millares, with his squashed cap with the wire missing and his careless ways, had assigned him a number and a job: "Gervasio García de la Lastra, 377A, speaking tube." It was an important responsibility. He would transmit the officer's instructions to the antiaircraft guns through the tube: that is, from now on he would be that officer's spokesman. His friends had seen him smile beatifically when he heard his number, so that after Don Mario had left, Javier Medina the poet, veteran of the station, his curly head bare, his aquiline nose jutting above his prominent teeth, had asked him, "Do you like your number, 377A?" And when Gervasio nodded he added, "Don't worry; that's what we'll call you."

And this was the way Gervasio García de la Lastra became 377A, a number followed by a letter, a coded name like a spy's. Petty Officer Pita, head of his group, assigned him a locker, a hammock, and a blanket. Petty Officer Pita, short, bull-necked, and serious, was a man of few words. The first thing that Gervasio noticed about him was his laconic manner, the gloomy sadness of his face. He was shy and solitary, and always went around as if thinking about something else. His erratic gaze came from grayish-blue eyes of shifting color, lighted by a little self-absorbed flame and in any case rather vague. At mess times he hardly ate (he would visit his locker or the steward, always returning a bit flushed with alcohol), and while on duty he constantly read adventure novels, a practice that emphasized his isolation. But during his watches, when he was unable to read his novels, his somber stare would wander over the sea as if he were learning it by heart, and he could spend hours without moving a muscle of his face. Unlike the normal standard for his rank, Petty Officer Pita was not authoritarian; rather, he was irresolute, tolerant, flexible about rules. Despite the fact that it was forbidden ("After the portholes are closed, no cigarettes on deck"), he himself smoked during the night watches, not even bothering to hide the flame under the rail.

Petty Officer Tubío, the telemetry specialist, was not a pugnacious man either. His flat, contented face was all of a piece with his voice, which was soft and uninflected. He was chubby and round-faced, a good conversationalist, and very fond of games of chance. An Andalusian and an ex-seminarian, his clerical air, which he would probably never lose, showed in the gestures of his soft hands and venerable-looking combination of features. Luis Naveira, "El Cativo"—Nasty—a beardless second-class seaman with childishly pink cheeks, often teased him about the vocation he had abandoned, attributing his departure to sex, but Petty Officer Tubío flatly rejected this.

"My wife attracted me out of the seminary with her eyes rather than her breasts."

Because of his modest rank he felt a reverential respect for intellectuals, and that was perhaps the reason for his mildness in a fire control station where almost everyone either had a university degree or was on the way to getting one. He could foresee the future, and guessed that several of the boys now under his orders would become important persons someday. He was especially humble and deferential with Javier Medina, a fifth-year architecture student who wrote poems in his spare time; he used the formal mode of address to him, and on one memorable occasion even addressed him as "Don Javier." Actually Javier Medina was entranced by the sea and had decided to give up his architecture studies and enroll in the Naval Academy as soon as the war was over. Petty Officer Tubío knew this, and for him it was no trouble at all to leap forward in time and imagine Javier Medina already a lieutenant with two stripes on his sleeve. Petty Officer Tubío's conviction that his present subordinate would soon be his superior placed him in an inferior position in advance.

After the depersonalized promiscuity of the training ship, Gervasio found a joyous revival of individualism in the cruiser. Even Peter, when he could find a quiet corner, had taken up his cabinet work again. His skill with his hands aroused his companions' curiosity. In absorption under the rocord, using photographs that Javier Medina had given him, he now went to work on building a model of the cruiser. He worked tirelessly in his miniature shipyard, and his activity became a collective pastime. It was a rare sailor who, when he came off duty, didn't ask about the progress of his work.

"Hey, Nauta, how's it going?"

For Peter, also by an inspiration of Javier Medina's, had ceased to be Peter and become "Nauta," seaman par excellence, not only because of his skillful hands but his knowledge of naval tactics and strategy. Little by little Nauta became Station H's center of gravity, so that it turned into a replica of the club. Not even the poker sessions were lacking; these were presided over by Petty Officer Tubío, and Miodelo, skinny "Santoña," and Fermín Linaje, "Escorbuto"—Scurvy—also participated in them.

Olive-skinned Fermín Linaje was an apprehensive, hairy, short-armed fellow who believed that lack of vitamins was still the chief scourge of sailors. His thick negroid lips and his nutritional obsessions reminded Gervasio of Papa Telmo's body type and his manias.

"What rations don't give, the sun supplies," he would say.

And in accordance with his creed, on sunny days he would lie on the rafts on the spar deck and spend hour after hour there, dressed in shorts, taking the sun. In poker he was a fearsome and imperturbable opponent. Few dared to call Scurvy's hand when he doubled the bet and his mulatto lips bent downward in a scornful grimace. As lecherous as Nasty, he often asked José Antonio Lago, "El Pintor"—Painter—to draw "a string of great broads" in the nude, which he then reviewed with lascivious delight, larding his contemplation of them with obscene comments. Painter, on the other hand, was as delicate as a porcelain figurine and seemed like a rare example of another race. He wore a size six shoe, and his whole neat, fastidious figure was in harmony with the size of his foot. He was the same age as Javier Medina and had studied fine arts; he never stopped drawing figures, either imaginary or from life, on a sketch pad. On calm days he would set up a little easel on the spar deck, the right size for his stature, and paint marine watercolors, pictures that departed from the norm for such paintings by not being pretty-pretty but instead contained a tormented beauty, perhaps because of the gloomy tones of the sea, the opacity of the light, or the dismasted ships that figured in them. When he was in a good mood he would invite the sailors with the strongest faces to pose for him (Scurvy, Javier Medina, Bartolomé Roselló, or "Rubio Colino"—Blondie—of the seraphic features), and made grotesque caricatures of them which were highly praised by the rest of his companions.

After the overcrowding of the training ship the cruiser meant the recuperation of individual life, a return to privacy. Separation of the ship's company into small communities (fire control, turrets, machinery, antiaircraft) meant replacing the training ship's miscellaneous promiscuousness by an attempt at domestic existence. But besides this division, Station H's autonomy was determined by its location on the upper deck, with only two means of access: one, the direct, was the iron ladder over the ventilator shaft, and the other a Jacob's ladder behind the stack, reached by the spar deck. This meant that Station H was not a place on the way to anything else, but that there had to be a deliberate reason for going there.

Contrary to what Gervasio had expected, shipboard practices did not change after they put to sea. Aside from watches, which naturally bore more responsibility, everything was the same. He had experienced the moment of their departure with great emotion, and now, on the vast and turbulent sea, he had the vivid idea that peace had been left behind, that he was entering the adventurous zone of war (there was no reason why he might not spy the periscope of an enemy submarine in the depths of the tossing water, for it was their duty as lookouts to discover them).

Buffeted by the wind, leaning on the chain on the spar deck, which he had previously been clutching with both hands, he regarded in astonishment (as a child examines its favorite toy) the black machine gun that fired tracer bullets. The nearness of the thing, the fact that it was ready for use, the solitude around him, awakened his dormant heroic fantasies. He took one step toward it and sat on the iron seat, turned the crank, and the gun barrel obediently moved from one side to the other. Trembling with emotion, he rested the padded butt against his shoulder, pressed his cheek against it and, peering up the tube, said in a low voice amid the wind's roar, "Brrrrrrp, brrrrrrp, brrrrrrp."

He pursued imaginary airplanes across the cloudy sky through the sights and felt powerful and invincible. Amid the tumult of that heavy cruiser his was the only clear head. He repeated the gun's movement from port to starboard and imitated three more bursts: "Brrrrrrp, brrrrrrp, brrrrrrp."

A small smile appeared on his face. An enemy airplane, hit in the nose, tried to gain altitude, went into a spin, and crashed on the sea's surface. Afire with enthusiasm, Gervasio pressed the machine gun against his shoulder, got another airplane into his sights, and just as he was about to fire a new burst felt a sharp shock on the back of his neck; but before his hair could rise he heard the mocking voice of Bartolomé Roselló, "Mallorquín," behind him.

"Hey, 377A, playing war?"

His enigmatic, interrogative eyebrows seemed to repeat the question. Gervasio stood up and timidly pointed toward the machine gun.

"I'd never seen one of those things close to."

Bartolomé Roselló started toward the station.

"Let's see if you show the same desire for action when the planes really come."

Gervasio, alone again, his balance disturbed by the listing of the ship, grabbed the spar-deck chain. The ship was bucking; it made him feel like going down on his hands and knees. Frightened by the whistling of the wind, he took refuge on the lower deck, but the swaying of the bulkheads, the shifting level of the floor plates, increased his confusion. Supporting himself on the lockers, he moved toward the bow, but as he took a step the deck seemed to slide out from under his bare feet, and when he tried to set his foot down, the ship moved toward him; he stumbled and almost fell. While he was still confused a sudden lurch to starboard threw him against the storage bins. He was breathing in short bursts, gasping. He tried to calm himself, to match his steps to the ship's oscillations from side to side by anticipating them, but the attempt was useless. The sea never repeated its previous motion and was growing more violent. He felt cold sweat in his armpits and his stomach contracted with a feeling of nausea. Convinced that fresh air would help, he staggered up on deck again. A gust of wind, strengthened by a yawing motion, threw him against the rail so violently that

Gervasio thought for a moment that the sea was going to swallow him and stood for a while trembling, clutching the railing, until the opposite movement returned him to his original position near the superstructure. He fastened the earflaps of his cap under his chin in the vain hope that it would be easier to control his brains that way. The waves beat against the ship's sides and swept over the deck with a noise like surf, but smothered by the howling of the storm. The gusts of wind were so violent, the ship's lurches so abrupt, that the boy slid or stopped, impelled by an irresistible force. The menace of the sea, the wind's howls, his own feeling of uneasiness, caused him to return to the lower deck, but the diabolical arrangement of the ladder's steps (which either made him stumble or sit down, according to the tilt of the ship) increased his confusion. He could hardly understand the bugle call over the loudspeaker.

"Set up tables," he said to himself in surprise.

The very thought of eating contracted his stomach. With a pasty mouth and a dry tongue, the sight of his friends chatting in the ship's well as if nothing abnormal were going on completed his demoralization. He retreated toward the stern, staggering. The repetition of the bugle call made him curl his lips in a grimace of repugnance. He hopped from table to table, leaning on their edges. In addition to his mental confusion and the sense of blockage in his stomach, now he was beginning to feel nausea. Dizziness assailed him, and without thinking he hastily climbed upward through the first hatchway he could find. There was no dividing line between the dirty, ragged sea and the sky, just as in José Antonio Lago's seascapes: they were one and the same. He tried to walk along the inner passageway near the superstructure, but the constantly fluctuating waves made him stagger like a drunken man. On the stern the shredded flag was whipping against itself; but that torn and ragged ensign, which had formerly aroused such emotions in him, now seemed to be a replica of himself. He thought that if he could vomit he might feel better, but was afraid of being thrown over the rail. He squatted near a scupper hole, out of the wind, and tried to bring on nausea by pressing two fingers against his tongue, but his stomach rebelled and contracted uselessly. There was nothing to throw up: all he felt was nausea. Mechanically he climbed to the spar deck, and as he opened the door of his station a convulsion clutched his insides; he heard his mates' protests as if in a dream, and among them, perhaps because it was the loudest, Scurvy's hoarse voice as he grabbed some coats, "You look more dead than alive, 37 . . . !"

The slam of the door left his sentence unfinished; Gervasio laid one coat on the planking in the lee of the rafts and covered himself with the other, drawing up his legs, seeking a fetal position; but since his nausea did not decrease he stretched them out and lay face down. That way the ship's movement was more bearable, with his stomach supported and his head and body adjusting themselves to the rhythm of the waves and offering them no resistance. But even though it lessened, the sensation of anguish persisted. He opened his eyes and found Peter kneeling beside him.

"You ought to eat something, you're seasick."

Nauta's sympathetic, single-minded, maternal, ubiquitous attitude humiliated him, but Gervasio was too far gone to pretend he felt well. He shook his head.

"Leave me alone. I'm not hungry."

He felt that it was shameful to let Peter see him in this condition, while the rest of his mates were leaving the station chatting indifferently, as if nothing were happening. He cursed the day he had enlisted in the Navy and realized that in any other place, even in the Legion, his behavior would have been worthier. He closed his eyes, avoiding Peter's commiserating stare, but when he opened them again he saw Petty Officer Pita's face over his friend's shoulder, his eyes screwed up against the wind's blasts.

"Bring him up some fruit, Nauta. Apples will do him good. As soon as we're through the Strait the sea will calm down."

Next day the wind shifted to the east and died down after the ship had passed the Strait of Gibraltar. The seas calmed and, like a magician's trick, a milky, smooth, sparkling blue sea appeared under the bow. The effect on Gervasio was electrifying: first his nausea decreased, then his mental confusion, and lastly his vital operations (glandular functions, secretions). It could be said that the ship's almost instantaneous stabilization had resurrected him, and with the resurrection came a return not only of his desire to live but also of his self-esteem. Hours later Javier Medina was instructing him at his station.

"Seasickness is like childbirth, 377A. You suffer while it's going on, but then you don't think about it again until the next time."

Gervasio nodded. Now that it was over he not only realized that Javier was right, but thought that his complaints while it was happening had been excessive. He was absolutely certain that if the storm should be repeated some day, he would be able to face it more worthily. He no longer lamented his fate. He even thought that his tendency to seasickness might render his conduct still more noble some day, for if heroism meant rising above adversity, a seasick hero would be doubly a hero because he had had two things to overcome. And so he smiled an indulgent smile every time that Dámaso Valentín, recalling his month and a half of ostracism in the training ship and his disastrous initiation into the cruiser, would tell him, "What the fuck, you don't have any luck, sailor; things just don't work out for you."

But Gervasio smiled because he knew that the deed of the fighter of whom great deeds are least expected was greater than that of the person apparently most able to carry it out. That was why Dámaso's comments, or any other scornful remark about his weaknesses, made him proud instead of cutting him down to size. There were even some nights in his hammock when he deliberately fought off sleep solely for the pleasure of imagining Uncle Felipe Neri beginning to write his biography (using as material the notes in his oilcloth-covered notebook): "Physically, given his lack of martial attributes and his tendency toward seasickness, he would have been thought unprepared for naval warfare; and yet Gervasio García de la Lastra . . ." Now he reveled in this idea. His future deeds, during which he would successfully overcome his physical weaknesses, acquired a special importance in his eyes. He often remembered what Eduardo Custodio had confided to him in the club one afternoon, months before: "When I was fourteen I tried to imitate Arizona Jim, the sheriff, with his eagle eye and his nerves of steel; but when I was fifteen I realized that I could hardly see anything at a distance and that a door slamming was enough to unhinge my nerves." Eduardo Custodio had said that one day less than a year ago, and yet there he was on the list of heroes of the *Baleares,* nominated for the Military Medal that all the survivors were to receive.

For Gervasio, whose travels had been confined to childhood

summer vacations, the first contact with the island of Mallorca, with its seamless dark blue sky, its transparent coves, its palm trees and windmills, gave the impression of an exotic, very remote tropical country. They had scarcely dropped anchor when he wrote a letter to Manena Abad that was full of shimmering adjectives: "This is a picturesque, paradisiacal part of the country; it makes you feel drunk . . ." But immediately following this, anxious to have the girl believe that he was in danger, he described the dramatic location of the base, an enclave in enemy territory, so that "at night the city is plunged into darkness, with just a little blue lamp on each corner to guide you, for fear of bombardments . . ." The girl answered by return mail, "How I envy you! Ever since I can remember I've dreamed of traveling. What wouldn't I give to change places with you!" Gervasio was discouraged; he had gone too far. He couldn't understand how anyone could treat a fighting man's hardships so frivolously. He deplored Manena Abad's character. He would have preferred a grief-stricken sponsor, making offerings to on high for his personal safety, begging God for his return. But Manena, far from trembling for him, couldn't see any merit at all in his action. War was a party; she was crassly confusing a warrior with a tourist. In his circumstances, to be envied and not pitied by a beautiful girl made Gervasio feel superfluous and useless.

At anchor in the bay, during his watches, he thought about Manena as he used the spotter to review the city's silhouette: the beach, the cathedral rising loftily above the old quarter, the finely balanced lines of the Exchange, the Almudaina Tower, Bellver Castle, and along the same line but lower down, the Marine Promenade flanked by palm trees, the elegant Terreno district, and the Hotel Mediterráneo (with its terraces descending to the sea) closing the city view on that side. Always the same. From time to time he might see a Nordic tourist sunning herself all alone beside the hotel pool, indifferent, like Manena Abad, to the ravages of war.

That lazy calm, more appropriate to a watering place than to a warship, was interrupted one day by the appearance of enemy planes. The metallic voice of Station A announced the news:

"Attention, Station H. Eight planes astern."

The loudspeakers spread the alarm, the bugle called to battle

stations, the crew mobilized, and the red flag of danger was raised
on the Almudaina Tower. Gervasio, huddled beside the speaking
tube with his helmet on his head and his heart beating wildly,
watched Don Mario's back and his crumpled cap with the wire
missing, visor pushed back, legs flexed, binoculars held high. Javier
Medina sang out the target, and as if his words had been the signal
they were waiting for, the station went into action. Petty Officer
Tubío, who had swung the telemetry tube toward the stern, began
to call out distances which Nasty transmitted to Lago on the rocord,
while Petty Officer Pita and Medina gave the location angle to
Blondie, who in his turn transmitted it to Bartolomé Roselló,
crouched in front of the Perozzi board. It was organized confusion.
Glances, words, information were transmitted, mingled, but no one
made use of any but those assigned to him. For some time they had
heard the faraway crump of the bombs and the dull explosions of
the minelayers at anchor near the line of buoys. Don Mario, keeping an eye on the planes' movements, ordered defensive fire, and
Gervasio, swelling with pride, notified the guns through the speaking tube. Bartolomé Roselló—"Mallorquín"—swung the ruler over
the board and yelled, "Defense zone four, defense zone four!"

Gervasio spoke the order through the tube. They could hear the
thud of bombs nearby and the brisk reply of the ship that was
being attacked. In the midst of the confusion Don Mario ordered
the guns to fire, and Gervasio put his lips to the brass mouth of
the tube and yelled "Fire!" with all his heart and soul. He drew
courage from the guns' immediate reply, the deafening salvo from
the starboard battery. A thunderous roar enveloped the bay. Bartolomé Roselló frowned in irritation as he realized that the squadron had passed safely through the first obstacle. He yelled for
defense zone three, but before Don Mario could repeat his words
a frightfully loud crash shook the cruiser, rattling the rings around
the cables, and flakes of paint from the bulkheads rained down on
Gervasio. He crouched still lower, his mind confused. "We're hit,"
he thought, but he heard Don Mario shout "Fire!" and, making up
his mind to die fighting, crossed his arms over his stomach to
protect it and yelled "Fire!" The antiaircraft guns on the starboard
side went off and he felt little electrified snakes crawling in his
belly. Bartolomé Roselló sang out "Defense zone two," and simul-

taneously the machine guns on the spar deck began to chatter. Gervasio's hair stirred under his helmet. The vibration was strong and unbroken. He could see the tracer bullets over the top of the rail, cutting the sky like rockets, shining in the sun. The explosions from the rest of the ships at anchor in the port, serving as counterpoint to their own, accentuated the confusion. When the airplanes had crossed defense zone one the station's crew grew more nervous. Don Mario, shoulders hunched, knees bent, eyes alert, scanned the sky unceasingly. Bartolomé Roselló, after singing out "Zero defense!" in an exhausted voice (which meant that in spite of their opposition the enemy planes had succeeded in getting into the vertical, into the mathematical center of their objective), stopped watching the board and covered his eyes with his arm. Petty Officer Tubío's soft hand clutched the telemetry cylinder, Miodelo looked sidewise at Don Mario, and Javier Medina's clenched jaws knotted. Gervasio clutched his knees in anguish, his face pressed into the mouth of the tube (as if he were trying to make himself smaller and take refuge there), and in that position heard the crashing series of bombs. Jets of foam as tall as cathedrals sprayed him like rain, but before their clamor had subsided, two dry, deafening, consecutive explosions shook the ship, flakes of paint fell again, and Don Mario's cap flew through the air. Gervasio loosened his grip on his knees and seized the tube desperately with his heart pounding like a drum. "My God, they're going to sink us," he moaned. But despite the violence of the last two explosions his companions seemed to be recovering their composure. Mallorquín, squatting, had picked up the ruler again and skidded it across the board, Petty Officer Tubío (his puffy hands swollen) was giving distances to Nasty again, and he in turn was giving them to Lago, Painter. Petty Officer Pita and Medina, through Blondie, were giving location angles to Mallorquín, and Don Mario, with his squashed cap once more on his head, was offering quiet instruction to observers and telemetrists. And when Bartolomé Roselló said routinely, as if they were on maneuvers, "Defense zone one, defense zone one," and a little later "Defense zone two, defense zone two," and Miodelo confirmed that the planes were retreating, the atmosphere became completely relaxed. The greatest danger had passed. An acrid cloud of smoke hung over the blue bay, dissipating as the airplanes disappeared in the distance and the rhythm of the guns decreased. Some explosions, sounding aborted, were still coming from the coast, while on board the firing stations, turrets, antiaircraft guns, and machine guns entered a phase of watchful inactivity. The calm infected Gervasio, who noticed that his guts were gradually unknotting and that his internal secretions were becoming more regular. But as he recovered his composure he asked himself about the silence, why no one mentioned the bombs' targets on the cruiser. Nor did he hear a stir on deck, or confusion, or cries of the wounded, or orders for abandoning ship. The shore batteries' fire at regular intervals was the only thing he heard, and the wispy little clouds of the antiaircraft guns floated like balloons in the clear sky. He felt a need to find out something, to discover with his own eyes what the situation was. He could see Don Mario's placid silhouette beside him, squashy cap pushed back on his head, with the binoculars in his right hand. As the quiet continued, Gervasio got up from his seat little by little until his yellowish eyes peered over the rim of the bulkhead. He was surprised by the order that reigned on the ship. Everything seemed intact there: forecastle, bridge, turrets, antiaircraft guns. He turned his head in astonishment. Astern the situation was the same. He couldn't see the slightest damage. How was that possible? And those tremendous explosions that had shaken the cruiser three times? What had that been? He sat down again, disconcerted. The barrages from the shore batteries sounded farther and farther apart. Dámaso informed them that the airplanes were flying over the beach, and seconds later Petty Officer Tubío, who was following them by telemetry, announced their disappearance toward the west. Peter notified Station A; they agreed. Nasty took off his helmet and wiped the sweat from his brow with the sleeve of his work uniform. He was smiling innocently. Bartolomé Roselló took a deep breath and lighted a cigarette. Don Mario reminded him that the action wasn't over, and Mallorquín ground out his cigarette on the deck. A short time later the loudspeakers announced the all-clear. With their helmets off, the danger past, their faces looked relaxed and jovial. And like the members of a funeral procession after leaving the corpse in the cemetery, loquacity and irrepressible desires to live came back to them. They laughed about nothing, exchanged theories about the action, cracked jokes. Javier Medina winked at Gervasio as he swung down from his observer's perch, his hair crisp, his nose curving above his big teeth.

"Well, 377A, how did you like that baptism of fire?"

Gervasio smiled, elated and nervous. He talked compulsively about the action, about Don Mario, about the speaking tube, the defense zones, and finally touched on the matter that was troubling him: those dramatic crashes that dominated the bombardment, that rattled the rings on the cables and made the bulkhead paint flake off and Don Mario's cap fly through the air: what could they be but bombs? Javier Medina listened to him ironically from the heights of his age and experience.

"Those are the turrets, 377A."

"The turrets?"

"The salvoes from the antiaircraft guns in the turrets."

Gervasio's attention was so concentrated that Javier Medina added in a melodramatic tone, "Just to give you an idea, the shock wave from the four guns firing all at once can gut a man at a distance of fifty meters."

CHAPTER 18

After his baptism of fire Gervasio again debated with himself, this time from a different viewpoint, the problem of whether he had really received a sign. That mental confusion, that dry throat, that gnawing sensation in the gut that he had felt during the engagement: were they symptoms of emotion, nervousness, or fear? He regretted Uncle Felipe Neri's absence, for he wanted to consult him, and in view of that absence appealed to his friends; but unwilling to have his privacy invaded, he invented an intermediary: Esparza, an Asturian in the mess stores. According to Esparza, during the engagement he had noticed a choking feeling, trembling hands, dry mouth, and blockage of the gut. What could have caused those symptoms? Were they manifestations of nervousness, emotion, or fear? Dámaso Valentín, leaning against the storage bin in Compartment 3, nodded eloquently and said, caressing the notch in his tooth with the tip of his tongue, "Not fear, sailor, panic; that's what your friend in the mess stores feels; nobody could have described it better."

Gervasio was gloomy and perplexed, for if the symptoms were really those of fear, how to reconcile them with that tentative rising of his hair which was a sign of courage? Months ago, Peter had remarked one day in the club that any man with sensitivity and imagination felt fear at some time in his life, and that courage didn't consist in not feeling fear but in controlling it. But Peter had said this some time ago, and now, because it was more recent, Damasito's opinion prevailed: "Panic; nobody could have described it better." But by attributing his own sensations to a straw man Gervasio had omitted an essential piece of information: that his hair had begun to rise. At this point in his reflections he reached the conclusion that, despite this capillary movement, his reactions in combat were not those of a courageous man, because on that occasion he had not enjoyed the sensation and still less had it led to a heroic action. Nor did he want to draw all the enemy's hostility on himself; he preferred to share it. And lastly, in the heat of battle, his most fervent desire had not been to shoot down the attacking planes one by one, but more modestly to have them go away.

One afternoon four days after the air attack, when he was at the movies, projection of the film was interrupted and a notice was inserted telling all the cruiser's crew members to return to their units. They left the theater in alarm. Groups of sailors were streaming toward the pier. The soberer ones took care of those who were drunk, but no one seemed to show concern.

"This happens every so often, 377A," said skinny Santoña; "just things that happen in war."

"But can you tell me where we're going?"

"Navy Radio says we're going to Pantelleria; I don't know."

After they had put to sea, during the first night watch, Gervasio asked Petty Officer Pita about Pantelleria.

"It's an island in the Sicilian channel, off Tunis. What else do you want to know?"

"And what are we doing in Sicily, Petty Officer?"

"Naval Command knows that, 377A. I suppose there's some question of capturing a ship."

"Do the Red ships go as far as that?"

Petty Officer Pita's mournful blue gaze seemed to fix itself on Gervasio's lips.

"Why do you say 'Reds,' 377A? You always say 'Reds'; you never say anything else."

"But they are Reds, aren't they, Petty Officer?"

"That depends on what you mean by Reds."

"Well, just that, Reds; Communists, Marxists . . . Aren't we at war with them?"

Petty Officer Pita's face remained impassive, though his expression darkened and changed completely. That happened sometimes. The secret lay in the blue of his eyes, as changeable as the sea and sky. His voice sounded more conciliatory when he answered.

"Communists, all right. There are Communists on the other side, but that doesn't mean that all of them are."

The moon sparkled on the sea and its light formed a huge cross with the ship's wake. The cruiser was sailing without lights, slipping through the water like a furtive shadow, and the engines' vibration scarcely left a trace of its existence on the sea's surface. Wrapped in the rough, wide-sleeved coat, leaning on the rail with the binoculars at his eyes, Gervasio yawned twice, so hugely that he almost dislocated his jaw. He was sleepy. That always happened to him during the middle watches. Night watches, coming between the first watch and the morning watch, interrupted his sleep and left him unsatisfied. "Sleeping in two chunks is a drag," as Damasito said. Peter, however, adjusted to the rotation of watches without making a fuss. Gervasio was touched by his friend's accepting smile every time he woke him up in the dead of night to change watches. He had only to touch him on the shoulder for Peter to throw back the blanket, sit up in his hammock, and put on his boots as he asked, "All quiet? Is it cold?" He would finish dressing and go up on deck by the galley ladder, after silently threading his way through the hammocks. Dámaso, a few hours later, was the other side of the coin: he would cling to the blanket, grunt, turn over, resist, swear, and when Peter at last managed to get him up he would be in a terrible temper, complaining like one possessed.

On the metal stool on the starboard side, Miodelo was playing the harmonica as usual. He played softly, without trying to compete with the noise of the engines and the ventilator's hum. He played by ear, unaware of how skillful he was, like a child reading a book he doesn't understand without a stumble. Skinny Santoña was rubbing his skeleton against the bulkhead, sweeping his forty-five-degree sector through the binoculars. He said, "Miodelo, play me 'The Love the Sea Brought Me.' "

And Miodelo obligingly played the tale of the unfortunate girl abandoned by the sailor with a lover in every port. Then Santoña asked for "Chaparrita," "The Man Who Deceives a Girl," and "Love Me, My Mulatto Girl." The music sounded nostalgic in the darkness, and in his corner Gervasio visualized Manena Abad, regretting that the girl couldn't see him crammed into that heavy coat, scanning the sea with his binoculars, keeping vigil over her sleep. Sometimes Petty Officer Pita, who even when he was a little drunk usually liked to listen to music, pretended that he had to keep up with the responsibilities of his job.

"Miodelo, stop playing your flute and keep watch."

"I am watching, Petty Officer Pita."

"You can keep watch while you're playing the flute?"

"I've got two hands, Petty Officer Pita. One for the binoculars and the other for the flute, as you call it."

The petty officer said no more, his face grave, his blue eyes lost in the darkness, waiting for Gervasio's turn to ask. 377A's military enthusiasm was curious: "Miodelo, play 'Death's Sweetheart'; 'The Volunteers,' Miodelo; Miodelo, 'Warrior Spirit'; Would you mind playing 'The British Flag That Waves o'er Gibraltar?' " Petty Officer Pita was getting impatient. He looked Gervasio over from head to foot with his vague eyes.

"Why do you always ask for military music, 377A?"

"I like it, Petty Officer; light music doesn't do anything for me."

Petty Officer Pita shrugged his shoulders and drew himself up. Miodelo continued to play. Miodelo, who had married at seventeen "because he didn't want to run out on a big belly," now had the responsibility, at twenty-one, for a woman at least ten years older than he, three children, and a little grocery store in Betanzos. "Doesn't it scare you, having three kids at twenty, Miodelo?" "Kid, that's why I play the harmonica, to forget that I have them." Skinny Santoña, who had been engendered by a sixty-year-old father, made fun of everything, beginning with himself; sometimes, referring to his almost translucent thinness, he would argue, "Since I'm the son of a grandfather it seems like the witches sucked me dry." At other times he consoled himself by appropriating virtues like prudence, temperance, patience, an even disposition, and experience, which were characteristic of older folks, ascribing them to the old man's genes. The daily contact imposed by the watches, shared watches in the middle of the night as the ship slept, invited confidences; and although Petty Officer Pita, who was more experienced, had nothing to say, Gervasio did not hold back. He talked and talked about his childhood and adolescence with almost complete honesty, omitting two crucial points: the phenomenon of his hair and Papa Telmo's political ideas. Petty Officer Pita was interested in the personality and death of his uncles, Norberto and Adrián, while Santoña and Miodelo, working-class boys who were used to doing things for themselves, listened open-mouthed to his domestic tales, in which the chauffeur, the laundress, the gardener, or the maids often figured.

"What the hell, 377A! You can tell a mile off that you're fine folks," Santoña would comment, while Miodelo waggled his index finger in admiration.

But as soon as Petty Officer Pita consulted his watch and said, "Hurry up, 377A; it's ten to," Miodelo would consider both the conversation and the recital at an end, and would blow through the holes in his harmonica, wipe it on the lining of his coat, and put it away wrapped in a handkerchief, as in a shroud, in the pocket of his work uniform.

Peter and Dámaso's private meetings with Gervasio took place in Compartment 3, over the bow storeroom. The limited space in Station H made private conversation impossible, so that every time they wanted to talk alone they would agree to meet there, at the little corner table under Dámaso Valentín's locker. These chats had become so usual that every time one of Dámaso's friends asked him to come to a meeting he would ask ironically, "Is there a controversy?" And so the conversations at the corner table began to be called by that name. On this afternoon Peter, with his careful, didactic clarity, was trying to justify their being sent to Pantelleria, which Dámaso was complaining about.

"It's easier this way. The blockade only works in the straits. The Red coast is too long for our little squadron."

Gervasio smiled, as if he had caught him out in an error.

"You said 'Red.'"

"Sure. You think maybe it isn't the right word?"

"Petty Officer Pita doesn't like it."

"Pita doesn't like us to say 'Red?'"

"No."

"What do we say, then?"

"I don't know; Republicans, I suppose."

The fight was on. Dámaso shared Petty Officer Pita's views.

"Reds or not, they respect the constitution that they swore to defend. We're the ones who're the rebels."

Peter, who accepted Dámaso's reasoning as a point of departure, argued that without rebels the history of humanity would have stagnated. Gervasio was confused by these high-sounding and subtle sentences. He was used to thinking about things on a lower level and liked to use domestic examples. He had noticed that Pita agreed with Papa Telmo on one key point: he called the Crusade a pronunciamiento, which led him to the conclusion that the petty officer might well be a camouflaged Red.

"He's a funny guy. He doesn't like to have us call the Reds Reds, and he smokes on the station when he's on watch."

"Does Pita smoke on night watches?"

"Whenever he comes on duty drunk."

"And how do you know he comes on duty drunk?"

"He smells of it. He doesn't have to talk, he only has to breathe."

Next night, when Peter was on watch, the alarm sounded. The sleepy sailors bumped into each other, crowded in hatchways and at watertight doors, but before the order was given to close portholes everyone was at his combat post. As he climbed the iron ladder Gervasio heard the noise of a motor and said without stopping, jerking his head toward Dámaso, who was behind him, "Airplanes."

Above, on their dark station under a starry sky, all was confusion. The roar of motors alternately increased and diminished, and while Petty Officer Pita swore that they were torpedo boats, Miodelo scanned the sky with binoculars looking for airplanes. Both of them angrily defended their point of view at the tops of their voices, until Don Mario reached the station, panting, and demanded silence. The noise of motors was ubiquitous, seemed to come from all sides, and as Gervasio huddled beside the speaking tube he felt the anguish of being surrounded. A sudden shock at the back of his neck (not followed, as was usual, by the rising of his hair) was the beginning of a process of choking sensations, drying of the throat, blockage of glands, and an empty place in his gut. He crossed his arms over his stomach to protect it and raised his eyes imploringly toward Don Mario, as if only he, like Christ on Lake Tiberias, could save them from the waters. But the commander hesitated, took no decisions, only ordered them to intensify their surveillance. Javier Medina's high-pitched, hollow voice from his observer's perch startled Gervasio.

"They're planes, Don Mario! We've got them on the vertical!"

Indeed, the roar of motors now seemed to come from above, and Gervasio, who had stood up in obedience to Don Mario's order, leaned his elbows on the rail and raised his binoculars toward the sky, just at the moment when Miodelo, who was standing beside him scanning the sea, corrected him.

"They're fast launches, Don Mario! Target sighted! Sixty-five degrees to starboard!"

Don Mario ordered the crew to their stations and told Peter to transmit the news to the bridge; but at the moment when he contacted Station A a sudden, blinding white light shone in the dark sky, hung over the cruiser for a few seconds, and then gradually descended, illuminating it like daylight with the livid clarity of a lightning flash. The rhythm of the boilers accelerated, the bulkheads vibrated, and the cruiser began its turn. Three new rockets, whose intensity of light increased as they descended, now opened like flowers above them, and simultaneously a spotlight which appeared to have risen from the depths of the sea slid over the cruiser's hull from bow to stern. There was a short burst from one of the machine guns on the spar deck. Don Mario repeated nervously, "Every man to his post."

Crouched beside the speaking tube, Gervasio closed his eyes and half opened his lips waiting for an explosion, but none occurred. What they did hear was the repeated shrilling of Station A's telephone.

"Station A."

"Station H."

"Attention! We are sailing in the territorial waters of Malta. British airplanes and fast launches. Avoid any action."

"Received."

Immediately, the cruiser's location lights went on, and as if by agreement the three torpedo boats that were circling around them also turned on their lights. Bartolomé Roselló, Mallorquín, with his blanket over his undershirt, pushed back his helmet and wiped the sweat from his forehead with the back of his hand.

"Those bastards sure took their time about telling us," he said.

The buzz of the motors was gradually left behind and the cruiser, its location lights again extinguished, was swallowed by the darkness. Hours later, during the dawn watch, Petty Officer Pita found Gervasio asleep. It wasn't the first time that the boy had nodded off during a watch. Sleep was so contagious at that hour that some of his mates, like Scurvy or Blondie, boasted that they could sleep standing up, binoculars at their eyes, without needing to lean on anything. The incident with the British had thoroughly awakened Gervasio, who could have sworn that he had just gone to sleep when Nasty's hand shook him by the shoulder.

"It's time, 377A. Hurry."

He got up drowsily, almost sleepwalking, and on the station a few moments later, wrapped in the rough coat, lulled by the noise of the engines, elbows on the bulkhead, he put the binoculars to his eyes and fell asleep. He would never know how many times Petty Officer Pita had waved his hand in front of the lenses to prove that he was asleep; but once awake, conscious of the enormity of his offense, he silently got to his feet beside Pita, letting the stool fall to the deck.

"I'm sorry, Petty Officer, I fell asleep," he said. "I couldn't help it."

To port the sky was beginning to lighten, dispersing the darkness. Petty Officer Pita shook his thick-necked head from side to side reprovingly.

"This is serious, 377A," he said. "A thousand sailors are asleep on board, trusting in the dozen who are on watch. But if they don't do their duty, everything can be lost in a moment. Try not to let it happen again."

In the red-tinged light of dawn Gervasio looked at him contritely, expecting him to add something else (that he would report him or not report him, that he would excuse him because it was the first time, or that the matter wouldn't go beyond the two of them), but Petty Officer Pita said nothing more, merely turned his back and raised the binoculars to his eyes as if reminding him what his obligation was.

When he went off duty, in the breakfast line in front of the galley, mug in hand, Gervasio looked for Peter to tell him the news. He was frightened; his negligence had been serious. He even thought that a court martial might be called for. Peter calmed him down. At times like these Peter was unique. He believed that Pita, despite his ambiguous behavior, was no tattletale and would never report a subordinate without telling him beforehand. But apart from what Pita might do, Gervasio's carelessness was inexcusable. He had betrayed the confidence placed in him, endangering the cruiser. Gervasio agreed docilely, with nothing to say for himself; he understood that he would not be punished for his negligence, but on the other hand his image had been tarnished in his friend's eyes.

At noon they encountered the freighter, at first a dark dot on the horizon surmounted by a plume of smoke, and later, once they had overtaken it, a shabby black merchant ship with high rails, her hull painted a dirty, faded red. The ship saluted, lowering and raising the Greek flag on the stern (under which her name, *Dilos,* appeared in widely spaced white letters). But the cruiser did not respond; it made a complete turn and began following the same course. The polished blue sea swelled between the two ships, so close to each other that even without binoculars Gervasio could see a little black dog running around on the Greek ship's afterdeck. The heliograph winked on the bridge, ordering her to halt, but the *Dilos* did not do so; rather, she increased speed as if the whole maneuver had nothing to do with her. The bridge repeated the order, but the freighter, seemingly deaf and dumb, turned sharply to port and increased her distance from them. The explosion of the warning gun caught Gervasio on the spar deck. A spout of foam flowered in front of the Greek ship's bow, and the black smoke from the stack thickened abruptly as she stopped. Gervasio could not conceal his surprise.

"Why that ship and not another?"

Javier Medina, his curly head bare, smiled complacently.

"Somebody informed, 377A. Spying is what's involved in these matters. Before she ever put to sea, you can be sure that up there"— and he pointed toward the bridge, on the other side of the stack— "they knew the ship's tonnage, her capacity, her color, and even the name she was going to be rebaptized with."

And he explained with eloquent gestures that these pirate ships often raised anchor with the original name on their stern, and a few miles out of port, far from prying eyes, a couple of sailors in boatswain's chairs would change it for another, usually in the language of a country that had nothing to do with the war. And he finished his explanation by saying good-naturedly, "Turkish and Greek names are the Russians' favorites."

A boat was lowered from the starboard gangway and the prize crew took their places in it. A ladder was thrown over the freighter's side to carry out the exchange of crews. From the boat the sailors of the *Dilos,* hands in the pockets of their blue peacoats, gazed indifferently—neither surprised nor intimidated—at their captors, who crowded along the rails to watch them. After they had been taken by a detachment of sailors to the officers' wardroom under the bridge, the cruiser gave some instructions to the freighter by heliograph and both ships started off again.

The *Dilos,* stern to the wind, sailed slowly, so that from time to time her escort got several miles ahead and had to go back to meet her. After ten days at sea the cruiser's crew was happy about returning to port, and made plans for the first foray ashore. In Station H Scurvy and Nasty, who had come up from the steward's stores slightly drunk, talked loudly about their plans and, between giggles, about women. Their aims were very specific: they were going to spend the afternoon in the house of "La Cubana." Making a great show of it, they scorned other peoples' plans and urged everyone to go with them. And so the appearance of the minelayer *Vulcano* and transfer of custody of the *Dilos* by the cruiser, and its subsequent complete turn, bow to the east again, was a bitter disappointment.

"Damn it all; to Pantelleria again."

"Who said so?"

"Our course says so, 377A. Don't you have eyes in your head?"

Fermín Linaje, Scurvy, spit out an oath, and Javier Medina took advantage of this to remark in a jocular tone that "he didn't see the future of the new Spain very clearly if, as seemed obvious, the only thing its youth cared about was whores." Scurvy, his personal philosophy attacked, replied with a speech made more heated by alcohol, according to which women were necessary after the age of thirteen, masturbation was degenerate, and a man's whole manner of being was to be found in the secretion of his testicles. Gervasio listened with an indulgent half-smile. Scurvy's ideas and the tone of his voice made him think, with a little pang of tenderness, of Papa Telmo.

"It's like listening to my father," he said.

"Gee, kid, does your father talk about women with you?"

"That's not what I mean. My father doesn't talk about women. He talks about the sun and the light, but in just the same tone you use to talk about your testicles."

Gervasio's contribution strengthened Scurvy's position, and he accused conventional medicine of tolerating masturbation and giving no importance to the carnal act. He turned to Gervasio and asked him what his father thought about that, and when Gervasio replied that he didn't know, Scurvy turned the question on him: What did 377A think about masturbation and the carnal act? What did he think about women in general? In the face of this attack Gervasio retreated, but the other insisted so much that he ended by admitting that he was a virgin, although, less shamed by being one than by having to confess it before an audience composed of Station H, corrected himself vaguely, "Well, a good many years ago I had an adventure with a maid."

"Did you go all the way with her?"

He didn't have the courage to say either yes or no, or to tell how old he had been at the time. Scurvy interpreted his silence as acquiescence.

"And you haven't been with a woman since then?"

"No."

"As soon as we're back on land I'll introduce you to one. You won't be disappointed."

Late in the day the sea rose, and at sunset the weather turned much colder. The cruiser was buffeted by the mistral (which put whitecaps on the waves) and gradually lost stability, but Gervasio maintained his composure by staying in the open air. He slept on his station, and next day they sighted the *Berezina,* a motorship a hundred and fifty meters in length. It obeyed the order to stop, and the exchange of crews took place without incident. The capture (observed by the sailors, as usual, from the deck and upper parts of the superstructure) held a surprise for them this time: there was a woman in the motorship's crew, a frail-looking girl in trousers who leaped easily to the gangway and walked calmly down the path opened for her by two rows of boisterous sailors. Gervasio, who was looking on from the spar deck with the binoculars, saw Petty Officer Pita in the first row, head bare and looking nervous. He had come to attention, and as the woman approached, he made her an imperceptible bow. But his gesture, which she undoubtedly took amiss, made the girl turn around and stick out her tongue at him. A loud whistle greeted her action, which increased until her slender figure disappeared down the hatchway in the bow. When he came down from the spar deck Gervasio found the deck in a turmoil (jokes, shouts, obscene speculations). He saw Peter among the groups of sailors and taking him by the arm drew him away from the crowd. His friend looked at him in surprise.

"Do you want a controversy?"

"Never mind controversies now."

"Then what's going on?"

"The petty officer . . . Didn't you see? He bowed to the Russian girl and she turned around and stuck out her tongue at him. Didn't you hear the whistles?"

"The petty officer? Which one?"

"Pita. What are you thinking of?"

"A bow? It must have been a joke!"

"Never mind jokes. I tell you, this guy's not to be trusted."

On their way back to the base the wind increased, made the little swell into a big one, and hours later the big swell into a rough, tossing, stormy sea. It opened in deep gulfs and the bow went up and down, submerging and rising alternately. Its pitching, as violent as in the Atlantic, eventually beat down Gervasio's resistance. He lay on a coat like a beggar (with two apples in his cap) in the lee of the rafts on the spar deck. He thought again about how mistaken he had been to enlist, and when at nightfall Scurvy stopped beside him and told him jovially that next day La Cubana would cure him of his seasickness, he closed his eyes in humiliation. In his situation Scurvy's boasting and the idea of La Cubana made no sense, because at the moment all he wanted was to die.

CHAPTER

19

Gervasio stood up, feeling limp and defenseless. He covered his genitals with the middy blouse that lay on the chair next to the bidet and hid behind the couch to dress. He had tried in vain with La Cubana, and now, when he saw her lying naked on the bed with a corner of the bedspread over her belly, devouring a cigarette, his awkward attempts rose to his mind again. Though on a different scale, everything had been a repetition of the wild ride with Amalia in the storeroom of the palace ten years before: the sudden lack of sexual desire, then the nervous compulsion, and finally loss of confidence and fear.

"He's a virgin, Cubana; take good care of him." There had been a competent smile on Scurvy's thick lips as he turned him over for his first performance.

"Has La Cubana ever not taken good care of a guy?"

Gervasio smiled in a conciliatory way, but when he was shut into the bedroom with her his spirit failed him, and instead of feeling desire for the girl he was overcome with a sort of repulsion and disgust for himself. And after the girl took off her robe and showed her black armpits, her pale tormented skin, her flabby breasts, her sparse pubic hair, his imagination came to a halt; lying beside her with their sweaty bodies intertwined, the memory of Amalia came back to him—her spasms, her erotic fever, her coarse language, so vividly and sharply that his sexual aggressiveness vanished, he realized that his flesh was shriveling and that the naked girl's nearness, far from exciting him, depressed him. However, he did not resign himself at once. Knowing that Scurvy and Nasty were waiting downstairs (in the moments of euphoria that followed his arrival in port, now recovered from his seasickness, Gervasio had promised to celebrate the fact), he tried again and again to kindle his virility. Finally he stopped and lay motionless, defeated. She did not change position when the boy got up, but when she saw him standing fully dressed at the foot of the bed she ground out her cigarette in the ashtray on the night table and sat up reluctantly, her blue robe over her shoulders. She appeared to be neither disappointed nor annoyed. Gervasio, feeling miserable, fought to hold back tears. All he wanted was to get far away from there.

"How much do I owe you?"

"Give me two duros; you didn't do anything."

He took out his billfold and timidly gave her three.

"Do me a favor, will you?" he added. "Don't tell my friends. I'd be the laughingstock of my station."

"Don't worry. What happens up here is a professional secret." La Cubana's tone of voice was wearily obliging.

Cheered by her promise, Gervasio played the man, drank, sang, and danced until the shapes of things began to look fuzzy and the room to turn round and round. Between dances Nasty would wink at him and laugh. When La Cubana came into the room and was

accosted by Fermín Linaje, she had said, pretending to an enthusiasm she did not feel, "Your little friend came through; now he's a
man." And Scurvy broke into applause, clapping very rapidly with
his short forearms. Two hours later in the shore-leave launch,
Peter, falling victim to belated adolescent jealousy, had scolded him
for his weakness.

"What have you got to do with Scurvy? Why do you let him lead
you around by the nose?"

Early on the following day their squadron fired up boilers. The
ships' stacks smoked faintly in the quiet blue morning. Navy Radio
broadcast contradictory rumors, though all of them were connected
with the arrival of Nationalist troops in Vinaroz on the mainland
and the splitting of the Republican zone into two parts. The fleet
would try to prevent evacuation of two regiments trapped at El
Puntal. The fleet was preparing to provide artillery support to the
forces that were advancing on Catalonia. The fleet was going to
mine the seaports closest to the theater of operations . . . However,
the squadron did not put to sea until just before dawn on the
following morning, cruisers at the head, flanked by the old coal-
burning destroyers; behind them came minelayers and gunboats.
When Gervasio went on watch he met Peter on the spar deck, eyes
shining with enthusiasm.

"Do you know where we're going?"

Gervasio shook his head.

"To the Columbretes. It's a landing. The *Vulcano* is carrying three
units of Marines."

"Are the Columbretes islands?"

"Well, they're insignificant little islands, but they're important
strategically, only forty miles from Castellón."

Small geographical details that had never been included in his
high-school manuals of study were becoming familiar to Gervasio.
The broad geography of his school days and the little geography
of war coexisted in his brain: Pantelleria, Grosa, Alborán, the
Chafarinas, and suddenly an archipelago that he'd never heard
spoken of before: the Columbretes.

A bright, clear atmosphere accompanied their course. Little
shoals of slippery, shiny tuna, displaced from nearby shallow
water, leaped in the sun. The sailors congregated on deck, stroked

255

by a soft breeze, talking in groups. The coal-burning destroyers, proudly smoking, drew ahead of the cruisers. In the distance, in the light mist, the rugged silhouettes of several crags emerged, standing out against the vague blue line of the coast. Javier Medina, binoculars hanging around his neck, was instructing Peter on the spar deck.

"The biggest one is Columbrete Grande. Behind it is Ferrera and to port is Horadada, you can see the hole in the rock with the naked eye. A bit to the left are twin islands, Churruca and Bergantín."

Peter nodded, inquired about details, and asked Javier Medina for a nautical chart (he didn't know the archipelago, and after the operation wanted to add the chart, with an account of the landing, to his naval archive). Javier promised to give it to him. From Peter's first day on board he had regarded him as a prize pupil, and had become his mentor.

From the top of his post of duty after the call to battle stations, surrounded by his mates, Gervasio adjusted the binoculars and focused them on the objective, which was acquiring volume and color as they entered shallower waters. The destroyers, on an antisubmarine course, cut zigzags across the wakes of the cruisers, which along with the minelayer *Vulcano* were approaching Columbrete Grande. The rough architecture of the lighthouse shone whitely, houses topped with windmills lay below it (only one of them, with smoke in the chimney and curtains at the windows, seemed to be inhabited), and whitewashed walls topped with brush prolonged the rows of buildings. Keeping in the lee of the island, the cruiser headed for the tiny beach where an alarmed band of seagulls rose in flight as it approached, only to settle on the other side of the rocks. On board everything was as quiet as if they were performing a mere gunnery exercise. Station A had circulated the order to use the lighthouse as a target, and Gervasio, looking over the rail, watched the synchronized swiveling of the turrets, the starboard antiaircraft guns set for surface firing, the aiming preparations of the *Vulcano* and the other cruisers. The defenseless little island, so savagely threatened, gave an impression of pathos. Dámaso Valentín, who was following this unusual show of force in amusement, turned toward him and said jokingly, "We're not going to shoot the island, are we?"

The heliograph on the *Canarias* blinked without receiving a reply. It tried twice more, but in vain. Unexpectedly the warning gun went off and the band of seagulls took flight, squawking, and headed for Ferrera. Columbrete Grande still lay silent. A burst of machine-gun fire stitched the rock where the buildings were, and then two thin figures came out of the house, stopped on top of the rise, and nervously waved a white sheet between them. At the telemeter, Petty Officer Tubío said in his rich clerical voice, "They're two old guys, Don Mario."

Behind him Damasito began to laugh, caressing the notch in his tooth with his tongue.

"Why don't we declare war on them?" he joked under his breath.

At first Gervasio felt mortified. Those powerful batteries ready to open fire on two helpless old men struck him as unnecessary showing off. But when he looked toward the *Vulcano* and saw the detachment of Marines drawn up on the deck with fixed bayonets, a febrile excitement washed over him. The Marines in perfect formation, boarding the boat and heading for the shore, evoked scenes from some novel or other that he had read in his childhood. With his naked eye he could see the red-and-blue uniforms ascending the path in single file, and the two old men who had been standing motionless at its top coming down to meet them. The captain spoke with them for a few minutes, then turned toward the sergeant who was with him, and the sergeant went into the lighthouse, emerged on the balcony, and raised the Nationalist flag. At that instant all the crews of the ships came to attention as the flagship's signal gun paid honors to the flag by firing the regulation twenty-one salutes. Something warm seemed to dissolve in Gervasio's breast and the hair on his temples stirred, but Dámaso's hearty slap on the back brought him to himself.

"I like these kinds of wars, sailor. What do you think? Did you see how to conquer an archipelago?"

During the past few weeks Gervasio's congenital ability to change reality, to make the most trivial events into splendid deeds, to magnify the purest banality, had become more active. Inspired by his imagination, Operation Columbretes (islands of whose existence Uncle Felipe Neri was also unaware) became a full-fledged landing. In his letter he wrote, without actually lying, of previous strategy (antisubmarine course, artillery preparation), subsequent machine-gun attack, landing with fixed bayonets, occupation of the island, and as a pleasant coda, "the stunning moment when our country's ensign was raised in the archipelago's capital, accompanied by the regulation twenty-one salutes." As he wrote of the thrilling ceremony Gervasio's pen ran away with him: "At that grandiose moment, Uncle, what came to my mind was the picture of the old conquistadors taking possession of infidel lands in the name of His Majesty, king of all the Spains."

Gervasio had a growing passion for making literature. He loved to swell like a peacock, to let his emotions show. The vague realization that someday those letters might serve as background for drawing his portrait as a hero made him more careful, forced him to watch himself, to measure his expressions. Uncle Felipe Neri answered him by return mail, in glowing letters overflowing with patriotic ardor, inevitably headed by the familiar philosophical premise "Who but God?" "Thanks to your heroic sacrifice, our Fatherland is beginning to be reborn," he said. They were warm, gratifying missives, but Gervasio would have preferred to read Manena Abad's spiky, energetic, nervous handwriting. The girl with streaked blond hair, whom he exalted in his memory, continued to endow his historic efforts with a sporting cast: "To live on the sea, heavens! The dream of my whole life." Gervasio fumed, disapproving of the girl's frivolous opinions. All the same, when they returned to base after the ridiculously overblown operation, he forgot about the girl and her opinions when he received a devastating letter from Mama Zita. Eduardo Custodio was not getting well. The terrible infection had left him practically blind, barely able to distinguish light from dark. He was learning to read the Braille system for the blind. She could tell him nothing about his state of mind because Eduardo refused any interference. Mama Zita ended her letter by exhorting him to pray for Eduardo. "I'm so afraid for that boy," she wrote. "What ideas are stirring in his unhappy mind?" These last sentences, which he gratuitously connected to his unsuccessful skirmish with La Cubana, plunged Gervasio into a corrosive religious crisis. He had to pray for his friend. But was his conscience in any condition to pray for anyone? How

long had it been since he had gone to church, since he had taken
communion? Was it consistent for him to spend an afternoon in a
brothel while his friend was going blind? Was such behavior worthy of a crusader? To justify himself he appealed to his loneliness,
to human infirmity, to the weakness of the flesh; but in any case,
was it consistent for the hosts of Christ the King to live in sin, to
fight in sin, to die in sin? Did he even know whether Tato Delgado
had died in a state of grace? And the rest of those who had died
in the *Baleares*? Would the Lord recognize contrition in their sacrifice and save them, perhaps? Why did the words of the crusaders
of the Crusade go one way and their conduct another? And if their
behavior was unworthy, disloyal to their principles, what made the
crusaders different from the Reds?

He spent several days in religious instability before he made up
his mind to confess. Dámaso Valentín was surprised by his decision.

"Don't tell me you're going to kill the afternoon in a church,
sailor."

There was emphatic pride in Gervasio's answer.

"Then what are we fighting for?"

He went into the cathedral at five in the afternoon and spent two
hours sitting in a pew under the multicolored light of the stained-
glass windows, repeating childishly, "Lord, let Eduardo see; don't
let my friend be blind." After an hour, in an attack of mysticism,
Gervasio offered the Lord a curious exchange: the sight of his left
eye for his friend Eduardo Custodio's right eye. He was tempted
to offer both but lacked the courage, fearful that the Lord would
take him at his word, though to silence the reproaches of his conscience he told himself that it wouldn't be fair either for Eduardo
to recover the sight of both eyes (and moreover without myopia),
while he stayed blind for the rest of his life. Despite the conditions
attached to his vow he was moved by his own audacity and felt
sublime, like Saint Martin, who gave half his cloak to a poor man
on a chilly day. He was sure that Peter's sense of philanthropy and
solidarity would never reach such heights. To give up one eye
would mean giving up the Naval Academy, and Peter wouldn't do
that for Eduardo Custodio or anyone else. These charitable fantasies, like his previous epic musings, made him more important in

his own eyes, led him to believe that he was superior to the rest of humankind.

The immense deserted naves, isolated from urban noise by their thick stone walls, helped Gervasio to concentrate. First he mentally arranged his sins in alphabetical order: La Cubana, God, Papa Telmo (his standoffishness, his distance from him). But he immediately decided to classify them according to the Commandments: he claimed to love God above all things, but more than God he loved Manena Abad, and the more she scorned him the more he loved her. He claimed to keep the Sabbath holy, but on many a Sunday he had lain in the sun on the spar deck, beside Scurvy, instead of going to the mass said by the padre in Compartment 4 at eleven o'clock. He claimed to honor his father and mother, but in the best of cases he honored only the latter; he scorned Papa Telmo, was ashamed of him, hated his convictions, thought him a bad patriot, and disdained his advice. He claimed not to fornicate, but he had tried to with La Cubana and had been greatly annoyed by the failure of his action. Coming to terms with his conscience gave him a soft, comfortable feeling, though an inner voice told him that despite the mysticism aroused by special circumstances, things would not change too much in the future. A door banged a long way off, and to the right of the main altar a thin priest appeared, dragging his feet as if he were senile. Gervasio confessed to him, shouting and gesticulating to offset his deafness. And on the following Sunday, back at sea, he took communion at the shipboard mass along with four dozen of his mates. As he returned to his seat, instead of giving thanks to God and petitioning him for his blind friend, he was working out sums, establishing proportions. If there were fifty communicants among twelve hundred, the conclusion could not be more devastating: the ship contained only about four percent of crusaders, hence the war necessarily had to be something quite different from what Uncle Felipe Neri said. At the last minute he succeeded in concentrating, and rocked by a sea that was choppy but not rough, offered the Eucharist for his friend Eduardo Custodio (without alluding to the exchange of eyes) and for Papa Telmo, not for his safety, but once more for him to be converted.

"Clothed in the new man," he ascended to the spar deck full of comprehension, abnegation, and solidarity; also altruistic, generous, and quick to pardon. Near the port machine gun he met Luis Naveira, Nasty, who was from the same village as Petty Officer Pita, and talked to him straightforwardly. What had happened to the petty officer? What were the reasons for his sadness, his remoteness, his bitterness, his melancholy? Nasty looked at him with his innocent blue eyes, loudly cracking his knuckles.

"Don't ask me, 377A. I don't know anything."

Gervasio continued to insist, and Nasty retreated.

"Look, 377A, everybody has his own story. I don't like to interfere in other people's lives."

But in his state of beatitude, in his zeal to help his fellow man, Gervasio persevered. What about solidarity? And feeling for shipmates? And mutual aid? What are we fighting for here if it isn't to help one another? Finally Nasty, with his childish face and chubby pink beardless cheeks, let fall the remark that Petty Officer Pita's unhappiness was incurable. His only brother, Máximo Pita, father of seven small children, had been assassinated in the village soon after the war began. Gervasio, who felt that the information was not sufficient, besieged him, pressed him, insisted. But Nasty refused to talk; he didn't know any more, what he had said was what his father had told him, because he hadn't been there when the murder took place.

During the afternoon watch the cruiser approached the recently conquered coast, near Vinaroz, and intercepted a small French ship, the *Balbec,* which was fleeing north with refugees. Two hours later it turned over its prize to the armed merchantman *Mar Negro,* made a complete turn, and sailed parallel to the coast, so close that soldiers and sailors exchanged greetings by waving caps and handkerchiefs. At nightfall three Martin bombers dropped their bombs on them. They were flying so high, at more than three thousand meters, that in spite of the surprise attack they didn't hit anything. Bartolomé Roselló, Mallorquín, of the almost imperceptible eyebrows, had directed the defensive fire; and Gervasio, crouched over the speaking tube with his mouth dry and his stomach in a knot, his insides in turmoil, his fear tempered by the conviction that in the worst of cases he could swim to shore (where the soldiers who were bivouacking on the beach would give him a hero's welcome), shouted the order, "Fire, fire, fire!" until he was hoarse. That night

during the second watch, tired out, and with a cloudless sky, a calm
sea, a clear conscience, and a serene mind, he fell fast asleep for the
second time. When he awoke he saw Petty Officer Pita's thick-
necked silhouette beside him in the shadows, wrapped in his wide-
sleeved coat, covering the outer lenses of the binoculars with his
hand. He shrank into himself abjectly, and just as he done the first
time, slid his buttocks off the iron stool until he was on his feet,
standing shamed and confused beside Petty Officer Pita.

"What did you go to war for, 377A? To sleep?"

"To fight, Petty Officer Pita. I enlisted as a volunteer to fight for
Spain."

"Do you Castilians fight for Spain with your eyes closed?"

Gervasio did not reply; he felt trapped, without an idea in his
head. Miodelo was playing "Carrasclás" in the other group, while
skinny Santoña watched over the bow. Petty Officer Pita looked
him over from head to foot, waiting for an answer. Gervasio decided to close his eyes and stake everything on one throw.

"You won't make a written report, will you, Petty Officer?"

"I don't make written reports, 377A; get that through your head
once and for all; I'm not that kind. But that doesn't mean you can
abuse my patience."

After his communion of the day before, Petty Officer Pita's
magnanimity completely softened Gervasio's heart; he felt tender,
companionable, and bold. And when at last he blurted out that he
knew how he suffered on account of his brother and was sorry for
it, Pita's eyes, two dark smudges in the half-light, shone in stupefaction for a moment, but he was unable to answer. Then Gervasio,
suddenly confidential, spoke to him impassionedly about the thing
he had hidden in shame ever since the war began: that Papa Telmo
was in prison, that Papa Telmo was a Republican, a nonconformist,
a traitor to his class, that he had been imprisoned in the bullring
of his home city ever since the early days of the Uprising. He was
surprised by the heat with which he spoke of his father, with an
undertone of enthusiasm, of affection. The boy established a point
of affinity between Papa Telmo and Pita. And the petty officer
listened to him in confusion, not knowing what to say. For the first
time, in the climate of incomprehension that was so habitual for
him, Gervasio was able to speak proudly of his father's civil con-

duct, convinced that it was judged in the light of different principles. At last he had found, among his circle of friends and acquaint-
ances, someone capable of valuing Papa Telmo's attitude. And
suddenly it became clear to him that no man ought to infringe
another man's freedom of thought. But a desire for balance led him
to talk about the death of Uncle Fadrique, murdered with ten other
members of his party on the Cerro de los Angeles at the foot of the
statue of Christ. ("A militiaman said, 'God's dead, so there's no
need for altar boys.' They stood them facing the pedestal and fired
shots into them, what do you think of that, Petty Officer Pita?")
Disconcerted, the petty officer lowered the hood of his coat as if it
bothered him or was too hot or kept him from hearing and began
to speak, first hesitantly and then calmly and with conviction, even
with fervor: "the others" too, in his village, had made his brother
Máximo do the stations of Christ, the Way of the Cross, around
the hermitage, and at each station they had beaten him brutally, so
that when he reached the last one there was no need to crucify him
because his skull was fractured and he was dead. Petty Officer Pita
trembled, clutching the front of the bulkhead under the stars, and
added, his voice growing stronger, "That's why I believe that it's
one thing to say the name of Christ and another to believe in him.
Because what Christ preached was that we should love one another."

Gervasio realized that he was in a corner, with no escape, but
feeling fraternal as he did tonight he said in a small voice, "That's
war, Petty Officer."

"I know it's war, 377A, but who invented this damned war?"

Gervasio writhed mentally. He recalled Uncle Felipe Neri's
denunciations in the drawing room of the palace, declaiming, like
the nearsighted prophet with stomach ulcers that he was, against
the excesses of "the horde." Not finding any other reply to give,
he repeated what he had heard his uncle say so many times.

"My uncle, who's an army officer, said that the war really broke
out in 1934 at the time of the October revolution. According to
him, what came afterward was inevitable."

"Even if it was, 377A, something went wrong. If it's the job of
priests and Christians to pardon, something important went wrong
then."

They were so absorbed in their conversation that the first time Miodelo announced in an urgent tone that he saw a shadow off the port bow, neither of them moved; and then, when he repeated it and skinny Santoña called to the petty officer, now frankly in a tone of alarm, a lively commotion was produced on the station. The four of them talked all at once, piled into the bow, trying to follow Miodelo's finger with their eyes over Santoña's shoulder.

"A shadow, Petty Officer . . . Holy God! Ten degrees to port. I'm keeping it in sight. Notify Station A. Make it snappy, Petty Officer Pita, it might torpedo us."

The petty officer, Gervasio, and Santoña focused their binoculars in the direction he had pointed out. Pita spoke after carefully examining the sector.

"I can't see it. It wouldn't be your imagination, Miodelo?"

A black, rigid, bristling silhouette, silent, high in the bow, suddenly seemed to emerge from the depths of the sea before Gervasio's astonished eyes.

"Great heaven, it's true!" he exclaimed in terror, his gut twisting, a slight stirring of the hairs at the back of his neck under the wide-sleeved coat. "There it is, a little more than a mile away, Petty Officer, twenty degrees to port!"

The black shadow on the black sea slipped in and out of sight at fleeting intervals, the pale mark of her wake the most perceptible sign: a blunt, solid, high silhouette with a lot of superstructure. As if his desire for precision would be a guarantee, Gervasio added, "Too high for a destroyer and too low for a cruiser. Shall I contact Station A, Petty Officer Pita?"

"Wait."

"And what if it lets go with its torpedoes? We don't want what happened to the *Baleares* to happen to us, Petty Officer!" shouted Miodelo in alarm.

Petty Officer Pita had fallen silent, his binoculars hanging on his chest, leaning on the telemetry apparatus with his bull-necked head bent a little forward, looking into space, as though he were offering a sacrifice. And as if he had remembered something all of a sudden, he put a cigarette between his lips and took his lighter out of the front pocket of his blouse to light it. Miodelo made a rush at him, striking it down.

"You're not going to smoke now, Petty Officer! Do you want them to send us to hell?"

The nervous shrilling of the Station A telephone startled him. Miodelo sat down on the iron stool.

"Station A."

"Station H."

"Didn't you see a shadow to port? Right now it's falling astern. Answer. Over."

Miodelo's words sounded neutral, rambling, as he looked out of the corner of his eye at Petty Officer Pita, who was still leaning on the telemetry apparatus.

"Station H here. One of us thought he saw that shadow, but we couldn't agree. We couldn't see it clearly. That's why we didn't report it."

The membrane of Station Λ's transmitter vibrated as if it had been slit.

"Station A here. You ought to know that any abnormality you have observed has to be reported to the bridge. Your failure is serious. Who's in charge of the group?"

Miodelo looked at Petty Officer Pita, who seemed abstracted and detached from the conversation. He lowered his voice to say, "Station H here. Petty Officer Pita."

"Station A here. By orders of the captain, Petty Officer Pita to the telephone. Over."

Petty Officer Pita shook his head two or three times before he sat down, cleared his throat, and said in a hoarse voice, "Petty Officer Pita, sir." Then he crossed the edges of the coat over his stomach and waited impassively for the reply. His conduct, in view of his experience, was unacceptable. Why had he concealed the suspicion of a shadow from the bridge? The shadow had been real: it was the minelayer *Marte,* deliberately assigned by naval command to test the efficacy of the cruiser's watches. Stations A, B, and C had replied immediately. What was the reason for Station H's obstinate silence? If the ship's safety had depended on that station and the enemy had been real, by this time we'd all be at the bottom of the sea. "There is no excuse for your conduct, Petty Officer Pita," concluded the metallic voice. "Disciplinary measures will have to be taken. Be on the bridge at eight o'clock tomorrow morning."

"Aye, aye, sir."

He did not change his position when he turned off the switch. Miodelo, Santoña, and Gervasio regarded him with a certain detachment, a mixture of accusation and and indulgence, as if they were watching a predatory animal caught in a trap. Petty Officer Pita said stiffly, without turning his head, "I'm sorry. I didn't see the minelayer and I didn't trust the rest of you either. If I'd seen it we would have reported it. I'm the only one who's to blame." He stood up, consulted his wristwatch in the starlight, bringing his eyes very close to its face, and added, "Hurry up, 377A. It's twenty minutes past the hour. Call your relief."

CHAPTER 20

Petty Officer Pita was punished with ten periods of confinement to the ship, a punishment which, in view of the rhythm of shore leaves, meant two or three months without setting foot on land. Almost nothing was learned of his interview with the captain. In addition to being evasive, which was habitual for him, the petty officer returned crestfallen, like a schoolboy caught in some flagrant offense. He gave explanations to no one, nor did anyone dare to ask him for them; he isolated himself, literally removed himself from the others. Navy Radio praised his gallantry in assuming responsibility for the affair by excusing the other members of his group. However, his offense produced bitter disappointment on Station H. Its loss of prestige with the other fire control stations was more than obvious. Station H had been the only one not to alert the bridge, and that meant that its crew's competence was diminished. In any case a tacit rivalry among the stations meant that each tried to be the best, and Petty Officer Pita, with twenty years of naval experience, knew this. Perhaps because of it, because of knowing that he was responsible, he was even more remote and secretive. Gervasio observed the petty officer's process of moral decay, and watched him. In the hours before the incident of the minelayer he had been sure that he could overcome his reserve, but now he realized that Pita's confidences were not based on a need for communication but on a momentary weakness arising from those of Gervasio himself. During subsequent watches he waited in vain for the unfinished dialogue to be resumed, but Pita maintained his silence, indifferent to the outside world to the point that when someone had to speak to him he inevitably seemed to be taken by surprise, and to return to reality cost him genuine mental effort. Peter, whom Gervasio had told about the death of Pita's brother, advised him to use some subterfuge to make him take up the subject again, but Gervasio's attempts along those lines were unsuccessful. "Pita," as Damasito said, "didn't charge the red rag." Apparently unaware of Gervasio's efforts, he continued to be immersed in his private world, so absentminded that he could let a whole watch go by without speaking a word, merely smoking an occasional cigarette or drinking a swallow of cognac from a flask that he had carried in the side pocket of his work uniform ever since the famous night. Gervasio confined himself to observing him at a distance, and Miodelo, who had taken Pita's part with a funereal respect for his silence, stopped playing the harmonica until one night when for unknown reasons, maybe because he was a little drunk, Pita was more open than usual and said, as if he hadn't noticed the interruption of the concerts, "Miodelo, why don't you play 'The Priest's Hat'?"

Miodelo, pleasantly surprised, took his harmonica from the folds of his handkerchief and played "The Priest's Hat" in a low key with a great deal of sentiment. This was the unexpected way in which Miodelo's harmonica solos returned to the night watches.

During mess hours Petty Officer Pita sat at the head of the table, reserved and distant. He scarcely ate, smoked all the time, and drank one glass of wine after another. His lack of appetite, which Gervasio had noticed ever since he came aboard the cruiser, had increased and became total a few weeks after his confinement. The petty officer was getting thinner, the seat of his trousers grew baggy, his face became sunken, the back of his head more prominent, and he developed a repeated, mechanical tic in his right eye, like an incomplete wink. Gervasio was greatly concerned for him, and although he knew that the petty officer did not share the ideals of the Uprising, he was reluctant—despite the evidence—to attribute the incident of the minelayer to bad faith. In fact, he had contradictory ideas on this point which varied with the circumstances. Sometimes he would say to himself, "He's a spy. He saw the minelayer's shadow like the rest of us, but chose to say nothing. And when he leaned on the telemeter and tried to light a cigarette, he was offering the cruiser to the Republican cause." But if he looked straight into the shifting blue of those wandering eyes he would conclude that when Petty Officer Pita refused to inform the bridge about the presence of the shadow, he had behaved nobly, trying to save the good name of Station H from being held up to ridicule. Certainly, during the summons to battle stations and firing practice that followed the incident, Petty Officer Pita often arrived late and sometimes a little drunk, delayed fixing the target, and often his figures did not agree with those of his shipmate Javier Medina. Gervasio's observation of the petty officer, which he had begun out of curiosity, became a systematic, diligent, almost professional kind of spying. He stealthily watched his walks on the deck, his sporadic visits to the lockers, his inroads on the ship's stores, his wanderings through storerooms and compartments. It was in this way that he discovered a friendship of Pita's that he had not known about: Petty Officer Poncela, the paymaster of the aft storeroom in Compartment 2. They met there every day, conversed, exchanged notes and papers; and one afternoon, minutes before the sailors went ashore wearing their dress uniforms, Gervasio followed Pita to the heads and saw him give a bulky envelope to Poncela over the top of the low bulkhead that closed off the enlisted men's toilets. Petty Officer Poncela, with his dress cap on, ready to go ashore, hastened to hide the envelope in his white laundry bag. Gervasio's heart came up in his mouth. He followed the petty officer to the shore boat, and after it landed to one of the last houses on the beach, from which he emerged minutes later without the white bag and with another striped one in his hand. After that the petty officer, still all alone, took two turns around the promenade before seating himself on the terrace of the Granja Reus café. From another table inside the café Gervasio observed him through the window, pretending to read a newspaper. Petty Officer Poncela had ordered coffee and a pastry, and before he had finished his snack a tall man with no eyelashes and red-rimmed eyelids, dressed in a loose black-and-gray-striped jacket, sat down at the next table and ordered black coffee. In the midst of paying his bill Petty Officer Poncela dug into his striped bag, took the bulky envelope out of it, laid it absentmindedly on the empty chair that separated him from the lashless man, and stood up. Gervasio's heart beat so violently that he nearly choked. He watched Petty Officer Poncela walk away and lose himself in the crowd, while the lashless man picked up the envelope from the wicker chair, placed it in the inner pocket of his jacket, and stood up too. Gervasio followed him to Calle Cifré, then turned onto Calle San Cayetano, which was very crowded, and hastened his step to keep from being left behind. Though he turned his head twice, the man with the unprotected eyes walked along confidently, unhurriedly, stopping from time to time. Gervasio followed him, pausing at corners and in dark vestibules, and as they entered the maze of little streets in the old quarter of the city and the traffic began to thin out, he let the distance between them increase. Suddenly the man in the striped jacket stopped and turned around, so rapidly that Gervasio barely had time to go down on one knee and pretend to be tying his bootlace. When, after nightfall, they drew opposite the Corredera de Tous y Maroto, on the Calle San Nicolás, the man in the striped jacket speeded up (his footsteps sounding rhythmically on the worn stones of the street), but when he saw out of the corner of his eye that Gervasio was doing the same he unexpectedly started to run. The long flaps of his unbuttoned jacket slapped against his buttocks as Gervasio ran after him, confused by the sound of his own footsteps on the pavement, but when he reached

the second corner he lost sight of him. Gasping for breath, never
pausing, he ran as far as the corner, looked both ways, and when
he did not see the man unhesitatingly doubled back through the
Calle de los Cestos. He ran down two other narrow streets at
random and at the end of the second stopped, panting, in the
shelter of a doorway, peering to one side and the other. He thought
that the strange man in the striped jacket had shaken him off, and
eagerly breathed in through his mouth. For the first time since he
had begun to follow him, he asked himself the question, "And if
I catch him, what then?" His stomach contracted. He felt his heart-
beats pounding in his neck. He was gasping. He thought he
glimpsed the familiar silhouette under the opalescent light of the
streetlamp on the corner, but did not move. "Am I crazy?" he asked
himself, to justify his inaction. In the half-dark of the Plaza de
Santa Eulalia the shadow disappeared again. He waited, sheltered
in a doorway on the Calle Arquitecto Reyes, until his wildly beating heart slowed down, and returned to the promenade.

Next morning after the spar deck had been scrubbed, Gervasio
hastened to convoke a controversy at the table near the lockers in
Compartment 3, to inform his friends about his latest discoveries.
When Dámaso heard his story he ran his red tongue across the
notch in his tooth, head bent, as he rolled a cigarette. Peter, his chin
resting on his closed knees, adopted an attitude of extreme solemnity. He ran his hand the wrong way over the hair at the back of
his neck before he spoke.

"Pita's a concealed Red; no two ways about it."

Dámaso Valentín suddenly raised his head, with his red tongue
poised to move across the gummed edge of the cigarette paper.

"You're seeing enemies where there aren't any," he said. "Can't
a man under arrest have any friends on land? Why not a woman?"

Gervasio rejected the suggestion.

"If that were true, why didn't he give the letter to Poncela in
front of everybody instead of doing it secretly in the heads?"

Dámaso Valentín, assuming a crafty air, blew smoke rings without replying. Gervasio was annoyed by his joking, flippant attitude. He had succeeded in making Peter suspicious, but Dámaso,
obstinate in his frivolous irresponsibility, had escaped him; there
was no way to make him concentrate, make him think. He tried to

shock him out of his skepticism by a number of hard-hitting questions: Why this daily socializing between Pita and Petty Officer
Poncela? Why did Poncela serve as a contact with strange civilians
outside the ship? Why didn't Poncela speak to the man in the
striped jacket instead of leaving the letter on the empty chair as
though they didn't know each other? The spark of amusement did
not disappear from Dámaso's eyes, while the shade of seriousness
in Peter's increased; he ended by expressing the opinion that Pita
had switched allegiance and that his failure to act in the presence
of the minelayer *Marte* had undoubtedly been deliberate. Gervasio's voice hesitated as he asked the necessary question.

"And . . . and what can we do?"

"Accuse him. Report him to the Command. I don't see any other
way."

"Don't count on me for that."

"Do you intend to cover up for him?"

"Call it what you want to, but I *can't* do it. It would be like
informing on my father."

Gervasio was aware of the inconsistency of what he was doing.
It was paradoxical to pile suspicion on the petty officer and then,
when the time came to make decisions, to excuse him, disregard
them, become his defender. And when Peter called this to his
attention he did not deny it, but repeated emotionally that to
inform on Pita would be like placing him in front of a firing squad
with his hands tied. He had spent several days thinking about Papa
Telmo's last note in reply to the compassionate letter he had written him on the day he took communion. Papa Telmo had respected
his ideas, but as soon as Gervasio had given him an opportunity he
had written him in deeply emotional terms, full of tenderness.
"Nothing is important enough," he had said, "to separate a son
from his father." Gervasio turned this sentence over and over in his
mind. Papa Telmo's position was clear: neither politics nor religion
nor war were sufficient cause to place distance between a father and
his son. His heart softened. He accepted his father's cautious sentimental approach as a natural process. And he remembered something Uncle Jairo had said in one of the Saturday gatherings in the
palace, whose meaning he had not fully understood until now:
"The spirit of the mother dominates in the child until adolescence.

After that, the father's (usually more reasonable, less instinctive) begins to displace that of the mother, and in the end it prevails." Was it pure chance that he should remember this sentence almost on the eve of his eighteenth birthday? Was it also chance that on the verge of reaching that age he had written Papa Telmo his first really open-hearted letter, inspired by spontaneous love? On some nights, when he went off watch and unhooked his hammock, in the few seconds before sleep came he tried his best to form a picture of his father's face; but he could not bring the features to mind, they faded in his memory, and in the end he pictured a face that vaguely reminded him of Petty Officer Pita's. He looked at Dámaso, lying on the linoleum with his fingers entwined behind his head, observing the iron bars that held the tables and benches to the ceiling. He felt himself floating, out in the cold, alone. And perhaps if Peter had spoken an affectionate word to him at that moment, he would have started to cry. But Peter, with impeccable reasoning, insisted on the expeditious solution. After a long pause he bit his lower lip and said, "I'm not unaware that a war is hard, even cruel, but the minute we let sentiment in, we may lose it."

Gervasio's outburst was unexpected. He was the first to be surprised by his spate of loquacity, in which passion prevailed over common sense. And in his impassioned speech he mingled the names of his uncles Norberto and Adrián with those of David and Fadrique, described their respective deaths, "the very same death," he said; and, as the only viable way out of the vicious circle of his argument, he unloaded his animosity on Peter, called him a "cold, calculating strategist," accused him of taking the war like a chess game, with no human beings involved ("One ship against another ship, one plane against another plane, one trench against another trench," he said), when in fact there was a sordid, dirty facet of that war that Peter knew and in which he was not ready to participate. It was the first time he had raised his voice against his friend, and when he finished he was trembling, frightened by his own vehemence, under the astonished gaze of Dámaso, who had risen to his feet, while Peter lowered his eyes in confusion and pretended to play with the earflaps of his cap, whose snap he mechanically opened and closed. After a while he raised his head and said, by way of excusing himself, that sometimes war with all its horrors demanded being a "cold, calculating strategist," a statement that touched Gervasio and induced him, not to apologize, but to promise him solemnly ("I give you my word of honor," he said) that he would not leave Petty Officer Pita by day or by night, and if worse came to worst he would convince him of the need to leave the ship.

Faithful to his promise, early next morning he followed Petty Officer Pita to Compartment 1 on the bow, the farthest from Station H, and there watched him write, on a hammock from the storage boxes, a message on a pad of paper, fold it into four, and slip it into the crack of a locker in the passageway leading to the boilers. An hour later its recipient, Petty Officer Poncela, the paymaster, appeared. After reading the note he wadded it up and stowed it in the upper pocket of his work uniform. Immediately, leaning against the bulkhead without moving from the spot, he wrote several hasty lines in reply and stuck them into Petty Officer Pita's locker. Until the cruiser put to sea three days later Petty Officer Pita and Poncela did not see each other again, and Gervasio deduced from this that the man in the striped jacket had alerted them.

The cold weather had returned, and gray waves wrinkled the sea's surface. During those days the newspapers spoke of a bloody battle on the Ebro, at first favorable to the Republicans, who had crossed the river, and in the end becoming a new Nationalist victory. What was the point, then, of their actions in the south, where the flotilla of cruisers was heading? On this occasion Navy Radio was both laconic and reliable: the destroyer *José Luis Díez,* which ever since hostilities began had been sheltering in a French Atlantic port, was trying to break through the blockade and reach Cartagena. As they came into the Strait the sea rose. The waves struck against the ship's stern, buffeted by an east wind, on a transparent day of perfect visibility. To starboard rose Gibraltar, the rock's top aflame in the sun, three dark destroyers below it, and to port the smoky silhouette of the African coast. Standing out against it like cutouts were the four stubby, heavy minelayers, immobile in the vast perspective. Dámaso Valentín, after examining the formation with his binoculars, said slyly as he turned toward them, "What would Petty Officer Rego think of this? Would he call it a valiant action or a cowardly ambush?"

He laughed in bursts, in hiccuping giggles, his head moving up and down as hens' do when they drink. Gervasio, who to forget his sensations of seasickness had avoided the close air of the lower decks for two days, grabbed the chain of the spar deck. Peter came and stood beside him.

"I'd like to know," he said, "what that guy is thinking about right now."

"Who? Pita?"

"Pita of course, who else?"

Gervasio's reply was accompanied by an evasive smile. Since their confrontation his attitude toward Peter tried to be conciliatory.

"On the high seas a man is the same as a prisoner."

"Don't be so confident. Remember the *Baleares.*"

The cruiser split the waters of the Strait in long sweeps, from La Línea de la Concepción to Trafalgar, back and forth, like a gigantic sentry. Day and night it repeated the same itinerary. To port and to starboard the flotillas of minelayers and destroyers also sailed the same waters over and over. On the third night, when they had lost hope that the destroyer would appear, they were awakened by the call to battle stations over the loudspeakers. When the alarm sounded Gervasio's feeling of seasickness disappeared. Seated on his stool next to the tube, huddled into his blanket, mouth dry, he tried to fight off a new attack of paralysis. Station A announced a shadow to starboard. Gervasio wrapped his blanket around himself, bent over the tube, and repeated Don Mario's order to the guns.

"Prepare for surface fire!"

But something was not going well in the observers' perches; neither Javier Medina nor Petty Officer Pita had succeeded in identifying a target (in the starlight Gervasio could see Pita's clumsy movements, his struggles, the useless turning of the crank). The cruiser made a turn and gathered speed. From the vibration of the bulkheads they deduced that they were sailing at the top capacity of the engines. No doubt the bridge was trying to combat the *José Luis Díez* with her own weapons: speed. Faster than her opponents, if she succeeded in breaking through the blockade line no one could stop her; she would leave them behind in an instant. Gervasio felt his hands trembling under the blanket; he shuddered when he heard the first salvo from the guns on the bow and again looked toward Petty Officer Pita in anguish. Tubío had been calmly calling out distances for some time, and Javier Medina had located the target. But Pita was clumsy: "I don't see it, Don Mario. I can't get it." The explosion of the stern guns shook the ship and illumined the station like a lightning flash. Other units were banging away from the starboard side, the firing became general, but Pita continued to struggle with the crank, blinked one eye and then the other, raised his head in despair, flung open his empty hands as a sign of impotence, while Don Mario fumed.

"Come on, Pita, get going, Pita; we're waiting for you."

The cruiser listed as it made a new turn, and the guns on bow and stern roared. They could hear the barrage from the minelayers, and Gervasio, crouched by the tube, looked unblinkingly at Petty Officer Pita, observing his hasty movements in the shadows. The bombardment did not cease, and when Miodelo shouted that the *José Luis Díez* had been hit, had a gash in her bow, and was sinking, silence grew heavy on the station. There were no signs of jubilation but rather the opposite; they all had a feeling of frustration. Don Mario sat down at the spotter and said, "Confirm." Station A's telephone explained that the destroyer was seriously damaged and, a short time later, that she had entered British territorial waters and that no rash action was to be taken. Don Mario turned around, swiveling his seat toward them.

"Waiting status," he said, controlling his anger.

Dawn was coming up over the bow, a pearly, chilly light. And the destroyer's black silhouette, listing to port, escorted by two British patrol boats, stood out against the whiteness of the rock, under whose shadow it took refuge a few minutes later. The all-clear had sounded and the crew of Station H went disconsolately down to the spar deck, once more overcome by a sensation of failure; and Miodelo's festive attitude as he played "The British Flag That Waves o'er Gibraltar" on his harmonica did not serve to dispel it.

Gervasio found Peter in the galley, in the coffee line. He was beside himself. He called Petty Officer Pita a traitor, and when Gervasio tried to excuse him Peter persuaded him that his own behavior was as guilty as Pita's disloyalty, and that he might even be shot for it. Gervasio hesitated, but continued to use his arguments: Don Mario had also witnessed the petty officer's conduct. He was head of the station. Why not let him take the initiative? Peter turned on him.

"And if he doesn't? He doesn't have the proofs we do. It's our duty to offer them to him."

"All right, if he doesn't take action I'll talk to Pita. I've given you my word, and I'll do it."

The victory over the *José Luis Díez,* which appeared in dispatches and was exaggerated by the press, resulted in a clamorous reception at the base: parades, banners, military music, and an elaborate military mass on the quay. Out of gratitude the owners of theaters and nightclubs gave the sailors free tickets to their shows for three days, and a fifty percent discount on drinks in the bars. It was a foretaste of the euphoria of the war's end. In the midst of this triumphant atmosphere came a telegram from Uncle Felipe Neri: "Thrilled glorious deed proud to have hero in family stop joint letter follows stop give details many congratulations and kisses." Gervasio reread the telegram, feeling perplexed. Then he swelled like a peacock. His childish and almost forgotten aspiration was ratified on the folded blue paper: as far as the world was concerned, he was a hero. Uncle Felipe Neri had just added his name to those of the famous, immortal warriors. His tendency to admit favorable opinions as true led him to accept his uncle's words verbatim. Manena Abad was also pleased, though she did not hide the reservations she felt: the cruiser's victory over the *José Luis Díez,* though brilliant, was after all a victory of Goliath over David, a logical and predictable one. Such niggling objections, after Uncle Felipe Neri's incandescent applause, caused him to tear up the letter and throw the little pieces into the sea. The judgment of an experienced man, and moreover a career military officer, must necessarily prevail over that of a girl not much past her fifteenth birthday. Gervasio paraded his vanity up and down the deck with Uncle Felipe Neri's telegram in the left-hand pocket of his work uniform, over his heart. That paper meant an explicit recognition of his courage, as definite as the wax seal giving him the San Fernando medal for heroism would have been. He gave some thought to the best way to answer his uncle. Boasting would lower the tone of his heroism (which consisted precisely in clothing the exceptional deed in the everyday word); but on the other hand it would be disappointing to admit his constraint in combat. Once again he chose hyperbolic objectivity: these were the facts, let the reader draw his own conclusions. By locating him outside the action, his own modesty made him even more admirable. Uncle Felipe Neri would attribute his remoteness to bashfulness. He was not lying when he spoke of tense waiting, of heavy fire, threat of torpedoes. And in view of his circumspection his uncle would mentally locate him in the place of greatest risk and responsibility. And he put so much fervor into the description of the battle that there was a moment when the hair began to rise on his neck, just as in his best times. He wrote in such a state of exaltation, with such burning conviction, that if at that moment someone had reminded him of the simple truth of what had happened (that Station H did not fire a single gun because Petty Officer Pita, the chief observer, presumably a concealed Red, couldn't find the target during the whole course of the action), he would have refused to believe it.

During the next few days the cruiser's activity did not decrease (east coast of Spain, Pantelleria, back to Spain), which made Petty Officer Pita's confinement to the ship seem likely to go on indefinitely. At mid-month the cruiser went to sea again with a specific mission: to escort a convoy of captured freighters to Málaga. Petty Officer Pita, after the battle with the *José Luis Díez,* had not returned to the mess table. His cheeks grew more and more sunken and sometimes, during night watches, he talked to himself in unintelligible words which Gervasio tried in vain to decipher. After they were at sea he began to meet Petty Officer Poncela again, either in the storerooms on the lowest deck by day or on the forecastle at nightfall. Gervasio spied on him. In view of Pita's absentmindedness he no longer took any precautions, and one afternoon at suppertime, as he was going down the hatchway to the stern storeroom, usually deserted, he bumped into him at the foot of the ladder.

"Did you want something, 377A?"

Gervasio was so startled that he didn't answer. He turned around and hastily returned to his station. He tried to avoid the petty officer, but the fact that they both had the next watch made seeing him inevitable. However, when Pita saw him again he had looked at him absentmindedly, as if to say, "Where have you and I seen each other before?" He was losing his head. He smoked at night without taking precautions, shamelessly lighting cigarettes with a lighter that showed the flame. Santoña and Miodelo, behind him on the other side, watched him in consternation and whispered under their breath. At dawn on the second day they were surprised by two enemy squadrons, ten Katiuskas and six Curtises. The attack was so unexpected (none of the observation posts had announced their presence) that the loudspeaker gave an unprecedented order to the crew: "Down on the ground!" (But what ground? thought Gervasio as he pressed his nose against the iron plates of the spar deck, trying to smother the muffled beating of his heart), while the bombs exploded and Gothic spouts of foam sprang from the sea. Once they reached their station, Don Mario's self-possession helped to restore the crew's composure, and as soon as Petty Officer Tubío swung the telemetry cylinder and began to sing out distances, and the commander (with his squashed cap on his square head) gave the order for defensive fire on the Curtises that were flying over them, Petty Officer Pita pronounced that lapidary phrase which would be engraved forever in the Navy's annals, as an emblem of stubbornness and refusal to follow orders:

"Don't fire on those, Don Mario; those are fighters. The ones we have to fire on are the ones that shit bombs."

Amid the explosions from the turrets and the chatter of the machine guns on the spar deck, a wave of stupor washed over Station H. The scene that followed was very rapid. A blunt, black, shiny object appeared in Don Mario's well-kept, hairy hand (what came to Gervasio's mind as he huddled over the speaking tube, shrunken by the noise, was the picture of Lucinio Orejón, with his incipient mustache and his baggy pants, emptying the magazine of his pistol on the attackers of the Lepanto barracks, back home in the Alameda district), which he coolly aimed at the petty officer's chest from five feet away and warned him, "Pita, obey orders or I'll put a bullet in your belly." A hellish noise was going on around them. Gervasio looked fearfully at Don Mario standing there, pistol in hand, giving no impression of melodrama, and then at Pita, his face sunken and twisted, the back of his neck prominent, his left eyelid twitching over his blue eye. He doubted that the petty officer would obey the commander's orders, and also that the commander was capable of putting a bullet in his belly. The very short period of time that the tension lasted seemed interminable to him. But before the bow turrets had a chance to fire again, Petty Officer Pita turned the crank, got the Curtises into his sights, and as if nothing had happened began to give data to the Perozzi board and Bartolomé Roselló to repeat in differing tones of voice the order of defense zones (one, two, three, and four), while the starboard team, led by Gervasio, fired on the fighters until they disappeared over the horizon.

On this occasion the all-clear did not produce the immediate clusters of men and conversations that usually marked the end of combat. The station's crew descended to the spar deck in silence, feeling dejected and downhearted. No one made any comment, not even about the remarkable incident of the pistol. Petty Officer Pita disappeared down the ventilator hatchway, and Gervasio and his friends, without previous agreement, met in Compartment 3 at the table below the lockers. Peter, very excited, his usual coolness gone, opened and closed the snap of his cap and demanded immediate action on Gervasio's part: the cruiser could not risk its safety by confiding its defense to "that lunatic." Gervasio nodded. He surrendered at last.

"Tonight I'll talk to him without fail," he said.

He was terrified by the idea of facing that erratic blue gaze, the conspiratorial wink of the left eyelid, but was ready to keep his word. However, during the evening watch he did not find Pita at his post and Javier Medina was there in his stead, bareheaded and with a severe expression on his aquiline profile. Miodelo and Santoña, who came up behind him chatting to each other, were also surprised when they reached the station.

"What's happening? Where's the petty officer?"

Medina slipped the strap of the binoculars over the hood of his coat and said in a low voice, "Pita's been arrested on the bridge, till further orders. He won't be coming back here. Meanwhile I'm chief of the group."

CHAPTER
21

Though in small measure, Petty Officer Pita's arrest changed the organization of Station H, Javier Medina, promoted to Petty Officer Second Class, became chief of the fourth group while Peter became observer and Fito Iroa, a blond, pink-cheeked boy with soft gray eyes, came from Station A to take over the telephones. Petty Officer Pita had left the ship one afternoon, guarded by Marines, while his brigade was off duty. Only Lago, Painter, had seen him leave, and the tips of his little red mustache drooped every time that he described his departure, with the squad of Marines around him, in

a motor launch from Naval Command: "When he got to the gangway he turned his head for a moment and saw me painting on the
spar deck. He smiled and gave a sort of wave with his hand, as if
he were saying good-bye, but the marine behind him gave him a
push, and then he went down a couple of steps and we lost sight
of each other." Petty Officer Tubío blinked when he heard this and
shook his head ambiguously, agreeing without agreeing, denying
without denying, an eclectic attitude that he found appropriate
between the two factions that had formed on the station. Encouraged to do so by skinny Santoña, Nasty (with his beardless, rosy
face over his broad swollen neck) now told them about the martyrdom of Máximo Pita, the petty officer's brother, in his village.

"They took him out in his underpants with a cross on his shoulders, and made him do the Way of the Cross around the hill. At
every station they beat him with sticks and stones, so that when
he got to the last one his head was broken and he was dead."

Gervasio listened to both sides in silence, but if the comments
were unfavorable to the petty officer and Miodelo resorted to his
harmonica and played "The Priest's Hat" to make amends, his eyes
grew wet and he would feel a slight prickling in the hairs on the
back of his neck. But except for Gervasio, Nasty, Miodelo, Santoña,
and perhaps Lago, Painter, for strictly sentimental reasons (maybe
because he had been the only one to say good-bye to him), the rest
of the station and the whole ship's company reviled him, convinced
that his treason could have meant sinking the ship and perhaps the
death of them all. For weeks Navy Radio attacked Pita, accusing
him of a whole series of transgressions which Naval Command,
preoccupied with the demands of a war that was drawing to a close,
did not bother to confirm or deny. According to Navy Radio, Petty
Officer Pita's disloyalty dated from the time he shipped on the
armed gunship *Apóstol Santiago,* in the Bay of Biscay, during the
early days of the Uprising, and was not out of principle (for he had
no concern with any ideology) but out of vengeance, an emotion
he had harbored in his heart ever since his brother's murder. Dozens of papers, letters, and compromising documents that proved his
treason had been found in his locker, in addition to a code in cipher
that he had been using for two years to communicate with a Red
transmitter in Marseilles. Navy Radio did not exclude the possibil-

ity that it had been he who, using prearranged signals, had guided the torpedoes toward the *Baleares* in the early morning hours of March 6, 1938. (Santoña got furious when he heard this theory: "That night he was right beside me. What kind of signals could he have given without my knowing it?") A group of saboteurs had been arrested in Mallorca at the same time as Pita, as well as Petty Officer Poncela, who apparently was the person in charge of giving information by Morse code about the cruiser's movements. Now kept prisoner in the castle of Bellver, Petty Officer Pita would leave it only to be tried by the summary court-martial in which the sailors who had worked most closely with him would be witnesses, especially the members of the fourth watch group of Station H. At the table in Compartment 3, Gervasio rebelled.

"I don't have anything to say against him. And besides, why should I do it? Don't they have proof enough already?"

Four days later Navy Radio offered a correction: Petty Officer Pita, having confessed and declared himself guilty, would be tried as a pure formality and without the presence of witnesses, for they were superfluous following his confession. Apparently the petty officer gave no signs whatever of repentance, was very calm, and according to his jailers did not think of himself as a traitor to the fatherland, but as condemned by traitors. At first Navy Radio had indicated that the trial would take place early in January, "out of respect for the holy season," but after Christmas, it spoke in vague terms of the last week in February.

Petty Officer Pita's arrest made Gervasio feel responsible, for although the accusation had not come from him, his delay in warning Pita had certainly kept him from escaping. As for Peter, he believed that when Pita realized how the war was going he had sacrificed himself voluntarily; he had literally immolated himself. But Peter's opinions did not soothe Gervasio, who had lost faith in words and was struggling with a profound crisis. Not even Uncle Felipe Neri's fervent letters kept him from realizing how mediocre he was. Could he consider himself a hero because of the simple fact that Uncle Felipe Neri said so? Who was Uncle Felipe Neri to have opinions about courage and cowardice? Was there anyone besides himself who could have an opinion about a soldier's motives? However, Uncle Felipe Neri's impassioned letters continued to flatter him, even though they did not convince him. He enjoyed reading them, although his subsequent reflections were more and more devastating: he was nothing but a paper hero (blue telegram paper), an impostor. If heroism meant offering oneself wholly and unconditionally, there was only one hero on the cruiser, Petty Officer Pita. And the cause? Was heroism possible in the service of any cause? Years earlier Uncle Felipe Neri had demanded a noble cause of the hero, but Gervasio's own experience had shown him that it was possible to invert the order of the process; that is, the soldier who died with his face turned to the foe, disinterestedly, might well be the one who ennobled the cause that he served. Alarmed by his conclusions, he took refuge in reading Uncle Felipe Neri's letters: exultant letters suffused with victory. The battle of the Ebro had been decisive. The enemy forces were weakening, their resistance was breaking down everywhere. The end of the war was coming. On this point Uncle Felipe Neri established a connection. He could not detach these happy prophecies from Gervasio's participation in the conflict, and often used the exploits of his nephew's ship as points of reference: before and after the landing on the Columbretes; before and after the *José Luis Díez* was put out of action. But despite the secret pleasure that such allusions produced in Gervasio, they did not stir his whole being as had the legionnaires in the past when they paraded down the Avenida de la Constitución, or as listening to the program "On the joyous path to peace" had done. A sort of immense fatigue had made him listless ever since Petty Officer Pita's imprisonment; something fundamental was growing cold inside him, disheartening him and opening the door to disillusionment.

Ordinarily Uncle Felipe Neri's letters arrived along with others from Mama Zita, Manena Abad, Doña Guadalupe Rueda, or Peter's parents, telling them about life in the city and the ups and downs of existence behind the lines. In her last letter Mama Zita told him that Papa Telmo would soon be freed, "in view of our troops' triumphal advance in Catalonia." All the prisoners who had someone of importance in Nationalist Spain to vouch for them would be released along with him (Gervasio asked himself whether Petty Officer Pita could count on a person of importance in Nationalist Spain, and whether, in his case, this support would be sufficient to save his desperate situation). Mama Zita also gave him a surprising piece of news: his sister Cruz had just become engaged to an Italian captain, Guido Fratelli, "who has been billeted with us for the last six months. He seems to be a responsible young man," she wrote, "though to judge from the jars of cosmetic stuff in the bathroom, very proud of his physical appearance." In Mama Zita's opinion the most serious obstacle would be Papa Telmo's reaction to his future son-in-law's Fascist ideology, the fact that he had long been a member of the Black Shirts.

For her part Doña Guadalupe described to her son Dámaso the misfortunes of his friend Eduardo Custodio.

"It isn't easy to have to write this," she said, "but his blindness has been almost providential. His face, with his nose eaten away by fire, puckered by the scars from his burns, two-thirds of his hair gone, is a monstrous face. I tremble at the mere idea that some day he might look at himself in a mirror." News from their respective families, especially news referring to Eduardo, whom they would soon have to face, temporarily distracted Gervasio from his gloomy reflections about Petty Officer Pita, as well as the fleeting pleasure that Uncle Felipe Neri's flatteries aroused in him.

One morning toward the end of March the cruiser embarked as part of the most impressive fleet Gervasio had ever seen. Along with the three cruisers and four minelayers, the old flotilla of coal-burning destroyers, three submarines, the gunships *Dato* and *Canalejas*, and the armed merchantman *Mar Cantábrico* put to sea. Later that afternoon they were joined from the mainland by the *Castillo de Olite*, the *Castillo de Peñafiel*, and two other transports loaded with soldiers. There was no mystery this time. The war, now almost at an end, was rusting the greased springs of military censorship. Their destination was Cartagena. A body of troops had mutinied and occupied the shipyard and some of the coastal batteries, and they were urging the Navy to take over the city without a fight, which on the one hand would prevent the Republicans from dismantling their fleet and on the other would help to open a new front behind enemy lines.

The squadron had scarcely taken positions before the city when the first aerial attack occurred. Twelve airplanes flew over them sprinkling them with bombs. A tremendous noise, like a thunderclap, enveloped them, and Gervasio, crouched before the tube, his stomach contracted, yelled "Fire! Fire! Fire!" almost mechanically. Minelayers and destroyers sheltered the freighters and a heliograph winked from a signal tower, urging them to make a landing. As the airplanes departed, a gigantic, spreading spout of water the size of a cathedral rose off the starboard bow. The cruiser veered, pitching, turning her back to the coast, whose batteries were giving the *Canarias* a hard battle. Farther out the merchant ships were moving with the current. Night was falling when Station A's telephone rang: "Locate coastal batteries in enemy hands." Before they could answer, the bombs of a new squadron of airplanes exploded. The Martin bombers were flying very high, and for a quarter of an hour the crash of bombs and the guns' replies kept Gervasio in a state of tension. To port, half a mile away, two spouts of water went up. The cruiser veered again, and when Miodelo announced that the airplanes were departing, the *Canarias* turned its bow resolutely toward the city with her location lights on, just as the *Castillo de Olite,* full of soldiers, drew away from the other three merchant ships and joined her. At a given moment they separated. The *Canarias,* lighted up like a transatlantic liner and with the obvious intention of attracting attention from the shore, turned sharply to starboard firing from her turrets, while the *Castillo de Olite,* furtive and un-lighted, headed for the coast under cover of darkness. Gervasio feverishly followed with his binoculars the merchant ship's bold penetration, its vague shadow; he saw it pass the line of buoys and suddenly lift into the air in an explosion, victim of a mine or a projectile. Petty Officer Tubío, at the telemetry machine, confirmed the tragedy even before Station A's telephone bell rang. After the explosion the *Canarias* stopped firing, put out its lights, and rejoined the squadron. The transports followed her wake, in convoy with the old destroyers. The darkness was total (only a faint glow from the city showing on the black line of the horizon), when the cruiser turned forty-five degrees to starboard and headed straight out to sea. A mortal silence reigned in the station. The consciousness of failure, the wreck of the *Castillo de Olite,* the sudden retreat, weighed on its crew. Don Mario, immobile at the spotter, scanned the sea in front of the ship. Minutes later the fleet divided: the transports, along with the smaller ships, headed north, parallel to the shore, in search of a port where they could take shelter, while the three cruisers in single file, sailing in zigzags, started east toward their base. But this separation did not bring the end of battle readiness. A pale, oblique new moon shone on the sea and the tuna swam silently in its light. There was something sad about the night's perfect calm. Don Mario continued to concentrate on the spotter and the sailors on their observation posts. Misgivings grew in Gervasio's heart. With the plan for a landing repulsed, fifty miles off the coast, what was keeping them there? Why didn't they sound the all-clear and let everyone go to bed? Why couldn't they at least give them a reasonable explanation of the situation? The sea opened before them in broad furrows, but did not rise. Like an answer to his thoughts, Station A's telephone rang. "We continue to be on battle status. Intensify surface watch." Don Mario assented without moving from the spotter. Gervasio could hardly see the vague shadows of his shipmates as they leaned on the rail of their station, binoculars at their eyes, as motionless as stones. The cruiser was sailing at top speed and the superstructure's vibration drowned out every other noise on deck. Gradually, Gervasio's initial uneasiness became anxiety. He felt that his tongue was woolly, his belly contracted, his brain confused. The metallic brilliance of the moon on the water, the silent fish, the prolonged silence, increased the anguish of waiting. What was happening? Whom were they escaping from? Were they trying to avoid an ambush? Suddenly the hum of a motor (muffled but growing louder) tightened his chest. There they were! Station C's announcement of airplanes was immediately corrected by Station A: "They're torpedo boats," it said. "Increase surface watch." Gervasio clutched the binoculars with such somber vehemence that he could feel the strap pressing against his neck. His companions, in silence around him, also did their best to locate the enemy. Sometimes the hum seemed to decrease and then return louder than ever. Without turning his head, Don Mario said, "Observers at their posts. Guns ready." The tossing seas opened like craters in the moonlight, and the buzz of the motor seemed to surround them stickily, in successive waves, in smaller and smaller circles, like the fan of water from a hose. Gervasio, completely defeated, his legs limp, could scarcely transmit the order, and when he raised the binoculars to his eyes again he was looking not so much for the objective as for protection, like a defenseless child who rubs his tightly closed eyelids against his mother's lap in panic. The roar of the motor seemed to die away after a new turn, but it was a vain illusion, for immediately the bridge discovered a torpedo boat off the bow and the machine gun on the spar deck fired two bursts of tracer bullets into the darkness. The bell of Station A shrilled again. A frightened, almost angry voice left the life of Station H in suspense.

"Two torpedoes astern!"

Overcome by an impression of catastrophe, Gervasio bent over at the waist and clutched the edge of the bulkhead with both hands. His temples were throbbing painfully and his veins, unable to maintain the flow of blood, seemed to suffocate him. The rhythm of his breathing was short and smothered, and his body seemed so fragile that his neck could hardly bear the pull of the binoculars. It was fright in a pure state, as if all the fears that had lain in wait for him since infancy had come together on this night to crush him. He gasped in distress, opened his legs in a V, and stared through the binoculars in a childish attempt to escape from himself. He cast a random glance over the waves illumined by the moon, and then he saw it: two white parallel tracks (the compressed-air wakes of the propellers) were advancing inexorably toward the cruiser. At intervals they disappeared in the swell only to reappear, whiter still and stylized, the left-hand track a little behind the right-hand one, at an unchanging speed. Terror stopped his mouth. He tried to announce the discovery of the torpedoes but produced only a dry sound in his throat, like a death rattle. His tongue was tied. In tenths of seconds he remembered Tato and Eduardo Custodio, and convinced that he was going to be blown up like them, that his hour had come, he took a prosaic, hardly warlike decision: he put two fingers in his ears and half opened his lips to soften the effect of the explosion. For an instant he could see the torpedoes themselves as they skipped between two waves: two shining metallic fish, spindle-shaped and incisive, which as they dived into the sea again became two effervescent wakes once more. He stood quietly, rigid, upright on the deck plates, his mind empty, fingers in his ears. All consciousness of his surroundings had vanished. His fear was so profound that he noticed neither the presence of his companions nor the incandescent bullets of the machine gun on the spar deck. In this situation of absolute confusion his hair began to rise: the shock crackled on the back of his neck with the violence of a short circuit, and immediately his body became electrified, he turned into a battery of opposing charges which stood his hair on end and made his skin prickle. It was a sort of unstoppable energy generated by his own terror. And he noticed that force in his head, struggling to expand, the individual hairs like wires pressing on his steel helmet so strongly that at last they succeeded in loosening it, raising the helmet little by little over the rigid spikes, pushing it off. With the shiny steel helmet hovering on the ends of his hair, his body hair pressed down by his clothing, the muscles of his abdomen tense, he did not blink; powerless, he watched the progress of the torpedoes, and when the moment of explosion came he closed his eyes and gasped for breath. But the maddening explosion that he expected did not occur. And as if he had split into two persons, he half saw the abrupt turn that almost threw the ship over on her side, the swish of the torpedoes brushing past the screws, their progressive departure toward the horizon. A warm tangle (control of urine lost) slid between his legs and descended, scalding the insides of his thighs, loosening his muscles. And at the same time his hair gave up, surrendered, and the steel helmet slowly lowered itself onto his head like a parachute until it settled there. Instantly the life around him returned. He heard an unintelligible cry of joy, perhaps from Javier Medina on the observers' perch. Behind him Damasito and Nasty were hugging each other exuberantly, he heard cheers and radiant voices around him, and on the deck below the exultant hubbub of the gunners, drowning out their battery chiefs' calls for order.

When the all clear sounded half an hour later, Gervasio (with his knees stiff inside his damp trouser legs) descended the ladder, stumbling like an old man, and took refuge on the spar deck out of the moonlight, completely undone. He sensed that someone was following him.

"Where are you going? Is something wrong?"

He slipped out of Peter's compassionate hands, and almost without realizing it found himself sobbing, his head resting on the rafts, murmuring incoherent phrases about his hair, Papa Telmo, and

Uncle Felipe Neri. His gaze was unfocused when he raised his face to his friend and said desolately, "It was fear, Peter; my father was right."

He almost shouted it, and when his friend made a sign to him that the duty station where the lookouts were was over their heads, he lowered his voice and began to talk very fast and low, in whispers. And so, between sobs and inconsistencies, a dialogue of mutual incomprehension ensued in which Gervasio spoke of his "paralyzing fear" and Peter assured him that every intelligent and sensitive person felt fear at some time in his life. They were talking about different things, for when his friend said specifically that everyone had felt fear that night, Gervasio made it clear, with his eyes fixed on nothing and with terrifying lucidity, that Peter was mistaken, that his fear was not circumstantial, a fear that would have disappeared with the torpedoes, but a fear that was installed here (he pressed the tip of his index finger hard against his forehead), and that it would stay there if he lived a thousand years.

That night, as if to confirm his words, he refused to sleep in the compartment below the waterline. He seemed to hear the lapping of the sea, the waves beating against the steel hull, and visualized the torpedoes riding those waves, the sensitive fuse poised ready to explode. Dámaso Valentín, unaware of his friend's psychic state, couldn't get over his surprise: "Sailor, where do you think you're going in this cold?" But Gervasio silently unhooked his hammock before Dámaso's astonished eyes and moved to the spar deck with it over his shoulder, in the lee of the stack, where he slept. On the following night he repeated the operation, and when his friends tried to dissuade him he turned to face them with a disturbed look in his eyes, his gestures showing derangement.

"I can't stand *knowing* that the sea's behind the bulkhead," he said with cold logic.

After they had dropped anchor at the base Gervasio continued to sleep in the open air, and Peter, alarmed by his perturbed state of mind, usually watched over him until he fell asleep. Two nights later Navy Radio broadcast the news of the collapse of the Republican army on all fronts. For all practical purposes the war was over. Despite the lateness of the hour the ships anchored in the bay replied with their sirens to the pealing of the city's bells. On the heights of Bellver rockets tore through the night, and their small, regular explosions created a climate of exaltation. Discipline was relaxed and pandemonium reigned on the cruiser. Groups of sailors roved from one place to another with bottles and guitars, drank and danced under the stars, and when the lights went up on board they were greeted with a storm of applause and exclamations. From the forecastle the ship's band led off with "The Volunteers," and a crowd of sailors followed it along the deck, singing the tune. Jubilation spread, bottles and musical instruments appeared from nowhere, a noisy string of firecrackers went off on the Marine Promenade. On Station H champagne corks popped and the sailors, sitting on the floor, drank straight from the bottles, and stimulated by Miodelo's harmonica, sang "Chaparrita" at the tops of their lungs. In the center of the circle Nasty and Scurvy were performing a loose-limbed dance, and Bartolomé Roselló, Mallorquín, raised his diabolical eyebrows when he saw Gervasio come in and handed him a bottle.

"Drink, 377A, the war's over!"

Gervasio drank a long swallow, feeling out of step, and when he had finished rubbed his uniform sleeve hard across his mouth. He felt alien. He had sunk into an abyss, and watched life pass over him without feeling strong enough to participate. Without ceasing to dance, Scurvy grabbed the bottle and raised his short, hairy arm, stamped energetically on the deck plates, staggering, and yelled, "A month from now, everybody at home!" And he drank and drank insatiably until Nasty, eyes sparkling, tried to snatch the bottle away from him. They struggled and the champagne eventually spilled over the piled-up coats. "Never mind, never mind!" Alcohol increased the animation, but the more the gaiety grew, the smaller and more withdrawn Gervasio felt. José Antonio Lago, Painter, sitting cross-legged, wondered aloud where Javier Medina was. Petty Officer Tubío's broad face split open in a red, watermelon smile.

"He must be in the Naval Academy already!" he said.

His sally was met with giggles. Nasty, barefoot and with his hairless chest bare, was strutting around rhythmically. "Come on, Miodelo, play us one of your Galician songs!" And Miodelo obliged; he played the harmonica as loudly as he could, and the little group supported the music with their strong, tuneless voices. Fito Iroa, the new one, passed him another bottle, but as Gervasio tipped back his head to drink he had a dizzy spell and his knees buckled. He got rid of the bottle and went out to the spar deck, frightened of himself.

On top of Bellver rockets and fireworks were still going off, and the city with its unaccustomed illumination (full of noise from strings of firecrackers, bells, and automobile horns) seemed to be on fire. Near the port machine gun where Gervasio had sat on his first day at sea, half a dozen sailors were passing a carafe around and breaking out into wild cheers. From the deck below, as crowded as the main street of a provincial capital on a holiday, rose songs, the strumming of guitars, the stamping of feet, cheers, oaths, the metallic sounds of the band. In his desire to flee from the general euphoria Gervasio started for the spar deck ladder, but before he reached it the curly head and long, somber face of Javier Medina appeared on it. When he saw Gervasio he stopped, a spark of seriousness in his eyes, and put a protective hand on his shoulder.

"I'm sorry, 377A. They shot Petty Officer Pita this morning," he said contritely.

Gervasio could not reply. Petty Officer Pita's shifting eyes, his evasive silences, his firm bull-necked head, came to his mind as he climbed down to the deck. And with him the disfigured masks of Uncle Norberto and Uncle Adrián, of David and Fadrique, of his friends Tato and Eduardo Custodio. On the dark afterdeck the noise was dying down. Some shapes were restlessly sleeping off their drinking bout in the lee of the superstructure, and Gervasio picked his way between them, snaking along, until he reached the stern taffrail. Once there, with the hubbub behind him, he leaned on the rail next to the little mast with his face in his hands. Slack, gentle waves lapped against the screws, and from the brightly lighted city came a noise of joyful crowds, counterpointed by the explosions of rockets and the pealing of bells. He was not surprised to see Peter beside him; he had been his shadow for a week. Peter leaned his elbows on the rail to his right in silence, and to mask his interference stuck the toe of his bare foot into the scupper hole as if he were trying to unstop it. Gervasio looked at him sidewise.

"He really was a hero, wasn't he?"

"Who? Pita?"

"Yes, Pita."

Peter hesitated. With his proverbial equanimity he weighed the pros and cons.

"Yes, he was," he said. "In a way, he was a hero."

"Why do you say 'in a way'?"

"I don't share the cause that he served."

"You talk just like my Uncle Felipe Neri."

"Don't you think that he was?"

Gervasio thought for a moment.

"And couldn't it be the other way around?" he said. "Couldn't it be that the man who dies generously is the man who ennobles the cause he serves?"

Peter's glance sank into the night, rested on the barely illuminated Castle of Bellver.

"Maybe you're right," he said thoughtfully.

"And the others?" Gervasio added stubbornly. "My uncles Norberto and Adrián, the ones who had the motorcycle, haven't they been heroes too?"

"Why not?"

"The same as Uncle Fadrique and his friends on the Cerro de los Angeles?" implored Gervasio, on the point of tears.

A painful pause ensued. They could still hear music and songs behind them. To port the lighthouse at Cala Figuera winked, and each time it did so it illuminated a triangle of sea on which the sails of two fishing boats shone whitely. Over Santa Ponsa a shooting star tore through the sky like a rocket and was lost in the night. Peter took Gervasio by the shoulders and led him gently, among the sleeping drunks, toward the lighted deck.

"Just the same," he said at last. "Why should they be different?"

Born in Valladolid, Spain, in 1920, Miguel Delibes is perhaps the leading Spanish novelist alive today. Winner of the prestigious Nadal Prize for his first novel in 1947, he has gone on to win numerous other literary awards and distinctions, and his previous novels have been translated into a variety of languages. *The Stuff of Heroes* is, by all accounts, his major work to date.